THE
MINSTREL
BOY

THE MINSTREL BOY

■

Dennis Jones

Random House
Toronto

Published in Canada in 1991 by Random House
of Canada Limited, Toronto.

Canadian Cataloguing in Publication Data

Jones, Dennis.
The minstrel boy

ISBN 0-394-22134-6

I. Title.

PS8569.0495M5 1991   C813′.54   C90-095609-7
PR9199.3.J65M5 1991

Typeset by Leaper & Gard Limited, Great Britain
Printed and bound in Great Britain by
BPCC Hazell Books
Aylesbury, Bucks, England
Member of BPCC Ltd.

The minstrel boy to the wars has gone,
In the ranks of death you'll find him;
His father's sword he has girded on,
And his wild harp slung behind him.

Thomas Moore

PROLOGUE

Bolivia
October 8–9, 1967

■

Michael Conroy knelt behind the trunk of a fallen mahogany tree a few yards from Captain Prado's command post and listened carefully to the gunfire echoing through the wooded canyon spread out below him. He was quite sure that the rattle of automatic weapons was coming closer.

Just visible in the undergrowth to Conroy's left, Prado was speaking rapidly into the radio handset. Conroy couldn't hear the words, but he guessed that Prado was ordering his men to increase the pressure on the guerrilla band trapped on the canyon floor.

The fighting had been going on for almost two hours, since one of Prado's patrols had been ambushed by the guerrillas farther up the narrow, steep-sided valley, which was called the Quebrada del Yuro. The patrol had lost two dead and several wounded. But Prado had maneuvered his Ranger company skillfully, and the guerrillas were in a hopeless position, surrounded and forced inevitably toward the hill that blocked the only remaining exit from the canyon. Prado had fifty men on that hill, waiting in ambush.

The undergrowth rustled to Conroy's right. Gonzales, his face shadowed by a floppy bush hat, was working his way along the mahogany trunk toward the American. He favored Conroy with a savage grin. Conroy, with less enthusiasm, grinned at the Cuban exile. The depth of Gonzales's malice made him uneasy.

"He's down there," Gonzales whispered in Spanish as he

reached Conroy's side. "I can smell him, by God."

"Is he?" Conroy asked. He felt he had to defer to some degree to the Cuban's self-professed field experience; Gonzales was several years older than Conroy's twenty-three, and had worked for the CIA considerably longer. Conroy had heard that Gonzales had gotten out of Cuba just ahead of Castro's secret police in 1960 and fought at the Bay of Pigs the following year when CIA-backed Cuban exiles tried to reconquer their country, but Gonzales never talked about it.

Gonzales was cautiously lifting his head to peer through the screen of leaves over the fallen tree trunk. "Oh, he's there, all right," he repeated. "Someday you'll be able to sniff out a Marxist as I can. Listen. They're a lot closer."

"*Si*," Conroy replied in a low voice. He looked over the tree trunk, down the steep forward slope of the hill. Leaves dappled his line of vision, but he thought he saw flitting shadows in a thicket of thorn bushes. He checked the safety catch of the Uzi submachine gun he was carrying. He was keyed up, nervous. It was hard to convince himself that there were real bullets flying down there, fired in fear and anger, and that men were actually trying to kill each other in the shaded depths of the Quebrada del Yuro.

"There they are!" Gonzales whispered urgently.

Eight or ten men had broken out of the underbrush and thorn trees on the valley floor and were running hard into a small clearing at the foot of the hill. They obviously had no idea that their escape route was blocked. There was silence for two beats of the heart, then Conroy heard Captain Prado's shouted order.

"Open fire!"

Automatic weapons hammered deafeningly to both sides of Conroy. Bullets sleeted down the slope, clipping branches from the thorn trees and striking sparks from bare stone. One of the guerrillas stumbled and fell, then another. Two of the survivors swerved and fled to Conroy's right, toward the nearer wall of the canyon. Gonzales had his Uzi resting on the tree trunk and was shooting at them as they ran. Conroy held his fire. His orders — and likely Gonzales's — were to stay out of combat.

Somehow the pair of fugitives reached the valley wall without appearing to be hit and disappeared into the under-growth at the wall's foot. By this time Prado had ordered a squad of soldiers into pursuit, and they went racing down the hill after the guerrillas. Covering fire crackled from the Rangers' positions on the hillside.

Gonzales had stopped shooting and was yelling something at Conroy. The gunfire prevented Conroy from hearing more than a scatter of words.

"... him. It's him — over there ..."

Gonzales jumped to his feet and tore off into the trees to Conroy's right. Conroy looked into the canyon. The squad of soldiers was shooting into a dense thicket. Through a narrow gap in the thicket canopy he could just make out the forms of two staggering men, one with the other's arm slung over his shoulders. Then they were gone.

Conroy thought: They're going to try to climb out.

He got to his feet and set off in a stooped run in the direc-tion Gonzales had taken. Branches lashed at his feet and arms, and his boots skidded on rough ground. He pelted down the right flank of the hill, from which Prado's Rangers were sniping at hidden guerrillas, then ran across a lightly timbered saddle and up its far side toward the heights above the thicket where he'd seen the two fugitives. As he reached the crest of the ridge, he caught up with Gonzales, who had tired quickly and was gasping and stumbling his way over the rugged ground.

"What the devil are you doing here?" Gonzales panted at him. "Go on back."

"They're coming up the canyon wall," Conroy told him. He was also short of breath. "Hundred meters on —"

"*Hijos de las chingadas,*" Gonzales swore, hurrying onward. "How many?"

"Two I saw."

"Where are Prado's men? Ah, there."

Just ahead was a sloping clearing that overlooked the canyon. In the center of the clearing Rangers were setting up a mortar. They turned quickly when one of them saw Gonzales and Conroy, but the two CIA men were wearing army uniforms and were plainly not guerrillas. One of the soldiers started fitting the mortar tube to the base plate.

"Look out!" Conroy shouted in Spanish. Two stumbling figures had appeared among the trees at the edge of the clearing. One was bleeding from the legs and obviously in pain. There was a breath's pause as the adversaries saw each other, then one of the soldiers called out:

"Surrender! Drop your guns!"

The uninjured guerrilla stood quite still, shocked into indecision. But the other supported himself against a tree trunk, swung up his carbine and fired. The shot missed. The soldiers fired just as wildly, one bullet glancing off the barrel of the guerrilla's carbine and smashing into his right forearm. The gun dropped from his grasp. Conroy saw the defeat in his face as he raised his hands above his head. The soldiers held their fire. The other guerrilla tossed his gun onto the ground and also put his hands up.

"Stop," the wounded guerrilla called out. His voice was colorless, drained of energy. "Don't shoot any more. I'm worth more to you alive than dead." He gave a gasping heave for air, then another.

Asthma, Conroy thought. They say he has asthma. It's really him.

With what sounded like his last scrap of breath, the wounded man added, "I am Che Guevara."

The soldiers brought the guerrilla leader down from the hills on a stretched-out army blanket carried by four men. The unwounded captive — his name apparently was Willy — stumbled along after them, hands tied behind his back. Conroy and Gonzales followed the carrying party at a distance of some dozen yards, Gonzales looking good-humored for a change.

Conroy was feeling considerable satisfaction mixed with traces of surprise at the ease with which Guevara had finally been captured. The Bolivian Army had been struggling to catch him since last March, when the government first realized he was in the hill country with a guerrilla band and trying to raise an insurrection. Guevara must have been in the country for months previous to that, preparing his bases, training his men and planning strategy. He'd been reported dead at least twice by the government. The poorly equipped and badly trained Bolivian Army appeared to be no match for him and his men; finally the Bolivians had asked for American specialists to train a counterinsurgency unit, and the Rangers were the result.

The CIA's involvement was not so direct, but nonetheless real. There had been genuine fear in Washington that Guevara's actions, coupled with a bitter miners' strike in the north of the country, could bring down the Bolivian government and start a full-scale popular revolt that would turn into a Communist insurrection. Guevara was too important to be left entirely to the Bolivians, so the CIA station chief in La Paz had assigned a number of field personnel to act as liaison between the CIA and the Bolivian anti-guerrilla campaign. For Conroy it was at least partly a training mission; he'd only been in the country eight months when he was ordered to work with Gonzales in the field.

But it's over now, Conroy thought as he tramped along behind the stretcher party. We got him. There won't be any Communist revolution here in the foreseeable future. Now the Bolivians can have a real chance at democracy. That'll really piss off Moscow. And Fidel.

He took off his bush hat and scrubbed perspiration from his forehead using the back of his hand. He was a big young man, with the powerful shoulders and broad hands of his Irish ancestors, but his features and coloring were not those of a Celt. His great-grandfather had come from the west of Ireland to New Orleans in 1845, and Conroy's great-grandmother and grandmother were Cajun. The old French blood had asserted itself in Conroy, and he was dark-eyed and fine-featured. He had had his hair cropped for this expedition, but when it grew out it was black and wavy. He could pass in appearance for Spanish, and his command of the language was good and getting better, if not yet idiomatic.

He jammed his hat onto his head and said in English, "Gonzales?"

"What?"

"What'll the Bolivians do with him, do you think?"

"I know what they'd like to do," Gonzales answered.

"Yes?"

"Shoot him."

"Are we going to allow that? He's got a lot of information about the Cuban Reds we could use."

Gonzales shrugged. "How do you propose to stop them if they decide to do it?"

Conroy looked up the trail ahead. The outskirts of the hill village of La Higuera were coming into view. "Persuasion?"

Again the shrug. "Bolivia has no death penalty. Do you think they want him in a jail in La Paz for the next thirty years? He'd attract nothing but trouble."

"I suppose so." Conroy studied the swaying blanket a few yards ahead, and the white-faced man lying on it. He'd like to see Guevara preserved. There was a lot the man could tell the CIA, assuming he could be persuaded to let it out. But neither Gonzales nor Conroy had the authority to tell the Bolivians what to do.

The column of soldiers tramped into the village. La Higuera was just another hill settlement, made up of adobe houses with tile or thatched roofs scattered around a dusty plaza; facing the square were a couple of public buildings, a kind of an inn, the inevitable small church, a telegraph office and a two-room schoolhouse, which was separated from the telegraph office by a narrow lane. The telegraph office had been taken over by the army as a field command post, and some enterprising Ranger lieutenant had added to its front a thatched lean-to furnished with a few broken-down tables and chairs, to serve as an officers' canteen.

Captain Prado led his men into the plaza, halted them and spoke briefly with one of his sergeants. The sergeant saluted, barked at his squad, and both the soldiers and the two captured guerrillas disappeared into the schoolhouse. Conroy waited apprehensively for shots, but there were none.

Prado marched over to Conroy and Gonzales. He was looking extremely pleased with himself. "He's locked up tight," Prado informed them. "I put Willy in the other room. They can't talk together and cause trouble."

"What's next?" Gonzales asked. "You were on the radio earlier."

"Colonel Zenteno and some other senior officers are

coming here from divisional headquarters in Vallegrande. To question him."

"When will they be here?" Conroy asked.

Prado glanced at him. The Bolivian officer's expression was carefully neutral. Conroy sensed dislike behind it. No matter how much we help them against their enemies, he thought, we're still foreigners. Gonzales as much as myself. It stings their pride. That's so damned silly. They need us; they ought to be prepared to like us a little.

"Not long," Prado answered. "They are coming by helicopter. There may be more prisoners or bodies by then. Sergeant Huanca's men are still searching for bodies in the canyon."

"Fine," Conroy said.

"We'll wait in the canteen." This was Gonzales, turning away from Conroy and Prado and moving toward the lean-to. Conroy followed the Cuban, glancing at his watch. It was six o'clock. In New Orleans right about now, Marguerite would be sitting down to Sunday dinner. Maybe she'd gone over to her parents' home, as she often did. He wondered what she'd think if she could see him here, know what he was doing. The difference between their two worlds, at this moment, was abyssal.

The boy who hung around the officers' canteen was waiting expectantly. "Beer," Gonzales ordered as he sat down on a backless chair. "Pilsener." He glanced at Conroy. "You?"

"Beer," Conroy said, nodding as he unslung his Uzi and put it on a rickety wooden table near the Cuban. The boy started to scuttle away in the direction of the village inn, which provided food for the unit's officers. Gonzales called him back. "I want to eat. Bring me something. It doesn't matter what."

Conroy told the boy to double the order and sat down at the table. Prado had disappeared, probably into the schoolhouse to gloat over his catch. Apart from the soldiers and a half dozen vehicles, the square was deserted; even the church door was shut fast, although it was Sunday. Except for the boy, the villagers were staying out of sight.

Conroy stretched happily, the wooden stool creaking

under his weight. He was tired, but Guevara's capture had given him a tremendous lift. Bolivia was Conroy's first foreign posting. It was a wonderful piece of luck, being present at the capture of the legendary guerrilla fighter.

The boy brought two bottles of beer, uncapped them and squatted against the telegraph office wall a couple of yards from Conroy. Conroy judged him to be about twelve, of Spanish ancestry with some Indian thrown in, a mestizo. He had chatted to the child a couple of days ago, when the Ranger unit first arrived in La Higuera. The boy had giggled at Conroy's occasional slip in Spanish, but was otherwise friendly enough.

Conroy fumbled a pack of cigarettes out of his bush tunic, extracted one and lit it. He took a pull at the beer. It tasted perfect.

"They're bringing in somebody else," Gonzales said, sticking a cigarette into the corner of his mouth.

Conroy followed his gaze. A squad of Rangers was marching a prisoner into the village square. While Conroy watched, the soldiers took him into the schoolhouse.

"He's for the high jump, too," Gonzales said.

"You really think they'll kill them all?" Conroy asked. Prado had emerged from the schoolhouse and turned toward the canteen.

"How should I know what they're thinking in La Paz?"

Conroy dragged on his cigarette, watching Prado approach. The Bolivian didn't stop to talk to them, but went into the telegraph office. From its interior Conroy could hear the crackle of an army radio. The shadows were lengthening rapidly, bringing the fleeting dusk of the tropic zones. The boy stood up suddenly and trotted away in the direction of the inn.

Suddenly Conroy heard the beat of helicopter rotors from the north; that would be Colonel Zenteno and the other senior officers arriving. Conroy drained his beer bottle and stamped the cigarette butt under his heel as a pair of choppers flew right overhead and settled out of sight beyond the buildings to the south side of the square, where the Ranger company's base camp lay.

Gonzales stood up. "I'm going over there," he said. "You stay out of it."

"What?" Conroy couldn't keep astonishment out of his voice.

"Stay out of it," Gonzales repeated. "Guevara will see you're American. He'll be even less likely to talk if you're there."

"Go to hell," Conroy snapped. "I'm going, with or without you."

"No, you're not."

Prado was standing in the telegraph office doorway, brought there by the sound of the helicopters. "What's going on here?" he asked Gonzales.

"The American doesn't need to be at the interrogation," Gonzales said. "He'll only make Guevara shut his mouth tighter."

"I'm CIA, damn it," Conroy broke in, hot with humiliation.

"So am I," said Gonzales. "And I have been here a lot longer than you have."

Prado was regarding Conroy frigidly. "I know you are CIA," he said. "You don't have to remind me. Gonzales is right. You're not needed. Stay away from the schoolhouse."

"I need to know what Guevara says, for Christ's sake. That's my job. Don't patronize *me*. Who the hell do you think you are?"

Prado stiffened. Conroy, too late, realized that he'd said far too much. He cursed his temper.

"Stay away from the schoolhouse," Prado repeated. "If you approach it, my men will have orders to turn you away. If you persist, they'll lock you up like Guevara." He removed his gaze from Conroy and stalked into the square.

"Stupid," Gonzales said to Conroy, and went after the Bolivian captain. Two jeeps, crowded with army officers, were rolling into the square.

"Son of a *bitch*," Conroy swore. He was awash with help-less fury and mortification.

Prado and Gonzales had disappeared into the school-house. Conroy sat down heavily on the stool, then realized that the boy was hovering nearby. He'd brought the food, *sajta del pollo* by the smell from the covered iron saucepan. Spiced chicken.

Screw Gonzales, Conroy thought, and motioned the boy

to put the food on the table. Conroy ate his own portion, and
then, just to get even, Gonzales's as well.

Darkness fell with tropic abruptness. Conroy had the boy
bring him another beer, then another, paying as he drank. He
smoked one cigarette with each bottle of beer; after a while
there were three butts ground into the dust under the table.

Conroy wasn't sure how much time had passed when he
finished his fourth bottle. He was, however, aware that he
was very slightly tipsy. There was one naked forty-watt bulb
in a holder over the door of the telegraph office, and in its
dismal light he surveyed the empty bottles in front of him.
The boy had disappeared. Beerless, Conroy lit another cigarette and began to smoke it halfheartedly. Occasionally he
heard raised voices from the schoolhouse, and once the
sound of a blow, but only once. The interrogators weren't
being as rough as Conroy had imagined they would be.
Probably, he thought, they realized there was no point in
trying to beat information out of someone as tough as
Guevara. Gonzales, the asshole, would come out of the
schoolhouse as ignorant as when he went in. The thought was
somewhat cheering.

Conroy realized suddenly that his bladder was uncomfortably full. There was a privy inside the adobe building
housing the telegraph office, but Conroy didn't feel like
encountering any of Prado's junior officers. He decided to go
along the laneway between the schoolhouse and the telegraph office and find a dark piece of wall.

He threw away the half-smoked cigarette, picked up his
Uzi and headed for the entrance to the lane. Prado had
posted a guard in the laneway, but the man recognized
Conroy in the dim light filtering out of the schoolhouse
windows and let him pass.

An alley intersected the lane at the rear of the schoolhouse, on Conroy's right, and a similar alley led away to his
left. Another of Prado's men was patrolling the back of the
schoolhouse; Conroy could make out his dark form against
the lighter adobe of the walls.

Never pee on a soldier's boots, Conroy told himself, and
turned into the alley to his left. His bladder was full enough

to hurt. He hurried along a few yards to a kink in the alleyway, stopped and unbuttoned.

He was doing himself up when he heard the faintest of sounds along the alley. He couldn't identify it for a moment, and then it came again: a quickly indrawn breath, followed by a soft, sharp exhalation, almost a gasp.

Conroy unslung the Uzi and stepped around the bend of the wall. Not two feet from him was a robed and hooded figure. It turned and tried to run.

Conroy caught up in two swift strides and grabbed, catching the fugitive by what he guessed was the upper arm. The person stumbled and half fell, the hood falling away from the head and face. In the starlight, Conroy saw that it was a woman. None too gently he pulled her to her feet, keeping a firm grip on her arm.

"What're you doing back here?" he asked in Spanish.

She wasn't struggling. "Please let me go," she whispered. She didn't sound like a campesino to Conroy's ear; her voice betrayed education.

"Who are you?" he asked.

"Marita Linares. Please let me go." She gave an ineffectual tug, which Conroy resisted easily. "I am the village school-teacher," she added in explanation.

"Why are you back here?"

"I needed to walk."

"You'd better come with me," Conroy said. Not far ahead he could see the end of the alley opposite the one he had entered. He pushed her toward it. She went with him, resisting only for the first few steps. He thought briefly about searching her for weapons but dismissed the idea. The villagers, self-effacing though they appeared, might react violently to a gringo doing a physical search of the village schoolteacher. And he suspected that Prado wouldn't be particularly quick to protect him.

The alley ran along the back of the telegraph office and ended at one of the side streets leading into the plaza. Conroy propelled her around the corner to the canteen lean-to. The boy had returned, squatting as before in the dust by the adobe wall. His eyes widened at the sight of the woman in Conroy's grip.

She stopped without warning and Conroy almost ran into her. She was making that sound again, the indrawn breath followed by the gasp, but this time louder.

He loosened his grip and said, "What's the matter?"

She got her breath back and said calmly, "I am going to have a baby in a little while. Likely tomorrow."

"What?"

"I am almost at my time. That's why I walk. It makes the ... tightness easier."

"Oh," Conroy said stupidly. He looked at her midriff in the light from the telegraph office. She was heavily pregnant. "I'm sorry, senhora." He dropped his hand hastily from her arm. "I didn't know —"

"May I go now?" she asked.

Wait, Conroy thought. He looked at the boy. "Who is this?" he asked.

The boy blinked. "Senhorita Linares. The schoolteacher."

She's not married, Conroy thought. That must be rough in a place like this. He looked down at her face. She was about twenty-five, and quite beautiful in a Spanish-patrician way. Her eyes were pleading with him.

"May I go now?" she repeated. "See, I told the truth. Please let me go home, I need to lie down."

Conroy nodded. She turned and vanished into the darkness of the street leading away from the square. Conroy looked after her for a long moment.

The boy was at his elbow. "Beer, senhor?"

"No." He looked at the child. "She teaches you?"

A shrug. "When I go to school. She comes from La Paz." He added confidentially, "My mother says she is a —"

A word Conroy didn't know. He could fill in the sense, though. "Why doesn't the father marry her?" he asked. As though the kid would know. "Is he from here?"

"No. Nobody knows who he is. Everyone says it is someone from La Paz. Do you want some more beer?"

"No. You can go home."

The child trotted away across the plaza and was swallowed by the night. Conroy, head full of beer fumes, made his way out of the town square toward the company bivouac. He reached the tent he was sharing with Gonzales, crawled into it and lay on his back in the darkness. He began thinking about the humiliation Gonzales and Prado had inflicted on him. Improbable ways of getting back at them, of reasserting his authority, danced through his head. Keep them from shooting Guevara? How would he do that? Gonzales would just laugh at him, and Prado would lock him up. But there had to be *something* he could do.

Still gnawing at it, he fell asleep.

He was awakened by the dawn birds, racketing in the trees. Conroy sat up slowly, his eyeballs gritty and the inside of his mouth tacky and sour. Gonzales's bedroll was unoccupied.

Oh, shit, Conroy thought, scrambling out of the tent. Are they still at it? Or have they killed him already?

He stuck his head into the tent long enough to rinse his mouth with water from his canteen and grab the Uzi. He was only three minutes' walk from the town plaza; when he reached it, he saw Prado and a group of junior officers standing around underneath the thatch of the canteen. Their postures betrayed tension. Gonzales was leaning against one of the lean-to's support posts.

"What's going on?" Conroy asked him.

"Zenteno's talking to Army HQ in La Paz."

"This is it, then," Conroy said. His spine tingled.

"Likely," Gonzales said.

"Can't we stop them?"

"It was a stupid interrogation. I tried to persuade them to take Guevara to La Paz where we could work on him properly. But Zenteno isn't interested."

"Shit." For an instant Conroy saw himself abducting Guevara at rifle point from Gonzales and the Bolivians, taking the guerrilla leader single-handed to La Paz somehow. Then he imagined how Prado would calmly shoot both him and Guevara, not a blink. Stupid, stupid, Conroy told himself.

"Will the villagers try to interfere?" Conroy asked. "The guerrillas might have had supporters here."

Gonzales gave a sharp snort of contempt. "Hardly. One of the peasants came around to the schoolhouse a few minutes ago and told Zenteno the village schoolteacher was helping

Che's band. The band was here last autumn, and he said he saw her taking food to them out in the forest. Prado's men have gone to get her now."

Goddamnit, Conroy thought, that's why she was snooping around last night. What the hell was she trying to do?

He almost told Gonzales he'd seen her near the schoolhouse, but then decided to keep his mouth shut.

Colonel Zenteno came out of the telegraph office and motioned Prado to come near. After a moment's interchange, which Conroy couldn't hear, Prado drew himself to attention, saluted and drew a small bunch of dried grass stems out of his tunic. He held them out to the group of noncommissioned officers who were waiting under the lean-to. Each of them drew one and examined it. The third to draw, a sergeant whose name Conroy vaguely recollected to be Teran, grimaced and compared his straw to that of the man next to him. Teran's was the short one.

"Go and get rid of him," Prado ordered.

Teran saluted, cocked his carbine and marched to the schoolhouse. A dozen Ranger privates trailed after him and waited outside the door while he entered. There was a long silence. Prado began to fidget.

The schoolhouse door opened and Teran came out, his face pale. Even from a dozen yards away, Conroy could see that he was extremely agitated.

"Get back in there and kill him!" Colonel Zenteno shouted.

Teran turned on his heel and went inside. The soldiers outside the door milled around excitedly.

Conroy heard a burst of gunfire from inside the schoolhouse. Then, without warning, the soldiers at the entrance surged forward and burst into the adobe building. Confused shouting sounded from the interior, then more shots, a fusillade. Conroy felt nauseated. The men's discipline had vanished, replaced by blood lust. Zenteno wasn't taking any action to stop it.

"Serves the bastard right," Gonzales muttered at his elbow. There was satisfaction in his voice. "He had a dozen of my friends shot when he purged the army in Cuba."

Conroy could only grunt in reply. He heard more shots.

"There go Willy and the other one," Gonzales said. He straightened away from his leaning post. "That's that. Now we can clean up the mess and get back to La Paz."

"You —" Conroy began, and stopped. A sergeant and a pair of Rangers were coming out of a side street, dragging the schoolteacher between them. Conroy could tell she still hadn't had the baby.

"Ah, you caught up with her," Zenteno said, stepping forward as the men and their prisoner reached him. From the corner of his eye, Conroy could see the executioners boiling out of the schoolhouse, shouting in exhilaration.

The sergeant nodded. "She had this, colonel," he said, producing a Walther automatic pistol from his trousers pocket.

Zenteno regarded Marita Linares, who was standing quite still between the two Rangers. Her mouth was quivering. Her eyes flicked to Conroy's, and he read the fear behind them. She'd have heard the shots, would know what they meant. There was something else there, too: a pleading. *Don't let them kill me. Please.*

"You were trying to reach Guevara with the gun, weren't you?" Zenteno said expressionlessly.

Marita looked at the ground. Conroy held his breath. The soldiers from the schoolhouse had stopped a few yards away and were waiting expectantly, hopefully. Conroy knew they wanted someone else to kill.

"Weren't you?" Zenteno repeated.

"Yes," Marita said softly, with the slightest tremor in her voice.

"Red slut," Zenteno said in a flat voice. "And a schoolteacher, in the name of God."

"What do you want to do with her, colonel?" one of the officers asked Zenteno.

Zenteno's brow furrowed for a moment. Then he said, "She's a guerrilla. Prado's soldiers can have her."

Prado glanced at his executioners. One of them shifted his carbine furtively.

"We can attend to her," Prado said. But he sounded reluctant. Conroy could imagine what was going through his head. Executing a guerrilla who was responsible for many soldiers' deaths was one matter; doing the same to a young, unarmed and pregnant guerrilla sympathizer was another. With rape thrown in, probably. But Conroy had no doubt the soldiers would do it if ordered to. Their blood was up.

"Good," Zenteno said indifferently. "Bury her out in the woods with the other two. Guevara we're to take to Valle-grande."

Marita's knees buckled. The Rangers on each side of her had to hold her up. She put her hands to her distended belly. "My baby's coming," she gasped. "Let me have my baby first, for the love of God. Please don't kill me."

Zenteno raised his eyebrows; he seemed to have ignored the fact that she was pregnant. Prado was looking even more reluctant than he had before.

Conroy, not even conscious of making a decision, found himself stepping forward. "There's no reason to kill her," he said. The sound of his own words surprised him "Leave her be."

"Who the devil are you?" Zenteno snapped.

"He's with Gonzales, colonel," Prado said. "CIA. American."

"What's this got to do with you?" Zenteno asked coldly. "Keep out of it, if you know what's good for you."

Two of Prado's men unslung their carbines. The muzzles were not quite pointing at Conroy.

"She's pregnant, for God's sake," Conroy said. "How can you kill her like that?" Mixed with his fear was pride; he was doing the right thing.

"She had a gun," Zenteno said. "You think she wouldn't have killed any of us, including you, if she thought it was necessary?"

She must have had the gun last night, Conroy thought, but she didn't use it because she'd have known shooting me would bring the soldiers. She waited to try again. But we can't just murder her.

"We are not Communists," Conroy said. He sensed Gonzales standing next to him.

"You idiot," the Cuban muttered. "This isn't the way to do it."

Conroy half turned toward him. "Back me up, damn it," he snarled under his breath in English. "We've already lost

Guevara to them. Let's bring something back to show La Paz we were out here. We should show at least some result."

Gonzales's eyes narrowed slightly. Conroy could see him thinking: the CIA wants information, not bodies.

"Do it," Conroy urged

The Cuban shrugged. Zenteno, who did not understand English, was regarding them with suspicion. "Colonel Zenteno," Gonzales said coolly, "Mr. Conroy wants to take the woman to La Paz for further questioning. It's always possible she's part of a subversive network we don't know about. I agree with him that she should be interrogated. Her knowledge shouldn't be wasted. With your permission, she can be sent back with Mr. Conroy from the Villegrande airstrip."

Zenteno appeared to be considering. Come on, Conroy thought. You can afford to be generous. You wouldn't give us Guevara. Just give us a small fish instead.

Zenteno seemed to reach the same conclusion. He made a dismissive gesture. "Very well. Put her in one of the helicopters. Get her away from Villegrande as soon as you land. I don't want her anywhere near the journalists who will be there. Lock her up in La Paz. Is that understood?"

"Yes, colonel," Gonzales said.

"Go on," ordered Zenteno, turning away. "Get her out of here."

Conroy crossed the open space between himself and Marita Linares. Her eyes met his. They were full of horror and despair.

"Come with me," he said, taking her by the arm to lead her away from the crumbling adobe schoolhouse. He was delighted with himself. He'd done it. He'd pulled it off.

Gonzales was looking at him with faint disgust. "Stupid American heroics," he muttered. "When are you going to grow up?"

Conroy just grinned at him.

Puerto Real, Cuba
September 7

■

Marita Linares sits at her bedroom window, waiting for her son. Her bedroom is on the second floor of the house, which is made of soft, yellowish stone; through the bedroom window Marita can see the dusty lane down which Ramon will come, when he comes, if he comes. There is a low stone wall on the far side of the lane, and beyond the stone wall lies the beach, very white and stark against the blue Caribbean. On the beach are a few palm trees and an abandoned American automobile, a 1955 Buick, with its hood raised as though waiting patiently for a mechanic who never comes. The car has been on the beach for three years. Marita has been here for much longer than that.

She shifts in her chair. The bedside clock ticks, clearly audible over the distant mutter of the surf. The surf is not too high for bathing today, but there are no tourists at Puerto Real. The beach is not on the tourist maps, although a few Canadians sometimes stray from the resort area near Playa Geron to the west and find themselves, surprised and slightly apprehensive, alone among Cubans.

Two weeks ago today was her fifty-third birthday. Marita Linares knows that on her fifty-fourth birthday she will not be here, looking out at the dusty lane or the beach or the rusting automobile lying axle-deep in the white sand under the palm trees. She will be lying in the cemetery behind the village, on the edge of the sugarcane fields. She knows exactly the spot where she is going to be after she is dead. Sometimes she goes and looks at the grass growing over the place, trying to imagine herself two meters down in the earth.

That is where I am going to be, she thinks. Right there. Under those very grass blades. In a hole in the ground.

Almost never can she imagine it properly. When she occasionally succeeds, she becomes very frightened at the idea of being left so alone under the earth in the cemetery, the idea that she will have to stay there forever. She has hardly ever been afraid of anything, but this is different. She cannot fight against it, she cannot somehow rip the crazily dividing cells out of her bone marrow and make her body clean again. This time it is really going to happen.

The first time was a year ago, when Ramon was last home. Her thyroid. They removed it, gave her pills, and the cancer seemed to be gone. Now it has returned, searching out another weakness in her, the very center of her bones. She found out about the recurrence a month ago. After they told her, the doctors at the clinic gave her some medicine, but it made her unbearably nauseated. The medicine was not a cure, it was only going to give her more time to feel sick, so she declined to take any more. Most of the time she doesn't feel badly, just rather feverish once or twice a week. They have found another teacher for the village school, so she is able to rest a good deal. The doctor at the clinic has said she will stay alive for about a year, perhaps less.

The shadows of the palm trees are growing longer, and the sea has become a deeper blue with the change in the angle of the light. It is possible Ramon won't be able to come today. The ship from the Middle East docked three days ago and he telephoned her as soon as he was ashore, but he said that his leave wouldn't start until his men were all settled in the barracks. Today is the first day she can expect him.

He knows she is ill again; he asked on the telephone and she told him. She has never hidden anything from him (except one thing), and he knows that this time she is going to die, because of what the doctors said when the cancer seemed to go away: if it comes back again, it will remain.

Because of this, she has resolved to tell him the one thing she has never told him. Because it is necessary for what he is going to have to do.

Marita Linares folds her arms under her breasts and continues to wait for her son.

*

Major Ramon Linares gets down from the bus just outside
Puerto Real, near the intersection of the highway with the
dirt road leading toward the sea a kilometer away. He is still
in uniform, although his week's leave has begun this
morning. He carries a small imitation-leather briefcase,
which contains a set of army fatigues, shaving gear, a filigree
silver bracelet from Yemen and a bottle of rum. The three
weeks' voyage home from the Middle East hasn't put any
weight on his spare frame; he is still skinny and tough from
hard living, skin deeply tanned from the Yemeni sun. He
grew a beard during the fighting — there was little enough
water to drink, let alone shave with — and after the
battalion's withdrawal he removed the beard but he has kept
the mustache, whose dark, tight curls accentuate his mouth
with its full and clearly defined lips. He has hazel eyes, a
straight, sharp nose and prominent cheekbones handed down
to him from some now-nameless aristocrat of Aragon or
perhaps Castile, come to the Indies four hundred years ago, a
forgotten imperialist of the Renaissance.

Linares begins setting one foot ahead of the other in the
rhythmic, unflagging march he has perfected over seven
years of tireless labor for other people's revolutions, as well
as for Cuba's. He spent two years in Angola, then returned
to Cuba to study military and civil engineering at the officers'
academy, passed a year in the People's Democratic Republic
of Yemen, returned to Havana to study the arcane arts of
military intelligence. Then came the posting to Ethiopia, then
Yemen again, now home. He has dug wells, built roads and
schools and medical clinics and airports, thrown earthen
dams across rivers, trained blacks and Arabs to do the same
and to fight into the bargain. South African soldiers have
mortared him in Angola, Eritrean insurgents dropped bombs
on him in Ethiopia, and not five weeks ago a counterrevolutionary army trying to overthrow the Marxist government of
the People's Democratic Republic of Yemen was attempting
to kill him with a deluge of shells. He is tired, and grieving,
and very angry.

After walking for a few minutes he sees the roof of the
house behind the row of low trees that screen its landward

side. His mother will be waiting for him, as she is every time he comes home on leave. He wonders what she will think of the reasons for his return. He wonders if he will see the sickness in her face.

The road turns into no more than a dusty lane that curves leftward toward the house. Linares picks up his pace a little. He is so close to home now that he wants to hurry. He tramps around the bend. There is the house facing the sea, the custard-colored stone and the rickety French doors opening onto the yard with its clothesline and sun-bleached wooden benches, the sloping tiled roof over the two upstairs windows. At the left window, a face: his mother.

Linares waves with his left hand, the one not carrying the briefcase. The figure in the window waves back and disappears. Linares hurries toward the house, the briefcase swinging awkwardly, out of rhythm with his pace, but he keeps going.

She meets him at the door. Linares drops the briefcase and embraces her wordlessly, and she him. After a moment she draws back, hands holding tight to his biceps, and looks up at him. He surveys her in return. Linares sees her in two ways at once, as he sometimes does: a woman with the delicate oval face of a hidalga, a noblewoman, the hair black but beginning to be streaked with white, tiny wrinkles at the corners of her dark, intense eyes, a faint palisade of lines across the olive skin above her upper lip. He also sees her as his mother. She is paler than he remembers, with an aura of fatigue he also does not recollect: the cancer. But over her present face are superimposed others from his memory: a much younger one looking down at him, teaching him to read; another, slightly older, glowing in lamplight at bedtime, telling him stories of the revolution and the brave soldiers who died in the jungle, fighting to the end for the freedom of the world. Always the stories, even as he grew older, the tales becoming more complex as he did, the stories taking on depth and breadth, betrayal, tragedy, death, power and glory, truth and lies. The lost revolution, the men and women who secretly lost faith with the dream, the dream fading, colors washing out of it just as the color left the world at sunset.

He cannot remember if she ever said that these were secret things. Much of what she recounted to him was not, on the surface, greatly different from the things he learned at school about the revolution and the forces that wished to destroy it, but when he was still quite young he recognized that there was a secret knowledge she was sharing with him: that over time the enemies of the revolution had penetrated almost to its center. Unable to confront it from without, they had taken on its very colors, seemed to become part of it, began turning the clock back little by little, each second's regress disguised as a step forward.

This he kept to himself; he knew intuitively that to speak of it was dangerous. Or perhaps she had warned him never to speak of it to others, as she never spoke of his father except to him, and that not often. He knows that his father, Jaime Camparo, was Bolivian, as his mother was, and that he died with Che Guevara in the betrayed revolution in that country, killed by the Americans and their eager Bolivian pupils. Linares does not know exactly how his mother got herself and him to Cuba; asked, she has always refused to answer. He understands; some of her rescuers are still alive, and she will not endanger them, not even by telling her son about them. She is still, whatever the others of her generation have become, a true revolutionary. Sometimes he still imagines, as he often did when he was a child, that his father did not die in Bolivia and that he will appear one day, tall and bearded and smiling, with a gun on his shoulder, to make his mother happy again and rekindle the beacon of the revolution of the world.

"You are terribly thin," Marita Linares is saying as she releases one of her son's arms and begins drawing him into the house by the other. "Haven't been taking care of yourself?"

He wants to ask how she is feeling, but doesn't. "The men have to be taken care of first, Mother," he says, picking up the briefcase and following after her. Inside the French doors is the living room, dim inside its louvered windows, with a long dining table at one end over which hangs a carved wooden candelabrum. Along the walls there are bookcases filled with books, almost all political or military history.

Seating arrangements are sparse: a cracked leather sofa, two cane armchairs with worn velvet seat cushions. A prerevolutionary brass standing lamp overhangs one of the cane chairs. This is the one his mother sits in to read. He puts the briefcase on the table and opens it.

"I know," she says. "But an officer isn't any good if he fails to keep his own strength."

"I'm far from weak, Mother," he says, placing the bottle of rum on the table and taking out the filigree bracelet, which is wrapped in a soft square of clean rag. He turns and takes a step toward her as she stands beside her reading chair. "Here," he says. "I brought this for you, it's from Yemen."

She takes the bracelet and unwraps it while he watches her anxiously. He has always yearned for her approval, especially when he has done something that might be construed as bourgeois.

She finishes unwrapping it and places the cloth on the back of her chair. The bracelet's silver glints dully in the light from the French doors as she turns the circlet of metal between hesitant fingers. "This came from Yemen?" she asks.

"Yes. There's a *souk* in Habban, a market. There're a lot of silversmiths in Habban."

She looks at him. "It isn't a black market?" He knows she wants to like the bracelet, but she hates the black market. It undermines everything.

"No, Mother," he answers, with an inward sigh of relief that this is true. "It's part of their economic plan. Or was."

She exhibits one of her rare smiles and slips the bracelet onto her wrist. Linares notices how thin her wrist seems to have become; the heavy metal hangs so loosely on her that he is afraid it will slip off. She notices him watching and pushes it farther up her arm, where it stays more comfortably. "It's beautiful," she says. "I'll wear it always."

Always? he thinks. How long will always be for her?

She realizes what she has said and regards him unfalteringly. "I have a little less than a year, Ramon," she says quietly.

He swallows hard, feels his eyes burning. "Mama? It's certain?"

"Yes."

He reaches out for her, but she holds up a hand to stop him. "No. I knew it might come. I've had time to get used to it. I don't want it to be over us like a cloud. Until I'm dead, I'm going to live."

He lowers his arms. "Yes, Mama."

"Now we should have something to eat."

He follows her into the kitchen, carrying the rum bottle, and pours them both a glass of it with water and sugar while she moves about, the gas stove hissing quietly like the sea wind outside. The old American refrigerator has been giving her shocks again, and he repairs it as she cooks. Beans and rice, eggs, a little pork. "How is the rationing?" he asks her as she spoons food onto two plates. Everything seems extraordinarily normal.

"No better, no worse," she answers, sitting down. "Bread and eggs and milk aren't controlled. Except that you can't buy a lot at once. They don't want people hoarding. I don't think it's changed since you were last here."

He finishes his rum, noticing that she has already drunk hers. This is not quite like her. "Fuel? Cooking oil?" he asks.

She gives a bitter shrug. "The Russians have raised their oil prices almost to capitalist market levels and they have reduced the sugar subsidies. The goods they export to us are worse than ever. There is still enough to eat, but no one who owns a car can afford the fuel to drive it." She puts her fork down and pours herself a little more rum, adding a very small amount of water from the pitcher. "Tell me what happened over there."

"In Yemen?"

"Yes. Of course."

"How much do you already know?"

"You'd better clarify most of it. Your letters were guarded."

He has not quite finished eating, but puts his cutlery down anyway. "All right. Since 1969 there have been two Yemens. The Yemen Arab Republic in the north, controlled by the Americans through the Saudis. And the PDRY, the People's Democratic Republic of Yemen, in the south. The southern capital is Aden. We've been sending aid and technical help for years. I helped build a lot of Habban. Schools, streets, water supplies."

"Yes."

"Two years ago Fidel also sent a battalion of combat engineers. I ended up commanding one of the companies when the old company major was killed in a rebel ambush. There was skirmishing along the border with the Yemen Arab Republic all last year, and then two months ago the YAR provoked a counterrevolution. The YAR had Saudi support and a lot of American weapons, which they sent across the border to the counterrevolutionaries. Some of the PDRY units were so infected by enemy agents that their officers led them over to the rebels."

Ramon looks at his hands, which are trembling with fury. "It was a disaster. We fought alongside the loyal Marxist units for two weeks, but we couldn't get supplies. We expected Russian support from the naval base at Aden, but they wouldn't do anything. They even pulled out the pilots who'd been training the PDRY air force. Then we heard our own brigades from Ethiopia were coming. We were holding the last line north of Aden; there were hardly any reserves at all. We thought we could hold out just long enough, long enough for them to reach us. It was the beginning of August."

"And then?" his mother asks, quiet and intent.

He tells her.

Major Linares focused his binoculars on the far slope of the valley a kilometer away, where rebel shelling had set the village of al Habilayn aflame. Thick columns of yellowish smoke bubbled into the clear air of early morning, throwing elongated shadows westward across the terraced hillside where the villagers grew their crops of millet and sorghum during the rainy season. Some of the terrace retaining walls had been smashed by shellfire during yesterday's bombardment, and dark streaks of soil spilled from the breaches down the tawny rock of the lower slopes. The shelling was still going on, but lightly, maybe only ranging shots. There were a few bomb craters on the valley floor, but the sky was clear of planes. Most of the air force had betrayed the real Marxist government in Aden right at the beginning of the insurrection, and had joined the counterrevolutionary forces. Only three air bases had been left under Communist control: Mukayris, Khormaksar in Aden, and al Anad. Mukayris had been lost during the second week. Al Anad, fifty kilometers north of the capital and about five kilometers behind Linares, was going to fall within the next two days unless the defenders were able to hold this last ridge before the open plain. The blocking force was made up of a badly weakened Yemeni mechanized brigade and the Cuban battalion to which Linares's infantry company belonged.

The position was not quite hopeless, provided reinforcements could be brought up from Aden to bolster the defense north of al Anad. And reinforcements were on the way: two full Cuban brigades, six thousand men, ferried over from Ethiopia across the Red Sea with all their equipment and supplies, in Cuban freighters. They were supposed to have sailed yesterday, which would put them into Aden harbor late today or early tomorrow. The advance guard could be at the al Anad front within twelve hours of landing. Once the brigades arrived in strength it should be possible to drive the forces of counterrevolution into the mountains, then begin to recover the territory they'd overrun in the Abayan governorate to the east.

Unless, of course, Linares reflected as he clambered over the wall of an empty gun pit and began to scramble down the rocky slope toward the company headquarters bunker, the rebels keep getting supplies and equipment from across the border. Then there'll be a stalemate. But at least the revolution here will be safe.

He passed his platoon strongpoint on the way to the bunker and paused briefly to exchange a few words with the lieutenant commanding the small unit. Linares's company consisted of three rifle platoons, and at full strength would have put a few more than a hundred men into the firing line. Casualties had reduced them to a total of seventy-six. The other two companies of the battalion were to the right and left of Linares's, with the battalion headquarters and the reserve — a very small one — on the crest of the ridge above Linares's command post, along with the mortar and artillery batteries. The tank company was at the airfield, a last-ditch defense. Last night they'd tried to get the tanks up onto the ridge to provide more fire support, but the terrain was too rough. The battalion's flanks were covered, or were supposed to be covered, by the Yemenis.

The shelling, which had been becoming more hesitant and sporadic for the past hour, had almost stopped by the time Linares reached his bunker, a shallow cave under a rock overhang, which had been improved by an earth and rock parapet. He ducked inside. The red power light of the radio, which was tuned to the battalion command net, gleamed in the dimness. Captain Menocal, Linares's political officer, was leaning over the radio operator's shoulder, the receiver handset clamped to one ear, taking down a message. A couple of maps were spread on the stony floor of the cave; Captain Portela, the company executive officer, was frowning at them.

"Reports?" Linares asked. His mouth was dry and he wanted a drink of water, but held himself back. He didn't need one yet; he only thought he did. What he wanted more than a drink of water was to bathe in it; he couldn't remember when he'd last been able to wash. Six days ago, or was it seven? They were all filthy and ragged, uniforms blotched with dried sweat and the lion-colored dust, blood-stained from scrapes and cuts and minor wounds. Unable to shave for a week for want of water, they were all growing beards.

Portela looked up from his maps. "Battalion's ordered a counterattack," he said tiredly. "Captain Menocal's getting the details from battalion now. We're to take al Habilayn back. We'll have 2nd Company in our support after artillery preparation. There'll be air support, as well."

"We'd better not count too much on help from the air," Linares said. He knelt beside Portela, feeling the cave floor hard and grittily painful under his knees. He'd lost too much weight in the past four weeks, as they all had. The tatters of his uniform were hanging on him like rags on a rake handle.

"Yes, sir," Portela said dutifully. He was an excellent executive officer, blessed with just enough imagination, completely professional, pragmatic. Menocal was a little different: the political officer, more of an intellectual, although he could fight as well as any of the men in the platoon strong points.

"When do we move?" Linares asked.

Menocal gave the handset to the radioman and held out the message flimsy. "These are the exact orders, major. Move off at 0830. Attack to commence at 0930."

Linares scanned the orders. They had about an hour to prepare. The artillery fire plan was straightforward, which was good. What was not so good was the need to cross the open floor of the valley, which would be swept by enemy guns and heavy mortars. But if the artillery did its job, the crossing might not be too bad. He opened his mouth to issue his first orders.

The ground suddenly shook. Linares found himself falling over, apparently deaf, for he could hear nothing. There was a brilliant white light outside and a sensation of intense pressure across his chest.

Barrage, he found himself thinking. A big one.

Then he was on the cave floor, mixed up with one of Portela's maps. There was sound again, a huge booming roar that seemed both to come from outside and to be transmitted through the earth itself. Bits of gravel shredded off the cave roof and fell down his collar.

Portela and Menocal were picking themselves up. The radioman lay inert on his face, bleeding from the back of his head, felled by a piece of rock peeled from the cave roof. Several heavy shells must have fallen just outside the cave entrance; more were thundering down not far away. That meant that this was no harassing barrage; the rebels were working up to a major assault.

At least we won't have to make that counterattack, Linares thought. He was still a little dazed.

"Can you raise battalion?" he yelled at Portela over the din of exploding shells.

Portela tried for a few seconds, then shook his head. The rock that had hit the radioman must have also struck the radio. "Doesn't work," he called.

Linares thought the shell curtain might have moved away a little. He had to see what was going on. "Outside," he ordered. He grabbed up the radioman's AK-47 assault rifle and headed for the cave entrance.

Portela and Menocal, white-faced, seized their weapons and followed him. Linares again noticed their fear and the absence of his own. It still puzzled him, that exemption. His body was as keyed up as theirs, the heart pumping hard and adrenaline flooding through the muscles, but for no apparent reason his brain failed to interpret it as fear. Death or mutilation seemed as unlikely as if he'd been at home in Puerto Real.

The blessing didn't make him foolhardy, however. He went as far as the parapet outside the cave mouth and looked carefully around its flank. From this position he could see down the slope to the valley floor some five hundred meters off. Smoke and dust from the barrage were drifting across the hillside, but he could still make out the bottom of the valley, sprinkled suddenly with hundreds of soldiers, all trotting toward the three-kilometer frontage held by the single Cuban battalion. Where the devil had the rebels gotten the men? And this quantity of artillery ammunition, for that matter?

He thought he knew the answer. The government of the other Yemen, the pro-Western Yemen Arab Republic north of the border, had finally decided to intervene on the side of the counterrevolutionaries. They'd sent troops and American munitions and weapons, supplied by the Saudi Arabians, who would like nothing better than to see the Marxist People's Democratic Republic of Yemen exhaust itself in an endless battle to preserve its revolution.

Sons of bitches, Linares thought furiously as the shells shrieked and boomed and the assault companies swept steadily toward the Cuban positions on the heights. But they won't get by us, we won't let them. *No pasaran.*

The first of the attackers had reached the bottom of the slope. Shells began exploding among them, the heavy mortars and 100 mm guns of the Cuban artillery support firing in reply to the rebel bombardment. Then the enemy barrage lifted and the shells began dropping farther up the slope, behind and above Linares's command post. The valley floor was speckled with the bodies of fallen men, but many of the assault wave had survived to reach the platoon strong points. Small-arms fire crackled across the slopes; hand grenades banged. Linares, from his higher vantage point, could see that small parties of the enemy were trying to infiltrate the positions and work their way toward the crest of the ridge. If they managed to get that far and dig in, the company would be in serious trouble. So would the battalion headquarters, just over the ridge line on its reverse slope. If the rebels took the ridge the battalion and the airfield were as good as overrun.

He glanced right and left. The riflemen and the single machine gunner of his headquarters section, dug in behind rock outcroppings close to the cave, were already in action, firing down the slope at the oncoming infantry. The battle had passed the point where he could exert any control over it, especially since he no longer had any communications with his platoon commanders.

"Find a position and start shooting," he called to his two officers, and crawled toward the machine-gun dugout. There was a *sangar*, a loopholed stone wall, near the dugout, and Linares slithered behind it and poked the barrel of the AK-47 through the loophole. He started squeezing off single shots at the shadows flitting through the smoke of the bombardment. A few meters away the machine gun hammered in short bursts. Enemy shells were still exploding along the crest of the ridge, but he thought there weren't as many as before.

Suddenly, cut off short, the shellfire stopped. Linares peered through the loophole. The enemy should have been right on the heels of the barrage, almost on top of him, but they weren't. The rebel gunners had overestimated the speed of the infantry advance, had ceased fire too soon and hadn't been ordered to open up again. They must be shooting a preplanned barrage.

They're having their own communication problems, Linares thought. Good.

He shoved a fresh clip into the rifle and listened carefully. There was still plenty of small-arms fire around his platoon strong points, although he couldn't see them for the smoke and dust. That meant the men in the strong points hadn't been overrun yet. Linares let his instincts take over, sensing the flow of the battle.

It's time, something deep inside him said. *Go.*

He jumped to his feet. A dozen meters away he saw Portela's white face staring at him from behind a boulder. "On your feet!" Linares screamed at him, at his riflemen and at Menocal. "Headquarters section! Immediate counter-attack! Go! Go!"

Without waiting to see if any of them followed, he sprinted down the hill. Veils of dust engulfed him, thick and tawny as a lion's pelt, eddying in the wind blowing along the valley. He sensed men behind him and threw a glance over his right shoulder. Portela was there, running through the murk as though the devil were after him, and beside him the light machine gunner, carrying the heavy RPK as though it were a twig. Menocal and the four remaining riflemen of the section were strung out in a rough line echeloned back to Linares's right.

A gust of wind twitched the smoke aside. Not a hundred meters ahead was the 2nd Platoon strong point. Linares's instinct had been correct. The attackers had gotten bogged down in the fire-swept zones between the three platoon positions, and were trying to overrun them instead of infiltrating all the way up the slope. At least a dozen were in Linares's plain view, kneeling or crouching with their backs to him.

"Shoot!" he yelled, but the machine gunner and his loader already had thrown themselves to the ground and were doing so. Portela and Menocal and the riflemen crouched behind stones and boulders and poured fire into the backs of the attackers. Grenades flew. Parts of men dissolved in sprays of red and gray and white.

Surprised by the unexpected counterattack from their rear, the attacking force around the 2nd Platoon position panicked, broke and ran. It was the worst thing they could have done. Others, whose units had already suffered dreadful execution in the frontal assault, saw the fleeing figures and concluded that they were the target of a counter-attack in strength. Ignoring their officers' shouts in their fear, they began to drop back down the slope, faster and faster as the Cuban strong points doubled their fire.

Linares saw them break and ran for the strong point, disregarding the danger of being shot mistakenly by his own men. But the platoon lieutenant had seen what was happening and was waving furiously at Linares, directing him toward a gap the shellfire had cut in the razor wire surrounding the position. As he scooted through the wire, followed by Portela and the others — not one of them appeared to have so much as a scratch — he heard the bump of mortar projectiles exploding on the valley floor among the fleeing insurgents. The attack, in this sector at any rate, had been broken.

"Are you in contact with battalion?" he asked the lieutenant as they crouched in the command dugout. Shells were falling again, to screen the rebel withdrawal. "We've got no radio up there."

"Yes, sir." The lieutenant gestured at the radio operator. "Gomez, help the major."

They were busy up at battalion, but he got through after a few minutes. The attack was fading away all along the front, the rebels streaming back across the valley floor, pursued by mortar and gunfire. All units were to hold their present positions until ordered otherwise. There was to be no pursuit.

Linares knew what that meant. Losses had been heavy. If the fresh brigades didn't reach them before the next attack, they'd be defeated. It was as simple as that.

The sun was down, and both dusk and the air temperature were falling rapidly. For all Linares could see from the crest of the ridge, where he was sitting on a flat rock that still retained some of the sun's warmth, the valley might have been uninhabited, except that al Habilayn across the way was still smoking dismally in the violet twilight. Both sides, exhausted by the battle that morning, were tending their wounds in private.

He spotted Portela and Menocal working their way up the slope toward him. Portela reached him first. "What's going on, sir?" the captain asked.

"I don't know," Linares admitted. "The colonel's orders. All officers captain and above to meet at battalion HQ at 1900." He glanced at his watch. "Three minutes from now. You're lucky you're not late. Let's go."

He got up from his rock and set off down the reverse slope

toward the battalion headquarters bunker. Everyone else was already there, but it wasn't as crowded as it would have been at this time yesterday. They'd lost several officers, including the major commanding 1st Company. He'd been hit in the head and wasn't expected to live.

Colonel Cardoso, the battalion commander, was leaning against the bunker wall, smoking a freshly lit cigar. His eyes were half closed against the smoke. A wide white scar ran from his right eyebrow high onto his scalp. No hair grew from the scar tissue. The old wound gave him a look of Mongolian savagery. He'd been hit in Ethiopia, fighting the Somali aggressors as a junior lieutenant back in 1977. Linares had a high regard for the colonel. He was a tough and vigorous commander, but he tried not to waste his men.

"Everyone here?" he asked around the cigar as Linares and his two captains took up positions along the back wall of the bunker. He took the cigar out of his mouth. "Good. We'll start. I'm sorry to have to tell you that Major Aguilar died an hour ago. Captain Ortiz will continue to command 1st Company until I make other arrangements. Any questions, comrades?"

A low murmur. It might have been any one of them.

Linares said: "Colonel Cardoso, with your permission."

"Go ahead."

"When may we expect the brigade reinforcements from Ethiopia?"

Cardoso put the cigar into his mouth, dragged on it and exhaled. "I was coming to that. There aren't going to be any reinforcements."

A stunned silence. "Sir?" somebody asked.

"They're not coming." Cardoso eyed his officers, measuring their reactions. "And we're not staying."

"Comrade colonel," Linares said, "it's true we need a rest. But until there's somebody to help the Yemenis hold up here —"

"You don't follow me, do you?" Cardoso snapped. "I said we're not staying. We're not staying in Yemen at all. We're being withdrawn entirely. Back to Cuba. Same with the Ethiopian brigades. They're on their way home, too."

"But," Menocal said, and stopped, mouth hanging open.

"But we've been here for two years," he managed to continue. "Why are they doing this?"

"Ask President Castro when we get home," Cardoso said. "I got orders, that was all. We're to pull out tonight. The Yemeni battalions on each side of us will have to extend to hold the line. I'll take it on myself to explain it to them. Company commanders stay here to cut movement orders back to Aden. The rest of you, get your men prepared. We move at 0300, and not a second later."

The junior officers filed dazedly out, leaving Cardoso alone with Ortiz, Linares, and Major Aranda, 2nd Company commander.

"Why?" Linares asked. "Why, really?"

"How should I know?" Cardoso said brusquely. Then, relenting, because he knew Linares's combat record: "I imagine it was Russian pressure. You know how the political situation's changed in the Soviet Union. No more support for armed revolutionary struggle out here. Moscow's feet have been getting colder since 1985. The Kremlin wants to climb into bed with the capitalists, the United States especially. Fucking revisionists."

Boots scraped on the stone steps leading down from ground level outside. They belonged to Major Eduardo Cruz, the battalion political officer. Alone among the men in the bunker, he'd recently managed to shave. His round, sleek face was glum.

"You've told them, colonel?" he asked after saluting.

"Yes," Cardoso snapped. "You're the political officer, you explain it to them. Why Havana's ordered this. Make some sense of it. If you can."

Cruz raised his hands, palms upward, in a gesture that was almost supplicating. "It's —" he began.

"Was this order directly from President Castro?" Linares interrupted, before Cruz could take flight.

Cruz and Cardoso exchanged the briefest of glances. "Yes," Cardoso said. "So I'm told."

"The colonel says it's Russian pressure," Linares said to Cruz. "Is that correct?"

Cruz nodded reluctantly. "It can't be anything else."

"That's why we haven't had any support from the Soviets

in Aden, isn't it?" Aranda chimed in. "They don't want to get involved. They're afraid of the Americans."

"And Fidel gave in to them," said Linares hotly. "Why *now*, of all times? Aden can't hold out against the counter-revolutionaries without help. Why not give us a month more? Just one month, and the brigades from Ethiopia?"

"Aden can't send us supplies unless the Russians provide them," Cardoso snapped. "You do know that, don't you, Major Linares? All the Russians have to do is cut off shipments to the Yemenis. They're going to do that soon anyway, some sort of agreement with the Americans and the Saudis. We'll wither on the vine here. Already we're short of ammunition, food, everything."

"Furthermore," Cruz pointed out, "we were supposed to be here as advisers and support troops only. We were never supposed to get dragged into combat. That only happened because we were in the way of the rebels' first attack."

Linares discovered that his fists were clenched. "Are we saying the revolution here isn't worth defending, then? Whose revolution is? Where do these things stop? Do they stop at home? When the Russians tell Fidel to kiss the American arse, is he going to do it?" Linares knew he should shut his mouth, but he blurted out the words anyway. "In anyone else ... we all know what it would be called. Betrayal. Treason. *Counterrevolution.*"

"Major Linares," Cruz warned icily. "You criticize too much."

Linares glanced at Cardoso. The battalion colonel was regarding him with eyes empty of all expression. The other two company commanders, Ortiz and Aranda, wore carefully blank faces.

"Is that all, major?" Cardoso asked politely.

"Yes, sir," Linares said. "That's all."

"Good," Cardoso said. "Whatever anyone feels about this, we've been given orders. We are going to obey them. Cruz, get the maps."

Linares's throat is dry from talking, and the rum bottle is half empty. He is not sure whether he or his mother has drunk most of it. He doesn't think it is her, for she shows no signs of intoxication.

"And after?" she asks.

"We were on the ship the next afternoon, those of us who were left. The rebels broke into the plain the day after that. Then everything came to a stop, while the Americans and the Saudis and the Russians made their deal. You know about that."

"Yes," she says quietly. "Provisional government. Bourgeois democracy. Another revolution destroyed from the inside."

"It's happening here," he says. He would never dare say it to anyone else. "It's already happened. Castro has given up. I knew it when the orders came to withdraw. He won't fight any more. Nobody will." He slams his clenched fist onto the table; the rum bottle and the cutlery jump. "What *happened*?"

"I think I can tell you what happened," she murmurs to him.

"What?"

"Listen, Ramon. I think everyone has two minds. A bourgeois one, and a revolutionary one. The bourgeois mind is very strong. It wants *things*, it wants comfort, it wants to be warm and fat, it doesn't want to struggle. It cares for nothing but itself, and it will do anything, once it has a few of those *things* and a little comfort, to keep them. A revolutionary, if he's going to keep on being one, has to struggle against it every instant. That is why the revolution has failed in eastern Europe, and in the Soviet Union, and why it will fail in China."

Linares nods. His mother looks into his eyes, then continues.

"The revolutionaries took power in the name of the people, which is right, but then they allowed themselves to have a few, even just one or two, *things*. As soon as they had them, they were afraid to lose them. Then they used their power, which was given to them by the people, to keep those things. Soon they began to fear the people. A gap opened between the people and the revolutionary party. Like magic, there is a class struggle again. The revolutionaries of the party have become the new bourgeoisie, and they behave like bourgeoisie. And the people, because they are infected with counterrevolutionary ideas from the capitalist world, think that destroying the party and replacing it with bourgeois democracy will bring them the things the party members have and they don't."

"But that's wrong," Ramon says.

"Yes, it is. The people think only of the wealth of the capitalist world, the *things*. They don't realize, or don't wish to know, that these things are purchased through the oppression of most of humanity. Remember how the capitalists once oppressed their own working class. Then Marxism came, and the workers began to realize what was happening. But the capitalists were clever, and they knew there would be revolution if they changed nothing. So they began to let their workers have a little more wealth, to keep them content and politically unaware, sleepwalking through the world."

"Like the factory workers in the United States," Linares says morosely. "All of them have cars, sometimes two in one family."

"Yes. But that wealth had to come from somewhere. Since the capitalists no longer dared squeeze all their wealth out of their own workers, they had to look elsewhere for it, outside their own borders. They found that even the poorest countries had wealth that could be forced out of them. And the people of those countries are brown, or black, or yellow. It's been easy for the capitalists to make their workers believe that such people are inferior, that it doesn't matter how many of them die so that the capitalist nations, the bourgeois democracies, can go on gorging themselves at the expense of the rest of the world."

She pauses; her voice has become low and fervid. She looks feverish. "The first revolution has failed because the revolutionaries broke faith with the oppressed, with themselves. They allowed themselves to be seduced. They have become what they fought against in the beginning. There are only a few of us left who haven't broken that faith."

She takes a deep breath. "And we have to begin again. There must be a second revolution. To begin it, we have to remind the world that the poor and oppressed have not gone away. We have to remind the poor and oppressed that the *revolution* has not gone away. The capitalists think they have

gotten rid of us, that we are powerless. We must show that
we can still inspire the masses, that we are still the leaders."

Spent, she slumps back in her chair. Linares observes her with
suddenly worried eyes. "Mother," he says, "are you in pain?"

She sits up again. "No. Only, I become tired sooner than I
used to."

"Jesus, Maria," he mumbles against all his training, putting
his head in his hands.

"I am the one dying, not you," she says sharply. She
cannot abide seeing him in pain for her. "Sit up."

He obeys her.

"We are all dying," she tells him. "Some of us have longer
than others. Mine is fifty-four years. It is twenty-seven more
than I once thought I was going to have. I think sometimes
that I have lived twice as long as I was supposed to."

He doesn't understand. He tells her so.

She reaches for the rum bottle, pours, sips rum neat from
her glass. "I have to tell you something important," she says.
"There was a time when I thought I never would, but
now...." She lifts her shoulders and lets them drop. Dusk is
falling outside the kitchen window, turning the sea indigo.
"It's necessary for you to know. Because of what we were
talking about. The revolution. The failure."

"Go on," he says as she pauses. Under his sorrow is an
intense curiosity. He has always suspected there was a secret
behind him, behind her, somewhere.

"As far as I am aware, there are very few people besides
myself who know this," she is saying. "One is Fidel Castro.
The second is a Bolivian like myself, Miguel Inciarte. There
is a third I know of. And the security service will have it
somewhere in their secret files."

Linares frowns. He is able to concentrate on what she is
saying, ignoring her sickness with an act of will, but none of
this makes sense to him. "Inciarte," he says. "He was the
Bolivian interior minister who pretended he was working for
the CIA, and then came over to the revolution. Che Guevara
kept diaries, when he was fighting in Bolivia, when my father
was with him. The diaries were captured. Inciarte smuggled
them out of Bolivia so Fidel Castro could publish them
here."

"That's right. But that isn't all he smuggled out. He also helped me escape, with you. You were only a few days old."

"I see," Linares says, and waits. Until now he didn't know who got his mother out of Bolivia, but he knows her too well to believe that this is the revelation toward which she is leading him.

"He did this," she says quietly, "because your father was not Jaime Camparo, as I have told you. Your father was Che Guevara."

It is stated so matter-of-factly that he accepts it without a blink, although he realizes that the knowledge is going to change him profoundly. He waits for her to go on.

She thinks he is in shock, for she hurriedly starts to explain related matters. "You are wondering why I went to such pains to keep this to myself. It was because of Fidel Castro. When I reached here, I told him who I was, who you were. He didn't believe me, of course, although Inciarte did. So Castro told me to make no such claims, or you would be taken away and put into an orphanage. I was afraid for you, so I obeyed. But because I had worked for the revolution in Bolivia, he let me stay here as a schoolteacher. When you were seven, he came to see me. He wanted to look at you. He watched you from this very kitchen one afternoon, when you were playing on the beach. After an hour, he knew I was telling the truth. Your father has come back in you."

"But why wouldn't he acknowledge it?" Linares asks. "Everyone knows Che Guevara was married twice. I have —" The thought was odd. "Half-brothers and sisters."

"Your father had been dead for seven years when Fidel came here. His legend was established. But there was always whispering that Castro hadn't supported your father in Bolivia as well as he had promised he would, even that Castro wanted him to fail. Castro was afraid of the whispers, because he was afraid of your father's memory. You see, Fidel already had begun to enjoy *things*. But your father was a true revolutionary, and Fidel knew it. We were a reproach to him. He ordered me to remain silent, and I have done so. Until now."

"Yes," Linares says. "I understand." It is starting to mean something. His mind is chasing fragments of images: himself out on the beach all those years ago, with Castro peering at him through the kitchen window. His mother and Che Guevara. His father alive in him again.

"Were you there when my father died?" he asks.

"Yes." She tells him what happened to her, almost happened to her, in the mountain town of La Higuera; about his birth on the aircraft on the way to La Paz. When she has finished, he says:

"The American knew who you and I were, and he saved us?"

"No, he didn't know. No one knew then. When we reached La Paz, the American's superior ordered him to turn me directly over to Inciarte, the interior minister. The Bolivian Army was giving out that Che died of wounds from the battle, you see, and I was too politically dangerous for the Americans to want to handle. But Inciarte hated the Americans and the Bolivian junta, and he hid you and me and told the army he'd had me secretly executed, and they believed him. He got us out as soon as he could. He fled the country himself just a few months later, after he got Che's diaries to Cuba. He was one of us all along."

Linares is oddly curious about the American. "But the American stopped them from murdering you in La Higuera," he says.

"Don't think too much of him for all that," she snaps. "He only saved me so the Bolivian doctors the CIA trained could pry my mind apart with drugs. It was only political luck I ended with Inciarte instead."

"Where is Inciarte now?"

"I don't know. He was in East Germany for a time. Perhaps he's still there in spite of their counterrevolution. He'd be very old. He may be dead."

"And the Americans don't know you escaped with me to Cuba? That we're here?"

"I don't know. The Americans might have found out later, after Inciarte got out. But it was so long ago."

Linares nods, a reflex gesture. He is emotionally far out of balance, and it prevents him from thinking clearly, a sensation he loathes. His mother is dying. He is Che Guevara's son. Everywhere the revolution has been betrayed; perhaps his father was betrayed. Something must be done. He must do something. He wants to burst into a shout, tears, anything.

Instead, he asks out of a tightened throat: "Was it Fidel? Did Fidel betray my father?" Already he thinks of Guevara as the man who with his mother gave him life.

She bows her head, then raises it. "I think it may have been. I could not believe it, not for a long time. But now.... Che needed help. Fidel must have known it. Monje, the chief of the Bolivian Party, knew it. But nothing was sent, no medicine, no food, no weapons. Monje stopped people from joining Che in the mountains. There was no one to help."

The sun is setting, and the kitchen is growing dark. Marita Linares gets up to turn on the electric light. When she snaps the switch the bulb glows dully yellow then fades into extinction. "You see," she says, resuming her seat. "There is no power. Fidel has sold the oil we need to make it. Yes, I think your father was betrayed. The Russians told Fidel even then that he must stop exporting armed revolution to Latin America. Che was an embarrassment to everyone." She looks down, clenches a fist on the table, strikes the wooden surface gently. "They all wanted him to fail, and so they let him die. I was the only one left who could help him and ... I failed —"

To Linares's horror, the words leave her in deep, racking sobs. He has never, never seen her cry. He reaches across the table, the dishes clattering, and takes both her hands.

Her long fingers lock convulsively around his. "I wanted to die," she whispers. "But I had you. I wasn't able to die."

She raises her head to look at him. Light reflected from the sea gleams in through the kitchen window. Her eyelids are swollen and inflamed with tears. Linares senses a slow, deep fracture taking place inside him. The world is transforming itself. It looks the same, but nothing is the same.

"Mother," he murmurs. "There must be something I can do."

Her eyes gleam, salt and wet like the half-illuminated sea beyond the beach. "Yes," she whispers. "Yes. There is. If you will."

"I will," he says, for her, for his betrayed and murdered father, for himself. "I will."

She is in possession of herself again. "I thought nothing less," she says calmly, after a moment. "We aren't quite alone in this."

"I would hope not."

"Do you know what GATT is?"

He frowns. "No."

"It's a capitalist organization, one of the ones they use to control the world economy. The letters stand for General Agreement on Trade and Tariffs. Its next meeting is in Miami, next May. It will be a major conference; many of the capitalist economics ministers will be there."

"And?"

"It has been suggested to me by someone I know that it would be an appropriate target for a revolutionary act. I'm afraid I can't tell you who the someone is. Enough to say that the person is of a like mind to ours. He has been aware of who you are for some time."

Ramon digests this. "He wants me to strike at the conference?"

"Yes. If you will. Because he believes you can do it, and because of who you are."

Ramon knows that he has, without realizing it, been waiting for something like this. Waiting to know that Yemen was not the end.

"I will do it," he says without hesitation. "How?"

"It will be very indirect. Wait for a little while."

"Yes, Mother."

"But Ramon."

He raises his dark eyebrows quizzically.

She is frowning, as she does when she concentrates hard. "I think," she says slowly and at last, "that the conference is insufficient. And it's always possible that the person I know ... well, suppose his security has been penetrated?"

Ramon nods. "It's always possible."

"There should be a different target. One even more striking than the conference. One that only you and I know about."

He regards her, eyes narrowed with concentration and excitement, as she tells him.

Lima, Peru — Washington, D.C. February 1–4

■

When Michael Conroy first managed to open his eyes, he thought he had been afflicted with some curious form of blindness. His visual field was a blank white. Then he saw a black fleck on the blankness. The fleck moved suddenly, stopped. Conroy realized that he was looking at a whitewashed ceiling, and that the black fleck was a fly.

"Michael?"

Conroy thought he recognized the voice. He turned his head slowly, realizing that he was in a bed and that his head was on a pillow. The pillow was soft, but the motion hurt nevertheless. He saw a white wall with a window in it; cheerful sunlight was falling in through the window. On a chair next to the bed, sitting partly in the sunlight, was Rick Saintsbury. His tanned, pear-shaped face wore an expression of concern.

"Michael?" Saintsbury said again, and added doubtfully, "can you see me okay?"

Conroy's vocal cords wouldn't work at first. He swallowed a couple of times before his throat was lubricated enough to speak. The muscle movement was painful. "Yeah," he managed. "Where the hell am I?"

"Anglo-American Hospital. Jesus, you're lucky. Do you remember what happened?"

"No." Conroy angled his head, trying not to wince. A plastic pitcher and a glass stood on a metal hospital table beside the bed. "Is there any water in that thing?"

Saintsbury shook his jowls dubiously. "I dunno if you

should have any. You've had a hell of a concussion. I should ask the nurse."

"Give me some water, or I'll get out of bed and pour it myself."

"Okay," Saintsbury said quickly. "It's your head. Stay put." He slopped a little water into the bottom of the glass and handed it to Conroy, who levered himself up on one elbow to take it.

"Last thing I remember is walking toward the car after I left the restaurant," Conroy said after a gulp of water. "Then what happened?"

"Car bomb. Triggered by a remote transmitter. About an hour after it happened, the Sendero Luminoso telephoned and claimed responsibility."

"Uh-huh," Conroy muttered, finishing the water and handing the glass to Saintsbury. He lowered himself onto the pillow. The Sendero Luminoso, the Shining Path Maoist guerrilla movement, had announced three weeks ago that they were declaring open season on Americans, particularly embassy or consular officials they suspected of being CIA. There wasn't a tourist to be seen in Lima; three had already been murdered, one an unfortunate Australian.

"You shouldn't have left the car on the street," Saintsbury told him. "They must have used a magnetized package, just slipped it under the chassis."

"Where the hell was I supposed to leave it? Are we all going to have to walk everywhere? That's just as dangerous. I hope Langley isn't going to tell Bate to issue some half-witted order like that." Bate was the Lima CIA station chief; Conroy, deputy station chief, was his second-in-command. Saintsbury was a senior case officer.

"No, he's not. But we're all going to have to be a lot more careful."

"I don't see how we can be unless we all quit working. How in hell did they miss me?" I might not have been here, Conroy thought. I might have been in bits all over a Lima street. Christ.

"You were lucky, like I said. To start with, it was a small bomb. Second, the triggerman fired it too soon. Something must have thrown him off — maybe he saw police doing a spot check. Anyway, you were still forty feet from the car when the damn thing went off. The blast pitched you into a wall, but the fragments from the car missed you somehow. You've got a couple of cracked ribs, a lot of bruises and a concussion that put you out for fourteen hours."

"This is tomorrow morning?"

"Yeah. Seven o'clock. I've been here all night, just in case they tried to take another crack at you."

"Thanks."

"S'okay. If you don't feel like throwing up, you can have some more water."

Conroy was in fact feeling a shade queasy. "No, thanks."

"I'll have the doc come in and have a look at you. If he says it's okay, we'll check you out of here tonight, after dark. Bate's worried Shining Path may have found out you're CIA and not consular. You're going to stay at the embassy compound tonight."

"I suppose so," Conroy mumbled. Talking hurt, and he was getting tired and wanted to go to sleep. "I'd better have Gord's staff check my apartment before I go back."

Saintsbury looked sideways. "Bate's had all your stuff except the furniture brought over to the embassy," he said.

"What? What the hell for?"

"Langley's recalled you," Saintsbury told him, still not meeting Conroy's eyes. "You're leaving for Washington as soon as you're fit to travel. A home tour. They've got fed up with you avoiding coming back. You were supposed to go back last year, remember? Now they're just going to yank you back."

Conroy let his head, which he had lifted off the pillow, drop onto it. "Ah, shit."

"Sorry. I know how you feel about desks. They'll likely put you onto training for a while. You know more than almost anybody about Latin America. After that they'll probably jump you to station chief."

"Who's going to take over my people? I've got a couple of good ones."

"I am, for the moment."

"Okay. I can live with that."

Saintsbury looked slightly relieved. "Fine, you wait right

here. I'm going to get the doctor to have a look at you."

Bate made Conroy stay at the embassy over the weekend, to make sure he was well enough to travel. Saintsbury was taking over as deputy station chief, and Conroy spent most of a day briefing him. Then Bate packed Conroy off to the airport under the protection of Saintsbury and two of the embassy guards, silent young Marines in civilian clothes with pistols under their jackets. Sendero Luminoso had bombed the car of an American businessman the day previously, killing the man, his wife and his two children. The U.S. Embassy was advising all Americans to avoid unnecessary travel. Saintsbury and the Marines accompanied Conroy into the transit lounge and waited with him until his flight was called. Conroy was annoyed at the precautions, and said so.

"I told Bate the same thing," Saintsbury confessed. "He told me to do it anyway. You're still not in great shape."

"It's not as bad as you're making out," Conroy growled. His head was clear, and he felt well again, although he couldn't breathe deeply because his ribs were taped. He stood up, shouldered his flight bag and turned for the departure gate where the line of passengers had almost disappeared into the maw of the boarding tunnel.

"You're sure you'll be able to connect with your sister at Dulles?"

"Yes, Rick, for Christ's sake, quit fussing." Gemma Conroy was a professor of art history at George Washington University. She was flying to Italy to spend three months doing research in the Vatican library, and she and Conroy would just manage to cross paths at the airport. She'd left a house key with a neighbor in case his flight was late, but he wanted to see her before she went.

"Well, anyway," Saintsbury said, also getting up. "I'll send you the check as soon as I've sold off your furniture. Shouldn't be too much trouble moving it. I'll try to get the rest of your stuff out in the dip bag, so the Peruvian post office doesn't steal it."

"Okay, thanks. No rush." Conroy stuck out his hand. "So long. Look me up in Washington."

"Will do."

He was traveling first class — it was almost empty — and had a window seat. The jet climbed and banked, swinging northward, and Conroy pensively watched the land drop away below him. Soon the flanks of the Andes thrust skyward through banks of cloud, peaks gleaming in the bright and bitter air. Down there lay the vast motley of Latin America, the successor states of the Spanish and Portuguese empires, those ramshackle realms hacked out of the Neolithic face of the continent by the conquistadores and the priests and the merchants of the faraway Iberian peninsula. Freighted with the twin millstones of colossal wealth and wretched poverty, its mingled human warmth and mindless cruelty had often driven Conroy to distraction, but at the same time the great continent drew him like a lodestone. Now he was leaving it, perhaps for the last time. If he got a promotion, it wouldn't necessarily be here.

He turned from the window when the stewardess served champagne, but refused the small bottle. Conroy now almost never drank. He had seen the hold alcohol could achieve over men and women in his profession, and the work could be hard enough without adding addiction to its other stresses. The food, however, was good when she brought it. He ate the meal and found himself sleepy again. He rebelled at the fatigue and dragged out the book he'd put into his cabin baggage. Saintsbury and his wife had given it to Conroy for Christmas and he hadn't got around to reading it yet; it was a recently published history of Francisco Pizarro's conquest of the Incan empire. Conroy lost himself in the author's examination of that fierce and blood-sodden age.

Lavender dusk was falling over the Virginia hills when the plane landed at Dulles. Conroy went through customs to find his sister, Gemma, waiting on its other side. She was almost as tall as he was, but not nearly so solidly built. She was also much fairer, with auburn hair and blue eyes. Except for a similarity of voices and intonation, they did not look like brother and sister. She was two years older than he was, and had never married. They embraced beside the cart onto which he had loaded his two suitcases and the flight bag.

"My God, Michael," she said breaking away and looking at his baggage. "That's not much."

"The rest is coming later. It's not much, either."

"You always traveled light, didn't you?"

"I guess so."

"Have you got a coat? We're having a cold snap." She was wearing a dark blue knee-length cape with slits for the arms and a jacket of the same material underneath. Looking around, he realized the garb must be a new winter fashion. He felt oddly out of touch, almost foreign.

"I've got one," he said. "How long before your flight?"

"I have to check in in just a few minutes. Security's taking nearly two hours nowadays. Here're the house keys. I left some dinner in the fridge for you. It's under foil. The car keys are on the hall table, and the car's in the laneway. It's just had its annual inspection, so you won't be bothered with that."

"Thanks," he said. He was disappointed that they wouldn't have more time together. Since their parents' deaths, she was the only person in North America he was close to. "You're too good to me," he added.

"Nonsense. I haven't laid eyes on you in a year and a half. I'm awfully glad you're here to take care of the house. I didn't want to leave it empty, but three months isn't long enough for a rental. You're sure you're all right by yourself?" He'd told her in his Saturday phone call that he'd been in a car accident. Gemma knew who he worked for, but she had always gone agreeably along with his public persona of a State Department employee.

"I'm fine."

"That's a relief." She looked at her watch. "Michael, I've got to go. Write to me. We'll catch up on everything when I get back." She leaned toward him and kissed him lightly on the cheek. "Don't forget to water the plants. Except the cactus, of course."

"I won't."

She left him with a dramatic swirl of the cape, stopping once to wave over her shoulder as Conroy was struggling into his overcoat. He waved back, and then she was gone.

He woke the next morning in Gemma's guest room, feeling back to normal again except for a dull ache where the two cracked ribs were knitting. The angry bruises on his torso had begun to fade, although they still looked quite virulent next to the white tape binding his rib cage. He took a sponge bath to avoid soaking the tape, then went downstairs to make breakfast. On the sideboard in the kitchen was a collection of framed photographs, among them one of himself and Gemma taken by their father in the back yard of the New Orleans house, just before Conroy went to Bolivia for the first time. Conroy gazed at it while he was eating his toast. Twenty-three years old, the man in the picture stared back.

What icebergs ahead you didn't know about, Conroy thought as he looked at the dark, arrogant, self-possessed young face that could have been black Irish, or French, or Italian, or Spanish. Bolivia and Che Guevara, Chile and Allende, Cairo and Sadat, Madrid and Franco, Uruguay and the Tupamaros, the colonels in Argentina, Sandinistas, Egyptians, Cubans, Russians, East Germans, disasters and a few victories. You still had Marguerite when Dad took that picture of you, in fact I think she was there that day, standing next to Dad, as I remember. You married her two years later, divorced three years after that. You didn't know that was going to happen, did you? Although if you'd stopped to think, you might have been able to see part of it. She wasn't equipped for that kind of life, the uncertainty, the deception, the foreignness, always moving somewhere else, although she tried bravely enough, she really did try. And you were up-country somewhere in Chile the day she had the stillbirth, eight months along she was, all alone in Santiago three weeks after we got there, not knowing a soul. That was the fracture that wouldn't heal. Losing the child like that. Her, our, daughter. Three months later she was gone. Remarried years ago. Her children would be grown by now. I heard somewhere she had two. And here I am, not much changed outwardly, hair not quite as black, a little gray in it but still lots left, more wrinkles around the eyes but my eyes are still just as dark, a big man but not a pound heavier than I was then, although my flesh is beginning to lose the fight with gravity just a little. I can speak half a dozen different shades of Spanish perfectly, Egyptian Arabic, a rough kind of Russian, Guarani. I can walk down a street in Rio or Madrid or La Paz or Asunción and blend in so well that even the natives will ask me for street directions.

Gemma said I traveled light. Could you have imagined, when Dad pressed the button and the shutter clicked that day in New Orleans, that it was going to be as light as this?

The kitchen telephone rang. Conroy put down his coffee cup and went to answer it.

"Hello."

A woman's voice. "Michael Conroy, please."

He'd given Bate this number as a contact for Langley, but he hadn't expected headquarters to be pursuing him quite so soon. "This is Michael Conroy."

"One moment, please, while I connect you with Mr. Vickery."

Jesus, I hate that, Conroy thought as the line clicked in his ear. If you want to talk to me, have the courtesy to call me yourself.

The line cleared and a man said, "Hello, Mike. This is Charles Vickery."

Conroy winced. The shortened form of his name always put his teeth on edge. "Hello, Chuck," he said.

A brief, startled silence. Conroy grinned. Then Vickery said, "Yes, well, I want to get you settled in as soon as possible. Can you come out here for one o'clock this afternoon?"

There was no need to ask where *here* was: the CIA headquarters complex outside Washington near Langley, Virginia. "Okay."

"Ask for me at the main desk. They'll show you up and we'll take it from there."

"Fine," Conroy said. "See you then."

Central Intelligence Agency, Langley, Virginia
February 25

■

" To put it in a nutshell," Conroy told the collection of youthful faces in front of him, "you can, at this level, bribe an official to do his job more quickly, or more slowly, or not to do it at all. What you cannot risk doing is try to bribe him to do something he knows to be illegal. To do that you need a closer relationship. Next Friday we'll work on the ways you can establish such relationships with Latin Americans without appearing to be what you actually are. Any more questions before we finish?"

Mumble, mumble. Apparently not, not even from the three hotshots in the class of twelve trainee officers. Friday afternoons were like that.

"That's all for this week, then."

Conroy had been lecturing without notes, as he always did, and turned to scrub a couple of diagrams off the blackboard while the class shuffled their papers together and began to file out of the lecture room. The smell of chalk and the dry scrub of the eraser reminded him of grade school and the competition to be allowed to clean the boards before recess. The memory made him smile. The best part had been taking the erasers outside to clean them, banging them together *whack-whack-whack* in big, satisfying clouds of chalk dust like miniature explosions. Pretending they were atomic bombs going off, nuking the Commies.

Bloodthirsty little bastard I was, he thought. Blissfully so.

He sensed someone at the classroom door as he made a last sweep with the eraser and dropped it onto the chalk trough. Somebody else got to clean the erasers nowadays.

The person at the door was Tucker Petrie, bald, bearded, narrow-eyed, torso too short for his legs. His trousers always bagged at the crotch because of the disproportion. He was, like Conroy now, on the staff of the Latin America division of the Directorate of Operations, DDO in the vernacular of the Company. Conway, who was fifteen years older than Petrie, had known him in Lima and in Santiago.

"Hi, Tuck," he said, dusting chalk from his hands. "What's up?"

"I was coming this way and Vickery asked me to ask you to stick your head into his office."

"Uh," Conroy grunted without pleasure. The Mike-Chuck incident three weeks ago had set Conroy and Vickery off on the wrong foot. Conroy thought he probably wouldn't have said it if he'd known that Vickery was the new head of the B/SO-IV section of the division, and therefore Conroy's boss. B/SO-IV was responsible for "special projects": covert action and espionage.

"Wazzamatter?" Petrie asked in his rapid-fire New York accent.

"Nothing." Conroy slapped a chalk streak out of his cardigan. "What's new on the ozone front?"

Petrie looked gloomy. "The new NASA figures came in last week, and Economic Research schlepped the projections over this morning. The holes over the poles, man, have lost another three-tenths of a percent in the last year, and there's a tenth-percent loss over the equator."

"Shit. What does ER think that's going to mean for crop deterioration in the southern hemisphere?" A section of the CIA's Directorate of Intelligence, the Office of Economic Research was trying to figure out what effects the slow decay of the ozone layer was going to have on food production in Latin America, and how that in turn was going to affect political stability there. Petrie's long-term project was to determine what sort of action, if any, the Agency could take to shore up fragile governments if the southern continent started to starve.

"They just don't know. There's not enough data on what happens to cereal crops when the ultraviolet levels increase this much. But none of it looks good. I'd buy stocks in suntan-lotion companies, if I were you. And don't expect much from the cherry blossoms this year. They were lousy last May."

"Thanks," Conroy said. "I won't."

"Don't mention it. Catch you later."

Conroy set off for the elevator and the long walk from the classroom floor to the domain of the Directorate of Operations. Somewhat to Conroy's surprise, since he'd expected to be kept waiting, Vickery's secretary sent him straight into the office when he arrived. Vickery was riffling around in a filing cabinet. He shut its drawer firmly and waved at a chair. "Afternoon, Michael," he said pointedly.

"Afternoon, Charles," Conroy answered, equally pointedly. The two men had maintained a cool, formal politeness since Conroy had joined Vickery's staff. Vickery was the younger by seven years, and was in line to be either station chief in one of the plum centers, like Paris or Vienna, or head of one of the divisional desks. He had not so far had much to do with Latin American operations, since most of his experience had been in Europe and the Middle East. Despite the coolness between him and Conroy, however, he had the grace to recognize Conroy's experience and make use of it.

"Couple of things," Vickery said, sitting down. His desk was clear except for a couple of file folders, a collection of family photographs, a walnut pen tray and a tennis trophy. The office, like Conroy's, was windowless although much larger and equipped with many bookshelves, all full. One enlivening touch was a small and exquisite model of an eighteenth-century English man-of-war, a thirty-two-gun frigate, in a glass case.

"Okay," Conroy answered, studying the department chief. Vickery was a sallow man with a yellowish mustache and luxuriant eyebrows that reminded Conroy of chives growing over the edge of a flowerpot. He had a different three-piece suit for every day of the week, but when he came to work on weekends, as Conroy was beginning to do, he wore old jeans and a Grateful Dead sweatshirt.

"To begin with the more important item," Vickery went on. "You're well overdue for a step upward. It's been discussed thoroughly since you got back, and the feeling is that there are two posts we ought to offer you. They are, however, immediate, so we'd be sending you out again soon. It's up to you to decide whether you want that."

"Uh-huh," Conroy said. He'd been expecting such an offer, although not quite so soon after returning from the field; he'd been a deputy station chief a good deal longer than was usual.

"You've been moved up more slowly than the average," Vickery said, as though guessing Conroy's thoughts. "You understand why that is, I guess."

Conroy nodded. "Yeah. Too much area concentration." The CIA preferred generalists to specialists. The fast-track people, in their zoom toward the best positions, worked all over the world, and on their home rotations switched from desk to desk and from area division to area division. Those who, like Conroy, preferred to concentrate on a smaller target tended to be promoted less rapidly. Knowing every-thing there was to know about Afghanistan might get you a knighthood in the British SIS; in the CIA it simply meant you were overspecialized and too narrow in your outlook. Until, as sometimes happened, the place you specialized in blew up in everybody's face, as Afghanistan had with the Soviet inva-sion in 1979. Then you were invaluable. Conroy had so far not been that lucky, if lucky was the word.

"That's right," Vickery agreed. "I've looked at your personnel record, of course. Just out of curiosity, after Cairo ... why did you take the Madrid posting instead of Vienna? You must have known you were narrowing your options."

"I always preferred Latin America to Europe. I don't know why. Madrid was a way to head in that direction. And I think now that Latin America is becoming the next major theater of operations."

"Do you think the Cold War's over?"

"No. Not necessarily. Could be having time out. But the north-south conflict is going to get a lot worse."

Vickery leaned back in his chair and clasped his hands

behind his head. "Yeah. The south is getting really pissed. You know that as well as anybody. Hard to blame them. The planet's going to hell in a handbasket, it looks like, so we tell them sorry, you can't cut down your rain forests any more, or hunt elephants for ivory, or turn nature preserves into farmland, and we won't finance dams for power to run factories, or roads so your campesinos can find markets in the cities, because we need the money for eastern Europe and our own mess. But by God you'd better keep up on your debt payments or we'll cut off *everything*. We got our piece of the action over the last two centuries, and too bad you missed it, and we know a lot of you will die of all sorts of things from malnutrition to AIDS, but you gotta realize there are too many people on the planet right at the moment, and some of us have gotta go, and it's not going to be us. Sorry."

Conroy was somewhat taken aback by Vickery's diatribe. "The question," he said, "is how long they'll put up with it."

"That's the question. Some of the Third World is sure to try to retaliate, or promote conflict between power blocs in the northern hemisphere so they can take advantage of it. That's got to be fended off."

"Yeah," Conroy said neutrally. "I suppose it does."

"I wanted to bring this up," Vickery said, "because it might have a bearing on your choice of posts. Do you want to be deputy station chief in Ankara, or station chief in Caracas? Or neither? We can always use you here, of course."

Turkey or Venezuela? Conroy thought. Turkey used to be a plum because it ran operations in denied areas, across the border in the Soviet Union. But those areas aren't so denied any more. And there's no doubt it's the Third World the troubles are going to come from.

"Caracas," he said.

"Okay. Caracas it is. Also you've got four months of back leave. You're supposed to take a month of it before you go, or the bean counters in Human Resources will get upset. The current Caracas station chief's tour is over in one month and one week."

"I'll go on leave next Friday."

"Fine," Vickery said. Conroy gathered himself to go, but

Vickery put up a hand. "One more thing," he said as he opened one of the file folders.

"Uh-huh."

"Have you ever had any contact with a woman named Keely Fitzgerald? Dr. Keely Fitzgerald, to be precise."

Conroy knit his eyebrows, trying to place the name. "I don't think so. Not as far as I can remember. Who is she?"

Vickery referred to the file folder. "Her full name is Keely Margaret Fitzgerald. Born Cork, Republic of Ireland, 1954, only child, parents now deceased. They were well off. Educated University College, Dublin, degrees in history and psychology. What a combination. Married an American named Francis Brock in Ireland. She emigrated with him to the United States the same year, in 1977. She's kept her Irish passport, though, never became an American citizen. She and her husband were divorced in 1982, no children. She did postgraduate work at Harvard, got her doctorate the same year as the divorce. Doctoral thesis published as a book, *The Collapse of the World Revolution*. Read it?"

"No."

"I have. It made quite a stir at the time. I suppose you were out of the country. She's too damned glib for my liking. She just published another one, *Latin America After Marx*. She's teaching at Harvard right now."

"Where's her ex-husband?"

"He died in a car accident in 1984, alcohol involved. We checked on him, he was a drunk, apparently."

"I'd remember somebody like her," Conroy said. "But I don't. What's she got to do with me?"

"She's got some important contacts," Vickery went on, as though he hadn't heard the question. "Among them is Rupert Lipton, the chairman of the National Security Council. He has personally put in a request for her to be allowed to interview you on the subject of Latin America."

Conroy became aware that his mouth was hanging open. "What?" he said after a moment.

"You heard me. She's got clout. I'm told Lipton wanted her on the president's Foreign Intelligence Advisory Board, and she had the grit to turn him down. She wants to discuss with you —" Vickery frowned at a sheet of scribbled notepaper "— the interfacial paradigms of armed revolutionary struggle and Marxist infrastructural political constellations in the Latin American tier from 1959 to 1973."

Conroy could imagine her just from the phrasing of the request: the kind of opinionated, pretentious academics he'd always loathed when they trickled into the intelligence field, as they sometimes did. Camouflaging trivial minds with frumpy tweeds and scholarly airs. Oh, God, he thought. Why me?

"Just to start with," he protested, "this is DDI territory, not ours. The Directorate of Intelligence is the analysis department. We don't hand out information, they do. Unless somebody's changed the rules."

"They haven't."

"Why, then?"

Vickery shrugged. "I suppose the director wants to scratch the NSC chairman's back for reasons of his own. This is a cheap way to do it."

"Okay," Conroy said. "So I'm the Chinese back scratcher. Then just to finish with, how did this Fitzgerald woman even know I exist?"

"That," said Vickery, "is the reason I didn't buck them on the request. I'd like to know myself. Find out, will you?"

Conroy sighed. "All right." Probably bad breath and dandruff as well as tweeds, he thought morosely. Jesus.

"She'll be arriving here at half past three today," Vickery said. "Give her till five, will you? And treat her with kid gloves."

"Fine. I will."

"Congratulations on the promotion. See you Monday."

Conroy returned to his office, or more precisely cubicle. It was one of a series lining both sides of a long, featureless, fluorescent-lit hall. The cubicle didn't have a window. It did have a gray metal desk, a gray metal safe, a set of gray metal filing cabinets, a gray metal wastepaper basket whose contents were collected every night and shredded, and a gray plastic computer terminal. The walls were off-white. The telephone was off-white. The thin upholstery of the desk chairs and the two visitors' chairs was maroon. The room was brightly lit and utterly without character.

At least I'll be on the move again soon, he thought. Promoted, that feels good. I think. Maybe it hasn't sunk in yet. I thought I'd get more of a bang out of it.

He looked at his watch. A quarter past three. He could just manage to get some coffee and be back in the office in time for the Fitzgerald woman's arrival.

His hand was on the doorknob when the telephone rang. Conroy muttered and went to the desk to answer it.

"Hello."

"Mr. Conroy?" A woman's voice, contralto.

"Speaking."

"This is Keely Fitzgerald. I'm terribly sorry, but my rental car has broken down. I shan't be able to reach you by half past three."

The Irish lilt was unmistakable. Her voice wasn't what Conroy had expected, although he wasn't sure what his expectations had been.

"That's too bad," he said, without meaning it in the least. "Do you want to try for Monday?"

"I'm leaving on the Boston shuttle this evening. I wonder —"

Here it comes, Conroy thought. Can you meet me somewhere in the city? "Yes?" he said.

"Could we meet somewhere in the city? I expect you'll be wanting to leave work in the not too distant future."

Kid gloves, Vickery had said. "That would be fine. Where are you now?"

"At the Avis office on M Street. Do you know where that is?"

"I can find it, but it's going to be a while before I get there," Conroy warned her.

"There's a coffee shop called the Caffeine Bean half a block east on the same side of the street. I'll wait in there. I'm wearing a green tweed cape."

"Fine," Conroy said and rang off. Just as I thought, he reflected. Tweed.

The light drizzle turned to light snow as he drove Gemma's Saab into Washington across the Chain Bridge. The Friday afternoon traffic was already starting to back up because of the weather; Conroy remembered being in the capital several years previously, when a sudden snowfall at rush hour paralysed traffic for hours. The city boasted that it got all its equipment out in force the very instant snow began to fall, and the boast was true. The trouble was that the force wasn't very large.

The potholes on the Whitehurst Freeway seemed to have deepened since he last bumped across them. At least most of the traffic at this time of day was outbound, streaming over the Potomac to Virginia or northwest along the great river into Maryland. The headlights looked yellow and wan in the encroaching dusk.

He swung onto M Street where the Key Bridge met the Whitehurst, and immediately was halted by a minor traffic accident ahead. It was well after four now. Conroy fumed. After five minutes of inching the traffic loosened up and Conroy scooted the small and nimble Saab ahead of a large black Mercedes with DPL plates, cutting it off. The Mercedes driver leaned furiously on the horn, and Conroy thought for an instant that the woman — it was a woman — was going to take advantage of her diplomatic status and ram him from behind. He accelerated, just in case, but she dropped back.

The Caffeine Bean was where Fitzgerald said it would be. He pulled into a loading zone, switched on the Saab's flashers, locked the car and went into the café. The inside was warm and steamy, heavy with the scents of expensive coffee and fresh cinnamon pastries. It wasn't very big, but the tables were crowded; Conroy could see a couple of green capes, but neither of them was tweed. He searched the tables again.

He'd missed her the first time because she was right at the back of the café, and because he was looking for his preconception. The cape was tweed, all right, but the face framed by the thrown-back hood and the mass of red-bronze hair was not at all what he had expected. It was oval, pale-skinned, with eyes set wide apart under arching eyebrows, a strong, straight nose and a somewhat overlarge mouth. Conroy made his way toward her among the tables, noting as he reached her that she had a sprinkle of freckles across her

nose, and that her eyes were green. His professional eye
picked up one thing that did seem in character with her scholarly background: she didn't appear to be wearing any
makeup.

She had been watching him approach. It was a cool,
unsmiling observation, quite self-possessed, and it made him
feel peculiarly awkward. "Hello," he said. "Are you Dr.
Keely Fitzgerald?"

"Yes, I am. And you?"

He had no idea whom else she would have expected.
"Michael Conroy."

"Of course. Could we find somewhere quieter to talk, do
you think?"

"Probably we should," he said as she got out of her chair
and heaved the strap of a flight bag over her shoulder.
Standing up, she was only a couple of inches shorter than he.
Conroy noticed that she moved awkwardly, as though she
found her height difficult to manage with any grace. "I've got
a car outside," he told her.

A delivery truck was waiting to get into the loading zone.
The driver glared furiously at Conroy and gestured angrily
with one arm. Conroy ignored him and opened the door for
the Fitzgerald woman. She maneuvered her flight bag into
the back and folded inelegantly into the front seat, gathering
her cape so Conroy could close the door.

As he pulled the Saab away from the curb he noticed the
faint light scent of the perfume she was wearing; it reminded
him of something, but he couldn't remember what. "Is your
luggage still at your hotel?" he asked, trying to force himself
to be companionable. "Maybe we should pick it up, if you've
got a flight this evening."

She gestured over her shoulder. "The flight bag is all I
have. I travel rather light."

The lilt was much less pronounced than it had been on the
telephone. She might almost have been born American.
"Okay," he answered. "Is there anyplace particular you want
to go to talk?"

"I don't know Washington all that well. You should
choose, perhaps."

She was gratingly formal and still hadn't cracked a smile.

Expressionless would be the word for it. "I don't know it that well any more, either," he told her. "I just got back and I haven't spent much time here for god knows how long. Look, if it's all right with you, we could go to my sister's place. It's not very far away, in Georgetown."

"Would your sister not mind? It's almost dinnertime."

"She's in Italy. I'm using her place till she gets back."

"That would be grand, then. But I have to be at National Airport before nine for the Boston shuttle."

Sorry if I'm inconveniencing you, he thought. But aloud he said, "No problem."

The snowfall was growing heavier as Conroy threaded the Saab through the congealing traffic into Georgetown. The wipers slapped dolefully at the mush trying to freeze on the windshield. Conversation inside the car was nonexistent; Conroy, still unused to driving in snow, was exerting all his concentration to avoid slithering into other vehicles. Their slow progress added to the irritation he already felt at having to submit to Keely Fitzgerald's questions. Finally he turned onto Gemma's street, a row of nineteenth-century brownstones that had been gentrified during Roosevelt's New Deal, and heaved a sigh of combined annoyance and relief.

"Are you from Washington originally?" Keely Fitzgerald asked as they were walking gingerly up the steps to the front door.

"No. New Orleans," Conroy said uninformatively as he unlocked the door and pushed it open. There had been a substantial estate when their parents died; Gemma put her share into the Georgetown property, which had doubled in value five years after she bought it. Conroy had put his portion into a mutual fund and left it there to accumulate interest. He had no clear idea of how much there was now, except that it was probably a lot.

Fitzgerald had obviously been expecting him to field a question back: *Isn't that an Irish accent you have, gosh, my ancestors were Irish too, what a coincidence, how long have you been here?*, but he didn't. The rebuff was plain as he saw her flush, mouth tightening, as she shed her cape and high leather boots. Underneath the cape she was wearing a blue moiré blouse, which looked like silk, and a calf-length navy skirt. The clothes had a distinct tint of money. She was long-armed and high-waisted, and again Conroy noticed the slight awkwardness of her movements, as though she was faintly worried that her knees and elbows might collide unexpectedly with her surroundings.

"We can talk in here," he said, leading her into the living room and turning on a couple of lamps.

"My good heavens," Keely Fitzgerald said, her pique momentarily forgotten. "It must be like this inside a jewel box."

Conroy nodded. Gemma was a collector, with a taste for small, finely turned work, but her acquisitions followed no particular pattern. Her living room was an indescribable anarchy of Persian miniatures, Greek icons, blue Iznik tiles mounted behind glass, snuffboxes from every corner of Europe, mosaics, English Regency crystal, enameled ceramic birds, old framed maps of the East Indies, and books, books, books.

"Sit down," he said, removing several issues of *Graphis* from one of the wing chairs in front of the fireplace. "Can I get you a drink?" he added in attempted hospitality and wondering what, if anything, there was in Gemma's liquor cabinet. He hadn't looked.

"No, thank you. I really shouldn't waste any more of your time."

In other words, get on with it, he thought. At least she doesn't look the way I expected her to. Thank God for small mercies.

Nevertheless he took the time to make coffee, which she accepted with some grace. When they were settled in the living room, she took a small tape recorder out of her flight bag and arranged a sheaf of notes on her lap. "The recorder is all right?" she asked.

"Sure."

She switched it on and started asking questions in her quiet contralto voice. Conroy found himself beginning to respect her in spite of himself; her questions about the old Latin American liberation movements were clear and intelligent, and had been carefully prepared. She didn't use the tortuous pseudoscholarly jargon her original information request had led him to expect. Nevertheless he volunteered nothing and kept his answers as short as he could without quite verging on rudeness.

There came a pause while she changed tapes. Into the pause she said sharply, "You're being extremely terse. This is *Washington Post* material you're giving me."

Conroy glanced out the front window; the snow was coming down in big, broad flakes under the streetlights. "You're working on a new book," he said, paying no attention to her charge. "Do you mind my asking what the thesis is?" He wasn't going to mention that Vickery had already told him.

She finished inserting the tape. Her fingers were long and slender, and he noticed that her awkwardness did not extend to the way she used her hands; her motions were deft and precise.

"Not at all," she said. "If it'll help convince you I'm not some kind of enemy. The evidence at the moment is that the ideology of world revolution is on its deathbed. It doesn't even get lip service from the Soviets or the Chinese any more. I'm trying to look back and identify clearly what's led to that. Then I'll try to predict what may replace the movement, or whether perhaps there's a way for someone to breathe life into it."

"You think either of those two possibilities will come out of Latin America?"

"Yes, or from somewhere in the so-called Third World," she said. "Better to call it the Southern World. Within a few years they may feel they have nothing to lose by attacking the northern civilizations as best they can. That may give the revolution movement a new lease on life."

And then we can enjoy ourselves fighting a few new wars, Conroy thought. "You don't think the movement's dead and buried, then?"

"Not quite. Although, interestingly enough, I think I can pinpoint the first clear symbol that it was starting to fail."

"What was that?"

Keely Fitzgerald touched the controls of the recorder. "The death of Che Guevara."

Conroy thought: And how did you know about me?

He had laid kindling and wood in the fireplace that morning before leaving for Langley. He stood up and lit one of the long matches that Gemma kept on the mantelpiece, opened the glass fireplace doors, touched the flame to the newspaper underneath the kindling. The fire caught with a fluttering sound. He closed the doors.

"You were there," she said.

He sat down again. "There were a lot of people there," he told her. "There were a lot of people who wanted him dead."

"Don't misunderstand me," she said. "I'm not accusing you of anything. He was executed by the Bolivians. I know the CIA didn't have a hand in that."

"That's a relief," he snapped. "But I think it's time I asked a couple of questions myself. I'm told you asked specifically to talk with me. Why did you do that?"

She sat up stiffly. "I don't think I have to answer that."

"And how did you know I was there in La Higuera when Guevara died?"

"Nor that."

Conroy shrugged. "Then I don't think we have anything left to say to each other."

She was nibbling angrily at her lower lip. She suddenly let go of it and said, "All right, then, I'll tell you. Three weeks ago I was in what used to be East Germany."

"Uh-huh." Conroy regarded her from narrowed eyes.

"I talked to a man there named Inciarte. You'd recollect him."

"Yes. He was Bolivia's Minister of the Interior at the time of Guevara's death."

"That's not all he was, as you know very well. He was a Castro sympathizer. He got Che Guevara's campaign diaries out of Bolivia so Havana could publish them and turn Guevara into a revolutionary legend. Then he fled. The last few years he's been living in Leipzig."

"None of that's ever been secret," Conroy pointed out. The fire was burning nicely now, and he looked at it without really seeing it.

"But there was someone else in La Higuera that day," Keely said. "A Bolivian girl, one of the support network Guevara was supposed to use. She was pregnant, and the soldiers were going to shoot her, but you stopped them. She had the baby on the plane to La Paz. You turned her and the baby over to Inciarte on the orders of your station chief. And before Inciarte fled, he got her and the baby — it was a boy — out of Bolivia to Cuba."

Conroy's fingers were clamped around the arm of his chair. He relaxed them. "Inciarte told you this?"

"Yes. He told me something else, too."

"What?"

"You didn't know?"

"I have no idea what you're talking about," Conroy said. His puzzlement must have shown in his voice, for she didn't seem to disbelieve him.

"The boy was Che Guevara's son."

"Well, I'll be damned," Conroy said. He was thinking back. "Che was known to be in the La Higuera region a couple of months after he reached Bolivia. She must have slept with him then. He always drew women."

"So I'm led to believe," Keely Fitzgerald said coolly. "She took a terrible risk."

"Yeah, she did." I saved Che Guevara's son for posterity, Conroy thought. How about that. "Inciarte told you all this?" he asked.

"Yes, he did. He's very old, and he rambles. Half the time I don't think he knew what he was telling me. But he was very canny about one thing. He wouldn't tell me her name."

"Which is why you've come to me."

"That's right," Keely Fitzgerald said. "I want to find her."

"What for?"

"Because I'm very curious. Guevara had four other children, clearly identified, no mysteries. Does the boy even know who he is? Why has he been so carefully hidden? None of the others has been, they're just more or less ordinary Cubans in spite of the name they carry. What's special about this one?"

"I can think of a dozen reasons," Conroy told her.

"So can I. I want to know which is the right one."

"You think this will lead to some revelation for your book?"

She glanced into the fire. "I have no idea. I do know that

whenever I've neglected in the past to follow up a line of research like this, I've regretted it."

Maybe, Conroy thought, if I tell her she'll get out of my hair. I don't see what security significance the name could have. Inciarte might have mentioned the name. I could cover my ass that way, if I had to.

"Give me the tape you just put in the recorder," he said.

Wordlessly, she extracted it and handed it to him. "Okay," he said. "Inciarte told you this, if the question ever comes up, which I don't think it will."

She nodded. He thought he saw a flicker of amusement deep in the green eyes. "Her name was Marita Linares," he said.

"Thank you."

"Don't mention it." He looked at the ormolu clock on the mantel. "It'll take a while to get to the airport in this. I'll drive you, if you like."

To his relief she refused in favor of a cab, and he showed her where the hall telephone was. Returning to the living room, he sat and stared into the fire. He was vaguely troubled about something, but could not identify what it was. Christ, he thought, I hope the airport isn't closed down.

"The cab's on its way," she said, returning to the living room. "I'd like to thank you for your help."

"Such as it was," he mumbled.

"No, really, it was good of you to see me. I didn't mean to inconvenience you as much as I have."

She was making him feel like a boor. "Look, Dr. Fitzgerald," he said with an effort, "I know we got off on the wrong foot. I'm not usually so ... irritable. I'm sorry."

She regarded him gravely. "I was rather scratchy myself. I'm sorry, too."

"Well," he said, and stopped, at a loss. Then, before he could stop himself, he found himself saying:

"I thought from the way your information request was worded that you were the wrong kind of scholar."

She burst out laughing. "You mean the part about interfacial paradigms and infrastructural political constellations?"

"Yes," he mumbled. "That part."

"I always use that language when I'm trying to get

something out of the bureaucrats," she said. "It works. I never use it for real things."

Conroy felt an odd, confusing relief. Outside a horn beeped.

"There's the cab," she said, turning away from him toward the hall. "Thanks again."

Conroy helped her on with her cape, then watched from the window as she hurried out to the taxi. The snow was falling more thickly than ever.

Gulf of Mexico
March 12

∎

Ramon Guevara peered into the darkness outside the cockpit windows and listened to the soft thrum of the engine a meter in front of his knees. The plane was flying very low, a bare hundred feet above the waves, and Guevara could just make out occasional whitecaps in the light of the half-moon. Beside him, the pilot kept his eyes riveted to the instrument panel and the faint red glow of its needles and indicators. Guevara knew from his previous two courier flights that they'd be at this dangerous height for another half hour, until the plane was well away from the Texas coast; only then would the pilot gain a little altitude, enough for him to relax his attention a little. This plane was different from the other two Ramon had ridden as courier in. He'd never seen it until this evening when he reached the Texas airstrip, which was really only a patch of smooth ground on the coastal plain north of Brownsville.

To a casual observer, and even in daylight, the aircraft looked like a Cessna 182 with its single engine and high wing and tricycle landing gear. Its appearance was deceiving, however. The plane had begun existence as an ordinary Cessna, but it had passed through the hands of a company that specialized in turning such airframes into almost undetectable night surveillance platforms. The Cessna now had a coat of radar-absorbent paint and a more powerful and fuel-efficient engine fitted with noise and infrared suppressors. A good deal of its internal structure had been replaced by materials almost transparent to radar. It also carried extremely sophisticated navigational equipment, and an extra fuel tank to extend its range to twenty-two hundred kilometers. In an earlier incarnation the plane had been part of the American-aided anti-drug war in Bolivia; somehow — Ramon had no idea exactly how — it had found its way into the hands of the drug cartel, and now served to carry the cocaine the Cessna's original owners had tried to destroy.

The Cessna was perfect for flights into and out of the United States because it was almost silent and virtually invisible to radar, but it had some major disadvantages. Two were its range and the fact that it was single-engined. Even with the extra fuel tank the Cessna had only a few minutes' reserve after reaching the clandestine airfield in northern Guatemala, so that every flight was a gamble with the possibility of a change in wind or engine failure, and the only concession made to the dangers of flight over water was the presence on board of two parachutes and a couple of life jackets. Moreover, its carrying capacity was limited to about four hundred kilos in addition to a full load of fuel and two crew members. This made it unsuitable for hauling anything but the most profitable of cargoes, and a cargo whose value if delivered was worth the risk of its loss: in a word, cocaine. The white powder was now far more precious than it had been a few years ago, when oversupply had driven the price down; the American war on the drug cartel had been partly successful, and moving cocaine into the United States in the face of naval patrols, satellite reconnaissance and Hawkeye surveillance aircraft equipped with powerful radars had become extremely difficult. The Cessna, in spite of its limitations of range and load, had one great advantage: it was very hard to detect. And several hundred kilos of pure cocaine, at the current wholesale price of twenty thousand dollars per kilogram, were worth more than seven million dollars. On the street the drug would bring several times that amount.

The front money for this shipment was in an attaché case behind Ramon's seat: three quarters of a million dollars in U.S. currency. Ramon judged that it would be just about what he'd need for the project. He sensed again the way in which Fate was directing his hand. Colonel Cardoso, not that he had realized what he was doing, had begun it three months ago in the beach house outside Varadero.

"And how have you been?" Cardoso asked, cracking open the rum bottle. "A lot quieter than the old days, isn't it?"

"Yes, colonel," Ramon answered economically. He hadn't had so much as a word with Cardoso for months, not since the battalion demobilized, the men sent to barracks or civilian life and the officers reassigned. He suspected he knew why his old commander had asked him to come out here to this windy beach and the ramshackle beach house that showed no sign of being permanently inhabited. The place had two rooms, one empty and the one they were sitting in, which contained a shabby wooden cupboard, a few age-bleached cane chairs and a wobbly table. The scratched plastic glasses Cardoso was filling had come from the cupboard.

"Your good health and the revolution," Cardoso said, raising his glass. He tossed down a mouthful of spirit neat. Ramon also drank, but more sparingly. "The revolution," he said. "Your health."

Cardoso set his glass on the table. "How do you like intelligence work?" he asked.

Ramon blinked and looked out the slatted window, which faced the beach. Between the slats he could see the breakers tumbling, their crests rosy in the evening light.

"Very much," he said guardedly. He might have expected that Cardoso knew about the reassignment.

"I hear you're being sent to the United States soon," Cardoso went on, studying him attentively.

"I am?" said Ramon. He was, but he wasn't going to admit it to anybody unless instructed to do so.

Cardoso swigged another mouthful of rum. "Yes, you are. Look, you can talk freely to me. I know exactly what you've been doing since we last met. Your reassignment to DGI. I'm kept informed."

"You're also DGI?" Ramon asked. The Dirección Général de la Inteligencia, the Directorate of Intelligence, had been organized and trained during the sixties with assistance from the East Germans. It had evolved into an effective and fairly sophisticated instrument of Cuban policy.

"In a way," Cardoso said. "There are close links between DGI and military intelligence, you know."

Ramon nodded. Cuba was a heavily militarized society, and the lines between civilian and military organizations were often blurred. Mother was right, he thought. The indirect approach. The man she knows arranges my transfer to the DGI, and at the proper time Cardoso takes over as the operations officer.

"How's your English now?" Cardoso asked.

"I'm told it's very good. My mother gave me a foundation to build on."

"Excellent," Cardoso said. He took out a pack of cigarettes and lit one. They were American, Camels. He offered one to Ramon, who took it gingerly. Cardoso was leading up to something.

"Your mother's not well, is she?" Cardoso observed as Ramon inhaled the heavy, aromatic smoke.

He'd know, of course, Ramon reflected. "No. Cancer."

"I'm very sorry. Do you approve of the care she's getting?"

"It's as good as we have."

"I suppose," Cardoso said thoughtfully, "that there are treatments we *don't* have. That we can't usually afford, except in special cases."

"What would be a special case?" Ramon asked, feeling sudden hope. Although the way Cardoso was going about this was curious.

Cardoso gestured vaguely. "It all depends. Let's turn to another matter. You're going to America next month. Dallas."

"Yes."

"And your assignment is to provide support and communications for our work in extracting high-technology secrets from the industries there. The information we provide for various clients."

This was why he was *supposed* to be going. The matter of the GATT conference had not been raised during his training. Security. Ramon was beginning to suspect that the strike was the project of a small cell of genuine revolutionaries inside the DGI, and that they were acting without official knowledge or consent. They'd use the industrial espionage cover against the DGI and against the Americans. It was very neat. He nodded and sipped at his rum.

"There's another matter involved. You would be the perfect man to help deal with it."

Now it comes, Ramon thought. "Yes?" he said.

"We are establishing a delivery pipeline for some valuable materials. One end of the pipeline is in Central America, the other in Texas. Not technological items."

Ramon managed to hide his bewilderment. Wasn't Cardoso part of the GATT project?

"Drugs?" he asked. He didn't really believe Cardoso's insinuation, that the DGI was involved in drug-running.

"I won't deny it," Cardoso said. "We both know the official position, but this is a matter of self-defense. The United States is our enemy, and any way of weakening our enemy is justified. The drug plague there also shows up the inherent contradictions of bourgeois capitalism. Furthermore, the trade provides us with a great deal of foreign exchange, hard U.S. currency. We need that money badly. We've been working with the South Americans for quite a long time, providing distribution in the United States, and it's been very profitable, I can tell you."

"What about 1989?" Ramon asked, to cover his confusion. There had been a drug scandal that year; General Ochoa and several officers had been arrested for involvement in the drug traffic, and the Minister of the Interior and the head of the DGI had been forced to resign. "Ochoa was a hero of the revolution, and Fidel shot him anyway, and three others. I thought *that* was the official position."

"There's more to that than you think," Cardoso said. "Ochoa was thinking about making a grab for power. And he and the others were holding back a lot of the money that was supposed to be going into the government accounts. And they were so blatant about it that Fidel had no alternative but to act. Since then everyone has been more discreet. There are no more shipments through Cuba. We've moved the operations offshore. The line goes Columbia–Panama–Nicaragua–Guatemala–Texas. It's difficult, but the returns make it worthwhile." Cardoso smiled. "The capitalists finance the revolution. It's much more sensible than robbing banks."

"What do you want me to do?" Ramon asked. He had regained his self-possession as Cardoso spoke, and was thinking hard. Cardoso wasn't working for the revolutionary cell after all. Ramon had to be cautious.

"We need someone completely dependable to act as a financial courier, as well as filling the support role for the technology acquisition. I've watched you ever since you came under my command. There's no one I'd trust more as a committed revolutionary."

"How is this to be done? The courier operation?"

"You'll be told later. Are you willing to carry out this assignment?"

If he refused, Ramon knew, he might never get off the island, no matter who was in the revolutionary cell that was sending him on the GATT strike. He dared not underestimate the power of the drug organization within the DGI. "Of course," he said.

"Good. What's your opinion of the two officers you had in Yemen, toward the end?"

Careful, Ramon thought. "Menocal and Portela?"

"Yes."

"The highest opinion. They're superb men."

"Committed to the revolution?" Cardoso asked.

"Yes. Without question." And more committed than you can know, Ramon thought as he answered. He had talked with them aboard the ship as it made its achingly slow way homeward, talked and talked, quietly, out of hearing, very carefully, feeling them out. The two junior officers were appalled at the withdrawal from Yemen, disgusted with the leadership and, when Ramon dug deeper, at the decay of the revolution. They thought much as he did, although without the depth and lacking the vision and determination to act on their anger. But he knew they'd follow him if he asked them to. He'd kept in touch with them since the return home. They were both being stifled by paperwork and boredom.

"That's encouraging," Cardoso said. "I want you to go and see them. Offer them a chance to work overseas again. If they say yes, let me know, and I'll instruct you further. Don't waste any time about it, though. And don't mention the narcotics to them."

"Yes, sir. But they're not —" He hesitated.

"What?"

"They're not DGI."

"That won't matter. Just speak to them."

"Yes, Colonel Cardoso."

"We'll have to see about improved treatment for your mother," Cardoso said casually, downing the last of his rum and pouring again. "Drink up. We'll finish the bottle before we go, comrade."

A few days later he was able to see his mother. They walked along the beach, in case the house had microphones, and he told her everything Cardoso had said. The revolutionaries had still not contacted him, and he was angry. "What is happening, Mother?" he finished. "Have you heard anything from your friend?"

She stopped and turned to face him. "Yes. Once."

"What?"

"He is in difficulties. It is going to be hard for him to help you further."

"What does that mean? Did he mention Cardoso?"

"No. He said that you were a good officer, and that he was giving you the objective. And that how you achieve it is your responsibility."

They walked on for a few meters. Ramon said, "Then appearing to help Cardoso is one way of approaching the objective. Not GATT necessarily. The other one. The important one."

"It will have to be. I don't see how you can refuse Cardoso safely."

"I was hoping your friend could supply the money I'm going to need."

"He didn't mention it. Ramon, you are going to have to do this very carefully. We can't trust anyone. There's always the danger of betrayal."

"As my father was betrayed."

"Yes."

"Very well," he said. "I'll do it alone. Well, not quite

alone." He told her about Cardoso's instructions regarding Menocal and Portela. When he had finished, he added:

"I thought the colonel was different. Cardoso doing this.... He was different in Yemen. A soldier."

"Perhaps you only saw him that way. These two officers of yours. Can you trust them? Will they keep their resolve?"

"Yes. I fought with them. They aren't like Cardoso."

He had approached Menocal and Portela the day after the meeting at the Varadero beach house. Disobeying Cardoso's instructions, Ramon had told them about the narcotics traffic and, more important, that he was planning a strike against the forces of counterrevolution. Although he told them nothing else, the two underemployed army captains had grabbed at the opportunity without a second's hesitation.

A thought struck him. "But will you take the treatments Cardoso arranges, Mother, as long as...."

"As long as he provides them? Yes, if only to live long enough to see you succeed. That much I'll take from them."

That much I'll take from them, Ramon thought, as the Cessna drummed onward into the night. Their money, and the chance they've given me to start the war again. My name is Ramon Guevara, and I am Che Guevara's son.

He glanced over at the rate-of-climb indicator. It was steady as the half-moon ahead. The pilot was still maintaining thirty meters of altitude; Ramon could sense the man's concentration as he held the little aircraft straight and level. He couldn't act yet. Taking the plane over at this height would be much too dangerous; one lapse of attention on the pilot's part and they'd be into the dark waves below. Portela and Menocal would be on their way to the rendezvous point by now, back there in the darkness that hid South Padre Island and the Laguna Madre behind it and the empty coastal prairie behind that.

"How long until we climb?" he said into the microphone of his headset.

"Just about now," the pilot answered, voice tinny in Ramon's earphones. He eased back on the control yoke. The Cessna slipped upward through the dark air. Seventy meters, a hundred. Three hundred. Still climbing. Eight hundred.

The pilot moved the yoke forward, checked his course, the turn and bank indicator. Then he reached out and moved a switch. "Autopilot's on," he announced.

Ramon said, "You're sure the radio's off transmit?"

The pilot checked switches. "Yah. We're okay. No leaks."

Ramon got out of his seat and slid into the aft part of the cabin, stretching the headset cord behind him.

"What in hell are you doing?" the pilot asked testily. "Don't go back any farther, or I'll have to retrim."

"Sorry," Ramon said. He was pulling the Browning automatic out of his jacket, slipping off the safety. Stooping to avoid the cabin roof, he moved behind the pilot and pressed the cold, round muzzle against the back of the man's neck.

"This is a gun," he said. "Keep quite still. Do you understand?"

A long moment's silence. The pilot remained absolutely motionless. Ramon pressed the muzzle a little harder into the flesh.

"Yeah," the pilot said. "I got you. Asshole."

"Be quiet and do as I tell you. First, when I tell you to, disengage the autopilot and take control of the aircraft. Don't try to throw it around. One quick motion and I will pull the trigger. Obey now."

The pilot did so.

"Good," Ramon said. "Now turn around, very gently, and fly a reciprocal course. We are going back."

"You must be fuckin' crazy," the pilot said. "You'll never get away with it."

"Do as I say."

The pilot moved his hands and the plane banked, gently, as Ramon had ordered, then straightened out.

"Good," Ramon said. "Now listen. There is a lot of money on board. A hundred thousand dollars of it is for you if you do exactly as I tell you, without argument. Eighty kilometers north of Port Isabel, between Padre Island and the mainland, there is a small island. Do you know where I mean?"

"Uh-huh." Surly, but interested.

"That is where I want you to go. Right over that island, on a due west course."

"You're out of your mind, you dumb spick."

"Just fly. I'll be watching carefully. If you miss the island, I'll shoot you."

"Won't do you much good unless you can fly a plane."

"You will be dead first. Is it worth it?"

"Aw, Jesus Christ. Okay. I'll find your goddamned island. Then what?"

"I'll tell you. Be still, now. I'm going to search you for weapons."

The pilot had a .357 Magnum in a shoulder holster. Ramon removed it and stuffed the revolver into his own jacket. "Okay," he said. "Go down below radar."

The little aircraft slipped downward through the night sky. At thirty meters the pilot leveled out and got Ramon's permission for two course changes to bring them over the island. Time passed.

"That's it ahead," the pilot muttered in Ramon's headset. "I have to climb."

Ramon could see the island racing toward them, a dark puddle on the moonlit water. The Cessna pulled up and the island passed underneath, featureless in the night. On the far side lay more water, and beyond it the coast of the mainland.

"Flash your landing light once," Ramon ordered.

The pilot snapped a switch twice. A patch of radiance appeared on the water ahead of them and then winked out. Off to Ramon's left came an answering flicker of blue light.

"Fly over the beach and go five kilometers inland. And slow down."

"How slow?"

"As slow as you can. Just above...." He searched for the technical phrase. "Stalling speed."

The modified Cessna would stay in the air at sixty-five kilometers an hour. After traveling at cruising speed for so long the little aircraft seemed to Ramon to be barely crawling over the ground.

"We're five klicks inland," the pilot announced. "You happy now?"

"Yes. Now climb to seven hundred meters and turn around. You are to go straight back out toward the sea."

"What the hell for?"

"Recognition." Ramon prodded him with the gun. "Do it."

"Jesus Christ, okay, just asking."

Ramon watched the compass and airspeed indicator and altimeter as the pilot obeyed. When the Cessna was settled at the right course and height he said, "Get your speed back down."

The engine quieted to a whisper. "Set the autopilot," Ramon ordered. The pilot tensed up; Ramon could feel the tension transmitted along the barrel of the gun. He jabbed the man hard. "Set it!"

The pilot reached out and clicked the switch. "What are you —" he began plaintively.

Ramon shot him in the back of the neck, grabbing him by the shoulder to prevent him from falling into the controls. The pilot's head lolled sideways, and the Cessna bobbed as his feet sagged on the rudder pedals. Then the autopilot caught the plane and it resumed its placid flight.

He had a little more than four minutes at this speed and height. As for the wind, he'd have to take his chances. When they took off it had been out of the east at about fifteen kilometers an hour. After making sure the pilot was secure in his seat, Ramon snatched up one of the parachutes and started to buckle it on, keeping one eye on the instrument panel clock as he did so. When he clicked the last strap into place he still had two minutes left. He opened the attaché case containing the money, removed the chain and cuffs and secured the case to his left wrist. Closed the case. A minute to go. He released the cabin door latch and waited. He'd parachuted twice before, in Angola, but both times had been in daylight. Never mind. At least he wasn't over a forest this time.

Best to allow fifteen seconds extra. He shoved at the door, ramming it open with difficulty against the pressure of the slipstream. It was going to be a squeeze. The Cessna yawed with the unbalanced drag of the opening door and yawed back as the autopilot tried to correct. Ramon pushed harder, forcing the door wide enough to admit his torso and the parachute pack. Then he braced his feet against the side of the dead pilot's seat and shoved hard. He popped out into space, felt a snatch at his boot heels as the door slammed in the slipstream, then he was surrounded by wind and darkness.

Tumbling a little, he thought. He straightened his legs out and saw the moon above him and to his left. Good enough. Holding the attaché case tight against his chest, he yanked at the D-ring of the ripcord, heard a flutter behind him as the parachute spilled into the air. The jolt as the canopy opened snapped his head sideways, stunning him for an instant. When he got his orientation back he saw the moon shining on water ahead of him, not a quarter mile away. Perfect. How high? Not very. Flex knees, a glimpse of the ground coming up, light earth, patches of sage.

Gravity whacked him into the ground. He fell with it, rolled, slapped the parachute's quick release with the heel of his hand and felt the straps give. In seconds he was on his knees, grabbing at the shrouds to collapse the canopy, which was billowing white in the gentle wind off the sea. He got it under control and started wrapping it in the shroud lines.

He had almost finished when he saw someone approaching. Still on his knees, he pulled out the Browning.

"Ramon? It's Joel. We saw the chute."

Portela. Good. Ramon put the Browning away and resumed gathering up the parachute. "Help me with this, will you," he said as Portela came up. They couldn't leave anything behind. "Where's Luis?"

"He's at the track inland, with the car. It was perfect, what you did."

"Did you see the plane?"

"No. We could hardly even hear it. It went out to sea."

"Good." Ramon felt himself relaxing at the news. He'd worried that the fuss of opening the door might tumble the autopilot and send the Cessna on some unpredictable course toward the land. Now, though, the plane would fly out into the gulf until it ran out of fuel or hit winds for which the autopilot couldn't compensate. One way or another, it would vanish at sea. The cartel would go looking for it, of course, suspecting that either Ramon or the pilot had run with the money, but the search wouldn't be pressed nearly as hard as it would have been if he'd left the plane for them to find.

Portela and he started making their way toward the car,
Portela lugging the parachute. "Now what are we going to
do?" Portela asked.

"I have to do some things. You and Menocal must go on
as normal. Go back to Dallas. The man named Faustino will
contact you when I don't come back. I'll be replaced. Just go
on as you were until I come for you."

"I would rather we were helping with the operation now."

"Yes. But if you vanish as I have, Cardoso and the ones
here will know we were robbing them. And I need you in
place for later. Don't worry, Joel. Your chance will come
soon." He clapped Portela on the shoulder. "We've come a
long way already."

Yes," Portela agreed. "I never thought I would get to the
United States. Not this way, at least. A spy."

Ramon nodded in the darkness. The DGI had infiltrated
Ramon into the United States by way of Canada. He had
entered the latter country as a Cuban national and exited it
by train as an American citizen of Puerto Rican descent. A
further sea change awaited him in Dallas. His contact and
control, a man who called himself Faustino and nothing else,
took away his documents and gave him new ones: now
Ramon was a legal immigrant from Panama, complete with
green card, Panamanian passport and driver's license.
Menocal and Portela turned up a couple of weeks later, sent
in by the same route. They never saw Faustino. Ramon,
acting as cutout, passed to them the new identities Faustino
had provided, and they got down to work.

Part of it was indeed technological espionage. There was
already a system in place, and it needed servicing. Portela
and Menocal loaded and unloaded dead drops with documents or money, rented safe apartments in less-than-
desirable neighborhoods, drove automobiles here and there
and left them, provided surveillance when needed, and
worked from time to time as casual laborers in Dallas's
construction boom. Ramon did some of the same things, and
in addition acted as cutout between the army captains and
Faustino, and occasionally between Faustino and a pair of
spies Faustino had already recruited. The spies were techni-
cians in Texas's burgeoning aerospace industry. Unknown to

Faustino and everyone else, Ramon also did a great deal of thinking and planning.

And then there were the drugs. Portela and Menocal had not been drawn in yet, but Ramon had made two money-carrying trips before this one, all the way down to Guatemala and back with the cocaine. He had not hijacked either of the first two deliveries because the amounts of money were smaller, and because he judged that his apparent death would be more credible if he waited through a delivery or two. He had a healthy respect for the traffickers. Their operations were carefully compartmented, and Ramon had never seen anyone at the airstrips in the United States except the man who drove him there, the man who gave him the money just before the flight, and the pilot. They all had been different people every time, and of different nationalities: Anglos, Colombians and one who Ramon suspected was Cuban. What the business arrangements among these groups were, Ramon couldn't guess. But he was out of it now. A free man, a revolutionary again. The more so because there had been no word at all, not the slightest contact with anyone who might have been a member of the cell of revolutionaries inside the DGI. Perhaps they'd been arrested. All the more reason to disappear as soon as he could.

"There's the vehicle," Portela said in an undertone, although there was no one for kilometers on this stretch of the coast. "Everything's there for you."

"Perfect."

The vehicle was a Bronco 4X4 with fat all-terrain tires. Ramon saw the glint of Menocal's grin as he climbed into the cab and pulled the door closed. Portela got into the rear and passed Ramon a flight bag over the back of the seat. The Bronco started to roll, bumping over the rough ground toward the inland road, lights off and Menocal navigating by the wan moonlight.

"Are you sure it's safe to use the Panamanian passport?" Menocal asked as he swung onto the asphalt.

"It will be for a while," Ramon told him. He was unlocking the money-packed case from his wrist. "There's a very good chance everyone will think I'm dead in the gulf somewhere."

"Also," Portela put in from the backseat, "they'll hardly ask the American authorities to watch for the passport. And neither DGI nor the cartel can watch every airport in the United States."

"I promise I won't try to go home for a visit," Ramon said. He was wondering whether he would ever see Cuba or his mother again. At the moment neither seemed likely.

Ah, Mother, he thought, if I can I'll come back. If I do not, it will be because I am in a revolutionary's grave. As my father was. But if I succeed, when I succeed, the people of the world will have something to remember the name Guevara by.

"Like Che," he said quietly.

"What?" asked Portela.

They did not know yet who he was. He had decided to tell them at a time when such a stimulus was needed. "I was thinking about Che Guevara," he answered. "I think he'd be pleased with what we're doing."

Havana–Puerto Real–Miami
March 14

■

"I have read all your works, including the journal articles," Oscar Torras said, exerting his considerable charm in Keely Fitzgerald's direction. "While I might disagree with some of your interpretations of events, I believe that you are not unsympathetic to our past."

"Or to your future," Keely pointed out. "That's why I'm here."

"Yes," said Torras. "Yes." He pressed his brown fingertips together and regarded them with what appeared to be affection. Keely noticed that he had long slender hands, almost womanly, the skin quite dark. He'd have black ancestry along with the Spanish. The latter genes showed in his deep-set eyes and the aquiline nose. He was nicely graying at the temples, mid-forties perhaps. Unlike other Latin men with whom she had dealt, however, he was obviously prepared to treat her as an envoy first and a woman second; although that had not prevented him from somehow transmitting his awareness that she was of the opposite sex.

"I gather you were asked to sit on the president's Foreign Intelligence Advisory Board," Torras went on. "But you refused," he added, as though hastily withdrawing some kind of accusation.

"You're very well informed," she admitted. She wondered exactly how the Cubans had gotten hold of that bit of information. It wasn't secret, but it was still surprising to hear it from an undersecretary in the Cuban Ministry of Foreign Affairs while she was sitting in the man's office in Havana.

"There was some doubt as to whether I was appropriate. That was partly why I refused."

Torras glanced out the window into the Plaza de la Revolucion and at the statue of José Martí at its center. "Ah, your Irish citizenship," he said. "Of course. Which does, on the other hand, make you a better and more disinterested envoy of Washington. Backdoor diplomacy, I believe it's called."

"Quite so," she said.

Torras ruminated on the far side of his brightly polished desk. His office wasn't large, but it was comfortable: the tall window with its deep maroon drapes through which the morning sun of the tropics streamed cheerily, deep leather chairs, also maroon, walls paneled in some light wood, Torras's desk with a rack of pens and three telephones. No paper on the desk; Torras wasn't that type of bureaucrat.

"When you were here last," Torras said, drawing himself up in his chair, "we discussed the possible normalization of relations between Havana and Washington. At that time the American State Department's position was that we should consider disengaging ourselves from certain revolutionary struggles here and there. As you are well aware, since that time we have, ah, disengaged certain supportive units from both the People's Democratic Republic of Yemen and from Ethiopia."

"Yes," Keely said. "That's been noted."

"I must be frank," Torras said with a rueful look. "There was a great deal of opposition here to our withdrawal."

You were bowing to Soviet pressure, Keely thought, but if you think I'm going to try to make you admit it, you're wrong.

"The problem in the United States," Keely told him, "is that while American leaders know that Cuba is not a security threat, the American public still believes otherwise. Politics being what it is, the current administration has been reluctant to propose dropping the trade and travel embargo until that perception has changed."

"Has it?" Torras asked.

"It's beginning to. The disengagement from Yemen and Ethiopia helped a great deal. Washington is prepared to continue talks on a more formal basis, beginning in June."

"Ah," Torras said. "That is indeed a step forward. But it will be delicate, on both sides."

"I know. That's why Washington would like your response through me."

"I have been instructed by the minister," Torras stated formally, "to tell you that we wish to pursue every avenue of reconciliation." He leaned forward over the desk. "There is a feeling in the leadership —" here he paused significantly "— that some aspects of the reforms that have taken place in eastern Europe might also not be out of place here."

And does that mean Fidel himself feels that way? Keely wondered with a jolt of surprise. I find it hard to believe. He's one of the last holdouts for the hard line. The east European Communist parties collapsed because Gorbachev let everybody know that Moscow wouldn't support them by armed force any more. But Cuba's different. The revolution here wasn't built on a foundation of Russian tanks, it's got its own roots. One of the things that's preserved it has been fear of the United States. If that was reduced by Washington lifting the trade embargo, establishing normal diplomatic relations ... *perestroika* and *glasnost* in Cuba? Maybe. The place is an economic shambles. It needs the United States. Maybe Castro's looking for a way out of his isolation, now that the Russians are cutting him loose.

"That news would certainly be of interest to the White House," she said.

"Excellent." Torras was smiling broadly. "There are many matters here for us to pursue at a later date. Now, I would be delighted to take you to dinner, but discretion obliges me to forgo the pleasure. May I be of assistance in any other way?"

He was moving toward ending the meeting. She flipped a mental coin and it came up heads.

"Well, in fact, yes," she said. "I am researching a new book. It's about the early days of revolutionary activity in Latin America. There is someone here in Cuba I would like to talk to if that would be possible, but I don't know where to find her."

"Oh?" Torras said. "What is her name?"

"Marita Linares."

He wrote it down carefully, using a silver fountain pen.

"She is involved in the book you are writing now?" he inquired delicately.

Keely had already decided to be honest, up to a point. Given who she was and why she was in Havana, she did not believe that there was any risk in asking.

"The book is an account of the early days of revolutionary activity in Latin America," she explained. "*Companera* Linares —" she used the revolutionary honorific, which in Cuba had replaced the older *senhora* "— was part of the network that was to support Che Guevara during his time in Bolivia. My best information is that she is now here in Cuba somewhere. I like to use original sources whenever I can, so if I could speak with her...."

"I didn't know that," Torras said with some interest. "In fact, I wasn't even aware of the existence of such a person." He smiled. "You're very well informed, too."

Keely inclined her head modestly.

"Very well," Torras said. "Let me check with someone. I believe your flight departs this evening?"

"I can delay it, if necessary." She had come over on what was coyly referred to as "the stealth shuttle," an officially ignored service run by Continental Airlines between Havana and Miami. Most of the passengers were Cuban exiles visiting relatives. You could only buy tickets at the airline counter; no travel agent carried them, and there were no telephone reservations. Keely's Irish passport allowed her to use the service with impunity, unlike natural-born American citizens.

"Perhaps you won't have to. She may live nearby. I will send the information around to the Monaco for you. Do you wish an interpreter? I can supply one if necessary."

Torras was going far out of his way to help her. She felt slightly guilty, knowing she was trading on her political importance for her own private ends. "No, thank you," she said. "My Spanish isn't really bad."

"Say something," he said, grinning at her. For a bureaucrat, he was peculiarly attractive. Warming to him, she switched to Spanish and gave him a few observations on the Cuban rebellion of 1895–98, and the leadership of José Martí during it.

He gave a little clap when she finished. "Excellent. Very good. Perhaps a little Castilian. Where did you learn it?"

"I learned it to do research on my last book. I spoke it all the time while I was doing the fieldwork."

"The book was *Latin America After Marx*?"

"Yes, that's right."

"There, you see, I really have read your books. They are very perceptive, although ideologically tilted perhaps. But I think that thirty years ago you would have been a Marxist. You worry about the downtrodden among us."

She suspected he was teasing her, but there was some truth in it. "Thank you."

He laughed, getting up. "I will have someone escort you down to the car to return you to the Monaco. I will let you know later today what I find out about Marita Linares."

Torras acted quickly, perhaps to impress her. Not two hours after the car delivered her to the Monaco Hotel, the desk called to inform her that someone was waiting for her downstairs. She went down by a staircase — the elevators had been behaving erratically that morning — and found her way through a dimly lit main floor corridor to the lobby. The Monaco had been built sometime in the early fifties, and had been nationalized along with almost everything else after the revolution; however, since it was used for guests of the Cuban government it had not declined quite to the level of shabbiness of other hotels of the same vintage. The lobby was clean and smelled of furniture polish, and there were still potted palms stationed against the tiled columns. The fifties furniture had long gone, however, replaced by imitation Danish modern settees and chairs. Light from the street filtered in through heavy double glass doors.

The female desk clerk smiled broadly at Keely and pointed to one of the sofas. The man sitting on it was about twenty-five, trim and dark, wearing an open-necked white shirt and navy blue trousers. As Keely approached, he stood up and gave a small bow.

"Dr. Fitzgerald?"

"Si."

"The undersecretary sent me," the man said in Spanish. "I am Miguel, his driver. He has told me to take you to see *Companera* Linares."

"Oh," Keely said, taken somewhat aback. She had envisioned herself renting a Lada and finding her own way to the Bolivian woman. "Very well. Is it far from here?"

"About three hours' drive. On the south coast. You should not try to get there by yourself."

She hesitated. It was just past noon. Her flight left at eleven. She could manage it, with two or three hours to talk to Marita Linares.

"Thank you," she said. "I'll be ready in a minute."

"You ought to bring a wrap," Miguel suggested. "There may be rain coming."

Miguel's weather forecast was accurate enough; rain did fall twice during the three-hour drive, once torrentially for five minutes just outside Havana, and again in spatters near Colon. But by the time the Chaika pulled off a secondary road onto a dirt lane, the midafternoon sun was shining brightly. Ahead, Keely could see blue water: the Caribbean.

"Where are we?" she asked.

"Near a village called Puerto Real," he said over his shoulder. "A very small village. Not on many maps."

"Oh," Keely said. She was stiff and cramped from sitting still for so long, and she was getting hungry. She hadn't eaten since seven o'clock. "How did you find it so easily?"

"The undersecretary gave me a map he drew."

Dumb question, Keely thought. Of course Torras would make sure I was going to the right place, once he or the Interior Ministry decided to let me go there.

That decision was worrying her at the back of her mind, in the place she put things she didn't want to acknowledge. The ease with which they'd agreed to her request was bothersome: she'd expected a polite and plausible excuse for not being able to talk to the Bolivian woman, especially if the ancestry of Marita Linares's son was being obscured for some reason or other.

But perhaps, Keely told herself, there's nothing more to it than the feelings of a woman who bore a child out of wedlock, a woman who wants to forget. Maybe nobody here knows who the boy's father was. Perhaps Marita Linares hid it from everyone for reasons of her own.

The Chaika was drawing to a halt outside a small two-story house made of light yellow stone. The house overlooked the beach and was separated from it by a low stone wall. A derelict car huddled in the sand near a clump of palm trees; beyond the palms the sea rolled in from an intense aquamarine horizon.

"Is she expecting me?" Keely asked Miguel.

"I am afraid I do not know. I will stay here. Please take as long as you wish."

Keely nodded and got out of the car. The size of the house, assuming it was inhabited by one person only, puzzled her. Someone was taking better than average care of Marita Linares.

She entered the yard and approached the worn French doors leading into the house. She thought she saw a flicker of motion inside, but wasn't certain. Surely, Keely reflected, Torras wouldn't send me all the way out here if she wasn't going to be at home.

She knocked at the door. For a long time there was no response, but just as she was about to knock again, a woman appeared quite suddenly on the other side of the glass. The door opened, squeaking on elderly hinges.

"Good afternoon," Keely said. "I'm Keely Fitzgerald. I'm looking for *Companera* Marita Linares."

The woman nodded. She was wearing a formless black dress and over it a gray cardigan. The wrists emerging from the cardigan sleeves seemed thin as the walking stick with which she supported herself, and her face was gaunt, the skin over her cheekbones hardly padded out by flesh at all. Her hair was gray and thin. But her dark eyes were alive with an expression that Keely could only describe as guarded. This woman is ill, Keely thought. Quite ill indeed. She can't be much over fifty and she looks as though she's dying. I think she may be. Why did Torras tell me I could see her? She ought to be in a hospital, not alone out here.

"Yes," Marita Linares said. Her voice was frail but there was authority in it. "I am Linares. Come in."

"I apologize for bothering you," Keely told her as she followed the woman into what must be a living room. The tip of the stick ticked on the boards of the floor. "I hope Oscar Torras told you to expect me?"

"Havana called," Marita said vaguely. She lowered herself into a cane armchair and pointed with her stick at a leather sofa. "Sit."

Keely sat. She hadn't known what kind of welcome to expect; clearly, though, it was not to be a gracious one. She sensed that Marita Linares was speaking with her under duress and for no other reason.

To gain mental breathing space she glanced around her at the room. There were windows with louvered shutters in the wall opposite the French doors, and a long dining table at the end farthest from the seating area. A wooden candelabrum hung over the table, and a brass floor lamp stood behind the chair in which Marita Linares sat. All along the walls were bookcases, and they were jammed with books. Keely could make out a few titles in the dim light. She recognized some of them: works of political and military history. On one of the bookcase shelves sat a black telephone, which looked new, and beside the telephone were a few photographs. One was of a young man in Cuban army uniform, staring directly and arrogantly into the camera. He was disturbingly handsome, but that was not what made Keely give a small internal start. She had seen photographs of Che Guevara, unbearded at twenty, and this young officer was the spitting image of the dead revolutionary.

"What does an American want with me?" Marita asked.

"I'm Irish, in fact, not American," Keely told her, recollecting herself. She took a notepad and pen out of her bag. She had decided not to bring a tape recorder; a sheaf of notes, buried among her official papers, would draw less attention on her exit from the country.

"Oh." A flicker in the dark eyes. "They didn't tell me that."

Who are *they*? Keely wondered. "I thought Oscar Torras would have mentioned it," she suggested, probing.

"No. I believed you were American. But do you live in America?"

"Yes."

"Are you an Irish revolutionary, fighting the British?"

"IRA? Oh, no. I'm from the south of Ireland. The republic."

"I see." Marita appeared to lose interest in the subject. "What do you want to talk to me about?"

"I'm writing a book about the revolutionary fighters in Latin America, from 1960 on. I gather you were in Bolivia in those early days."

Eyes like a cat, intent and watchful. "I was."

Careful, Keely told herself. "Tell me about what it was like in Bolivia then," she said. "How the people lived, what they thought of Fidel and the revolution here."

It seemed innocuous enough. Marita Linares began to answer in her fragile but peculiarly compelling voice, her sentences precise, her descriptions vivid and her thinking astute. Keely began to realize, even if the books surrounding her hadn't pointed in that direction, that she was dealing with at least her intellectual equal.

They talked for perhaps forty minutes before Keely remembered, with something of a start, that Marita was a sick woman and that she might be tiring. She had to come to the point.

"I gather also you were connected with the underground that was supposed to support the guerrillas in the field."

"I was a schoolteacher," Marita said after a pause. "I knew some people in the underground. Nothing more. You should talk to them. Those who aren't dead."

"But you were in La Higuera when Che Guevara was killed."

"He was murdered. Everyone in Bolivia knew the government soldiers shot him after he was taken prisoner."

She wasn't responding to the question. "But, *Companera* Linares, were you there at the time?"

"What does it matter now? He's dead."

"Yes," Keely said. "Did you know him well?"

"I knew who he was when they brought him to La Higuera."

"Was that the first time he was there?"

"Yes. As far as I know." The voice betrayed advancing fatigue.

She's lying, damn it, Keely thought. She glanced over at the bookcase. "Is that your son in the photograph over there? He's very handsome."

"Yes. That's my son."

"What's his name?"

Hesitation. "Ramon."

That was Guevara's code name in Bolivia, Keely thought. Oh, hell, how I hate prying into private lives. "He's an army officer still?"

"Yes."

"Could I talk with him?"

"You would have to ask the army. He's not here."

"He looks very like Che Guevara."

There was a long silence. "You have been talking to someone," Marita Linares said. "Who?"

"A man named Inciarte. He was once —"

"I know who he was," Marita cut in. "He had strange ideas about a lot of things. They'll be stranger now he's an old man." She raised the walking stick and slammed its end down on the wooden floor with a deafening crack. Keely started back.

"Now go. Get out of my house. Take your prying questions elsewhere. I have nothing else to say."

Humiliated, cheeks hot, Keely stuffed her notes into her bag. She'd gone too far and knew it. And she was no closer to learning anything about Marita Linares's son.

She felt the Bolivian woman's gaze hard between her shoulder blades as she opened the French doors and let herself out into the yard. Miguel was leaning against the Chaika, gazing out to sea. From the careful neutrality of his expression, Keely knew he had heard at least part of what had happened in the house. He got behind the wheel as she climbed into the backseat.

"Havana?" he said.

"Yes, please. I'll go back to the hotel now."

The Chaika had been gone for some twenty minutes when there was a tap at the French doors. Marita had been sitting quite still in the cane chair since the car left, and she didn't get up in response to the tapping. After a moment the doors

opened and Cardoso came in. He leaned against one of the
bookcases, the one on which the photographs stood.

"You should have been more astute," Cardoso said. "All
we have is the name Inciarte. We don't know why she is
interested in your son."

"Why are you worried about it?" she asked. "Perhaps
she's exactly what she says. A writer of books. An intellectual. But why should I let her pry into my privacy?"

"Perhaps she's not just an author. Is it something to do
with the fact that Ramon is Che Guevara's son? The woman
seemed to be aware of it."

Marita said, "You knew, then." She appeared angry at his
knowledge, but not surprised by it.

"Yes. It's in his file, of course."

"I have no idea why that fact would interest her."

"What did you and Ramon discuss before he left?"

She looked up at Cardoso. "He said he was assigned overseas again. That he wouldn't be back for some time."

"That was all?"

"Yes. What else would he have told me? He's a soldier."

Cardoso pulled at his jaw. "You weren't curious?"

"Of course I was curious. But I know better than to ask
some questions. Do you take me for a fool?"

Cardoso pulled thoughtfully at his jaw again. As though
the thought had just struck her, Marita exclaimed suddenly:

"He is safe, isn't he? Nothing has happened to him? He's
not in some kind of trouble —"

"No, no," Cardoso assured her. "He's fine. Everything is
all right. We were simply curious as to why this Fitzgerald
woman wanted to talk to you."

He's lying, Marita thought with satisfaction. Ramon has
disappeared, as he said he was going to do. They don't want
me to know it. And they're not being rough with me. So
they're not quite sure what's become of him. Perfect. But this
donkey has a point. Why *was* the Irish woman asking such
questions? Perhaps I should have let her go on. But I didn't.
And the less said the better, as things are. Not even the
person in Havana knows what Ramon is doing, what he's
going to do. Is he going to give Ramon any help at all? Or
has he just slipped my son from the leash to let him run?

"Very well," Cardoso said, straightening up. "We'll let it go at that. Perhaps she's just an intellectual snooping around for a book, as you said."

"Yes. Please keep such hyenas away from me in future."

"As you like. Has the medical care been satisfactory?"

"The nurse comes every evening. I am still alive."

"So I see," Cardoso said with a wry smile. "Very much alive. I must be sure not to come within range of your stick."

She smiled in return, to humor him: a sick old woman. He was such an ass, even if he had once been her son's commander. She had recognized him, from Ramon's description, when he first came to the house to tell her about the medical service. Colonel Cardoso, once a real combat officer and now only a narcotics trader, walking symbol of the corrupted revolution.

"Be sure you don't," she said.

Keely was worn out by the time Miguel pulled to a halt in front of the Monaco. For most of the way from Puerto Real she had been going over the interview again and again in her mind, trying to find a chink between Marita's words to let some light through. She couldn't find one. The woman hadn't even admitted that Ramon was Che Guevara's child, although she had not denied it outright.

Perhaps, she thought, as Miguel opened the car door for her, it's really nothing more than the feelings of a woman whose past hurts and who doesn't want to talk about it to anyone, especially a stranger. I imagine that's how I'd feel in her position. And Ramon isn't hidden for any devious political reason, it's just that no one wants to raise ghosts from the past.

Once inside the Monaco she trudged up three flights of stairs to her floor; the elevator appeared to be working again but her legs were cramped from the long hours of sitting and she wanted to work the knots out of them. Her room, which overlooked a quiet side street, was cool and dim, the evening light obscuring the worn edges of the fifties furniture. The room had a bathroom, with hot water that worked, and she went in to wash her face.

The soap she had brought was in her toiletries case. On

the point of picking the case up, she stopped. She was sure she had left it on the right side of the sink, not on the left.

She straightened up, looking in the mirror. Her eyes stared back at her, perplexed and a little frightened.

Wait a minute here, she thought.

She returned to the bedroom. Her suitcase was lying on the foot of the bed, zippered and locked as she had left it. She unlocked it and studied the contents. Her belongings were not precisely as she had left them.

Somebody's been in here, she thought. She quickly went through the suitcase. Not a thing was missing.

Not a thief, she thought, sitting down on the bed. But someone searched the room while I was gone. She felt unaccountably afraid, and very much alone. Her quasi-diplomatic immunity suddenly did not seem much of a protection.

Her watch showed eight o'clock. She had intended to have something to eat in the hotel restaurant — her stomach had been protestingly empty for hours — then go to the airport, but abruptly she wanted to be on her way out of Cuba. She packed everything quickly, locked the room behind her and went along the hall to the elevators. The long corridor, lit badly by twenty-watt bulbs, was deserted. She waited, hearing clicks and whines from the elevator shaft. Finally the machine put in an appearance and she stepped into the cubicle. Two large men and a small woman stared fixedly at her as she boarded. There was a lot of baggage around their feet. They didn't look like Cubans, and one of the men smelled strongly of rum. The woman eyed Keely's dress and open raincoat with some interest.

"Canadian?" she asked as the elevator cage groaned into motion. She had some kind of accent.

"No, Irish," Keely said. The woman turned to one of her companions and broke into a stream of what Keely suspected was Russian. She relaxed slightly. The men beamed at her. "Irish, good," the one who smelled of rum said. "We are from Leningrad. Have you been to Leningrad?"

"No," said Keely. "I haven't."

"You should come. Lots of people from west coming to Leningrad now."

"I'll be sure to try," Keely said as the elevator doors

opened. The Russians bustled out behind her. She hurried to the checkout desk and turned in her key; the Ministry of Foreign Affairs had paid for the hotel. It wasn't until she was standing on the outside steps in the semidarkness, suitcase in one hand and leather bag that served as a purse over her shoulder, that she realized she might have made a mistake. There was only one cab in the rank, and that was the one she was going to have to take unless another one turned up within seconds. The man in the cab might be waiting specifically for her. Visions of abduction and interrogation ran through her head. She briefly considered walking around the corner to hail a taxi, but remembered how few and far between cabs were in Havana. And a lot of them were allowed to travel only within fixed zones.

This is ridiculous, she thought. I'm shying at shadows. They wouldn't dare do anything to me, not when I'm under the ministry's protection, would they? For heaven's sake, I'm an envoy from Washington.

At home in Boston the idea would have seemed ridiculous. Here, in a dim Havana street without anyone close by, it seemed much less so. Maybe they, whoever they are, don't know that, Keely thought. Or maybe they don't care.

She tried to see into the cab's interior, but the inside light was off and the streetlights were too dim to make out the driver's face. As if that would tell me anything, anyway, she thought. Now what do I do? The airport bus went two hours ago.

The Russians tumbled out of the hotel entrance, laden down with their baggage, waving their arms around and shouting at each other. One of them saw the taxi and gave a loud whistle. The taxi remained quite still.

Inspiration. Keely called out to the Russian woman, "Airport?"

"*Da.* You also?"

"Yes. Do you want to take a taxi together?"

She spoke to her two companions. The rum-laden one beamed again. The other shrugged in acquiescence.

"Yes, yes, that would be good. There is only one taxi, we should share."

Keely stepped into the street and waved imperiously at the

cab. Reluctantly, it seemed to her, it rolled forward and stopped in front of the entrance. The driver was one of the few Cubans of Chinese extraction. With rather ill grace he opened the trunk of the Lada.

Somehow they all managed to cram into the little car. The Russian who smelled of rum was in front, the woman in the middle of the back seat with Keely on one side and the second man on the other. Keely had the impression that he would have liked to be sitting next to her. She was relieved that he wasn't.

José Martí International Airport was eighteen kilometers out of the city. The driver went as fast as possible, probably eager to be quit of the Russians, who talked nonstop at the tops of their voices. They found out where Keely lived and asked every question about Boston they could think of. The man in front produced a half-empty rum bottle from somewhere, swigged from the neck and offered it to Keely, who refused. The other two accepted. The journey became boisterous.

As they approached the airport the man in the back began trying to tell Keely some Russian joke by translating it, badly, into English. It seemed to be about a Ukrainian peasant, an egg and a KGB colonel, but she couldn't make head nor tail of it. She countered with the one about the English sports car driver, the two Irish farmers and the hayfield, but the Russian couldn't follow the joke's logic. By the time she finished, with the Russian looking puzzled, the taxi was drawing up at the terminal entrance. They piled out. The drunken Russian insisted on paying her share of the cab fare. Keely studied the driver as the money changed hands. He didn't seem concerned at her safe arrival.

Imagination, she thought. There's nothing to worry about. But why did they search my room? They didn't do it last time I was here. Was it because I talked to Marita Linares?

Keely and the Russians trooped into the terminal. It was crowded, with a lot of package tours on the way out. She heard German and Russian and some other languages she took to be Slavic of one kind or another, Polish and Czech, perhaps. There seemed to be more foreigners than Cubans.

The special visa from the Ministry of Foreign Affairs

would have allowed her to wait in the VIP lounge, but she felt safer amid a press of humans. The airport restaurant was closed so she found a small bar, ordered a glass of fruit juice and settled down to wait for an hour, until it was time to go to the departure area. She passed most of the interval thinking about who had turned her hotel room over and why. She thought it likely Torras had used the Interior Ministry to find out where Marita Linares lived, and likely the request would have gone through the police. Or maybe Cuban counterintelligence, the G2, had been listening somewhere along the line. Were Torras and his boss, the Minister, under the gun somehow, so much so that the security forces would ransack the belongings of an envoy from Washington?

She grimaced in frustration. There was no way she could tell.

Maybe, she reflected, Michael Conroy would know why my seeing Marita Linares would attract such interest. Something to do with her and Che Guevara and their son, perhaps? I think that as soon as I get to the States I'll ask him about this.

She had thought about Conroy quite a number of times since she left him looking out the window after her that blizzardy night in Washington. Thought about him, in fact, more frequently than she considered reasonable. He was just another CIA spook, after all; she'd met a number of them, and by and large they hadn't impressed her. But he had a kind of peculiar individuality under the blank CIA surface, as though he was conscious of a streak of eccentricity in himself and was concealing it by sheer willpower. Once or twice she had found herself intending to telephone him, then realized that there was nothing to telephone him *about.* They'd only just avoided disliking each other before they parted ways, and there had been no suggestion between them of getting in touch again. She was mildly annoyed that some part of her felt there had been, or should have been, such an arrangement.

Well, she thought, if I needed an excuse to contact him, I have it now.

The juice was warm and oversweet; she left it unfinished and started making her way toward the departure lounge and the Miami shuttle. Even — perhaps especially? — on the Cuban end there was no indication that such a flight existed.

She kept a watch for followers on the way to the lounge, but didn't detect any. I'm not trained for this, though, she reminded herself. There could be a dozen of them, and I might not know it.

Keely's VIP visa let her sail through the exit formalities without a pause, but she didn't start to feel secure until she was inside the departure lounge. The lounge was half full of Cubans returning to the United States after, she presumed, visiting relatives. Several of her fellow travelers regarded her curiously; with her bronze hair and fair complexion she plainly wasn't one of them.

A Cuban man sat next to her in the Boeing when they embarked, but he was easily sixty and his company didn't bother her, except for the faint odor of after-shave and cigars that came with him. Keely's father had occasionally smoked cigars but most often a pipe; she remembered him tramping up the long slope of the back lawn toward the old house, the pipe stuck in the side of his mouth, surrounded by his dogs, the mist lying over the river valley behind him or the sun falling on the river, gleaming silver in the green of the water meadow. For some reason it was that memory, more than any other, that brought her the pang of homesickness.

I feel it in the deep heart's core, she thought as the Boeing lifted from the runway. Yeats. Now there was a grand man, a man who knew what he was talking about.

She smiled at herself. How long I've been away, she thought, and here are my feet still planted firmly in six inches of Irish mud. I can feel it between my toes, I can.

Keely drowsed during the flight; the old man next to her fell asleep and snored gently. She didn't come fully awake until the approach lights of the runway were flicking past underneath the plane's belly and the necessity of effort again presented itself. One more flight, the run to Washington to take Havana's message to Rupert Lipton, then tomorrow evening on to Boston and home. She'd be glad to get there.

Lipton was going to be glad to hear what the Cubans had to say. He was coordinating the president's secret initiative to reform the American relationship with Cuba, and Keely was, in effect, the president's backdoor ambassador to Havana. Strictly speaking the State Department should have been handling the initiative, but according to what Lipton had told her the president wanted a more direct approach, one not constrained by the State Department's sense of protocol and its sluggish bureaucracy. Furthermore, Lipton had said, the Cubans probably wouldn't listen to the State Department anyway. They'd be much more likely to respond to a direct contact with the White House. When the groundwork was laid, Lipton thought, State could then be called in to formalize it and tidy up the loose ends. The Secretary of State, who was reported to be firmly under the president's thumb, had apparently gone along with the scheme and had not informed his underlings of what was happening.

The Boeing thumped onto the runway, trundled along for a while and stopped. Keely heard the rumble of the gangway connecting. Yawning, she gathered her belongings together, squirmed past the Cuban and after a few minutes found herself going through customs. Not even a cursory check of her baggage, such as it was.

At this hour, just past midnight, the terminal was fairly quiet. Keely located a bank of telephones on the upper concourse and dialed Lipton's home in Washington, using a credit card number he had given her.

"Hello."

"Dr. Lipton?"

"Speaking."

She thought he recognized her voice, but she wasn't sure. "It's Susie-Q," she said. It was a silly code name. Men. Irritated, she hoped for an instant that Lipton's wife was listening in on an extension.

"Oh, hi. How's everything? The kids?"

"The children are fine."

"Ah, that's good. Any problems?"

She hesitated. Not over the phone. "No."

"Okay. See you at one tomorrow."

"Bye." She rang off and stood for a moment, looking at the telephone. Then she rummaged in the leather bag and got out her address book. Conroy's number was under M for

Michael. She'd taken it from his sister's phone the evening she'd interviewed him.

She used the credit card number again. A sleepy voice answered.

"Hello, Michael?"

"Yeah. Who's this?"

"I'm the doctor who makes house calls in snowstorms. Remember?"

"What?" A pause. Then his voice again, very awake and alert. "Okay. What's wrong?"

He assumes something is wrong, she thought. Always a spook. "Nothing," she said. "I have something I'd like to talk to you about."

"Go ahead."

"Face to face, preferably."

"Okay. When and where?"

"Same place you met me last time. Ten tomorrow morning? Can you get away from work?"

"I'm on leave," he said. "I can pick you up."

"Good. Thanks. Bye."

"Bye," he said, but she could sense the curiosity in his voice. She hung up, feeling ridiculously conspiratorial. Now to get over to the charter terminal and the private jet Rupert was supposed to have waiting for her. She'd have to go down to the lower concourse and catch the airport shuttle.

A bus was pulling out just as she reached the transit point outside the glass doors of the lower concourse, and Keely sighed with annoyance. She set her suitcase on the platform beside her and pushed the strap of her leather bag higher onto her shoulder. She felt utterly weary, and she had a long way to go yet.

Even at this hour there was a certain amount of foot and vehicle traffic along the roadway and the platform. People were being picked up and dropped off by taxis and private cars; an airport security van cruised slowly past, the men inside scanning the concourse facade. Beyond the roadway the Florida night lay like a thick, damp blanket, pierced at ground level by the lights of parking lots and green directional signs, and in the sky by wandering speckles of aircraft lights. Keely could smell the kerosene odor of jet fuel, and under that the subtler, heavier scent of tropical vegetation and a trace of the sea.

A long black Chrysler was proceeding slowly toward her along the platform, parking lights on and headlights off. Keely paid little attention to it until it pulled to a stop almost in front of her and a man in a gray suit got out of the front passenger door. He was a young man; Keely noticed vaguely that he was nice-looking, with short blond hair and a neat blond mustache.

"Dr. Fitzgerald?" he asked.

"Yes?" she said, taken somewhat aback.

He was opening the Chrysler's back door. "We were sent to pick you up," he said. "Security."

She frowned and didn't move. "I wasn't told anything about this. Let me see some identification."

"It was Mr. Lipton sent us," the man said. "I can put your suitcase in the trunk."

"Oh," Keely said, relieved. "That's okay, it's light." She picked up her suitcase and stepped toward the open door of the car. And then she said, almost on impulse, "But I want to see some identification."

"Okay," the blond man said. "No problem." He reached under his jacket. And Keely was thinking, as the universe seemed to slow down, this is all wrong. He should have showed identification as soon as he got out of the car, and he should have met me inside if it's security, and Rupert would have said just now if he was sending someone, he's not from Rupert at all —

Keely flung the suitcase at him as his hand appeared with a gun in it. She turned and ran toward the automatic glass doors leading into the terminal. She heard a snarled "Shit" behind her as she reached the doors, the heavy panes sliding open just in time to let her through, and the clatter of the blond man's shoes on the pavement behind her. A hand tugged at the belt of her raincoat but she wrenched free, stumbling into the long hall of the lower concourse, and she glimpsed startled faces turning toward her as she finally got her balance. "Stop him!" she yelled at the top of her lungs. A long way off she saw the uniform of a security guard, and she ran toward it. To her right was a long wall of glass windows, and in its reflection she could see herself, coattails flying.

And no one behind her.

Jesus, she thought, slowing down. I got away from him. But are there more inside? Why didn't he shoot me?

She was trembling from reaction, and felt sick. Because they wanted me alive, she told herself. Who in the name of the Almighty were they?

The commotion had attracted the guard's attention. He was trotting toward her, his gun already drawn. Keely turned to look through the windows, toward the platform outside the doors. The Chrysler was gone. So was her suitcase.

Those bloody bastards, she thought, although her knees were weak. She wanted to sit down.

The guard was at her elbow, wearing a perplexed expression; the catastrophe he seemed to be expecting hadn't materialized. "What's going on here?" he asked, regarding Keely suspiciously.

"A man outside tried to pull me into a car," she quavered. For a second she thought she was going to fall over, but caught herself. "He took my suitcase," she added, suddenly infuriated all over again. The anger made her feel better.

"Okay," the guard said. He spoke briefly into a hand radio. "What kind of car was it?" he asked Keely.

"Black. Recent model Chrysler, luxury car. I didn't get the license number. There were at least two men in it. Just outside. They drove off."

He used the radio again. "Okay, ma'am, we're onto it. Could I see some identification, please? Then we'll go up to the security office so's I can make out a report."

She obliged. They were polite and agreeable enough at first, but when they discovered that she wasn't an American and that she'd come in on the Continental flight from Havana, the temperature cooled noticeably. The matter was made worse by the fact that she couldn't tell them why she'd been in Havana.

"Look, Dr. Fitzgerald," the security captain said at last as he leaned over his desk toward her, "we're trying to get to the bottom of this, and you're being no goddamned help whatsoever. You don't have any idea at all who these characters might have been?"

"No. I'm afraid not."

"Nothing connected with your being in Cuba?"

"I really honestly don't know."

"And there's a charter plane waiting to take you to Washington."

"Yes. I should be there right now."

"And these characters took your suitcase."

"That's right."

"You're sure there was *nothing* in the suitcase except personal effects?"

He thinks I had drugs in it and some other dealers stole it, she realized. "That was all," she snapped.

"No drugs, for example."

If he goes on like this, she thought, I'm going to have to call Lipton after all. I *really* don't want to do that. "No. No drugs."

He regarded her speculatively. "I dunno if I believe you."

"Suit yourself. But I really have to be on my way."

He sighed. "Okay. But first show me what's in your shoulder bag."

I don't have to do that, she thought. But anything to get out of here. "Okay," she said, and unloaded it onto his desk. "There. Satisfied?"

He nodded. She gathered up her belongings and said, "I don't suppose you'd be willing to let me make a couple of phone calls. I'll use my credit card."

He gestured at a vacant desk a few feet away. "Go ahead."

She needed to let Lipton know what had happened; he'd better have someone meet her at the Washington end. But when the number rang through, all she got was his answering machine. Keely hung up in frustration and growing nervousness. The blond man had known Lipton's name. So whoever had tried to abduct her had connections either to Havana or to Lipton's own people. She didn't like that at all.

I'd better not take any chances, she thought, and dialed Conroy's number. He answered after six rings, and he didn't sound pleased.

"It's the doctor again."

"Yeah?"

"Can you meet me at National? At the charter gate, in

about two and a half hours? I may be in trouble."

"Christ," he said, but she couldn't tell whether it was from consternation at her news or from irritation at being asked to pick her up. "All right. What line?"

"It's called Seaboard Charters."

"Okay. I'll be there."

She hung up and turned to the security captain. "I don't suppose," she said sweetly, "that you'd be willing to give me an escort to the charter terminal?"

He sighed. "Yeah, I suppose so. Who were you calling? The CIA?"

She started, then realized he was being sarcastic. "That's right," she said. "I was."

He shook his head tiredly and picked up his telephone.

Washington
March 15

■

Conroy knew something was badly wrong when Keely hurried through the arrivals gate; she looked frightened, which was an expression he hadn't until now been able to imagine on her face. Then she saw him, and her face cleared. Conroy felt subtly gratified. Knight in shining armor, he thought.

"Hello," he said as she reached him. "Trouble?"

"Yes. Thank you so much for doing this."

"I don't mind," he said, although that was not what he had been saying to himself two hours earlier. "No luggage?"

"Somebody took it. They tried to take me, too."

Conroy looked swiftly but unobtrusively around. There was no one nearby, and the terminal hall was almost deserted at this hour of the morning. He had checked the area carefully when he arrived twenty minutes ago, and he had no sense that there was anyone watching the arrivals gate, but after hearing what she'd said he was in a hurry to get out of the building.

"They were armed," she added as they started for the exit. "At least one of them had a gun."

Conroy nodded. He was carrying his Beretta 9 mm automatic in a belt holster under his raincoat. "So do I," he told her. "Where do you want to go?"

She passed the back of her hand over her forehead. "I hadn't even thought about it," she said. "I'm booked into a hotel, but...." She trailed off. "I've been awake for nearly twenty-four hours. I'm sorry, I'm not thinking straight."

"You'd better come to Gemma's place with me. Then we can work out what to do next."

"Yes. Good. I'd feel safer."

They trudged into the parking lot and located Gemma's car. Conroy checked the rearview mirror carefully as he pulled onto the George Washington Parkway; it was still some time till dawn and there wasn't much traffic. He detected no surveillance.

"Okay," he said as he settled down for the run into the city. "What happened, exactly?"

"I'd just come into Miami," she told him. "I was doing some research. I was waiting for the terminal shuttle bus when this car pulled up." She went on to tell him about the attack and the inconclusive interview with airport security. But she left out the matter of where she had been.

When she finished, he drove along in silence for a few minutes. Then he asked, "When are you going to tell me the rest of it?"

"What rest?"

"Do you normally charter planes to fly around on research expeditions?"

"Well, no."

"Who are you working for?" he asked. "Rupert Lipton? And where were you before you flew into Miami?"

She remained silent.

"Look," Conroy said, "I can find out in about three hours what planes flew into Miami last night, and who was on them. You came in on the Havana shuttle, didn't you?"

She slumped in tired defeat. "Yes."

"Backdoor diplomacy?"

"Yes."

"Why didn't you tell me that in the first place?"

"Because it's backdoor."

"Lipton's behind it? Not that it matters to me."

She nodded. "I was going to tell you about Cuba. It was the diplomacy part I wanted to be reticent about. I told you I'm just too tired to think straight."

"We're nearly there," Conroy told her. "When do you have to talk to Lipton?"

"One o'clock."

"You can get some sleep, then. We can talk later."

"That would be grand." She put her head back against the rest and closed her eyes.

"Here we are," Conroy said a few minutes later. He followed Keely as she stumbled up the steps to Gemma's front door. Inside, she stood unsteadily while he relieved her of her coat. He realized that she was weaving with fatigue.

"Before you do anything else," he said, "you'd better get some rest. At the top of the stairs on your right there's a bedroom. Use that. There's a bathroom next to it."

"'Kay," Keely mumbled, and without further ado began to totter up the stairs. Conroy waited until she reached the top and disappeared. Then he went into the living room, took off his gun, dropped heavily into an armchair in front of the fireplace and promptly fell asleep.

He woke up at ten past nine, with sun pouring in through the living room windows. No sounds from upstairs. He washed his face in cold water in Gemma's downstairs powder room and wandered blearily into the kitchen to make coffee. While the percolator bubbled he sat at the pine table in the breakfast nook, chin on one hand, and stared blankly through the glass patio doors into Gemma's back yard. It had been an exceptionally cold winter, and there was still some dirty snow along the north side of the privacy fence, where the sun didn't reach this early in the year. The lawn and flowerbeds were bare, brown dormant grass and dead-looking earth with no sign of the living roots and seeds underneath. A couple of sparrows were aimlessly pecking among last year's matted flower stalks, looking for food. Conroy had carefully filled the bird feeders with sunflower seeds, but the sparrows didn't seem to be interested. He'd been at Gemma's a couple of winters back, for a Christmas visit, and he seemed to remember that there had been more birds then. Small ones, looking like sparrows dipped in raspberry juice, purple finches Gemma had told him. And a couple of waxwings, and some blue jays, and a type of small bird that insisted on going down tree trunks head-first, a nuthatch. He hadn't seen any this winter except a half dozen of the finches early one morning, and one nuthatch the same day. Other than that there were only the dingy sparrows, and occasionally a starling.

The percolator bubbled into silence. Conroy filled a mug, slopped milk into it, a little sugar. Standing at the kitchen sink and looking out the window while he sipped at the coffee, he wondered whether to wake the woman upstairs. She might not appreciate it; she'd been out on her feet when they arrived at the house.

He was vaguely flattered that she'd called on him for help, although he didn't quite understand why she'd resorted to him; with her connections she probably could have rustled up a platoon of Secret Service agents if she'd needed to. That, however, would have attracted all sorts of unwelcome attention to where she'd been and what she'd been doing. Probably there were a number of other things she could have done, but for obscure reasons of her own she'd chosen to call on him.

Conroy couldn't make any sense of it unless Keely Fitzgerald was somehow connecting last night's events in Miami with something that had happened in Cuba. What the latter might be Conroy couldn't imagine. He supposed he'd find out when she finally got around to talking to him.

Marita Linares, he thought suddenly. It's something about Marita Linares.

He sighed and drank the rest of the coffee, trying to remember when last he'd been alone in a house with a woman who wasn't married. He'd had a brief relationship, a couple of years after Marguerite pulled out, with the daughter of a British diplomat in Rio de Janeiro, but it had eventually dried up and blown away. Since then he'd not had much to do with women on an intimate level. He worked too hard, for one thing, and after the mid-eighties and the spread of AIDS, casual liaisons had become much too dangerous. The mortality rate from the disease wasn't nearly as high — yet — as those of the great plagues of history, but the psychological effect was similar. Closeness could kill you. Finding normal human intimacy in a town as full of ambitious transients as Washington had always been a problem, but Conroy knew from the personal experience of the past few years that it had become even worse.

I'm glad I'm not going to be stuck here for two years, he thought. It'd drive me crazy, I'd probably end up resigning. What would I do in that case? I could afford to retire, if I were careful. Go to a small town, get a dog, watch the seasons go round and round.

He heard footsteps in the hallway and turned to see Keely Fitzgerald standing uncertainly at the kitchen door, fully dressed. Her eyes were puffy, and although she'd obviously brushed her hair she still looked bedraggled.

Jesus, Conroy thought suddenly, I forgot to shave. I must be a wonderful sight. "Morning," he said brusquely. "Coffee?"

"I'd kill for coffee," she said. "And a change of clothes."

"The coffee I can manage," he said, pouring as he spoke. "The clothes are another matter. I can probably find something of Gemma's to fit you. She jogs or something."

"No," she said. She seemed alert enough. "But thank you. I'll go and buy something before I see Rupert. It can be casual, I suppose."

He shrugged and handed her the coffee. "Fine. You've got a few hours yet. Cream and sugar on the table."

She put away one cup and started another while they made light and inconsequential conversation. Then she said, abruptly:

"Cuba. Marita Linares."

"What about her?" Conroy leaned forward, remembered his unshaven jaw and leaned back.

"I found her. With some help from the Ministry of Foreign Affairs. A man named Torras."

Conroy nodded. "I've heard of him. He would have gone through the Interior Ministry to locate her. Did he show any reluctance to help?"

"No. None at all. He even gave me a car and a driver. She lives a long way from Havana, down on the south coast, a place called Puerto Real."

"Did she talk to you?"

"For a while." Keely recounted the conversation in detail and told him about the photograph. "And I think she's sick," she ended. "Very sick. Cancer or something like that. She was using a cane, and she can't be even close to sixty."

"And the boy's name is Ramon, and he looks like Guevara."

"Yes. But she wouldn't admit that Guevara was the father. She admitted she knew who Inciarte was."

"So you said," Conroy reminded her. "Then you went back to Havana. Did you notice whether anyone was following you? Either out or back?"

"I wasn't watching for it," she confessed. "In either direction. I'm sorry, I'm thick as a wall."

"You wouldn't likely have spotted it, anyway," he reassured her. "If it's done well, it's even hard for a professional to detect."

"Oh. Well, anyway, when I got back to the hotel, I realized my room had been searched. It wasn't robbery, because nothing was taken."

Conroy rubbed his chin thoughtfully, oblivious to the scratching sound it made. He caught Keely grinning at him.

"What?" he said, smiling uneasily.

"Us," she said. "We are discussing matters of state and high policy, and we look as though we'd each been dragged through a bush backward."

"Sorry," he said. "I forgot to shave."

"Doesn't matter," she informed him. "But why was my room searched? I've been to Cuba for these reasons twice before, and that never happened."

"They were looking for information, I think," Conroy said. "But exactly what, I have no idea. Was there anything else? Anything Torras said? Anything the driver Miguel said or did? Anything at the airport or on the plane?"

She told him about the Russians and the old man who sat next to her on the flight. "After I got to Miami, you know the rest."

"All of it?"

She bristled slightly. "Yes. All of it."

"Sorry," Conroy said. "Once bitten, twice shy."

"All right, I deserved the question. But that really is everything."

"I wonder where Ramon Guevara is right now?" Conroy muttered.

"Would that be significant?"

"Might be. Look. The only time you've run into any trouble, it coincides with asking questions of Ramon's mother. Somebody is curious about how and what you know about Marita Linares and her son. Curious enough to risk grabbing an unofficial United States envoy."

"I know. That frightens me." She gave a small shiver. "Would they have killed me?"

"No, I don't think so." Privately, he did not believe this. For a moment he imagined her lying with a bullet in her head in some hidden grave, never to be found. Earth closing her open green eyes.

"But who would do such a thing?" she was asking. "Are you sure it's not political? Would part of the Cuban government kidnap me to make me tell them what the ministry and Washington are talking about?"

"No, I don't think so. There'd be much better ways of doing it. Although ... I suppose if they really wanted to screw up negotiations, taking measures against an American envoy would help do the job."

"Taking measures meaning murder?"

She wasn't about to be soothed. "Yes. Possibly."

"My God, this is infuriating. I'm supposed to go back, you know. If it's needed."

"I wouldn't do that just yet." Conroy ruminated for a few moments while Keely glared into her coffee mug. Finally he said, "Let me do some checking at the office. Maybe there's something in the bowels of the computers, or Registry."

She looked at her watch. "Yes. I'd better get going. Can you drop me off somewhere I can shop for some clothes?"

"Yeah. Look, I'll give you my spare key to the house. Come back to change, if you like. Can you meet me here when you're done with Lipton?"

"Yes. That should be by late afternoon."

"Fine," Conroy said, getting up. He paused. "One last thing, just a little one. Why did you call me rather than someone else?"

She looked confused. "I couldn't get through to Rupert. I didn't want. . . . This is supposed to be very quiet. I knew I could trust you. I'm sorry about dragging you in like this."

"I don't mind," Conroy said, and went upstairs to shave.

*

He dropped her off in central Georgetown and drove out to Langley. In the main building he ran into Tucker Petrie just outside the latter's office and followed him into the cubicle. "What're you doing here?" Petrie asked suspiciously. "I thought you were on leave."

"I am. I came in to chase something around. Actually, I was going to ask you to give me a hand."

Petrie looked doubtful and owlish. "I've got a hell of a big report due at the end of the week."

"If you promise to help I'll tell you about the purple finches."

Petrie eyed him even more suspiciously. "What about the purple finches?"

"They're disappearing."

"No shit," Petrie said. "So's the ozone layer. What do you want help with?"

"A Cuban. I have to find out where he is."

"Good luck. Do you know how many Cubans there *are*?"

"This one's special. He's Che Guevara's son."

"Che's got four kids total, and they were all in Cuba last I heard."

"Not this one, Tuck. He's a wild card."

Petrie's eyebrows migrated toward his hairline like two Vs of Canada geese. "Oh? For this I should screw up my chances of promotion? Because Che Guevara couldn't keep it in his pants when he should have?"

"Ah, come on, Tuck," Conroy pleaded. "I really could use some help. Give the ozone layer a break for the rest of the day. It could probably use it."

"Oh, all right." Petrie sighed. "Just let me lock up. Christ, you're persuasive."

"That's good."

"What do you want to find out?"

"I want to know everything about a Cuban army officer named Ramon Linares. Linares is his mother's name. Marita Linares."

"What's the father's?" Petrie wanted to know. The Spanish naming convention was to add to the given name the father's surname and then the mother's surname. Castro's full name, for example was Fidel Castro Ruz.

"I don't know. Maybe Ramon never used it."

"Sort of waving your bastardy on a stick, to do that."

"Maybe he doesn't care. I don't know. Anyway, what I'd really like to know is where he is now and what he's supposed to be doing, if possible."

"Mind if I ask why?"

Conroy considered this and then said, "Okay. A person I know was in Cuba and went to see Marita Linares, Ramon's mother. Research for a book. On the way back the person's baggage was searched and the person ran into some trouble in Miami. I'm trying to find out if the events are connected."

"Hokay," Petrie said. "Where do you want to start?"

"Central Reference. If that doesn't give us anything, I'll get Vickery's clearance to work on back case files. I can give you one piece of hard information. His birthdate was October 9, 1967."

"You know that for sure?"

"Yes," Conroy told him, remembering. "I know that for sure."

"That might help," Petrie said. "Let's get on it."

The Office of Central Reference maintained a vast collection of biographical intelligence on foreign and domestic person- alities, as well as map and photographic libraries, huge quan- tities of books, newspapers and journals, and a variety of less sensitive intelligence reports and studies. A lot of it was stored on microfilm or in an elaborate computerized inform- ation retrieval system. Petrie and Conroy logged in, each found a research cubicle with microfilm readers and computer terminals, and they went to work.

Around three they broke for coffee. Conroy was feeling the effects of his disturbed night; his eyelids on the inside felt as though they'd been roughened with fine sandpaper. The coffee came from a machine in the lounge down the hall from the library and left a thin, vile-tasting coat of whitener on the tongue.

"Anything?" Petrie asked Conroy over the top of his white paper cup.

"Not yet."

"Just how serious was this trouble your, ah, person had in Miami?"

"Serious," Conroy said, feeling momentary distress. "Maybe wet work."

"DGI?"

"I don't think so."

"The person isn't mixed up with drugs, is he?"

"No."

Petrie tossed his cup into a wastebasket. "Let's go back. I'll try overseas troop commitments. Maybe he served overseas. Or have you already done that?"

"No. I'm working on the FAR staff college placements. The damn things aren't complete."

An hour went by, then another. Conroy, usually possessed of endless patience in the pursuit of information, was beginning to feel restless. Keely would be at the house soon, and he wasn't sure how long she'd be willing to wait before going on to Boston. He leaned back in his chair, clasping his hands behind his head, stretching the kinks out of his shoulders.

Petrie said from behind him, "I've got something. I think."

Conroy turned around. "Ah, good. What?"

Petrie handed him a sheet of scribbled notes. "It's in this. Sketchy, but it's there. A Ramon Linares was in Yemen last year before they pulled out. A major, and it looks like he was an infantry company commander. He was in Ethiopia some time before that, a captain in charge of an engineering unit. Probably some combat as well. Served under a man named Cardoso in both places. Cardoso was the infantry colonel commanding that brigade in the PDRY."

Conroy studied Petrie's small, neat handwriting, wondering who had obtained the information and how. "So he wasn't in Cuba last year. But he probably is now, assuming he came back with the brigade."

"Yeah."

"Hm. He's a tough one, then."

"Look a little farther on," Petrie told him. "I did some snooping around Cardoso. He seems to have DGI connections, although the documentation isn't sure what exactly. He was also one of the officers under a cloud in the drug scandal that involved General Ochoa back in '89. But he seems to have survived it intact."

"Is there any photography on Cardoso or Ramon?"

"Yeah. That's the file reference number at the bottom."

"Could you get copies for me? I want to finish off the FAR records."

"Okay."

Petrie disappeared and Conroy returned to the keyboard. He found only one nugget in the slender information about the Revolutionary Armed Forces officer schools: one of the students at the Havana school, a certain Lieutenant Ramon Linares, had been cited for excellence in intelligence studies. Conroy's mouth pursed. Intelligence background, too. And engineering. And infantry combat. Major Ramon Linares had packed a great deal of experience into a relatively small period of time.

But there the trail went cold. Nothing about what he might be up to now. Maybe he was languishing in a peacetime paper-shuffling job, dreaming of the good old days, an old soldier at twenty-six. Conroy, stretching again, stared moodily at the terminal screen until Petrie returned with the photographs.

"I had it enhanced before printing," he said. "The originals were pretty grainy. These are the two best ones."

Conroy studied the pictures. One showed two uniformed men standing a yard apart in front of a row of metal wheels, the running gear of some kind of armored fighting vehicle. They weren't smiling, but seemed to be in the middle of a conversation, their faces in profile.

"The one on the left is Cardoso," Petrie said. "This was taken in Ethiopia three years ago. The other shot is better. It's supposed to be Ramon. Captain's collar insignia. Probably taken in Addis Ababa."

The second photograph showed a young soldier half turned toward the camera. He was smiling and gesturing off to his right at someone or something out of frame. The background this time seemed to be a masonry wall with a small, barred window in it. In the right of the photograph was the rear third of what had to be a donkey.

"That's Cardoso on the right," Petrie joked, indicating the

donkey. "He's in civvies."

"Um," Conroy said. The young soldier's face jolted him. It was so like that of the man he had first seen in the Bolivian jungle so many years ago, the face of Che Guevara. The man won't lie down, Conroy thought.

"That what you wanted?" Petrie asked.

"Except where he is now. Let me think. Drugs, drugs. Cardoso. Look, Tuck, I've been out of the country for a while. Do you know anybody at DEA who'd be able to help? Maybe they have something on Cardoso. If Ramon's mixed up with him ... there might be a connection I could use. I don't know what. Something."

Petrie threw up his hands in mock despair. "The Drug Enforcement Agency? Sure. If you can wait two years for the request to go through channels. One of their people told me he was in on a search of a stockbroker's office, the guy was drug dealing, and an IRS agent was in on it, too, you know, if they couldn't get him on drugs they'd get him on tax evasion. The rules were that the IRS guy and the DEA guy couldn't disclose information to each other at the investigative level. So here they are, both going through the same goddamn filing cabinet, elbow to elbow, the same files, and neither of them could tell the other what he was looking at. So they'd each open a file and go through it while the other was like, literally looking over his shoulder. They couldn't talk to each other. I don't know how they ever manage to jail anybody."

"I thought that mess was going to be cleaned up," Conroy said in disbelief.

"That incident," Petrie told him sardonically, "happened four months ago."

"Shit." Conroy paused. "However, you *do* know somebody in DEA."

"Yeah." Petrie looked at the ceiling, and then down. "Are you going to be around this evening?"

"My sister's place."

"Give me the address and phone number. You never know what people are going to leave lying around on their desks. Let me take the photos and my notes. I'll get them back to you tonight."

"Okay," Conroy said. "Thanks."

"You owe me. I want regular reports on those finches."

Conroy returned to Gemma's house shortly before seven, having stopped to buy beef tenderloin and sour cream and mushrooms. The beef was touted as additive-free, and was inordinately expensive because of it. Keely wasn't in the house, although she'd been there to change clothes; the skirt and blouse she'd been wearing last night were neatly draped over the chair in Conroy's room. She'd left a note to say that she would be back about seven-thirty. It was a peculiarly intimate touch, although he was sure she hadn't meant it that way. He wondered if she was going to tell Lipton and her other high-powered contacts what had happened in Miami.

Half-past seven came and went, and she still hadn't turned up. Conroy started to worry. He knew it was irrational, but he did so anyway. To distract himself he puttered in the kitchen, filleting the beef just so, slicing the mushrooms, mincing garlic, setting the table in the dining room. It was with considerable relief that he heard a cab pull up outside just before eight o'clock, and then the click and creak of the front door. He hurried out to the hall, wiping his hands on a dish towel as he went. Keely was shrugging her raincoat off.

"Hi," she said. She sounded tired.

"Hello. You made it. Everything all right?"

"Except that it's starting to rain. It's a desperate miserable night. It's a lot colder than it was this morning."

"Come on out to the kitchen. I was just putting together some supper."

"You don't have to feed me, you know."

"Have you eaten?"

"No."

"Well, then."

She dutifully followed him into the kitchen where he set a pot of water on to boil then tossed oil and garlic and chopped onions into a pan and began to sauté them.

"You can cook," she said.

"Yeah. Beef Stroganoff. With egg noodles and peas on the side. Okay?"

"It sounds grand." She was sitting at the kitchen table, legs crossed, massaging the sole of one slender stockinged foot.

Conroy looked quickly away. "I made coffee," he said. "Or there's Scotch, gin, bourbon, wine. Would you like any of the above?"

"Coffee. You're busy, I can get it."

He showed her where the mugs were. She filled one for herself, then hesitated. "You, too? Or I can make you a drink if you point me to it."

"I'll have coffee. Please."

"You're not a drinker, are you?" she said, coffeepot poised.

"Almost never."

"Neither am I," she said. "I saw my father die of it." She sloshed coffee into the mug, spilling a little. "I'm so damned clumsy," she complained. "Especially when I'm tired." The topic of her father, opened for a moment, seemed to have slammed shut.

"Everybody is. Were Lipton and company happy with your trip?"

She was sitting again. "Yes. The prognosis for better relations is good. I'm sorry I can't be more explicit for you."

"I don't really want to know," Conroy told her. He dropped noodles into boiling water and adjusted the heat. "Did you tell them about Miami?"

"Yes."

"What did they think of that?"

"Well, Rupert was annoyed with me for going off and doing what I did. I told him it was my research, and the reason he was using me was that I did that kind of work, and that I had no idea the subject of Marita Linares was sensitive for anyone. That cooled him down a little. Then he got worried about my safety. He said he thought it might be a drug connection I'd stumbled across."

"Uh-huh," Conroy said. He dropped strips of beef into the pan with the garlic and onions and began to stir the mixture around. "What's he going to do about it?"

"He wants to provide me with a guard until they find out what's behind it. He suggested Treasury Board. That's the Secret Service, right? Right. He doesn't even want me to go home until I've got some protection. I told him I wanted to talk to you first."

Conroy stopped stirring the things in the pan. "What about?"

"I wanted to ask if you'd do it. I know you. You understand what's going on. About Ramon and the rest of it. I'd.... To be frank, I'd feel safer with you than with someone I don't know."

"I'm being posted to Caracas in a few weeks," he told her. "I don't think I could avoid going."

"Even that long," she said. "Maybe they'd find out who was after me before you left." He realized, to his consternation, that her voice was shaking. "I'm an academic," she said. "I'm not used to this sort of thing. It terrifies me that I might have been dead by now if I hadn't.... I know what those drug people are like. Michael, I'm frightened half out of my wits."

He sensed that she was on the point of tears. She had also, for the first time, called him by name. If this is manipulation, he thought, it's a brilliant job.

"Okay," he said. "Maybe you'd better stay here for a while. I'll stand in for the Secret Service as long as I can. Will Lipton go for that?"

"I think he'd jump at the chance," she said. "He didn't really want to pull in Treasury. This is all supposed to be backdoor work. My getting protection would involve all sorts of questions being asked. The negotiations are extremely sensitive just now." She was recovering her poise.

"That settles it, then," Conroy said. "We'll set it up officially tomorrow, then go to Boston and pick up whatever you need to stay here for a while. Harvard won't be a problem?"

"No. I was on a kind of research leave." She hesitated. "Did you find out anything today, about Ramon?"

"A bit. He spent a lot of time overseas." He told her what he and Petrie had found out about Ramon Linares, or Ramon Guevara, as Conroy was beginning to think of him. "Tuck has a friend in DEA," Conroy finished. "He's going to check with him. Under the table, because of one of those bureaucratic problems. He's bringing over the photos and anything else he can find this evening sometime."

"I don't know how to thank you."

"Well, dinner's just about ready. Maybe you could put on the peas?"

They had finished eating, and Conroy was loading the dishwasher, when the doorbell bonged. Keely was on her way in from the dining room with some cutlery. She stopped, her whole body tense.

"I'll get it," Conroy said. "Stay here."

It was Tuck. Conroy let him in. "I've got a few possibilities," Petrie said, shaking raindrops from the brim of his hat and waving a damp manila envelope in Conroy's direction. "Some of it's in here. The rest is in my head. Boy, it's raw out there," he added pointedly.

Conroy gave him a Scotch and brought Keely in from the kitchen. "This is the person from Miami?" Tucker asked, regarding her appreciatively.

"Yeah," Conroy said. "Keely Fitzgerald. Tucker Petrie."

"That's all I want to know," Petrie said, sitting down. "Open the envelope."

Conroy did so. In it were the two photos Petrie had found that afternoon, the notes and a computer facsimile of a third photograph. "Telephoto lens," Petrie explained, gesturing at the last item. "The two people by the plane are members of a Cuban–Colombian drug-import pipeline. The plane's got the wing flaps of a Cessna 182 modified for clandestine work. First time the DEA's ever seen it. It flew out of the airstrip right after dusk, about ninety minutes after this picture was taken. My friend said the DEA was planning to move in and collect the cocaine and the traffickers when the plane came back, but it never returned. So the DEA had to leave the runners alone. No evidence. That was about two weeks ago."

"What happened to the plane?"

"Nobody knows. Not even the narcotics runners, apparently, from the DEA's informants. The DEA thinks it went down at sea, on the way to wherever it was going or maybe on the way back. It might have. Single engine's not a way I'd want to cross a lot of water."

"Who was on the plane?"

"Two guys. The pilot and a passenger. Likely the passenger was there to make sure the pilot didn't rip the cartel off. That's happened."

"Was one of these men the passenger?" Conroy asked, indicating the photograph of the Cessna.

Petrie swigged at the Scotch. "DEA isn't sure. But one of them hasn't been in evidence at all since this flight. And they'd never spotted him before. They have no idea who he is. He wasn't the pilot, because the pilot arrived after that picture was taken."

"Which one's missing?" Conroy passed Keely the photograph.

"The man on the right," Petrie said. "In front of the engine cowling."

Keely was bent over the fax, studying it intently, tilting it to catch the lamplight. Finally she said, "That's him. I'm almost sure of it. The man in Marita Linares's photograph. Ramon Guevara."

Petrie got up hastily. "I think that's all I want to know right now," he said. "Thanks for the drink, Michael. I can let myself out."

Keely waited until he had gone, and then said, "Why is he so nervous?"

"He shouldn't have the information," Conroy explained. "And the DEA man shouldn't have given it to him. Tuck's getting uninvolved as fast as he can. It was a favor to me that he did it at all."

"I see," she said gravely. She picked up the other photographs. "That's him, too, in that one. There's no doubt at all. Who is the older officer in front of that tank, or whatever it is?"

"A Colonel Cardoso. Ramon's CO in Yemen and Ethiopia."

She laid the pictures down on the coffee table. "What do you think all this means?"

"I think," he said slowly, "that when Ramon disappeared, the drug people assumed that the plane went down at sea. Then, two weeks later, you turn up, a secret envoy from Washington. But you also want to see Ramon's mother, for no clear reason. Somebody wants to know why, so they let you talk to her. They make it easy, in fact. You can bet that as soon as you left they were asking Marita Linares what you wanted to know. Likely pretending to be DGI, the state police. Or maybe the DGI's mixed up in it, too. She'd have told them what you discussed, no reason for her to refuse. Or maybe they had microphones in the place. But they don't know *why* you were asking these questions, and they want to. Maybe they're worried that Ramon has turned his coat, and you're filling in background to establish his bona fides. They search your hotel room and find nothing. Then they decide to ask you personally. Somebody in Havana talks to somebody in Miami, by radio, not telephone. Coded messages. These organizations have lots of technology, they could do it, especially if the DGI's involved. Somebody is told to meet you at the airport."

"But I was sent by the White House," she protested. "They wouldn't dare."

"They used to kill judges and attorney generals in Colombia," he said. "Then the Bolivians and the Peruvians took over the trade, and they murdered the Bolivian justice minister last year. They don't play by any rules at all. When the old Mafia killed one of its members for whatever reason, it still made sure the man's family was cared for afterward. These people kill the family first. That's why Lipton's worried about you."

She shivered. "It's horrible. I don't know anything at all that's useful to them. But they think I do, so...." She closed her eyes and opened them again. "What are we going to do?"

Conroy drummed his fingertips on the photographs. "I'm not convinced that Ramon is dead."

"Why not?"

"There's no proof. No wreckage, no body. Somebody with that background.... Does he know whose son he is, do you imagine?"

"I have no idea."

"Suppose he disappeared on purpose. There might have been a lot of money on that plane, payment for the cocaine."

"He did it for the money?" Keely ventured.

"Maybe. What do you think?"

She stared unseeing past Conroy's shoulder. "It's possible. But the way he might think, given the little we know about him ... it's also possible he'd decide to disappear for other reasons. He'd fit a terrorist profile reasonably well."

"Yeah. I was thinking that."

"On the other hand," Keely observed in a matter-of-fact tone, "he may really be dead."

"Maybe," said Conroy. Part of him wouldn't accept it so easily. "But I think we'd better try to find out. Because if he's dead, then you'd be off the hook with the cartel as soon as it was public."

"That had occurred to me," she observed wryly.

She's brave, Conroy thought, looking at her profile in the lamplight. I know a lot of people, men included, who'd be basket cases if they were facing what she is. Tuck notwithstanding, I'd better take this to Vickery.

"I don't know about you," he said, smothering a yawn, "but I ought to get some sleep. You must feel the same way."

"Yes," she said. "Where do you want to put me?"

"Same room as last night. Do you want to borrow some nightwear? Gemma wouldn't mind."

"That's okay," she said. "I'm fine."

"All right." He stood up. "I'll put out some fresh towels."

She seemed hesitant. "You don't think they can find me here, do you?"

"No," he told her, "I don't. And Gemma has an alarm system. I'll set it before I go to bed. Just don't come downstairs in the morning until I've turned it off, it's got motion sensors down here. I'll show you how to use it tomorrow."

"Okay."

She went upstairs and Conroy closed down the lower floor of the house, lights, furnace, door locks. He could hear water running, her footsteps above him. Not quite like hearing Gemma. Different.

He sighed, set the alarm system, then started quickly up the stairs before it activated itself. A few minutes later he was in bed in Gemma's room, with the light out. The noises of Washington filtered in through the window mixed with the tap of rain on the glass. Tree branches rustled. Conroy began to drop off; then he heard the sound from down the hall. It was very faint, but he knew she was crying.

He threw the covers back, sat up, then stopped. No, he

thought. That's private. He slid under the sheets again and closed his eyes. After a couple of minutes she was quiet again, and Conroy fell asleep.

Dubai, United Arab Emirates
March 16

■

The KLM airliner tilted to port, allowing Ramon Linares to look along the great swept wing, past the wing tip, down to the sea below; salt white at the wave crests, incandescent blue glare in the troughs. Eastward, land the color of ground cinnamon, fading to tawny haze where the desert lay.

Ramon straightened up in his seat, tightening his safety belt a little. The cabin crew was all tucked away in preparation for the landing, leaving the passengers to their own devices. The human cargo was by no means all Arab. A significant proportion was European, with a sprinkling of Americans, expatriates returning to the shores of the Arabian gulf to work for the banks or the oil companies or the construction consortiums that had sprung up in the United Arab Emirates in the course of the oil boom years ago. The boom had receded in the eighties, but because of clever financial management the Emirates had managed to hold on to much of the prosperity it had brought them, diversifying away from oil into investment banking, shipping, natural gas liquefaction and, in the case of the Dubai emirate, aluminum smelting. Dubai had remained the most prosperous of the Emirates, and the city slipping into Ramon's view as the jet straightened out reflected this fact. Spread out on both sides of the waterway known as the Creek, Dubai gleamed white with the towers of luxury hotels and trade complexes, and the domes and minarets of new mosques floated above wide boulevards that ran between squares shaded with palm trees and cooled by fountains.

The Creek was one of the main axes of the city. Dubai was far from a new place, although oil had transformed its outward aspect; for centuries it had been a fishing center and trading entrepôt, and the dhows had sailed year after year from the Creek's mouth, dropping their nets in the Arabian Gulf or riding the monsoon winds to India and Iran. The dhows still put out from Dubai in the dawn, and Dubai still traded from east to west and west to east, but most of the wares now traveled in huge container ships that called at the new port of Jebel Ali, twenty kilometers south of Dubai.

The air terminal, however, looked much like air terminals everywhere, with the cosmetic difference of signs in Arabic. Ramon had one suitcase in the hold of the aircraft and one item of cabin baggage. The latter was a fabric carryall sized exactly to qualify as carry-on luggage, and inside it, under a layer of spare clothing, was the money. Transporting so much loose cash into the UAE in this manner was a calculated risk; there was nothing illegal in it, but if the money was found he would be subjected to a conversation he would rather not have. Banking it in the Caymans would have been the ordinary answer to the problem, but he had not dared risk going there; too many drug traffickers used the no-questions-asked Cayman banking system, and Ramon didn't want to encounter anyone who might have heard that he was supposed to be dead. There were going to be several times in the future when he would have to take such risks; they had to be accepted.

Before going through customs he had to obtain his visitor's visa. Five days ago, in New York, he had telexed the Sheraton Dubai to request the document; most of the major hotels would arrange one for incoming guests if they provided birth date, religion, entry date and passport number. Again, giving the false Panamanian passport number was a risk, but at this remove from the Americas Ramon judged it to be a minor one. His confidence was justified: the visa was ready at the immigration counter. He showed the passport, signed for the visa and left without any complications.

Customs turned out to be just as straightforward. A bored officer chalked his suitcase and the carryall with only a cursory glance into the former, and Ramon was through. In Dubai.

He began to relax as he changed money and then sauntered toward the taxi loading area. If I were Muslim, he thought, I would now be saying that this is the will of Allah. As a Marxist I consider it the inevitability of history. No matter which, I won't object to a healthy ration of good fortune. I've spent too long on battlefields not to believe in luck.

He stepped outside into the Dubai afternoon, and the heat poured over him, into his lungs, the light searing his eyes. I'm not acclimatized any more, he thought. Too long since I left Yemen.

Several hotel taxis were waiting in the cab rank outside the terminal, along with several of the more battered street taxis. Out of the habit of security more than for any need of it, Ramon opened the door of one of the street cabs and put his head into the air-conditioned interior. He thought the driver was Pakistani rather than Arab.

"Sheraton Dubai," he said, and then in English, "how much?"

The driver eyed him. "Hundred dirham."

Ramon snickered. "Forty. I have been here before."

The driver shrugged. "Everything get expensive, more. Seventy."

"Fifty." Ramon began to close the door.

The driver threw up his hands. "Okay, okay, fifty-five."

It was still too much, but Ramon nodded and climbed into the back. The driver set off with a squeal of hot tires on broiling asphalt and headed out of the airport onto Al Maktoum Road. Like all drivers in the Emirates, he drove very fast and didn't pay much attention to lane markings. At the Clock Tower roundabout he took the left exit and headed for the Creek. Ramon kept an eye on him, but he didn't try to go on across the bridge; instead he turned right on Bin Yas toward the Sheraton. "Fixing buildings on Al Maktoum," the driver explained. "Too much heat, too much salt. All these big places going to fall down someday."

"Yes," Ramon agreed absentmindedly. He was thinking about the rest of the day.

The driver remained silent until they reached the Sheraton. Ramon paid him and went inside. The lobby was vast, its ceiling made up of huge curved triangles of concrete faced with tile and supported on massive round pillars; the groins between the ceiling panels were pierced by triangular windows that illuminated the interior with a cool indirect light. The lobby formed a mezzanine above a lower level, in whose center a fountain jetted ten yards into the air, filling the great room with the sound of falling water.

Ramon checked in without difficulty and went up to his room. He'd taken the least expensive available, but it was luxurious even by the best North American standards. He found himself resenting the luxury as he washed and shaved in the gleaming tile bathroom; the place was a monument to capitalist extravagance.

Nevertheless the bed was inviting. He closed the drapes, threw himself onto it and promptly fell asleep.

Two hours later he awoke, refreshed. It was time to start moving.

He went downstairs with the carryall, and found a bank of public telephones just off the main lobby. They were still free, a fringe benefit of the oil boom. Ramon dialed a number and waited. After a few ring tones a man answered.

"Yes?"

Ramon summoned his best Arabic, trying to lose the Yemeni pronunciation as well as he could. "I would like to speak to Rashid al-Bakr, if that is possible."

A pause. "He is not here at this time."

"I would not wish to disturb him. But we have done business in the past."

"What is your name?"

"Major Perez."

"Please wait."

Ramon waited. After perhaps two minutes the voice came back on the line. "Where are you?" it said.

"The Sheraton."

"A car will come for you in an hour. It is a blue Mercedes."

"I will be at the entrance."

Click.

Ramon hung up and returned to his room, where he
waited for precisely fifty minutes. Then he went down to the
lobby and strolled to the glass doors at the front of the hotel.
He had been there for no more than a few moments when
the blue Mercedes arrived. Ramon got into the back and the
Mercedes pulled away from the hotel onto Bin Yas Road.
The driver, an Arab wearing a white *dishdasha,* did not
acknowledge him, and Ramon did not attempt to open a
conversation.

The Mercedes headed up to the Corniche then followed the
coast road northward. The city fell away behind, and they
were rolling through semidesert specked with patches of
salt-tolerant plants: hammada bushes, patches of sea
lavender, the odd acacia and calotropis. The sun was
beginning to drop away to the west.

After they had been driving for a good half an hour, a tall,
square tower appeared ahead, standing between the road and
the sea. At its base was a large compound whose walls ran
right down to the water. Greenish-blue roofs, exactly the
color of the shallows beyond the white beach, were visible
above the tops of the walls. The Mercedes slowed down,
swung off the main road onto a narrower asphalt one and
drew up in front of a heavy metal gate set into the compound
wall. The driver waited patiently for a few seconds, until one
leaf of the gate slid ponderously back into the wall. The
Mercedes glided through the opening, and the gate closed
behind it.

Inside the compound was an oasis: date palms, lawns,
vine-draped trellises, a long garage with accommodation for
half a dozen vehicles, a flagged plaza on whose far side stood
the square tower, and next to the tower the main house. Two
stories high, the latter was built of smooth cream-colored
stone in a U-shape, with the two side wings stretching
forward to make a spacious courtyard in front of the main
entrance. Large windows with louvered shutters looked into
the courtyard, which was dotted with flowering shrubs set in
stone planters. The Mercedes stopped in front of the
courtyard; the driver got out and opened Ramon's door for
him. Ramon stepped onto the pavement and began to sling

the carryall over his shoulder. Very politely and firmly, the Arab took it from him. Ramon neither resisted nor protested.

The main door of the house opened, and a man hurried down the steps. It was al-Bakr, and he was smiling broadly.

"Major Ramon Perez, your presence honors my house," he said in Arabic as he approached and embraced Ramon, who returned the greeting. As they separated, al-Bakr added, "I did not expect to see you again for a long time."

"I am honored to be in your presence," Ramon answered in Arabic. The tongue was beginning to come back. "It is truly good fortune that has permitted me to stand within your house again."

"Yes," al-Bakr said. Like the driver, he was wearing a snow-white *dishdasha* and a red-checkered head cloth held in place with the twisted black coil of fabric called an *aqal.* His face betrayed little of his age: he could have been anywhere between thirty-five and fifty. He had a huge beak of a nose and full lips surrounded by a short-clipped black beard and mustache. Two deep lines ran between the flare of his nostrils and the corners of his mouth. Carefully trimmed black eyebrows arched over gray eyes.

"Come into the house," al-Bakr said. "Have you belongings with you?"

Ramon inclined his head politely toward the Mercedes driver, who was standing a few yards away with the carryall at his feet. "That is yours?" al-Bakr asked.

"Yes, it is."

"Bring it," al-Bakr said briefly. The driver obediently picked up the carryall and followed them into the house.

"There is some concern about explosives," al-Bakr explained as they entered the cool dimness of the entrance foyer. Inside and beyond the foyer was the *majlis*, the main public room. The floor was green marble, veined with white, the walls were white marble veined with pearly gray, and the domed ceiling was inlaid with traditional Islamic floral motifs in tile and ceramic. Along the walls were benches piled with thick cushions. At one end of the big room the furnishings were more Western, with deeply upholstered chairs and divans and small tables. Al-Bakr led Ramon to the Western end of the room.

"Please be seated," he told Ramon and gestured to the driver. The latter silently put the carryall on the carpet beside Ramon's chair and promptly vanished through a door at the rear of the *majlis*. Al-Bakr placed himself in a chair across a low table from Ramon's and favored him with a white-toothed smile. Ramon smiled back, offering a slight bow. The house was silent; he and the driver and al-Bakr might have been the only three people in it, but Ramon knew that a finger snap would summon armed men within seconds. The trust al-Bakr had in him was measured by his disregard for the contents of the carryall; it could have had ten kilos of C4 explosive in it instead of money, but the Arab was assuming that it did not.

"You have come a long way?" al-Bakr ventured politely. He would never have been so rude as to ask from where; it was part of the ritual of etiquette. Ramon was very comfortable with the ritual, because it was not unlike the Spanish traditions that lingered in Latin America. Everything, at first, must be oblique.

"From Cuba," he said. "Now that I have come to the Emirates, I could not allow an opportunity to pass of meeting with an old friend and associate."

Associate, the key word. Al-Bakr now knew, if he had not already guessed it, that Ramon was here on business. They had indeed been business associates before, for a year in fact, during Ramon's last twelve months in the PDRY. That was when the Russians had begun cutting off the supply of arms to Aden. The government, desperate for weapons, had gone shopping in the international arms bazaar, and Ramon had been instrumental in obtaining Soviet-made weapons to bolster the PDRY's armed forces. His chief supplier, although not the only one, had been al-Bakr. The Arab was able to supply large quantities of everything from small-arms ammunition to light tanks, both Western and Eastern, and for reasonable prices. The UAE authorities were quite aware of his activities, but al-Bakr enjoyed protection in the right places and was careful never to offend his protectors by supplying weapons to the wrong people, for example Iran or

Israel. He was adept at moving shipments around the Middle East, using the Dubai free trade zone, which occupied part of the container port at Jebel Ali. The FTZ was a haven for all sorts of traders, excepting those whose merchandise was drugs; the UAE was quite willing to shoot drug traffickers. This suited Ramon perfectly; in the UAE he was unlikely to run into anyone who knew of his connections to the cartel.

Al-Bakr looked thoughtfully at the ceiling. "Friendship is an excellent foundation for good business," he observed, and left it at that as the door at the back of the *majlis* opened and a servant glided in, bearing a gold tray on which were minute Arabic coffee cups and a *dalla*, the traditional long-beaked coffee pot. Al-Bakr took up the *dalla*, poured and proffered the tiny cup to Ramon. Ramon waved gently to indicate that al-Bakr should be served first. The Arab declined with a polite murmur. The ceremony properly begun, Ramon accepted the offered cup.

"I trust that your family and sons are well?" Ramon asked after a sip of the strong, cardamom-flavored coffee.

"Very well. My eldest son has begun his education; I have engaged tutors for him. I believe one day I will send him to Oxford. He has a bent for mathematics."

"You are most fortunate."

Al-Bakr offered more coffee, and Ramon accepted. They exchanged pleasantries for a few minutes. On the offer of the third cup, Ramon oscillated the small container politely to show that he declined, and handed it to al-Bakr. The Arab studied him for a moment. Then he said:

"I trust I may be of assistance to you in some matter of importance?"

Ramon inclined his head. "It is an affair of some importance and also of some sensitivity."

Al-Bakr nodded. "I enjoy taking the air at this time of the day," he said. "Before the chill of the evening comes on. Would you care to accompany me?"

"Of course."

They left the *majlis* — Ramon didn't bother to bring the carryall — and strolled around to the left of the main house, where the square tower rose above the house roof and the compound walls. It was a wind tower, the ancient residential cooling system of the gulf. Louvered openings on the top story caught the prevailing wind and directed it down an air shaft to the rooms at ground level, and a similar shaft on the leeward side sucked the air up and expelled it at the tower's summit. There were not many left in Dubai, or anywhere else in the region.

Al-Bakr stepped through a door into the thick-walled base of the tower. Ramon followed. He could hear the rush of air above him and could feel the steady draft through the room in which he stood. The room was dim, lit only by the doorway and three narrow windows, one in each wall except that of the doorway. There were benches along the walls, and cushions on them; the plaster floor was partially covered by carpets.

"Here there are no ears," al-Bakr said comfortably, settling himself onto a cushioned bench and pointing for Ramon to do likewise. "In solid masonry it is hard to insert microphones."

Ramon nodded. "You are very wise."

"I am a businessman," al-Bakr said. "How may I help you, assuming my small resources can be of any assistance whatsoever?"

"I need to acquire a certain type of weapon," Ramon said. "It is not a common item. It is for this reason that I have come to you. There are few men who are able to match your ability to satisfy a client."

Al-Bakr exhibited an elaborate, self-deprecating shrug. "That may be so, although I would not say it myself. Nevertheless it is unwise to entertain unrealistic expectations of anyone's resources. Could you be more precise as to the nature of the weapon?"

"I need three hypervelocity missiles and the associated laser targeting equipment."

Al-Bakr folded his hands in his lap and appeared to be listening to the wind rushing through the air shafts of the tower. "These are not commonly available devices," he observed.

"I am uncomfortably aware of that difficulty."

The Arab's mouth pursed. "The Americans make them. So do the Russians, and the Iraqis have made a good copy of the latter. Of the two versions, the American is the more expensive. It is also more complicated and more subject to failure in the field. However, it is the most accurate of the two — assuming it can be made to work. Is range a consideration?"

"Three kilometers, minimum."

"Either version would provide that. Weight? The Iraqi copy of the Soviet weapon is about six kilograms heavier than the American device. The aiming system is some four kilograms heavier. But the Soviet design is more rugged."

"The weight is within my delivery capacity," Ramon observed.

"I can acquire an Iraqi-made Soviet version for you in about two weeks, or a little less. The American weapon would require much longer."

"I need the shorter delivery time. Can you quote me a price on three missiles and the targeting system?"

"I am ashamed to mention it. As I said, these items are not commonly available."

"I am aware that there would be exceptional expenses to be met."

"Hm," al-Bakr said. "How would you want delivery to be arranged?'

"Air freight, as far as Mexico City. If I might make a suggestion, they could appear to be light drilling and electronic surveying equipment."

"You would deal with customs in Mexico?"

"Yes."

"I see no difficulty with any of that. If I, too, might make a suggestion, however."

"I would be honored to hear it."

"If you do not have a compelling need for speed, sea freight would be less subject to interference. I could ship the merchandise air freight to Algiers, and from there it could go by sea to Tampico in Mexico. This would occupy perhaps three weeks from the time of dispatch. I can let you know exactly how long in a few days. Also there is the matter of a lower delivery expense by sea."

"That's true," Ramon said. The idea held considerable virtue. He was going to need to use up some time before the

target was in position, and having the weapons in transit for
three weeks instead of under the noses of the Americans
would reduce his risk. "I bow to your superior experience in
these matters," he said. "The ship would suit me perfectly. It
arrives at Tampico?"

"Yes."

"Good. Using that method of delivery, what would be the
cost of the package?"

"Again, I am humiliated to mention it."

"I understand that it is circumstance rather than desire
that forces this necessity upon you," Ramon said.

"Very well. I cannot make the transaction for less than
three hundred thousand American dollars."

The figure made Ramon blink. The hypervelocity missiles
— HVMs — were recent technology, but the weapons themselves were simple and inexpensive. The laser targeting
equipment would cost about sixty thousand dollars on the
legitimate market. The high price al-Bakr was quoting must
include substantial bribes to persuade Iraqi military officers
to part with the weapons. There were few other places to
obtain them; they were designed specifically to engage
heavily armored targets, and only governments likely to be
engaged in large-scale tank warfare were bothering to
acquire the weapons. For Ramon's purposes the weapons
were ideal: they had a range of more than three thousand
meters, they were extremely fast and they were quite light in
relation to their destructive power. But they did not, in fact,
carry any explosive at all. They depended for their effect on a
superdense slug of depleted uranium inside the missile body.
When the lighter casing of the missile disintegrated on
impact with the target, the uranium slug kept right on going.
It would penetrate any known armor plate, composite or
solid, and it had appalling effects as it bounced around inside
an enclosed space, such as the interior of a tank. There was
an added bonus: although the uranium was not detectably
radioactive when at rest, it produced a brief and lethal
shower of short-range radiation if it struck a hard target, such
as an armored fighting vehicle. But from Ramon's point of
view it was the speed and range that were the weapon's
strong points. The radiation burst was of little consequence

for what he was planning.

There would still be more than enough money. "That seems reasonable," he told al-Bakr. "Could you also provide about five kilos of C4 plastic explosive, and four pencil timer detonators?"

"Certainly. There will be a slight additional charge."

"I can pay you in cash, half now and the balance on shipment."

"That would be most satisfactory," al-Bakr told him, and then, to formalize it, "we have an agreement."

"We have an agreement," Ramon repeated. "There is one other minor item. I would like to acquire two alternate passports. Genuine, rather than forgeries. And a driving permit. I prefer to be mobile, in case of need."

"I can furnish Filipino passports without difficulty. Would those be suitable?"

"One would. I would prefer the other to be American."

"I believe I can manage it."

"Would they be available soon?"

"Within a few days. Considering the size of our transaction, there will be a charge for only the Filipino one. You will need to furnish passport photographs. I can direct you to a suitable establishment."

"Your generosity is greater than I deserve," Ramon said. He had decided not to ask al-Bakr to furnish him with a weapon; he had presumed far enough on the Arab's resources by requesting the passports, and in any case he was safe enough unarmed in the UAE.

"And your understanding is greater than I deserve," al-Bakr responded politely. "Now, as to payment. How would you like to arrange the cash transfer?"

"As it happens," Ramon said, "I have brought funds with me. They are in your *majlis*. In fact, I would be in your debt if you would keep all the money on these premises until it is time for me to leave. It amounts to approximately four hundred thousand dollars. I do not entirely trust hotel safes."

"Very wise," al-Bakr murmured. "I am flattered at your trust. I assure you it will not be misplaced."

Ramon knew this was true. There was absolutely no likelihood of al-Bakr keeping the money. His reputation was worth far more to him than the stacks of bills inside the carryall.

"Come into the house again," the Arab said to him, standing up, "and we can complete this part of the transaction. You wish to return to Dubai afterward?"

"Yes. I intend to remain there until the merchandise arrives and we have completed our arrangements."

"That would be most suitable," al-Bakr said. "I will contact you at the Sheraton when the passports are available. When the merchandise arrives, you may inspect it at my warehouse in the free trade zone."

Mexico City – Dallas
March 20–21

Colonel Dioclés Cardoso sat in the crowded Parador bar on the lower level of the Mexico City air terminal, drinking a Tecate beer. He was mildly nervous; it was a long time since he had played these passport games, not since he'd moved from the DGI into the combat forces at the beginning of the Angolan campaign. As he looked back at that period, he realized that the revolutionary wars had been the best time of his life. After only a few months at home he'd felt himself becoming restive, craving some kind of action.

This wasn't like planning a counterattack or a fighting retreat, but he was at least in some kind of action again. He'd get used to it quickly enough.

He glanced at his watch. His contact was a couple of minutes late. Cardoso frowned. The DGI prided itself on running precise and well-timed operations; of all the Latin American intelligence organizations, it was by far the most effective, and at least as professional and as ruthless as the Polish SB and the East Germans had been before the Communists lost power in Europe. Cardoso clearly remembered the East German SSD advisers who had trained the DGI in the latter's early years: precision and punctuality, punctuality and precision, they'd drummed it into Cardoso and the rest of the intelligence recruits day after day, month after month. It had been second nature to him ever since.

He rested his elbows more firmly on the folded copy of *El Dia* and ordered another Tecate. Inside the newspaper was the passport on which he'd arrived from Cuba. According to the passport he was a Costa Rican businessman in transit from Cuba to San Jose, with outbound ticket in good order. The customs police had made him open his one suitcase, but of course there was nothing in it that would arouse their suspicions to any degree.

Another minute passed. Cardoso began to consider the fallback meeting place, but he was reluctant to use it; he didn't want to waste time. Maybe the contact couldn't find him. Cardoso wasn't using a recognition signal; he'd been told the contact would spot him by sight and get confirmation from the newspaper lying on the bar. One corner of the paper was torn off in a V-shape to provide this confirmation.

Lighting a cigarette, Cardoso stared morosely at the bottle of beer. The process of infiltration was almost making him forget why he was carrying it out. Ramon Linares, who was perhaps dead and perhaps not. If not dead, then perhaps a thief and, perhaps, something worse, much worse.

The back-stabbing prick, if he was alive. And that mother of his. The woman was as cold as anybody Cardoso had ever laid eyes on. She must have been hotter once, though, to let Guevara poke her back in '67, assuming that had really happened. Her file referred to her allegation years ago that Ramon was Che Guevara's son, but there was no evidence to support or deny the claim. Only a woman knew for sure who her child's father was, and if she was a certain type of woman even she wouldn't be sure. Fidel obviously hadn't believed Marita Linares's story, or he'd have made some kind of propaganda out of it. Unless Fidel wanted the whole matter kept under the rug. He hadn't supported Che in Bolivia as well as he might have. But then dead heroes were often more useful politically than live ones.

Although, Cardoso mused, Ramon did bear an uncanny resemblance to Che, once you were looking for it. The same kind of charisma, the kind that made a superb leader. But there might have been a streak of venality in him that Che hadn't had, not to mention a generous helping of recklessness. Hijacking cartel money like that was sheer stupidity, if in fact that was what Ramon had done. It wasn't the quantity — what Ramon had had with him on the plane, Cardoso reflected, was like piss in the ocean compared to the cartel's cash flow — it was the principle. Any betrayal of the cartel had only one penalty, death.

Cardoso swigged more beer. As Ramon's sponsor, he was responsible for the major's actions. Although genuinely grieved when he first heard that Ramon was missing, he now hoped that the man was well and truly dead. Cardoso was high in the hierarchy of the Cuban division of the cartel, but not high enough to ignore the consequences of an error like recruiting a traitor, especially a traitor who for some reason seemed to have attracted the interest of the Americans. Or at least of someone working for the Americans: Dr. Keely Fitzgerald.

For some reason, but what was it?

DGI counterintelligence watched every move Fitzgerald made while she was in Cuba. This was not merely routine surveillance of an important foreigner; there was a good deal more at stake, and it had to do with the involvement of parts of the DGI in the narcotics trade. There was not, of course, a division of the DGI dedicated to the traffic. What did exist was a tight and secretive cabal of intelligence and military officers who were for the most part in the DGI's Branch G4 (Illegals — for illegal overseas agents), or in Branch G2 (counterintelligence), or in various military arms that could supply clandestine transportation or logistical support. Fidel knew about the cabal, of course, but he turned a blind eye to it, just as he'd turned a blind eye to General Ochoa's drug activities until 1989, when Ochoa started getting too big for his breeches and brought his fate on himself. Since then the narcotics traffickers had been much more discreet, and in addition had established an early-warning system against the possibility of another crackdown. Cardoso, an officer in Branch G2, was part of the warning system.

It was in this capacity that he had been keeping an eye on Dr. Keely Fitzgerald. Washington certainly knew that Cuba was still connected to the narcotics cartel, and one of the points of negotiation might be for Havana to put a stop to it. But Fitzgerald had put no such demand to Oscar Torras, and the cabal had breathed more easily. It appeared that they had a free run for the immediate future.

And then, on her last visit, she made the totally unexpected request to talk to Ramon's mother. She shouldn't have known the woman existed, nor Ramon either, for that matter. Torras had reported the request, as a matter of course, to Branch G2, and Cardoso called a hurried meeting of the senior cabal members available. They decided to let Fitzgerald run, and to put audio and visual surveillance on Marita Linares's house. The results of that, like the search of Fitzgerald's hotel room, were inconclusive. She might have talked to Inciarte, as she'd told Marita Linares, but then again maybe she hadn't. Then Guillois — head of G4, Illegals, and senior in the cabal — had got it into his head that Ramon had disappeared in order to go to the Americans and expose the Cuban cabal, and that Fitzgerald was questioning Marita Linares in order to establish Ramon's bona fides. But Fitzgerald could be forced to tell them why she was interested in Ramon and what the Americans were planning to do about him, or with him. The woman was an unofficial envoy, after all, and her death could be made to look like the random violence for which Miami was notorious. Over Cardoso's protests, Guillois had decided to order her picked up for questioning in Miami.

It was a counsel of panic, but the order had been transmitted before cooler heads prevailed, and before it could be countermanded the attempt had been made. The men sent to do it had failed dismally, so the cabal now had the worst of both worlds: Ramon (if he was alive) was still hidden, and the Americans knew that they'd touched a nerve.

There remained the possibility, as Cardoso had pointed out at the end of an acrimonious three o'clock in the morning meeting, that Ramon was indeed dead at the bottom of the Gulf of Mexico, and that Fitzgerald was merely researching a book, as she had told the Linares woman. Nobody was willing to believe this without further checking, not even Cardoso; there was too much at stake. And even if Ramon was no more than a thief, and not in fact a traitor, he still had to be punished.

Cardoso, who had recruited him, got the job.

His beer was almost gone. He consulted his watch again. Five minutes late. Time to go and use the fallback.

He was sliding off the stool when a man elbowed his way up to the crowded bar right next to him. The man was carrying a folded copy of *El Día*, which he dropped carelessly half on top of Cardoso's. The corner of the man's paper was torn off, the safe signal. Cardoso took out a cigarette, lit it and immediately stubbed it out in the ashtray, to show that he also was clean. "You're late," he growled out of the corner of his mouth.

"Bomb threat on the subway," the man muttered back. "It was slow."

"Who this time?"

"Maoists."

Some people never gave up, Cardoso reflected. He'd given up six years ago and decided to insure his own future. When Fidel died and the revolution fell apart, as it almost certainly would, Cardoso would be out of Cuba like a shot with a new identity, a great deal of money and a new future.

The bartender wandered over to ask what the contact man wanted. He ordered rum. Cardoso and he ignored each other until the liquor came and the bartender's attention was elsewhere. "Any special instructions?" Cardoso asked under cover of the bar racket.

"No. It's all in there. Look at it before you go." The contact downed the rum in one swift gulp. As he did so, Cardoso slid the man's copy of *El Día* to one side. The contact put his glass on the bar, picked up Cardoso's newspaper and vanished quickly into the crowd behind him.

Cardoso relit his stubbed-out cigarette and smoked for a few minutes while he waited for the contact man to get clear. Then he took his suitcase and the newspaper into a nearby toilet, entered a cubicle and sat down to see what he had.

An American passport, in the name of Enrique Carvajal, showing him to be a naturalized citizen, birthplace Saltillo, Mexico, profession business consultant. Naturalization papers ditto, dated two years back. A worn billfold, containing a New Mexico driver's license, also suitably worn, giving a street address in Albuquerque, and two credit cards, which he could use for identification or for checking into hotels but not for purchases, since they were forgeries. Mexican visitor's registration card, without which he could not leave Mexico. An envelope stuffed with American bills, five thousand dollars' worth in twenties and fifties. The return half of an airline ticket, Dallas to Mexico City to Dallas. The flight left in two hours.

It was enough to get started with. Satisfied, Cardoso went through the motions of using the toilet, flushed it and stuffed the wallet and passport into his topcoat. Then he left the cubicle and went to the concourse to find an out-of-the-way bar to wait in until it was time to board the aircraft.

Cardoso's plane thumped onto the runway just as dusk was turning into night. He could see, outside the porthole, the glitter of the terminal lights and off in the distance the blaze of Dallas reflected in the indigo sky.

On enemy soil, he thought. Behind the lines. He realized that he was beginning to enjoy himself.

I was starting to rust, he reflected. Now again I can shine in use.

He could not help comparing the interior of the terminal with that of José Martí outside Havana. There were hardly any soldiers, for one thing; the few he did see appeared to be men on leave, not guards. And the place was vast. Cardoso hadn't been in the United States since the late seventies, not long before he transferred from military intelligence to a combat command and went off to the Angolan war. And he had spent his time in the United States in Miami, where he had been operating, with East German support, against American military installations in southern Florida. The FBI had gotten on to him somehow, and after six months he'd had to run for it. He'd never been back since, and Dallas was a complete unknown to him.

Never mind, he thought, as the immigration officer took a cursory look at his papers and waved him through. It's just another big American city, from my point of view. Be careful, and everything will be fine.

In order to do just that he spent half an hour lugging his suitcase around the terminal, watching for surveillance. As far as he could tell, he was clean. Then, following the instructions he had memorized in Havana, Cardoso went down to the terminal's Airtrans station. A train was just gliding in, but Cardoso ignored it. He took off his topcoat, sat down on one of the benches, spread the topcoat across his knees and blew his nose with a white handkerchief. Then he balled up the square of cloth and carelessly let it fall to the ground by his left shoe.

The train pulled out. There was no driver. Cardoso watched with interest as it accelerated. Controlled by a computer somewhere, he guessed. How would you hijack something like that?

He thought about it idly for a couple of minutes, until another train slid into the station. Very carefully and without appearing to do so, he watched the people getting out of it. The sixth man off, one carrying an attaché case but no other baggage, looked like a possibility: the long-time illegal with the work name Faustino. Cardoso leaned forward, setting his elbows on his knees, and saw the man's eyes flick toward him and the handkerchief lying by his shoe. Then, to Cardoso's relief, he switched his attaché case from his left to his right hand: all clear. Cardoso stood as the agent sauntered over to him.

"Is the weather good in Saltilla?" the man asked. It was almost a formality.

"It's not time for the rains yet," Cardoso answered.

The man nodded. He was short and rotund, although powerfully muscled through the shoulders, with a pocked face and a graying mustache. He looked for all the world like a Hispanic heavy construction worker, or perhaps one who had worked hard enough to rise and form his own company. This in fact was his cover and had been for a long time. The company was quite successful, in an unobtrusive way.

"We'll get the next train," Faustino said. "It takes us out to the parking lots and the other airport terminals. I have a car."

"Good. You're cleaned off, of course?"

"Of course. You know my work name?"

"Faustino."

"That's right. Here's a train."

They did not speak again until they were in Faustino's car and rolling down the Northwest Highway toward Dallas. Great blocks of light, office towers, leaped into the darkness ahead of them.

"Where am I seeing them?" Cardoso asked.

"A safe house in the west end of the city. It's not a long way."

"Good. Is there any food there?"

"Yes."

After a while they crossed a bridge over a narrow river. "The Trinity," Faustino explained. "We'll be there soon."

Cardoso nodded, watching the lights of the city pass. So much wealth, so much display, so much waste. Once it had appalled him. Now, in middle age, he wanted as much as possible of it for himself. He did not want to end his life a superannuated army officer in a back-country village in Cuba, living on a handful of pesos every month, rationed food, three-year-old rum, watching his wife grow fatter and grumpier and uglier. He wanted good food, fine liquor, his own villa by the sea, expensive and beautiful cars and lots of women. The fact that he wanted these things and yet loved the danger and excitement and even the discomfort of war did not strike him as incongruous. The one side of him lent savor to the other.

"I presume they don't know it's me who's coming to see them," he said.

"No. They don't. I used a dead drop to tell them to be at the safe house. I've never made direct contact with them. It was always Linares."

"And they don't know Linares is missing?"

"No, they don't know that, either."

"How have they been doing?"

"They are doing all right. Linares managed that part well. One has found work at the new TRW plant. The other's working as a waiter and bartender. But he's acquired a secretary who works for a department head at Hughes Aerospace."

"That's excellent," Cardoso observed. Privately he did not care in the least. The Russians still wanted the industrial intelligence the DGI was so good at acquiring; Moscow wasn't averse, even in these days of cooperation with the United States, to taking shortcuts. But the demand was down a great deal, and the DGI was having to develop other markets, the Chinese and Taiwanese particularly. They would pay hard cash for information, which the Russians had never been willing to do. But that cash went straight into the treasury, and little of it stuck to the fingers of those collecting it. Compared to the sums generated by the drug trade, though, the amounts available through industrial espionage were like spit in a river. And the espionage operations provided useful resources and expertise for the narcotics traffic. Portela and Menocal, useful though their activities at Hughes and TRW might eventually be to the Chinese or the Taiwanese, were really in the United States to provide manpower for the cartel when it needed it.

"I assume they haven't had anything to do with the pipeline yet?" Cardoso asked. Occasionally some agents were reluctant to help with drug cartel operations. But once it was pointed out to them that they were already spies and hardly in a position to argue, they never refused.

"No. They haven't been needed. We were holding them in reserve until this came up. Here we are."

Faustino was turning the car into an alley between two three-story buildings. In the headlights Cardoso could see iron fire escapes dangling from the wall above. "This is the safe house?" he asked.

"Apartment. It's at the back, on the ground floor."

"I want a weapon."

Faustino handed over a flat black Walther, which Cardoso shoved into his waistband, under his suit jacket. Then they got out of the car, and Faustino led the way to the rear of the building. The cross alley was dimly lit by windows above it. Cardoso could hear the rumble of traffic, a siren far in the distance and an aircraft way overhead. The alley at the building's rear smelled of cat urine, although it was free of garbage.

Faustino produced a key and unlocked the steel-clad back door of the building. Inside was a dimly lit corridor with dirty yellow walls and threadbare carpeting on the floor. There was a fire hose cabinet in the wall, but its glass was broken and the hose was gone. Cardoso could hear music and raised voices reverberating from at least one apartment. The air was laden with the smell of old garlic and used cooking oil.

"This is not a dangerous neighborhood," Faustino said. "Only noisy." He stopped at the first door on the right and raised his hand to knock.

Cardoso reached out and held it. "I'll do this," he said.

Faustino blinked. "Alone? You're sure?"

"Yes. I don't want them to see you."

"Very well. There's a certain knock."

"What is it?"

Faustino clicked his tongue to demonstrate.

"Good," said Cardoso. "Fine, go and wait."

Faustino nodded and left. Cardoso waited until he had exited through the heavy outside door, then gave the knock. After a moment a voice on the other side said, *"Si?"*

"Cardoso," Cardoso said.

Bolts and chains rattled and the door flew open. Portela was on the other side of it. "Colonel?" he stammered.

Cardoso stepped through and closed the door behind him. "Hello, Joel," he said. "Is Luis here, too?"

"Yes, sir. Colonel, I didn't expect —"

Cardoso cut him off. "Drop the ranks, we're not in the army any more. Have you any rum, in the name of God?"

Portela was rapidly regaining his composure. "Yes. Come into the kitchen. Someone left food for you. As well as the rum."

Cardoso followed his erstwhile captain along the narrow hall. Portela's surprise at the door had been genuine enough. Cardoso tried to decide whether there'd been anything else in it, such as uneasiness or guilt. He didn't think there had been. It was always possible that these two men were unconnected with what Ramon had done — might have done? — in spite of the fact that he had recruited them. Cardoso rather hoped they were. They had served well under him, and he didn't want to order their executions.

The safe apartment was a small one, what Cardoso vaguely recollected from his Miami days was called a studio apartment. One larger room served as a bedroom and sitting room; it was featureless, sparsely furnished with a couch, a chair and a couple of lamps. The frayed rattan blind was closed. A bead curtain separated the room from the tiny kitchen, which contained a card table and three folding chairs. Menocal was sitting at the table. His dark eyes widened when he saw Cardoso, and he scrambled to stand up.

Cardoso waved him into his chair. "I don't want salutes," the colonel said genially. "I just want a drink."

Menocal subsided into the chair. Cardoso observed him closely, but he was reacting in exactly the same way Portela had: surprise, then something like pleasure. But Cardoso thought he sensed an oddity to the pleasure.

Is this something they expected to happen? Or *like* something they expected to happen?

Portela was pouring rum into a glass. Cardoso noted with gratification that it was Captain Morgan dark, the kind he liked best of all. He took the glass from Portela and sniffed the liquor deeply, with appreciation.

Menocal was grinning broadly, his astonishment fading. "Was it too boring in Havana, colonel?" he asked with a chuckle. "I have to warn you, it's pretty quiet here, too."

Cardoso laughed and sipped at the rum. "Well, there wasn't much to do," he said easily. "Have some rum yourselves. I don't plan to drink the whole bottle. Is there something to eat, Joel? You said there was. I'm famished."

Faustino had left bread and a box of fried chicken and some kind of salad made with potatoes. "It's Yankee food, sir," Portela said as he got it out of the scratched refrigerator. "But one can get used to it. It's not that bad."

"I could eat a horse and chase the rider," Cardoso told him, sitting down. The bread was already buttered. Cardoso tore off a hunk and began to eat, alternating bites of chicken with bread and spoonfuls of the salad, which he did not really like but consumed anyway, on the battlefield principle that you always ate when you could since you never knew when you would have another opportunity. The red and white striped box was soon empty. Cardoso sat back in the creaky folding chair, exhaled gratefully and took another nip at his glass of rum. "There," he said. "Maybe it's Yankee, but it's better than Yemen was sometimes. Remember how hungry we all were?"

They grinned at that. Both had followed his lead and were drinking, but carefully. Cardoso had been observing them while he ate, looking for changes. There weren't any clear ones; they were both the vigorous young men he had known in Yemen. Joel Portela, broad-shouldered, with great big hands and an engaging, straightforward smile in a solid jaw. Luis Menocal, smaller, more solemn, with his dark eyes set close together and his narrow face tapering to a chin that receded perhaps a little too .much. He was the more intense and talkative one of the two, as befitted a political officer. The only real difference Cardoso could see was that they looked better fed than they had in Yemen, which was hardly surprising.

"You're wondering why I'm here," Cardoso said abruptly.

Portela nodded. Menocal merely looked inquisitive.

"I am sorry to have to tell you," Cardoso said slowly, "that Major Linares is missing."

Shock spread over both their faces. Cardoso had rehearsed this many times since he learned he was coming to the United States, and he was watching them closely. But there was nothing in their expressions that should not have been there.

"When?" Menocal queried anxiously. "What's happened?"

"A few days ago," Cardoso told him. "We don't know exactly what happened to him." He was purposely vague, to see if they would betray themselves with too much knowledge.

"Is he dead?"

"We don't know that, either. I wanted to find out if he had spoken to you within the past two weeks. Perhaps he said something that would give us an indication of what happened."

They both shook their heads. "We haven't seen him for a long time," Menocal said. "Almost not since we arrived here. We always used drops. The last one was — let me see ... I serviced one four days ago."

That was no help; it was Faustino who had been keeping the drops going.

"It's very important that we find him, or find out what happened to him exactly," Cardoso said. "Unfortunately, we think he has turned his coat around."

Portela's mouth dropped open. "Mother of God," he whispered. "He couldn't have."

Menocal was looking worried. "You mean he's going to betray us to the FBI?"

"That's not likely. He wouldn't want to talk to *them*. It appears he joined some drug traffickers, got his hands on some of their money and stole it. The traffickers are after him."

"Drugs?" Portela said. "Ramon would never have done that. He wouldn't have dealt in drugs."

"People have given in to temptation before this," Cardoso said, aware of the irony of the words even as he said them. "Let me assure you he's done it. We have to get to him before the traffickers do. Or worse, what has Havana really worried, is that the Americans may catch him. If they do, he may bargain with them, give them everything he knows so they'll go easier on him. That would include handing over you two. Not to mention several other people. It would be a disaster. Is there anything you can tell me?"

They appeared to rack their brains for several moments. Then Portela said:

"Isn't it possible he's dead? You said he was missing. He *might* be dead. Was there some kind of accident?"

Either he is very clever or he really doesn't know, Cardoso thought. But which? Or maybe he doesn't know anything, and Menocal does. I can hardly start pulling out their fingernails on this much suspicion, can I? Some of us in the cartel would, but I've never gone that far. And they were my men, once.

"He might be dead," Cardoso conceded. "But we have to be sure one way or the other." He eyed them. "You both seem very certain he wasn't working for the traffickers."

"Colonel," Menocal said stiffly, "I know what you're thinking. Ramon recruited us both. But I swear he never involved us in anything like this. We had no idea what he was planning."

Cardoso mused for a moment. The major point in their favor was that they were here in the safe house with him. If Ramon and these two had stolen the money together, all three of them would have disappeared at once. Whatever Major Linares was up to, he was doing it alone.

"I want to go over everything that passed between you since he recruited you," he said. "Every last detail. Everything you can remember."

He pushed the rum bottle to one side.

The interrogation went on for a good three hours. "I know you're telling the truth," Cardoso said when it had finally finished. He felt exhausted mentally, although their cooperation had been total. "But I had to have every scrap of information." He reached for the bottle, poured rum for all three of them. "Let's have a drink to the days in Yemen. It's been a long time."

They did so, and then had a drink to the brigade, and then one to the battalion. Cardoso, relieved that if Portela and Menocal hadn't pointed him in the direction of Ramon they at least weren't working with him, found himself relaxing and enjoying himself. After a while the bottle was empty. "I have to go," he said. "Can't tempt the Americans by staying too long in one place. You two wait here for ten minutes, then leave five minutes apart."

Menocal nodded. He was looking gloomy again. Finding out that your old commanding officer had a bad streak was enough to make anyone gloomy, Cardoso reflected.

As Cardoso stood up Portela said, "But what are you going to do about Major Linares?"

"We'll find him," Cardoso said with conviction. Menocal looked even gloomier, and angry.

Portela saw him to the front door. "Good night, colonel," he said softly. "I'm sorry."

"So am I," Cardoso muttered, not meaning it. He had written Linares off as a soldier and a human being. He stepped into the hall and heard the door close behind him with a rattle of locks and chains.

He went out to the alley. Faustino was slumped down behind the wheel of the car, appearing to doze. Cardoso climbed into the passenger seat, realizing that he smelled rather heavily of rum, although with his hard head he did not feel it much.

"Well?" Faustino asked, straightening.

"They don't know anything," he said. "Even what they did tell me didn't help. *Is* he dead?"

"I don't know," Faustino said.

"I need to get some sleep. Where have you put me?"

"I booked a hotel room. It's paid for in advance by my company. All you have to do is check out whenever you need to. When are you going back?"

"I don't know. We have to do some more looking first. How can I contact you tomorrow? Telephone?"

"I'd rather you didn't use the telephone. Across from the hotel there is a bus stop. I can pick you up there whenever you like."

"Then be there at seven tomorrow morning. Are our watches at the same time?"

They synchronized, and Faustino started the engine.

Luis Menocal and Joel Portela did not obey Cardoso's instructions to the letter; they waited the required ten minutes, but instead of leaving separately they did so together. Menocal's Bronco was parked a block from the safe house. They got into it and Menocal started the engine, although he didn't set the vehicle in motion.

"Ramon didn't expect this," Menocal said. "What do you think we ought to do? Cardoso knows he's alive, I'm sure of it."

"I think we have to stop Cardoso from hunting him," Portela answered after a pause. "We don't know where Ramon's gone, so we can't warn him. But Cardoso might find out, he's got better resources than we have. He might ambush Ramon."

"Do you think Cardoso suspected us?"

"I couldn't tell. I don't think so, or he would have taken us. I think."

Menocal ruminated. "If we set the Americans on Cardoso ... the DEA or the FBI, maybe. If they catch him, he won't be able to go after Ramon."

"But suppose he told the Americans about us?"

"Why would he, if he doesn't suspect us? You know how many informants there are. He would likely think it was one of them."

"But Faustino would be after us in a minute, even if the Americans weren't," Portela warned. "It's too much of a coincidence."

"Yes," Menocal said slowly. "I suppose it is. But we can't

just sit on our asses and let Cardoso go after Ramon."

"I know."

"What we could do," Menocal said, "is just get out. Get out now and hide at the rendezvous. We have to get the other equipment there anyway. We could start early."

"You mean blow Cardoso and disappear."

"Yes."

"Are we going to sit here all night?" Portela asked. "I don't like sitting around."

Menocal put the Bronco in gear and started driving aimlessly through the streets. "Did you bring your car?" he asked. "I can take you to it."

"No. I used the bus. The car's not working right."

"That dealer cheated you."

"I know."

"If we give Cardoso to the Americans and then disappear," Menocal said, as though thinking out loud, "the DGI and the cartel will both be after us."

"That's going to happen sooner or later, anyway," Portela reminded him. "But you were right. We have to do something about Cardoso."

"Would Ramon want us to do it? Will we make a mess of his planning if we do?"

"Remember what he used to say," Portela said. "Sometimes you have to act, just jump into the dark. He hated people who hesitated."

"We'd better do it, then," said Menocal. "There's an FBI office here. We'll get out of our apartments right now and telephone once we're on the way. I'll tell them Cardoso's a big drug man from Cuba, that he's in town and that his contact is Faustino. Actually I'll tell them that Faustino's really Miguel Darias, the name Ramon found out. The Americans will track Cardoso through Darias fast enough. But we'll call in the morning, from out of town. If Cardoso does give the Americans our names, I want to have a head start."

"It's a good thing Ramon left us with some of the money."

"He trusted us. He told us what Faustino's real identity was. He wouldn't have given us a weapon like that if he wanted us to sit on our hands no matter what happened. We

have to give him all the support we can. And we don't have
to stay hidden for a long time, remember."

Portela remained silent.

"What's the matter?" Menocal asked. "The woman at
Hughes?"

Portela seemed to rouse himself with an effort. "No."

"Well, anyway, you'd better call her. Otherwise she may
report you missing after a while. We don't want that."

"I'll call her."

"Good. We'll pick your things up first. I want to be out of
Dallas in an hour."

Cardoso woke abruptly. Gray light was seeping around the
edges of the heavy drapes of the hotel room. He had a slight
headache from the rum, and words were chasing themselves
around in the back of his head. He had a feeling that they'd
been repeating themselves there for some time, but they
drifted away before he could make sense of them.

Something about the Fitzgerald woman. That was it. Last
night he hadn't mentioned her to Joel or Luis; perhaps that
was an error. It was most unlikely that either of them would
know anything about her, but he ought to verify it. It was the
sort of thing Guillois would ask if he had done, and Cardoso
wanted to be able to say yes.

His watch indicated twenty past six. He went into the
bathroom and shaved and showered, taking despite his
preoccupation a sensual delight in the unlimited hot water
and the soaps and the thick towels. Someday I'll be able to
do this whenever I like, he thought, as he toweled himself
dry. Where? Rio, maybe? Buenos Aires?

He dressed, checked the Walther and went downstairs.
The hotel lobby was quiet, as befitted a Sunday morning,
although Cardoso could hear the clink of cutlery from the
restaurant adjoining the lobby, and smell toast and coffee.
His stomach growled. He ignored it and went outside.

The street, like the lobby, was almost deserted. This made
Cardoso feel conspicuous, and he didn't like it. He glanced
surreptitiously at his watch. Two minutes to seven. Pretty close.

He sauntered across the four lanes of asphalt. A bus was
visible a couple of blocks away, and in front of it a car that

might be Faustino's. Cardoso stood beside the light standard that supported the bus stop sign, and waited. The car and the bus moved closer. After a few seconds, Cardoso could make out the driver: Faustino. Cardoso relaxed a bit.

The car pulled up to the curb. It was a dark green Ford, and nicely inconspicuous, a reassuring fact that Cardoso hadn't been able to note in the darkness last night. He got in, slamming the door behind him.

"What do you want to do?" Faustino asked without preamble as he accelerated away from the curb.

"I want to ask some more questions. This time I want you with me."

"Fine. Bring them back to the safe house?"

"No. One at a time will do."

"Portela's closest," Faustino said. "An apartment near Chalk Hill Road. He's the truck driver, the one I told you about who's poking the Hughes secretary."

"Go there, then."

Faustino turned the Ford onto a cross street and headed south. Cardoso didn't pay much attention to their surroundings even when they crossed the Trinity. Ramon had the faith I did when I was his age, Cardoso was thinking. He was very angry when we were ordered to pull out of Yemen. Just suppose he's decided to carry on the armed struggle all by himself. What would he do?

He'd follow the classic pattern. Money first, then weapons, then the first revolutionary act. Let's assume he has the money. Now he needs weapons. Where would he go to get weapons or explosives? To do that without getting caught, you need contacts. He has no contacts in the United States except the cartel people and us, and he would not dare use either. So he's probably going to make his purchases somewhere else. Where might Ramon Linares have contacts with no-questions-asked weapons dealers? Ethiopia. Possibly Iraq. Not Yemen at the moment, too risky since the collapse of the Marxist government there. The United Arab Emirates. Syria, even. They sometimes got rid of perfectly good third-line equipment.

"Needle in a haystack," Cardoso muttered.

"What?" Faustino asked. The Ford was cruising down a

residential street dotted with nondescript three- and four-story apartment buildings set among rooming houses, liquor stores and secondhand-car lots. The apartments were deteriorating, and the bright morning sunshine accentuated their cracked stucco and peeling window frames.

"Arms dealers," Cardoso said irritably. "We're going to have to check all the fucking arms dealers. Never mind, it'll keep till later."

Faustino parked on the street and switched off the engine. "The place is that one just ahead on the right."

"Come as far as the apartment with me. Then you can wait outside."

There was no security system for the apartment lobby, or if there were it wasn't working. The two Cubans ignored the elevator and went up the fire stairs to the second floor. Portela's apartment was the third on the right. Cardoso knocked on the door, using the special pattern from the safe house while Faustino stood off to one side, out of sight.

There was no answer. Cardoso frowned and knocked again.

Still nothing. He exchanged a glance with Faustino and tried the doorknob. It turned easily. Cardoso gave it a slight push and felt the door give. It wasn't locked.

Maybe he's gone out for a minute, Cardoso thought. He stood aside and gave the door a shove. It swung wide. There was no sound from the interior of the apartment. Cardoso drew his gun and gingerly stepped inside.

The door opened into the living room. A short hall led off to Cardoso's right with a bedroom at its end; he could see a white bureau with a few odds and ends lying on it. Reflected in the bureau's mirror he could see most of the bed; it was rumpled, but there was no one in it. The living room was scantily furnished: a couple of sling-back chairs with black steel frames, a vinyl-upholstered couch, a television set, a rack of cheap video and audio equipment. Cardoso listened carefully, but could hear nothing but faint traffic noises and the drip of a tap. He motioned Faustino to follow him. Faustino stepped inside and closed the door softly.

"Where is he?" Cardoso said. "At the woman's apartment? It's Sunday."

"Maybe," Faustino muttered. "Check the kitchen."

It was a galley type, divided from the living room by a thin partition. A few dirty dishes sat in the sink under the dripping tap. It was as empty as the living room.

"Fuck," Cardoso said. He knew intuitively that he'd made a serious mistake. He returned to the living room and stood indecisively, looking at the rack of electronic equipment. A couple of videotapes lay on the floor in front of it. Cardoso picked one up and inspected it. It wasn't labeled.

Faustino came back from the bedroom, looking grim. "His clothes are gone," he said. "So is everything from the bathroom. I think he's run for it."

"I know," Cardoso said absentmindedly. He was trying to imagine how he was going to explain this to Guillois. He'd had the links to Ramon right in his fist last night, then he'd opened the fist.

I have to catch the little shit and kill him, he thought. Now especially. This is a lot worse than it looked a day ago.

"What's the tape?" Faustino asked.

"No label." Cardoso handed it over. "A cinema film?"

Faustino turned the cassette over in his hands two or three times. "There was a video camera in the bedroom," he said. "I wonder."

"Play it."

Faustino deciphered the controls and stuffed the cassette into the player, pressed buttons. The screen of the television set blinked and flashed, turned grainy black and white. Then a picture appeared, in color but out of focus. The focus sharpened as someone adjusted it. In the picture was the bed in Portela's bedroom, and on it were Portela and a young woman with black hair, both naked. A half-empty liquor bottle stood on the table beside the bed.

Cardoso frowned. Who was adjusting the camera?

His question was answered almost immediately. There was a blur, then another man flung himself onto the bed. A very young man, blond, an Anglo; Cardoso judged him to be about twenty. His face was smooth, almost beardless, and he had huge eyes.

"A ménage," Faustino said. "The idiot."

"Is the woman the one from Hughes?"

"I think so. Yes."

"Who's the boy?"

"I have no idea," Faustino said. "Maybe the woman likes two lovers."

"I —" Cardoso began, then swallowed. Two bodies were entwining with each other on the bed, but neither of them was the woman. The couple was Portela and the boy. The woman was embracing Portela from behind, kissing the back of his neck, but he was ignoring her.

"Shut it off," Cardoso snarled. He wanted to vomit.

The screen went blank. There was a long silence. Then Cardoso said, "Did you know he was a faggot? Why didn't you report it? We would have pulled him out immediately."

"I didn't know," Faustino said. He didn't say anything else, but the words hung in the air: *It was your responsibility to know this, colonel.*

Cardoso dropped into one of the sling-back chairs. "He never showed any sign of it overseas," he said angrily. "He was a man, God damn him. How could he have hidden it so well?"

Faustino shrugged. "Lack of opportunity. Here he had the opportunity. Maybe the woman started it and Portela found out he liked this kind of ... I don't know."

"Where the devil have they gone?" He knew without even thinking about it that Menocal was gone, too.

"Maybe the boy or the woman knows. We could pick the woman up easily enough."

"No. He wouldn't have told her. He's not that stupid. And it might lead to complications if she disappeared." And God knows, he thought, I don't need any more complications. "But as far as I'm concerned now, Linares is still alive."

"What are you going to do, then?"

"I need to use your communications with Havana. Linares has gone overseas, I think. Havana will have to start asking questions around the arms dealers. While that's going on, I want you to look for the other two."

"Are you going after him, as well?" Faustino asked.

Cardoso was about to answer when he heard the rattle of a key in the apartment door lock. He was out of his chair in an instant, flattening himself against the wall next to the door on its hinge side, the Walther already in his hand. He noticed out of the corner of his eye Faustino disappearing into the kitchen.

The door opened, blocking Cardoso's vision, then began to swing closed. Cardoso stepped forward, slammed the door shut with his foot, clamped his arm around the throat of the person who had just entered and squeezed hard, choking off the windpipe. He thrust the Walther muzzle under the ear, grinding it hard into the flesh, realizing as he did so that the intruder was the boy on the videotape. The key tinkled to the floor and the boy made choking and groaning noises, trying to pull Cardoso's arm away from his neck.

"Be quiet," Cardoso hissed in Spanish, knowing his tone would be understood even if the words weren't. "Or I'll kill you. Come here, Faustino," he called.

The boy became still. Faustino appeared from the kitchen, his automatic in his hand. Cardoso jabbed the boy harder behind the ear. "Do you speak Spanish?"

The boy gave a terrified nod.

"Good. Keep quiet and I won't hurt you." Cardoso wrenched him almost off his feet, dragged him the two meters to the vinyl couch and slammed him down onto it. The boy whimpered. Cardoso, in a sudden fit of rage, slammed the Walther's muzzle against his mouth and felt the steel grate hard on the boy's teeth. "Shut up! Shut up!"

The boy closed his eyes and obeyed. Blood trickled from a split lip.

"Watch him, Faustino," Cardoso ordered. He sat in the chair across from the boy and placed his pistol on his lap. "What's your name?" he asked companionably.

"David," the boy whispered. "David Wright. What are you going to do to me?"

"Nothing," Cardoso said. "I'm sorry about your lip. The man who lives here. Where is he?"

"I don't know. I swear to God, I don't know."

"When did you last see him?"

"Friday night."

Cardoso touched the pistol.

"It was Friday night, I swear it was." A tear trickled down the side of David's nose. "Jorge said he was busy this weekend, but I could come Sunday morning. Today."

Portela had stuck to his work name, understandably. Cardoso asked, "He gave you a key?"

"Yes."

"He called himself Jorge Oliva?"

"Yes."

"Was he going on a trip?"

"I don't know. He wanted me here Sunday. I was away until this morning, he told me to come this morning. Have you ... What have you done with Jorge?"

"Nothing. We just want to know where he is."

"I swear I'd tell you if I knew. Just don't do ... do anything to me."

"We won't." He doesn't know where Portela went, Cardoso thought. He can't tell us what he doesn't know. "Fine," Cardoso went on. "Now we're going to leave. But we have to tie you up and gag you before we go." The boy looked strong enough, and Cardoso didn't want a lot of flailing around when he found out what was going to happen to him. "Just to protect ourselves. You understand?"

A nod, and faint hope in the blue eyes.

"Faustino," Cardoso said. "Use the bed sheets."

Faustino dragged a sheet into the living room and tore it into strips. Terrified and compliant, the boy lay on the floor and offered no resistance as Faustino gagged him, bound his wrists and ankles and ended by tying them together behind him.

"Good," Cardoso said.

"You really don't think he knows where they went?" Faustino asked.

"Why would Portela have told him, of all people? A faggot?"

Faustino shrugged. "I suppose. Use the gun?"

David's eyes widened in shock. He started to wriggle on the floor, making grunting noises around the gag.

"No. We don't want to leave a bullet behind," Cardoso said. "Strangle him."

"Look," Faustino pointed out. "You're probably leaving the country, aren't you? I'm not."

Cardoso grimaced. "Suit yourself. Give me some of that sheet."

It only took a couple of minutes. David made it quicker by struggling. Cardoso wished, as he was doing it, that it was Ramon thrashing around on the worn carpeting. After the convulsions and noises stopped, Cardoso checked for a pulse, found none and stood up.

"We can't leave him here," Faustino told him uneasily. "When the police find him, they'll suspect Portela right away. If they catch him ..."

"If they catch him, so what? Portela can't lead them to you."

"But do you want him caught? He might be going to Linares. If the American police got Linares, what then? *He* knows about me."

"Stop worrying about Linares," Cardoso said. "It's up to you to find Portela before the police do. Do you expect to run no risks in this business? And if you were really in danger, Havana would pull you out. Anyway, it'll be days before they find this creature." He prodded the body with the toe of his shoe. "There's plenty of time."

Faustino made an accommodating gesture. "Whatever you like."

"Good," Cardoso said. "Now we have to get through to Havana. Help me drag the guts here into the bedroom, and we'll close the doors and windows. When he starts to stink it won't get out into the hall so fast. And don't forget to get rid of that videotape."

Washington
March 22

■

"Are you going to be home this morning?" the voice in Conroy's ear asked him. "Hello? Hello, Michael, are you awake?"

"Uh," Conroy said. The voice belonged to Vickery. "Yeah, I'm awake. I think." He looked at the bedside clock; eight-ten. "What's the matter?"

"There's some business to discuss with some people. Would you mind if we came there? It's more central for some of them."

Conroy was fully awake now. "How many people?"

"Three or four."

He wanted to say, Why not out there? but didn't. "I suppose so. When?"

"Nine-thirty. We'd like the doctor to be there."

"All right. Come on ahead."

Conroy hung up and looked at the squares of light on the wall opposite the window. He could hear water running in the shower down the hall. The doctor, as Vickery had put it. It was Keely's turn to make breakfast; they'd been alternating meal preparation for about a week. Five days had passed since she and Conroy had gone to Boston to bring back her essentials, including about a hundred pounds of books and a portable computer. She was determined not to let her enforced concealment interfere with her work schedule, and had set herself up in a corner of the bedroom she was using. Conroy was beginning to be a little nervous about how Gemma would react if she knew about the arrangement.

He still hadn't written to her. He was, he knew, putting it off because he wasn't quite sure how to tell his sister that he'd allowed a woman to move in with him; no matter how urgent the necessity, it was still in some ways an invasion of Gemma's privacy.

Although, he reflected, Keely had been very careful not to spread herself any farther than the bedroom she was using. Except for that, there was almost no trace of her in the house barring her coat and rain boots by the front door. She wasn't even keeping any toiletries in the bathroom. For two days she'd avoided using the kitchen, until one morning he'd come downstairs to find her preparing two breakfasts.

"I hope you don't mind me using the kitchen," she had said. "But the least I can do is share the cooking. You've done it all so far. Will your sister mind me in her kitchen?"

"No," Conroy had said. "Gemma loathes cooking. This is probably the most the stove's been used since I was here last."

Keely spent a lot of time in her room working. Conroy hadn't left her alone in the house for more than a few minutes during the first few days; both he and she were nervous that another attempt might be made to abduct her. But nothing had happened, and despite Lipton's pressure on the DEA and the FBI to discover the reason for the incident, there was no information as to who had attacked her in Miami, or why. Conroy knew she was finally becoming restless, though. He judged that it wouldn't be long before she was demanding to return home. Whether Lipton would go along with that, Conroy didn't know.

He heard her go downstairs, spent a few minutes in the bathroom himself, dressed and followed her. Keely was stacking toast on a plate when he entered the kitchen. She was wearing jeans and a thick blue sweater. "Morning," he said.

"Morning. Coffee's ready. Sit down, everything'll be done in a minute."

Conroy slid into the breakfast nook and took a gulp of coffee. She made it strong, usually with a dash of cinnamon. "Listen," he said. "Did you hear about the Polish couple who got married, and then discovered they could only get along if they didn't live in the same city?"

She eyed him suspiciously, spatula poised over the eggs hissing in the frying pan. "No," she said. "I didn't. What about them?"

"They were Poles apart."

"Oh, God," she moaned, beginning to scoop up the eggs. "That really is *dreadful.* What on earth goes on in that mind of yours? Do you make them up that way on purpose?"

"It's no worse than the one you told me about the English weather report," he reminded her.

"That was at least witty."

"Well, yes."

She set his plate in front of him. He looked at the neat arrangement of eggs, ham, sausage and tomato. "You make me feel inadequate," he said.

"You make very good pancakes."

"Thanks," he admitted. "Keely, Vickery's decided to hold a meeting here at half past nine."

She looked at him, eyebrows raised. "Oh? That's rather nervy of him. Do you want me to get out of the house while it's on?"

"No. You're supposed to be part of it. Maybe he's got some bee in his bonnet about security." He wondered for a moment how Gemma would feel about her home being used as a safe house. Probably she'd think it was funny.

"What's happened?"

"I don't know."

"Maybe they've decided nobody's after me any more. My God, I hope so," she said feverishly. "Michael, it's no reflection on you, but this is driving me stone mad. How long am I going to have to hide? You can't go on like this indefinitely, either."

"I know it's getting on your nerves."

"Do you think perhaps something's happened that'll let me go home where I belong?"

"Maybe," Conroy said, unwilling to be too definite. He was unreasonably stung at her choice of words. They seemed to imply that she found being around him an uneasy experience.

Well, maybe it is, he thought. After all, I'm a spook who's

supposed to be her bodyguard. How did I expect her to feel? Every time she looks at me it reminds her of why she's here. We're doing well to be as friendly as we are, cooped up together like this. What did I expect? Something out of the movies?

They finished eating. "Do you want me to put on coffee for them?" Keely asked as Conroy began stowing the dishes in the dishwasher.

"No, I don't think so. I'm not feeling real hospitable this morning."

"I've really fouled up your leave, haven't I?" she said sadly. She handed him two empty juice glasses across the table, her long arms moving tentatively and with that trace of awkwardness that transformed her for an instant into a young girl on the edge of adolescence.

"It's not your fault," he assured her. "Nobody's fault. Actually it was those two bimbos in Miami, and whoever was behind them. To tell you the truth, I've enjoyed having you here."

She gave one of her brief, illuminating smiles. "Thank you. But it's still ... Do you know what my father used to say?"

Conroy closed the dishwasher. "What?"

"Fish and guests stink after three days."

Conroy laughed. "I suppose. But there are guests and guests." He wiped crumbs from the table with a damp cloth; she moved her arms out of the way to let him do it. Conroy felt an instant's vertigo, as though he had been displaced for a moment into an alternate universe in which he and Keely were a couple. Then the sensation was gone.

Ah, hell, he thought. Don't start that.

She was looking up at him. "What's the matter?"

"Nothing. I was just thinking of something. Were you close to your father?"

"I loved him dearly," she said. "He could charm birds out of the trees when he was sober. But he had trouble with his elbow. A taste for the poteen. I guess I mentioned that. It was what killed him finally — his liver went. I was fourteen. My husband died of it, too."

Conroy nodded. It was the first time she had mentioned her husband.

"In a car accident," she said. "You knew that, didn't you?"

Again he nodded. "Yes."

"A file on me?"

"It was in there." He was reluctant to elaborate. "Not much else. No private life."

"I felt after that that I was bad luck," she said, as though the file was an irrelevance. "It didn't make any sense, but it was there."

Conroy shook crumbs out of the cloth into the sink. "Do you still feel that way?" he asked.

A long pause. "I'm afraid so," she said quietly.

And that's a message if I ever heard one, Conroy thought, hanging up the cloth. "I'm sorry," he said, and the doorbell rang. The stove clock said nine thirty-two.

It was Vickery, accompanied by a younger man Conroy didn't know. The younger man was carrying a black attaché case. "Do you mind if Bob does a sweep?" Vickery asked, shrugging out of his topcoat. "It won't take more than five minutes."

"Go ahead," Conroy told the younger man, who set the attaché case on the floor and began taking bits of electronic equipment out of it. Conroy led Vickery into the living room, where Keely was already sitting in one of the armchairs by the fireplace.

"Hello," Vickery said. "You'd be Dr. Fitzgerald." He stuck out a hand and Keely shook it. "I'm Charles Vickery."

"Who else is coming?" Keely asked. Bob was wandering around the living room, studying the readouts on his sweep.

"A guy from the FBI," Vickery said, settling himself onto Gemma's brocaded sofa. "Name of Dick Claudel. And Kevin Garland, our assistant deputy director of operations, to represent the DDO. And Dr. Lipton."

"Rupert's coming?" Keely asked, sitting up straight.

"Uh-huh," Vickery said.

Conroy, too, was taken aback. He hadn't expected anything like this gathering. Something had happened to turn Keely's attempted abduction into a larger matter.

It had began to grow the night Tuck brought Conroy the picture of Ramon Guevara beside the drug traffickers'

Cessna, and the information about the aborted DEA intercep-
tion of the cocaine shipment Ramon was supposedly bringing
in, and Ramon's alleged disappearance. After some soul-
searching about exposing Tuck's DEA contact, Conroy had
decided to take the information to Vickery. He couldn't sit
on it, despite Tuck, who apparently hadn't thought the
matter through. Keely was Lipton's and the White House's
personal envoy to Havana, and if the CIA held back information that pertained to her safety, the consequences were not
difficult to imagine. Vickery had agreed, and wheels had
begun to turn. Both the DEA and the FBI were now looking
hard for Ramon. There was also a watch out for Colonel
Cardoso. It all looked very good in theory, but Conroy was
cynical about the commitment of the DEA and the FBI to the
search despite Lipton's pressure. If Keely hadn't become
involved, Ramon would be no more than another dime-a-
dozen drug courier, and Cardoso a target of uncertain value.

Tuck, of course, had been furious. But Vickery hadn't
pressed him for the identity of his source, and as far as
Conroy knew, the faceless DEA man — or woman — hadn't
come to jurisdictional grief. But Conroy knew it was going to
be some time before Tuck agreed to help him again, if indeed
he ever did.

"Are you sure it's safe for all these people to come here?"
Keely was asking Vickery. "They'd make a lovely target."

"It's convenient location-wise," Vickery said. "And the
FBI's been watching the house for three days. Nobody's
paying any attention to it."

"They have?" Conroy said with annoyance. "Somebody
might have told me."

Vickery's sandy eyebrows twitched. "I didn't find out
myself till this morning. This was just as much a surprise to
me."

"Oh," Conroy said.

The doorbell bonged again. This time Vickery went to
open it and came back with Garland, who was assistant DDO,
and the FBI man, Dick Claudel. Introductions were
performed. "Dr. Lipton's late," Garland observed. Garland
was as thin as a string bean, with a completely bald head and
silver-rimmed glasses. He would have been quite in place in a

university faculty club. Claudel, by comparison, looked like somebody who made a living by riveting steel girders together: short, wide and muscular, graying hair clipped short, huge hands. His blue suit did not sit well on him. He was carrying a small black briefcase, which he placed on the couch between himself and Vickery. After fiddling with the case for a moment, he removed its lid to reveal a cellular telephone. "Communications," he explained. "I'm patched in to New York, I hope."

Bob came into the living room, this time empty-handed. "Clean as a whistle," he said.

"Okay," Vickery told him. "Off you go." He looked out the front window. "Dr. Lipton's car just pulled up."

The chairman of the National Security Council came into the house unaccompanied, although Conroy knew he'd have somebody riding shotgun in the car outside. Quite naturally, he took the dominant position in the group, sitting in the fireplace armchair across from Keely's. Conroy observed him with some interest. Lipton looked fit and youthful, in spite of being, Conroy knew, older than sixty; his gray hair, which hadn't thinned noticeably, was carefully cut and styled, and he had a profile that would have been a good model for a classical Greek statue of Zeus. He was aware of his attractiveness, too; every movement seemed to possess a calculated grace.

There's a man who'd like to be president, Conroy thought. His opinion was reinforced by Lipton's voice: it was mellow and powerful, but with a slightly rough edge that gave it character. He had no distinct regional accent.

"Perhaps we'd better get started," Lipton was saying. "Thank you, Mr. Conroy, for extending us your hospitality."

It was Gemma's but Conroy didn't enlighten him. "You're welcome," he said.

Lipton inclined his head an inch in acknowledgment and said, "Dick? You'd better bring us up to date."

Claudel cleared his throat. "The FBI office in Dallas received a telephone call late yesterday afternoon. The call originated at a pay telephone in the El Paso dialing area. The caller stated that Colonel Dioclés Cardoso, of the Cuban DGI, was in Dallas on a mission connected with the drug pipeline through Guatemala. Even more important, the caller said that Cardoso's support in the United States was being provided by a man code-named Faustino, whose real name was supposedly Miguel Darias Benevides. The caller stated Miguel Darias's address, then hung up."

Claudel cleared his throat again, somewhat nervously, Conroy thought. "There unfortunately was a delay before this information was followed up," Claudel went on. "However, the follow-up was successful. Miguel Darias lives at the stated address. He owns a small construction and contracting company in Dallas, and has been a Dallas resident for fifteen years. He has never come to the attention of any law enforcement arm. We're still checking out where he was before he came to Dallas."

Claudel consulted a small notebook. "Because of the interest in Cardoso, the Dallas office put a watch on Miguel Darias's office and residence as soon as the identification was made, starting at ten o'clock last night, Dallas time. About one hour later Darias left his office at the construction yard and drove to the Granada Hotel. He was seen to be carrying an attaché case. An agent followed him into the hotel, but because Darias did not stop at the desk the agent was unable to determine which room he was going to and elected not to follow him upstairs because of the danger of detection.

"However, the Granada management cooperated by allowing the agent to station himself behind the reception desk. A check of reservations revealed that one room was being held in the name of Darias's company, and that the room was occupied, although the occupant had not checked in personally. Some twenty minutes later Darias came downstairs, unaccompanied and still carrying the attaché case. The agent outside followed Darias to his residence. A telephone call by the hotel manager to the room in question indicated that it was still occupied, so the agent inside the hotel remained behind the desk in case the occupant checked out. The occupant did at 6:00 AM, Washington time. He is now being followed. He has been positively identified, visually at least, as Colonel Dioclés Cardoso of the Cuban DGI. Darias has not yet left his residence. Cardoso, however, boarded an aircraft on a nonstop flight to New York at seven-thirty this morning, again our time. He paid cash for the ticket, under the name of José Garcia." Claudel grimaced in disbelief. "He must have picked that one out of the air. He arrives in New York at a quarter after ten, in about forty-five minutes. We'll pick up the surveillance at Kennedy. He wasn't booked through, so if he's going anywhere else he'll have to book an onward flight at Kennedy."

"Okay, everybody," Lipton said, "what's going on here?"

A long silence.

"Okay, then, nobody knows for sure. Any guesses?"

Garland said, "Charles? Your estimate?"

Vickery sat up a little at the assistant DDO's request. "Well," he said a trifle reluctantly, "we don't have much. Cardoso is connected to the drug traffic, and so was — or is — Ramon Linares. Dr. Fitzgerald was talking to Linares's mother, and appears to have been attacked because of this, but we don't know by whom or why. Then Ramon disappears, and Cardoso turns up in the United States, doing we don't know what. Then there is the question of the identity of the informant who told us Cardoso was here. That's a wild card. Right out of the blue."

And that was sheer luck, Conroy thought. If it hadn't been for that break, we'd be right where we were ten days ago, standing still. Who in hell was it?

"It wasn't any of your regular informants?" he asked Claudel.

"No. Not as far as we're aware."

"It's a mishmash," Garland said. "We don't have enough information, damn it."

"Do you suppose Cardoso is going to New York to meet Ramon?" Keely asked.

"Or maybe he's chasing him," Claudel said. "If he did hook a pile of cartel money, they'd want to nail him."

"Or maybe," Conroy suggested, playing devil's advocate, "Ramon is dead and Cardoso's here for some other reason altogether."

"Shee-it," Claudel said. "Pardon me, Dr. Fitzgerald. But it seems to me we're chasing our tails here. Darias hasn't done a thing out of the ordinary except go to the Granada Hotel, and we can hardly pick him up and sweat him for that.

Insufficient cause. All we can do is watch Darias and keep tracking Cardoso until he ends up wherever he's going."

"There is another possibility," Lipton said in that center-stage voice of his.

Everybody looked at him, which was precisely the effect he'd expected.

"I discussed this with the Secretary of State last night," Lipton went on. "It's quite likely there are Cuban political maneuverings behind this. We are trying to come to some accommodation with the Cuban government as a step toward normalizing relations. Even Castro has finally accepted the need for this. But I hardly need tell you there are plenty of people in Havana who have a vested interest in keeping Cuba at daggers drawn with the United States. If there's a rapprochement with the United States, it will open the way for us to pressure the Cuban government to allow the kind of liberalization we've seen in eastern Europe. That spells the end of the Party's monopoly on power, and of course there are lots of Party functionaries who are afraid of that prospect. What's on everybody's mind, naturally, is that Castro won't be around a great deal longer. If Havana and Washington can come to terms before he dies, there'll be a good chance that the Cuban reformers — and there are quite a few of them — will be able to take over. However, if American attitudes to Cuba were to become hostile again, and if Castro died while that was the case, the hard-liners in the Party will almost certainly be able to get rid of the reformers and tighten the Party's control of the island. We'll be back at square one."

He paused, looking significantly around at his listeners. "There is a very good chance," he said softly, "that what we're seeing here with Cardoso and with Ramon Guevara is the beginning of a maneuver of that kind. That it's not connected with drugs at all. Or that the drug matter is no more than a cover."

"Do you mean," Keely said, "that Ramon and Cardoso are going to do something violent to stop the normalization process? Some kind of terrorism?"

"That's what I mean."

"I kicked that idea around with the DDO," Garland said

thoughtfully. "It makes a certain amount of sick sense."

"Unless," Conroy pointed out, "it works the other way around. Somebody wants Castro in hot water with us so he can be gotten rid of more easily."

Lipton shot him a look of annoyance. "Pardon my saying so, Mr. Conroy, but that's a pack of nonsense."

Conroy shut up, his ears burning.

Vickery was nodding, but Claudel next to him was looking doubtful. "I dunno," he said. "With respect, Dr. Lipton, I've got a feeling it's no more than the result of a drug deal that got screwed up. If that's all it is, we're tying up a lot of manpower. There's no warrant out for Cardoso. Never has been."

"Maybe we should see where he goes after he gets to Kennedy," Vickery suggested. "Or we could always pick him up and deport him. He's in the country illegally."

"That leaves Ramon Linares on the loose," Garland said.

"What's your opinion, Keely?" Conroy asked. He had the distinct feeling she was being overlooked, and it annoyed him.

"Well," she said after a pause, "to start with, nobody seems to believe that Ramon is dead. Let's assume for the moment that he isn't. Mr. Claudel may very well be right about all this being no more than a theft by Ramon from the cartel. On the other hand, Dr. Lipton's ideas have a realistic ring to them. If that's what's going on, we're in a very dangerous situation. Ramon Guevara is the type of person who would be capable of a violent terrorist act, and presumably so would his old commander, Colonel Cardoso. If they have the backing of the DGI, or even if they're acting alone or for some faction of the Cuban Communist Party, they could be deadly. I don't think we can afford to ignore the possible threat. We only know about three people at the moment, remember: Ramon, Cardoso and Darias. It's only by accident that we found out about the last two. How many others are there? Who telephoned the FBI in Dallas, for example?"

"I should point out to everyone here," Lipton interjected gracefully, "that Dr. Fitzgerald is not only a historian of revolutionary movements, she is also a specialist in the psychology of revolutionaries. She has given us expert and useful advice in our dealings with the Cuban government."

Conroy glanced at Keely. She was quite expressionless.

"Maybe we should talk about what to do if Cardoso heads out of the country from JFK," Claudel said. "There's a limit to how far I can chase him with my people."

Garland rubbed his bald pate. "That's probably going to be up to us," he said. "But we haven't had much time to get things on line. A lot depends on where he's going. And he's moving fast. We can't just turn the stations loose on him without some kind of background. That's how things get fouled up."

Vickery looked at Conroy. "You want the job, Michael? Assuming he goes overseas?"

"What?" Conroy asked, startled. "What about Caracas? I'm supposed to be there in a week."

"Caracas could wait a bit. You've already got the background. It'd save time, which we haven't got a lot of."

"Is this a formal assignment?"

Vickery shrugged. "You can turn it down if you want."

The assumption that he might, after having come this far, stung Conroy. "All right," he said. "I'll go."

Keely was looking at him with an odd expression on her face, something like compassion. "I want to go, as well," she said.

That caught even the imperturbable Lipton by surprise. "I beg your pardon?" he said.

"I think I ought to go, too. As you said, Rupert, I'm a specialist in revolutionary psychology. If anyone can figure out what Cardoso or Ramon is going to do next, I can. It might give us a slight advantage when we need it most."

"But," Garland said huffily, "you're not trained for this kind of thing, Dr. Fitzgerald. Forgive me, but you'd be a liability from an operational point of view."

"Michael?" Keely said, turning to him. "You're the one who's going."

Conroy opened his mouth to answer, but Vickery interrupted him. "It's not Michael's option," Vickery said. "I'm sorry, but that's the way it is."

"If I were a man," she said fiercely, "you wouldn't object, damn it."

"Yes, I would," Vickery snapped. "Unless he were properly trained."

Conroy was infuriated with Vickery for cutting in on him, but he only said mildly, "We don't even know where Cardoso is going, yet."

"If I might put a word in edgeways," Lipton said, with clear annoyance. Everybody went silent, Vickery with his mouth still open.

"Keely, you're good at intuiting what these people will do next," Lipton admitted. "But it's true you're not trained in fieldwork. And it's possible that Cardoso knows what you look like. If he does, you'd be something of a liability. And you're already in some danger, as we know from Miami. This might be putting your head in the lion's mouth."

"It was you who suggested I get out of the country for a few weeks because of that," she retorted. "I refused because I didn't like feeling I was running away. Now I'm willing to leave, and you're telling me not to? And Cardoso doesn't necessarily know what I look like. You're assuming too much. Furthermore, I'm not suggesting I follow him around in the street. But I can't be much use to Michael or anyone else if I'm here hiding under a bed. The way matters are now, I might as well be in jail. I have to *do* something."

Lipton regarded her thoughtfully as she finished. "Well," he said. "I guess that puts it in a nutshell. Mr. Conroy, what do you think? You're the point man."

He was saved from an immediate answer by the chirp of Claudel's cellular phone. Claudel grabbed it and said, "Yeah?" He listened for a few seconds, his mouth tightening. "Okay," he said. "Can you stay on the line one minute?"

He tilted the receiver away from his mouth and said, "The man's plane got in early. He's just booked a KLM flight to Amsterdam, with a connection to Abu Dhabi in the United Arab Emirates. American passport, name Enrique Carvajal. The flight leaves in an hour. Pick him up or what do we do?"

"Jesus," Garland exclaimed. "He's really moving. No. I think we let him run. We can get somebody to pick him up in Amsterdam. Charles?"

Vickery nodded. Claudel looked at Lipton. "Let him run," Lipton said. "But make sure he gets on the plane."

"Okay," Claudel agreed. Then, into the telephone: "See him onto the plane. That's all. Advise me when the flight gets off the ground." He hung up. "The next dance is yours," he said to Conroy.

Everybody was looking at him. He realized he still hadn't decided what to do about Keely.

"Well, Mr. Conroy," Lipton said. "Do you think Dr. Fitzgerald can help you enough to take her along?"

He could leave her in one of the big Dubai hotels; she'd be safe enough there, and she could perhaps help him. She is, he reminded himself, as much of a specialist as I am. What she does isn't unlike intelligence work. With some on-the-job training she really could be a lot of use. And there's the cover angle — a couple traveling invites a bit less suspicion than a lone male.

"Okay," he said, taking a leap into the dark. "We'll go together."

United Arab Emirates
March 23

■

The desert glared into Cardoso's eyes. Looking down, he saw the shadow of the Mazda's roofline just appearing on the vehicle's hood. A little past midday, then. Ahead of him, the four lanes of shimmering blacktop stretched toward an eternally distant dun horizon. Above the earth, the sky: ground pearl at the horizon, shading gradually to azure in the dome.

Cardoso squinted at the temperature gauge; the needle was resting securely a few millimeters below the red. That was the only thing he was really concerned about at this point, a boil over. The Al Ain road was well patrolled, and good as his driving documents were, he didn't want to have to answer any probing questions.

Twenty minutes to the guest house, forty kilometers. Nothing at all in the air-conditioned cab of a four-wheel drive Mazda Jeep rolling along at a hundred and twenty kilometers an hour. On foot and away from the road, if you were foolish enough to leave your vehicle, you'd be dead in rather less than that distance. Cardoso had spent some time in the arid lands in Ethiopia, and they were dangerous enough, but this was the real, deep desert. The Bedouin nomads were at home in it, but it was sometimes too much even for them.

The man who had brought the Jeep to the airport for him — and the business visitor's visa and the other papers — had been careful to show him the survival pack, although Cardoso wasn't going anywhere off the beaten track.

Cardoso had found this reassuring. The PLO people were erratic sometimes and didn't prepare as well as they should for the unexpected. Whoever was arranging matters for him had to be among the more imaginative and therefore more careful men in the Palestine Liberation Organization office in Abu Dhabi; careful to the extent of locating this encounter well out of the city, although Cardoso felt that such precautions were probably unnecessary.

Five minutes from the guest house. The highway was now traversing a flat stretch of rock and sand, the dunes here less than a meter high. In the shimmering distance Cardoso could just make out a blurred patch of white. As he drew nearer, the patch began to resolve itself into a cluster of buildings, a handful of huge white sugar cubes tossed haphazardly into the lion-coloured dust.

Cardoso slowed down. The buildings could be nothing other than the Shaikh al-Mualla guest house, halfway between Abu Dhabi and Al Ain. The guest house provided both an emergency refuge from the desert, and accommodation for tourists and expatriates who wanted to see more of the emptiness than was provided by the air-conditioned excursion buses that whined along the baking black road between Al Ain and the sea.

Havana had sent him here straight from the United States. Other senior officers were checking elsewhere: Damascus, Tripoli, even Brussels. Cardoso was supposed to cover the UAE and, in spite of the collapse there, Yemen. Then Baghdad in Iraq. He didn't like any of it. Yemen was going to be dangerous. He was supposed to pick up documents for the next two countries from the PLO here; Havana was forwarding them.

Is Ramon somewhere here in this armpit of a country? Cardoso wondered as he wheeled the Mazda onto the access road that led from the highway to the guest house. Somewhere between here and the coastal cities, or in them? Once I catch up with him, if I catch up with him. . . .

Then what?

Cardoso, during the long, monotonous hours of his journey to Abu Dhabi, had had plenty of time to think. He had come to one conclusion: if Ramon had gone overseas somewhere to buy weapons, he was not working for the Americans. That was one worry disposed of. It left a nagging question, though: what was he planning to do with the weapons once he had them?

Cardoso had no idea. In a sense, the question was irrelevant. The long and the short of it was that whatever Major Linares was up to, he had to be stopped.

Not just stop him, Cardoso thought, pulling through a wide gateway into the walled car park of the guest house. He has to be dead. Not the least because he turned his coat on the cartel. And no matter how good the political reasons are for blowing up something that belongs to the Yankees. Anything else is second to the fact that he's a traitor. I'm going to have to kill him. I knew that when I left Cuba, I don't know why I keep dithering around the subject. Probably because he was one of my men once, and I keep hoping there'll be a good reason for what he's doing. The same sentimentality that made me lose Portela and Menocal. It could cost me my skin. Enough.

Half a dozen vehicles, mostly four-wheel drive, were drawn up in the compound under wooden lattices, which kept some of the sun off them. Cardoso stopped next to a dusty Range Rover and opened the door of the Mazda. Desert heat blasted into the cab, as though some eerily soundless bomb had exploded nearby. In spite of himself Cardoso gasped. He'd have to get acclimatized quicker than this if he was going to be good for anything. He took a couple of salt tablets from a packet on the dash and washed them down with water from his canteen while he studied his surroundings.

The parking courtyard was walled on two sides against drifting sand; on its third and fourth sides was the main guest house of the complex. The place had been constructed to resemble the traditional mud-brick architecture of primitive Abu Dhabi, and its upper story was pierced only by small square windows. The roof was flat. Four arched doorways, two in each wing, led from the courtyard into the interior of the guest house. The doors themselves, set back in the archways, were in deep shadow. Cardoso squinted into the dimness. He couldn't see anybody, and the courtyard was deserted.

He was swinging one leg out of the Mazda's door when a movement in one of the arches stopped him. Cardoso waited, watching. The man in the archway inspected him carefully, then stepped into the mottled shade under the lattices. Cardoso didn't recognize him, but then he hadn't expected to; his contacts with the PLO had been limited even in Yemen, where a significant number of Palestinian terrorists had taken refuge over the years. And this man might never have been in Yemen. The PLO had maintained representation in the UAE for quite a long time.

The man approached the Mazda somewhat warily, glancing at the license plate, then at Cardoso. He was wearing the local *dishdasha* and a white head cloth, and his hands were hidden. Cardoso, who was not armed, forced himself to relax.

After a few seconds' more inspection, the man seemed satisfied. He walked over to the driver's side and said in good Spanish, "Let me get in, please."

Cardoso suppressed a start of surprise and moved over. He'd expected to have to work in his rusty English or in Arabic, which wasn't much better. The man slammed the door and started the engine; a welcome draft of cooler air wafted out of the ventilation slots on the dash.

"Where are we going?" Cardoso asked.

"Just to drive," the man said. "My name is Ibrahim."

Of course it is, Cardoso thought. "You speak very good Spanish," he said.

Ibrahim grinned at him, teeth white in his dark, thin face. The wrinkles around his brown eyes were pronounced when he smiled. Cardoso put his age at about forty.

"I was an engineering student in Havana once," Ibrahim said. "A guest of Cuba. I learned Spanish there."

The Mazda was outside the compound now, but instead of heading for the main road Ibrahim drove past the white sugar cubes of the guest house outbuildings and swung the vehicle toward the north. Cardoso could barely detect the trail he was following over the stony ground.

"We won't go far," Ibrahim said as the Mazda mounted a rise and grumbled down the other side, gearbox whining in low range. Just left of the track on the far side of the rise lay a huge, deep bowl of smooth sand the color of ground nutmeg. Ibrahim gestured at it.

"Don't ever drive into one of those," he said. "You may be able to climb out, but likely your vehicle will not."

Cardoso nodded. He had no intention of driving in the deep desert if he could avoid it.

Ibrahim drove for about a kilometer, until the track descended into a shallow depression a few hundred meters across. In the middle of it he stopped, set the hand brake and put the engine into neutral to keep the air conditioner running. Then he turned to Cardoso.

"There," he said. "No one will come out here at this time of day, not even the *Bedu.* How can we help you?"

Cardoso looked out the windshield, at the silent ferocity of the desert. He was not certain precisely how much assistance he should in fact ask for, although Ibrahim's offer was genuine, for Cuba was among the last of the PLO's non-Arab allies. Once, the Palestinians had been trained and armed and supplied with significant help from nations of the East Bloc: the Czechs and Bulgarians provided training bases and weapons; the East Germans trained PLO men in intelligence and counterintelligence; the Russians, carefully in the background, siphoned funds to PLO treasuries. Cuba, as in Ibrahim's case, had taught PLO youths both civil and military engineering.

But with the collapse of the Communist governments in eastern Europe the support had dried up, and the Russians drew back from their former protégés. Even Libya had become less enamored of the PLO's struggle for a homeland, and many of the other Arab states were willing to honor the PLO more with the abstractions of words than with hard cash and weapons. Cuba's steadfastness, in the face of her own difficulties with the Russians, had brought Havana and the PLO closer together, and there was a very discreet PLO office of representation in Havana, rather like the one that existed here in the Emirates, in Abu Dhabi. The DGI had next to no power in the UAE, so the needs of Cardoso's journey were being met, and his way smoothed, by the arrangements made at Guillois's request between the pair of PLO offices.

"I need to find a man," Cardoso said. "He may be here in

the Emirates. I'm not certain."

"I presume he doesn't want to be found."

"No, he doesn't."

"Probably," Ibrahim said, "we can help you. The Havana office said there was no conflict of interest, so that's all right. You were to bring with you details of this person?"

Cardoso passed over a photograph of Ramon, the picture he'd brought with him from Havana to the United States. "There are physical details on the back," he said. "He may be traveling under a Panamanian passport, the name Manuel Diaz del Cristo." He handed over a separate slip of paper. "Here's the passport number."

"Diaz, Manuel," muttered Ibrahim as he inspected the information. "Where might he have entered?"

"I don't know. If he's here, he might be going to see al-Bakr."

Ibrahim propped the photograph on the dashboard and regarded it thoughtfully. "Why would he be trying to buy weapons?"

"We aren't sure. We think he may have an ideological dispute with the leadership. But we want to find out."

"Who is backing him? Al-Bakr can be expensive."

"He stole the money," Cardoso said curtly.

"Ah," Ibrahim murmured. There was a world of understanding in his tone. "I see."

"Can you obtain any assistance from al-Bakr?"

Ibrahim frowned. "It depends. If this man of yours is a valued customer, then no. Al-Bakr's success comes a good deal from his reputation for being closemouthed. Would your man fit that category? Valued customer?"

Cardoso nodded reluctantly, remembering the ease with which Ramon had dealt with the arms merchant in the days of the war. "I'm afraid so."

"Hm. We've never been able to get anyone into al-Bakr's organization, unfortunately, so that avenue's also closed.... How urgent is this?"

"Very," Cardoso said.

"I can have the hotels checked to begin with," Ibrahim said. "I'll also make other inquiries. Is there anyone else looking for him? The Israelis or the Americans, for example?"

"No," Cardoso told him. "There isn't." The question of the Fitzgerald woman's interest in Ramon was still unresolved, but Cardoso wasn't about to complicate matters by bringing the subject up with Ibrahim.

"Good. Now, there's an important matter. Assuming we find Mr. Diaz for you, assuming he's here at all, what do you want us to do?"

"Just tell me where to find him," Cardoso said. "I will deal with him after that."

"How?"

"I promise you won't be involved."

Ibrahim absentmindedly smoothed the cloth of his *dishdasha* over his knee. "That's important," he said. "Our office is here on the sufferance of the UAE authorities, and for no other reason. We have to be extremely careful."

"Can you help to the extent of a weapon and transportation? I also would like a set of handcuffs and if possible a strip of the metal prongs used to puncture tires."

"Caltrops, you mean. I think so. What kind of gun?"

"A revolver. I don't like automatics in sandy conditions. They jam."

"We can arrange that," Ibrahim said. "The vehicle is a little more difficult. We can't provide you with one directly. I'll arrange for you to steal one of ours. That way if you're arrested for something, there won't be a provable link. I hope you understand."

Cardoso nodded. "I understand. What about the hotel, though?" Reservations had been made for him before he arrived, and the visa had been awaiting him at the airport desk.

"If you're arrested, all such records will vanish."

Cardoso had expected nothing less. If he was caught, he'd be cut loose. "Fine," he said.

"I'll take you to the guest house now," Ibrahim told him. "Then you can return to the hotel. After that, I'm afraid you'll just have to wait until we find him or you're satisfied he's not here. I wouldn't advise you to go looking yourself. There are a lot of people in Abu Dhabi and Dubai. I assume no one knows you're here except us and the DGI?"

"That's right," Cardoso told him. "There's nobody else in the least interested."

United Arab Emirates
March 29

■

"We'd better take it easy," said Deakin's voice from the radio transceiver under the Range Rover's dash. "You see it?"

Conroy looked down at the display of the tracker, which was mounted on a clip next to the radio. The signal strength had been getting stronger for the past kilometer.

"I see it," Conroy said into the microphone. "He's stopped, or close to it."

"Roger that."

Conroy eased off on the accelerator and allowed the Range Rover to slow down to about sixty kilometers an hour. He was careful to keep several hundred meters between himself and Deakin's Daihatsu Jeep, which was in the lead. Ahead, the irrigated greenery of the Jebel Ali worker's town wavered in the noon sunlight; off to Conroy's left lay the low hill crowned by the futuristic buildings and parabolic dishes of a satellite ground station. More residential construction covered the slopes. High wire fences on the other side of the road surrounded the vast transformer blocks and towers of the main Dubai power station.

The bug monitor emitted a small chime. It was transmitting from the target vehicle, Cardoso's Suzuki, which was well out of sight and about a kilometer and a half away, according to the tracker display. The chime was the bell of the Suzuki's car telephone. It had rung twice before, but Cardoso had done nothing but listen before hanging up. Deakin hadn't been able to get a tap on the phone; they'd done well as it was to get the tracker beacon and the bug aboard the Suzuki.

This time, though, Cardoso said something after the chime. The words were hard to hear because of the Suzuki's air-conditioner, but to Conroy it sounded as though Cardoso was telling someone, in Spanish, that he would work by himself from here on.

In Spanish? Conroy thought. Is he talking to Ramon?

He started feeling hopeful. After traveling halfway around the globe on a speculation, they were perhaps about to come up with something conclusive.

"He's heading toward the Jebel Ali container port, I think," Deakin said.

"I see the cargo cranes," Keely said from the Rover's passenger seat. "Look."

Conroy could see them as well, spidery lattices dancing in the heat. The Rover was moving through a huge industrial complex: the Dubal aluminum smelter, an extrusion plant, a gas processing refinery, a steelworks, all on a monumental, pitiless scale that dwarfed the human and vehicle traffic moving along the main road and the narrower roads leading into the industrial areas.

"The roundabout's just ahead," Deakin observed. "If he turns right, he's going to the container port. Wait one. Okay. There, he went right. This is the only way out unless he goes overland. We'd better watch from here."

"Okay," Conroy said. He pulled over, got out and opened the hood to give a reason for the halt. "Could you tell if he was following somebody?" he asked, leaning into the Rover's cab through the open window. With the engine and the air-conditioning off, the interior was heating up in a hurry.

"No," Deakin answered. "But he's stopped. I can just see him, way up the road. Now he's pulled off, out of sight. We'd better shut up now. I'm getting out of the way."

Hurry up and wait, Conroy thought. Although this is the first time Cardoso's moved significantly. As far as we know. I should be glad we're moving at all.

"Is he waiting for Ramon, do you think?" Keely asked from the far side of the cab.

He looked at her. Like Conroy and Deakin, she was

wearing Arab's men's dress: a white *dishdasha* topped by a checked head cloth held in place by the twisted black cord of the *aqal*. She'd used bronzing cream to darken her skin, and with the sunglasses hiding her green eyes she could pass plausibly for a young Arab male. Conroy, with his darker coloring, looked quite natural in the garments.

They'd nearly had a row over the degree to which Keely could participate in the surveillance on Cardoso. The morning after Deakin — a CIA case officer working out of Abu Dhabi under U.S. Embassy cover — had set up the surveillance routine, she'd asked Conroy if she could accompany him during his spells of watch. Conroy had refused point-blank; there was too much risk that Cardoso might recognize her if he happened, through bad luck or his own countersurveillance, to catch sight of her. Conroy had thought she was going to blow up at him, but for some reason she'd simply gone silent and returned to her hotel room.

He found out why that evening. He came back from his watch — he and Deakin were alternating with a second team — to find an Arab sitting at the desk in his room, his back to Conroy and apparently quite at his ease. Conroy was armed with a Beretta in a belt holster under a loose shirt, but he hadn't drawn it in case the Arab was a hotel official. Then the Arab turned and took off his sunglasses. It was, of course, Keely.

"Jesus Christ," Conroy exploded. "Don't ever do that again. You might have got shot."

"It's that convincing?" she inquired, unalarmed.

"Yes, damn it."

"Then I should be able to go out with you, shouldn't I? After all, you and Deakin and his people are wandering around in the things."

There was more argument, but he'd known that in the face of her determination he was only postponing defeat. Finally, he'd agreed to it over Deakin's protests. There wasn't much trouble she could get into, anyway; they were supposed to do no more than track Cardoso and monitor any meetings with another party — they hoped with Ramon Guevara. No direct action was to be taken against either of the Cubans while they were on UAE soil.

"Well, maybe he's meeting Ramon," he told Keely, looking past her into the Piranesi landscapes of the industrial zone. "Maybe it's something else altogether. But he's sure as guns meeting somebody, and somebody he hasn't had to look hard for. Except for moving from Abu Dhabi to Dubai, he's hardly left his hotel room."

"But I wonder where he went that first day, before we got here?"

Conroy frowned. That was a fly in the ointment. There'd been a foul-up in communications, and the CIA station chief in Abu Dhabi hadn't put a tight enough surveillance on Cardoso after he arrived. He'd been trailed to his hotel all right, the Meridien, but only one man had been assigned to him after he'd been checked in for a couple of hours. Cardoso had suddenly emerged from the hotel's underground parking lot, driving a Mazda, and had vanished into the traffic while the single surveillance officer was frantically trying to get backup. He'd even missed the number plate, so they couldn't track the source of the vehicle, and when Cardoso eventually returned to the hotel he turned up out of nowhere, on foot.

Then, however, the Cuban stayed put for almost two days, until the day before yesterday, when he suddenly moved by taxi up to Dubai. There he checked into the Dubai Hilton. Conroy and Keely and the rest of the surveillance team had moved to Dubai with him, but in neither the Meridien nor the Hilton had Deakin been able to get a tap into the Cuban officer's communications.

But as soon as he reached Dubai, matters had begun to come to a head. That night Cardoso walked out of the hotel and down to a car park near the Creek, where he had simply climbed into the Suzuki he was now driving, and taken it to the Hilton car park. The station in Abu Dhabi ran a check on the license number: the Suzuki belonged to a Palestinian businessman who was known to do "favors" for the PLO representation office in Abu Dhabi.

"There it is," Keely had said when the information came through. "Ramon, Cardoso and the PLO. It fits the political scenario we put together in Washington. None of those people wants Havana to normalize things with the United

States. I'm sure they're working on a major terrorist strike."

On the strength of this, Deakin secured a bug and a tracker beacon from the Abu Dhabi station, and the following night got himself into the Hilton car park and installed both devices in the Suzuki. He reported on his return that the Suzuki was equipped with a car telephone, but he hadn't had the equipment to wire it. They decided to leave well enough alone and settled down to wait.

And the waiting had ended ninety minutes ago, when the Suzuki emerged from the cark park and set off southward through Dubai, toward the coast road. Now the wait was starting again, with Cardoso somewhere nearby, waiting for something or someone, and his watchers doing the same.

Five minutes passed. The tracker didn't budge, and the only sound from the bug monitor was the rumble of Cardoso's air-conditioning.

Damn his eyes anyway, Conroy thought. What the devil is he waiting for?

Ramon and al-Bakr levered the top off the long wooden crate and laid it on the concrete floor beside the satchel containing the cartel money. Above the two men the ceiling of the warehouse receded into shadows made deeper by the small skylights set into the roof. A dim shaft of sunlight from one of the skylights fell into the crate, dully illuminating a layer of plastic-bubble packing.

"The crate is lined," al-Bakr said. "And there's a dehydrator. You won't have any trouble with condensation."

Ramon nodded absentmindedly and began to strip back the layers of packing. Underneath the layers was a set of racks, in which were stowed long metal bars with hexagonal cross sections.

"The drill bits are on top," al-Bakr pointed out.

"Help me get them out."

The arms dealer bent over the crate; metal clanged as the two men removed the bits and put them on top of the crate's lid. Under the last layer of bits was a shorter rack, and in it were three slender greenish-gray rods about four feet long. Metal mesh covered each end of the rods.

"The mesh is for the X-ray machines," al-Bakr explained.

"It will prevent the fins and the shape of the warheads from being detected. The launch rails and ignition wiring are wrapped in mesh also, down on the crate bottom."

Ramon nodded again and pulled aside a section of mesh to reveal the smooth ogival taper of a warhead and the transparent eye in its tip, the viewing port for the missile's laser guidance system.

"Documentation?" he asked, letting the metal fall into place.

"The installation and field manuals are with the firing equipment. They will not be difficult for anyone with your experience of engineering and munitions. Also, the C4 plastic explosive you wanted — five kilograms — is in a canister shaped as are the drill bits. The detonators are packed separately, of course."

"Good," Ramon said. "It's very good." I'll get it all through, he thought, unless the crate is physically searched all the way to the bottom at the other end. But that is unlikely. "The laser guidance?" he asked.

"Over here."

This crate was smaller and squarer. Inside were various black boxes, cables and things that looked like telescopes. "The manifests are for electronic surveying equipment," al-Bakr said. "That, in fact, is what the top layer is. The lower layer is for the missiles." He smiled faintly. "Avoid confusing them. Again, the documentation is at the bottom of the crate. There is no charge for the real surveying equipment, by the way."

"Thank you," Ramon said. "The battery pack for the laser sight. Will it be necessary to recharge it before use?"

"The batteries hold their charge for several months without significant depletion. But it would be best to verify the charge before deploying the weapons."

"I'll do that," Ramon said.

They sealed the crates, and al-Bakr handed over the receiver's copies of the cargo manifests. "The ship sails this evening and is due in Tampico on April 19," he said. "Is that satisfactory?"

"Perfectly." Ramon knelt beside the satchel of money and opened it.

"I took the liberty," al-Bakr said, "of counting out the three hundred thousand dollars. Only to save time. It's in the plastic bag. If you would like to recount —"

Ramon shook his head. "No," he said. He extracted the plastic bag and handed it to the arms dealer. "I trust your reputation."

Al-Bakr executed a small bow. "Thank you. Were the passports satisfactory?"

"Yes. Very." Al-Bakr had delivered them on time, as promised. One was American, one Filipino; Ramon had immediately checked out of the Sheraton and moved to the Inter-Continental, using the Filipino passport as identification. If there was anyone remotely interested in his Panamanian identity, this effectively broke the trail. He had then used the forged temporary driving permit to rent a four-wheel drive Toyota Landcruiser.

Al-Bakr bowed again. "It has been a pleasure to do business with you, major. Let me know if I can be of assistance to you in the future. Now, it would be preferable if you were to depart first. Go with God."

"And you also," Ramon answered. "Shall I go out by the same way I came in?"

"Yes. Please."

Ramon turned from the Arab and retraced his steps, leaving the warehouse by the small side door where he had entered. Outside the warehouse's air-conditioned interior the heat and humidity were fierce, the sun just past its zenith. Under it the Jebel Ali container port and free trade zone baked in the incandescent light, the tall, spidery loading cranes down by the waterfront shimmering in vertical waves of superheated air.

Ramon brushed perspiration out of his eyes and got into the Toyota. He was packed, out of the Inter-Continental hotel in Dubai and ready to go; all there was left to do was drive the eighty kilometers south from Jebel Ali to the Abu Dhabi airport, book his flight to the Philippines via Singapore and be gone. He would stay put in Manila for two weeks, then go to Mazatlan in Mexico to collect the shipment from al-Bakr. By that time Portela and Menocal should have vanished from Dallas, collected most of the necessary equipment, and as soon as Ramon arrived at their base with the weapons they could start tactical training. There was enough time to complete all the preparations; not a great deal, but enough.

And then, Ramon thought as he wheeled the Toyota toward the zone's south security gate, we'll do it. I probably won't survive, and it's likely neither will Luis and Joel, but we talked about that, the revolution will live through our deaths if our deaths are necessary. My father acts through me. The oppressors thought he was dead, that he couldn't ever trouble them again, but they were wrong, and I'll show them how wrong they were. And after us there will be others like us. The Americans and the Russians and the bourgeois democrats of Europe think the revolution's over with, that it failed, it's garbage. Wrong.

He grinned ferociously, then the grin softened. He had yet to tell Luis and Joel who his father was. If their resolution were to need stiffening, that would do it. Neither did they know the identity of the target; that would come at the beginning of the training. He rather looked forward to their reaction when they found out. No one had ever dared such an act. It would make even their deaths worthwhile, if they died in the attack.

He checked out through the security gate, handing over the dated authorization al-Bakr had sent him along with the passports. Now he was clear. A few more hours and he'd be in the air; the plane left at eight this evening.

He drove slowly out of the port area until he was able to pick up the Jebel Ali bypass road that led southwest toward the old Dubai-Abu Dhabi border twenty kilometers away. The cranes of the port slipped out of sight below the horizon, leaving nothing on either side of the bypass road but scrub desert and the occasional corpse of a car-struck baby camel desiccating quietly under the blaze of the sun. At this hour of the day there wasn't much traffic, although what there was moved fast.

Ramon began watching the rearview mirror. There was a vehicle framed in it that had been there for some time. It was staying well back, so that he couldn't tell what kind of machine it was, but it was making him uneasy. He slowed down to eighty kilometers an hour, to force the other driver either to pass or betray himself by also slowing down.

For a minute he thought the vehicle behind had in fact cut its speed, but then it began to get larger in the rearview mirror. It flew by on his left, giving Ramon only a fleeting glimpse of the driver, a man wearing sunglasses and Arab clothing. There was no one else in the vehicle, a Suzuki four-wheel drive. Ramon made a mental note of the plate number. The Suzuki receded rapidly into the heat haze ahead of Ramon's Toyota, and he relaxed a little. But in spite of his earlier decision not to carry a weapon in the Emirates, he began to wish he was armed.

There's nothing to worry about, he told himself. In a few hours I'll be out of here.

He kept his speed down, though, watching the mirror.

Conroy drove at an even hundred and ten kilometers an hour, keeping Deakin's Daihatsu just in view. By experimentation he'd determined that the other vehicle was obscured by the heat waves when it was about two kilometers ahead, and he assumed that Deakin had made the same observation and was using the effect to keep out of Cardoso's sight. Following someone out here in the open without being detected was difficult. The desert wasn't dead flat; there were sweeping ridges from time to time, but they were too far apart to allow you to keep very close to a target. According to the beacon, though, Cardoso wasn't straying from the road. There had been no telephone contacts.

"Have you ever been in a desert before?" Keely asked.

"Yeah. Egypt. I did some cross-country stuff. It looked a lot like this, but rockier."

"It's dangerous, isn't it?"

"It can be."

Deakin's voice crackled out of the transceiver. There was a lot of static interference all of a sudden, as though there were a thunderstorm nearby, but in this place such a thing was hardly likely.

"Repeat, please," Keely said, thumbing the microphone switch.

"There's somebody moving slow up ahead. It's not the

target, target must have passed him. I'm going to do the same."

Keely clicked the switch twice in acknowledgment. "Got it," Conroy said.

Another car flickered in and out of the shimmer ahead. It was white, and moving quite slowly. Conroy closed the distance in a hurry, and when he was a dozen yards behind the other car he pulled into the passing lane. He noted without paying much attention that it was a Toyota Landcruiser. Then they were by it, and swinging into the right-hand lane. Keely was peering into the side mirror.

"Oh, my God," she said.

"What?"

"Michael, that's Ramon we just passed. I'm sure it was him. He's wearing sunglasses and his mustache is gone, but it's him."

"Jesus, okay. They're meeting out here." He snatched up the microphone, remembering to keep it in front of him in case Ramon was watching for such an action from behind. But the Toyota was well back. "Tic-tac," he said, "that was the secondary target you just passed."

Static, then:

"You sure?"

He glanced at Keely, who nodded. "Affirmative," he said.

"Okay," Deakin said. "Primary's still moving, though. They'll meet when he stops. Keep going."

Several minutes went by.

"Hold on," Deakin said suddenly. "Primary's dropped into view. Pulling off near a — a building. I'm too close, I'll have to go by. You, too. You're bracketed."

"Okay," Conroy said.

"Now what?" Keely asked.

"We go on out of sight. If they've both stopped, we're okay. If they're playing leapfrog, with Ramon passing Cardoso to see if we've stopped up ahead, we're in trouble. There's nowhere to hide out here."

Keely looked into the side mirror. "There's nobody behind us."

"It's a bloody good thing we've got the beacon," he said. "Get down in the seat. If Cardoso's watching for followers, I don't want him seeing you. Even if you look like an Arab."

She did so. The tires whined and hummed. Another minute passed, and up ahead Conroy saw the building Deakin had noted. Well beyond it, there was a low, sweeping ridge. Up there, he thought. Across the ridge. We can monitor from there, I hope. Where the hell is this static coming from?

The Rover shot by the small dilapidated building and as they passed it Conroy saw in the rearview mirror that Cardoso's Suzuki was parked on its blind side. The Suzuki would be invisible to Ramon as he approached the building. Cardoso was nowhere to be seen.

Another few kilometers passed under the Toyota's wheels. There were no other travelers in sight, ahead or behind. No one had passed Ramon since those three vehicles earlier. They'd gone by very fast, not hanging back a little as followers would have while they tried to make up their minds what to do. Ramon hummed tunelessly to himself, thinking of nothing, watching the road.

Well ahead there was a white blur by the roadside. As he approached, it resolved itself slowly out of the heat glimmer, a small derelict concrete structure, perhaps the ruin of a police checkpoint near the old Dubai-Abu Dhabi border. Ramon squinted at it suspiciously.

If there's an ambush before the airport, he thought, it's here.

He slowed down somewhat. The building appeared deserted, wavering in its envelope of heat. Nobody professional would try a shot from there, Ramon told himself, not at a car traveling at high speed. I'm jumping at shadows.

He pressed the accelerator to the floor and the Toyota jumped ahead, quickly gathering speed. The ruin drew nearer. He'd be by it in seconds. For a moment he thought of dropping sideways on the seat as he went by, but rejected the idea. At this speed it would be too easy to lose control of the Toyota. Anyway, the road ahead was clear, except that a thin black line was suddenly snaking its way across the lighter asphalt—

Caltrops.

Ramon slammed his foot on the brakes and wrenched at the steering wheel, entirely too late. Both the Toyota's front wheels ran across the spike-studded band of stiff fabric, and both tires blew out almost simultaneously. The Toyota's nose dropped and the vehicle spun, the front tires shredding off the rims and the rims grinding plumes of sparks from the road surface. Ramon yanked his foot off the brake and tried to fight the Toyota straight, but the vehicle was skidding sideways toward the verge of the road, and the wrecked front tires gave no purchase. He felt the back end hit the soft sand of the shoulder, and the world inverted itself, dust showering from the Toyota's floor into his face as the vehicle went over. He fell from behind the steering wheel onto the roof, striking his head violently, then vaguely felt himself slammed sideways across the back of the seat as the Toyota continued its roll. It smashed over onto its passenger side and tried to keep turning, but there was not enough momentum left and it fell back again to skid another ten yards in a shower of sand and gravel.

Ramon vaguely sensed that everything had finally stopped moving. He was not quite unconscious, crumpled up against the passenger door at the bottom of the wreck. His neck hurt, and he could smell gasoline and oil on hot metal. Something was rumbling faintly, and he realized through the haze that it was a wheel spinning little by little to a stop. A hot desert breeze floated in through the smashed windshield.

I must turn off the ignition, he thought. Fire.

The keys were still in the ignition lock on the steering column, at what seemed a long distance above his head. He tried to move, untangle himself from the gearshift. His body still seemed to work, although it hurt abominably, and nothing seemed to be broken.

He managed to sit upright on the still-intact side window and was reaching toward the keys when a shadow fell across the vertical wall of the Toyota's hood. Ramon realized that he had forgotten about the caltrops and about the other car.

The Suzuki's driver was peering into the Toyota at him, peering over the sights of a large black revolver. He had taken off his sunglasses. Ramon looked at him. It was Colonel Cardoso.

"I'm glad you're alive, Major Linares," Cardoso said. "Get out and come with me."

The Daihatsu and the Rover were well off the road on the west side of the ridge. There was absolutely no cover.

Maybe we can pass for Bedouin from a distance, Conroy thought as he clambered out of the Rover and went over to Deakin's Daihatsu. A lot of them use trucks and cars nowadays.

Deakin had turned off his engine and air-conditioning so as to hear the bug's transmission better. His Arab clothing made him look much heavier than he was; under them, Conroy knew, the man was thin as a bean. He was lantern-jawed, with somewhat bucked teeth. At this particular instant he was frowning.

"What?" Conroy said.

"Nothing at the moment. Maybe the second car hasn't reached Cardoso yet. It should have, though. Damn that air conditioner of his. I should have put the bug under the seat. But I heard him get out of the car when we were a few hundred meters past him."

Conroy sensed Keely come up beside him. "So did we," he said. "But as far as I can tell he hasn't got back in yet."

"There was that odd noise, a couple of minutes ago," Keely observed, "a kind of pop, and then scraping sounds. But it might have been him doing something with the engine."

"I don't know what the hell's going on," Deakin confessed.

"Ah," said Keely, with a quick intake of breath. They all heard it: the snick of a car door latch, thuds and bumps. Deakin reached under the dash and switched on the recorder.

"In," said a voice, in Spanish. Conroy thought it was Cardoso's.

More clicks, sounds of things moving.

"That should hold you," the same voice said. A pause. "Is this all there is left? Where's the rest of it?"

A second voice made an incomprehensible noise. Conroy saw Keely's lips move. *Ramon.*

"Answer me."

"Go to hell," the second voice said. "Why don't you just shoot me and get it over with?"

Conroy and Deakin and Keely looked at each other in total confusion. "What the fuck?" Deakin murmured.

"Not here," Cardoso's voice said. "Out in the desert. And there are some things I want to ask you. Although if you cooperate ... you were one of my officers once, Ramon. I do not really want to execute you."

"But you will," Ramon said. "No matter what I do."

"Think on it," Cardoso said, and Conroy heard the Suzuki's engine rev as the Cuban put it into gear.

"Jesus Christ on a bicycle," Deakin said softly, "They're not working together at all."

"Follow them," Keely said. "We've got to keep in bug transmitter range. What's that? Five kilometers?"

"In good conditions," Conroy said, "but there's a lot of interference today."

"There's a sandstorm somewhere not far off," Deakin said. "Sand grains rubbing together when it's dry. Makes static electricity. Sometimes you can see lightning."

"We *are* being monitored in Abu Dhabi, aren't we?" Keely asked.

"Not particularly. Not on a surveillance. But I should check in."

He changed transmitter frequencies and said, "Tic-tac to Rig. Over."

The only answer was a burst of static and something behind it that might have been a voice. Deakin tried twice more. Static.

"We're out of contact, damn it," he said. "We've been having a lot of radio problems lately. Solar flares. Sometimes it's worse out here."

"We'd better get moving before they're out of range," Conroy said. "We need to hear as much as we can."

"Okay," Deakin said. "Let's go."

Ramon's wrists were handcuffed to the grab rail above the front passenger window but Cardoso, taking no chances, was driving with his right hand on the steering wheel and the

revolver in his left. Occasionally, in order to change gears, he
had to put the revolver in his lap, but it was never out of his
hand for more than a few seconds. Ramon knew that he
might be able to deliver a kick at Cardoso at a vulnerable
moment, but with his hands secured awkwardly above his
head he wouldn't be able to put disabling power into the
blow. It was a bad idea, anyway; even if he did kill or incapacitate Cardoso, or manage to overturn the Suzuki by a judi-
cious kick at the accelerator, the handcuff key wouldn't likely
fall within reach. And Ramon did not want to be chained in
the oven of an overturned vehicle to die in an agony of heat
and thirst. He preferred the dignity of a bullet.

Cardoso had found an indistinct track leading southeast
into the desert, and was managing to sustain a good fifty
kilometers an hour over its rough surface. The Suzuki jolted
and bounced, the springs protesting. Outside the cab the
scrub thorn grew sparser as the land became more arid. The
horizon ahead was blurred and indistinct, as though the
desert tones were washing into the sky.

They traveled in silence for some twenty minutes. Then
Cardoso said, "Why did you take the money?"

"I needed it," Ramon said. Cardoso had tossed the money
satchel and Ramon's luggage into the back of the Suzuki
after handcuffing him to the grab rail. He obviously didn't
want any traces of Ramon left for passersby to find. Ramon
thought: If there were some way to kill him and escape, I still
have everything I need.

"What for? What was the money for?"

Ramon didn't answer. There was more sand than gravel
outside now, and a hint of dune formation. He could see
puffs of sand being picked up and dropped by the wind. The
puffs seemed to move in quick swirls and spirals, like dust
devils at home.

"You came here to buy weapons from al-Bakr, didn't
you? That's what you did with the cartel money. Some of it.
What is your target?"

"You'll find out," Ramon murmured.

"Even with you not there to handle the matter?"

Ramon shrugged.

"Menocal and Portela will carry on, is that right?"

Cardoso asked. "Is that what you think?"

"They will," Ramon said, although he knew that with him gone, they wouldn't be able to. They didn't know about the weapons that would come to Tampico, or the nature of the target.

"No, they won't," Cardoso said. "We've already grabbed them. There's nobody left, Ramon."

"Bluff away, colonel. How did you track me?"

Cardoso shrugged. "We're checking everywhere. I was sent here. You were here."

"No, I mean why did you decide I wasn't dead?"

"We almost did," Cardoso told him. "But a certain woman who works for the Americans came asking questions about you. Her name is Dr. Keely Fitzgerald. She went to see your mother. Why did she do that, Ramon?"

"I have never heard of such a woman."

"Haven't you? Or is it really the Americans you're working for? Is the CIA going to use you to attack the cartel? Maybe it isn't the Americans you're targeting after all?"

"You're too devious for your own peace of mind," Ramon said. "What I was planning to do is much more straightforward."

"And what is it?"

Ramon refused to answer. He wondered idly whether Cardoso would try to torture it out of him. He'd face that when and if he had to. For the moment he turned inward, thinking. Try as he might, he could see no way out of his impasse, unless Cardoso took the chance of removing him from the Suzuki before killing him. But the colonel would be very careful even then. It was the smallest of chances, vanishingly small.

I was so close, Ramon thought in a cold rage. Only a few more hours. And all because of that woman, the Fitzgerald woman, whoever she is. Who is she?

They drove on in silence.

A kilometer and a half behind the Suzuki in the worsening visibility, Conroy tried to contact Deakin. Although he was only fifty meters behind Deakin's Jeep the transmission broke up badly. Deakin stopped, and Conroy pulled up behind him. The lanky man came back to the Rover and Conroy rolled down his window.

"The bug's not getting much through in this," Deakin said. He had to raise his voice because of the wind. "The beacon's still good, though. What do you want to do?"

Dust blew into Conroy's eyes. "We'll have to get closer. Can we risk it?"

"I think so. We should be able to get within two hundred meters in this. At that range the beacon gives accurate distances."

"We can't let Cardoso kill him," Keely said urgently. "This isn't at all what we thought. Even if Ramon's dead, the others may go on without him. He's our only link to whoever they are."

"We weren't supposed to touch him," Deakin said doubtfully. "It could cause all sorts of problems. I don't even know where we'd put him."

"It could cause all sorts of worse problems if we don't do it," Conroy said. "Keely's right. We're going to have to intervene."

"Okay," Deakin said. "It's your diplomatic disaster. Shall we do it right now?"

Conroy thought for a moment and decided to take a calculated risk. "No. Let's close up as much as we can and still stay out of sight.That'll improve the bug reception. As soon as they stop, though, we'll have to go after them. If Ramon gets away from Cardoso into the desert, well, we'll have to take our chances picking him up later."

"Can't you sort of sneak up on them?" Keely asked.

"No," Deakin said. "Not in these conditions. This sort of thing, you have to go in as fast as you can. Get them off balance for a couple seconds, you've got the edge. Hit them hard and fast and keep hitting."

"What about Cardoso?"

"Let him go," Conroy told her. "We can turn the UAE authorities loose on him. He's a lot less important than Ramon is now. Let's go. We can't lose that beacon."

Ramon estimated that the Suzuki must be nearly thirty kilometers into the deep desert by now, and there was hardly any scrub vegetation at all. The track wound among three-meter dunes. Between the dunes, where the track didn't run, there was dun sand mixed with patches of gravel. The southeast horizon was pale lemon yellow, and the sun's disk was becoming indistinct.

"What's wrong with you?" Cardoso asked suddenly.

"Is that a stupid question, do you think?"

"That's not what I meant. I've been watching you. Most men would be showing some fear. You don't."

"It's because I'm not afraid," Ramon said. It was true. He'd never felt what the others seemed to feel in Yemen or Angola or Ethiopia. There was, he imagined, some kind of short circuit in his emotions, in his brain somewhere.

"I remember," Cardoso said. "You were always like that. I used to wonder if it was willpower."

"No," Ramon said. "It wasn't." There seemed to be a lot of dust in the air all of a sudden. Visibility wasn't much more than two hundred meters. Ramon couldn't understand why Cardoso wasn't taking any account of it.

"Why have you wasted yourself like this?" Cardoso was asking. "You could have done anything."

"This is what I'm doing," Ramon told him. "Why did you decide to do what you're doing? You betrayed the revolution. You betrayed what we were fighting for. You betrayed me."

"Oh, it's like that, is it?" Cardoso said with a short, ironic laugh. "The old revolutionary platitudes. There *is* no revolution, Ramon. There never was. There are only people trying to grab power for themselves. It's just a matter of different names for the same old things."

"I'd kill you if I could," Ramon told him.

"I know. Do you know who you are?"

"Yes. Do you?"

"Che Guevara's son. Your mother told you, didn't she? And not long ago. Is that what's sent you over the edge like this?"

"I'm not over any edge."

Cardoso grimaced. "There are none so blind as those who will not see."

"It's people like you who murdered my father," Ramon

snarled, fury getting the better of him for an instant.

"It was better it happened," Cardoso said evenly. "There's nothing sadder than an old revolutionary, gone to fat in the belly and babbling about the hero he was once. Like Fidel."

"Does Fidel know what you do?"

"How should I know? If he does, he doesn't care, or he'd stop me. There's your revolution for you."

"It isn't over. The revolution won't ever be over."

Cardoso only snorted. Then he said, "Almost fifty kilometers. This will be far enough."

"A bullet in the back of the head, is it?"

Cardoso was gearing down for a patch of soft sand that had blown onto the track. Wind-driven grains of it scratched at the windshield and the metal panels of the Suzuki. "You don't seem to understand," Cardoso said. "It isn't the money. And if it were only me, I'd likely let you go. But I recruited you. You betrayed the cartel. If I don't deal with you, I'll be executed. Be glad it was me instead of some of the others. They'd have tortured you to death."

The Suzuki stopped.

"We're about to have a sandstorm," Ramon pointed out. "Are you really going out in that?"

"There's still some visibility," Cardoso said. He switched off the engine, put the keys carefully into his pocket and set the hand brake. Then he opened his door and got out. Hot, dry wind, crackling with static electricity and loaded with sand, blasted into the cab. Cardoso slammed the door and walked around the hood to Ramon's side. Ramon watched him carefully. He's going to get me out, he thought. He doesn't want traces of my death in the car. Keeping things tidy.

He thought for a moment that he'd be able to slam the door into Cardoso's body as Cardoso opened it, but the colonel placed himself at its rear edge before swinging it open. "The revolver's cocked," he said to Ramon. "It will fire at a touch. Don't move."

He covered Ramon carefully as he leaned forward to wind down the passenger window. Then he slammed the door closed on Ramon again. This protected him from kicks. Cardoso then set the muzzle of the gun under Ramon's jaw, reached inside the cab and unlocked the handcuffs. They sprang free and dropped onto Ramon's lap. Cardoso backed quickly away.

"Open the door very slowly," he said, "and get out."

Even at two hundred meters' range the bug transmission was breaking up. Conroy strained to hear what was going on in the Suzuki. It was hard to tell if it was stopped or not.

There, the unmistakable sound of the engine switched off. Maybe Cardoso or Ramon would say something, a last scrap of information.

"— touch. Don't —" More static. Door banging again.

Let's go, Conroy thought. The Daihatsu Jeep didn't move. Deakin, Conroy thought, let's go.

He isn't hearing it.

Conroy let out the clutch with a rush and rammed the accelerator down. Get as much speed as possible on the harder surface of the track. Three yards from the Daihatsu Conroy wrenched the wheel and swung the Rover off the track to pass the other vehicle. He caught a glimpse of Deakin's startled face as the Rover lurched past, its tires slithering in the soft off-track sand, and sensed rather than saw Deakin belatedly start to move.

"Keep down!" he yelled into the backseat, where he'd put Keely for safekeeping. He should have known better than to bring her, he should have known it might turn into something more than surveillance. Never mind now, stay on the track, they couldn't be far away—

There.

He saw the humped shape of the Suzuki in the yellow gloom and two shadowy figures beyond it, then the Rover's front wheels had slipped off the left edge of the almost-invisible track and he was fighting to keep it from spinning. Deakin's Jeep, on firmer ground, went flying by on Conroy's right, toward the Suzuki and the shapeless men, one of whom was raising an arm, pointing it at the Daihatsu, and Conroy heard the dull double boom of the shots as he straightened the Rover and slammed the brakes on. It shuddered to a stop and he was rolling out the door onto the sand and gravel, part of his mind hearing two more booms, then clangs and thuds as the bullets hit the Rover's bodywork. Then a violent, grinding crash.

Jesus, Cardoso's good.

Counting the shots. Four. Useless without knowing what kind of weapon he had. Conroy was crouched behind the Rover. He couldn't see what had become of the Daihatsu and Deakin; they were hidden behind his vehicle. He couldn't remember having drawn the Beretta, but it was in his hand.

"Keely, slide out this side and onto the sand," he whispered. "Quick!" Vehicles were death traps in a firefight; any powerful handgun would punch a bullet through thin bodywork without difficulty. Or fuel tanks. You had to be behind the engine block, or at least a wheel.

She got out. Conroy was puzzled. Nothing seemed to be happening. Cautiously, he peered around the tread of a front tire.

He felt suddenly sick. The Daihatsu had slammed hood-first into a two-meter boulder, and Conroy could see Deakin slumped over the steering wheel. One of Cardoso's first two shots must have hit the CIA man, or the Daihatsu, or both.

Cardoso.

Conroy peered through the thickening murk. This wasn't just a high wind any more, it appeared to be the onset of a sandstorm. Through the driving grains Conroy could make out the prone figure of a man on the ground some thirty meters away. Cardoso or Ramon? Whichever one it was, the other was still on the loose, and maybe armed.

This is a royal mess, he thought. We were supposed to do nothing but track Cardoso and listen to him, and now we've got casualties and a chance one of them's Ramon. Christ, what a screwup.

He couldn't crouch behind the Rover for the rest of the afternoon. He had to see to Deakin, to start with.

"Stay here, keep down," he whispered to Keely. She nodded. She'd lost the sunglasses somewhere along the line, and her eyes were large and frightened.

Very carefully, he slithered from behind the wheel. Nobody shot at him. He ran in a crouch to the Daihatsu, whose radiator was steaming gently, and gingerly looked into the cab.

There was no hope for Deakin. A large-caliber bullet had hit him squarely in the throat.

That should have been me, Conroy thought. If he hadn't gone past me like that—

He dropped into a crouch again. Cardoso or Ramon?

Conroy scuttled toward the body in the sand until he was close enough to see that it was Cardoso. The back of his head had been smashed in with a rock. Ramon grabbing his chance. There was no sign of a gun near him. Ramon wouldn't have missed taking it, and he was still out there somewhere. How far would he have run?

You idiot, Conroy thought, he hasn't run far at all. We're fifty kilometers into the desert. He needs transportation.

He looked wildly around. Sand rasped at his cheeks, forced his eyes almost shut. He could see the Rover's outlines, just, but the Suzuki had vanished. Suddenly, over the hiss and howl of the wind, he heard the growl of a starter and the sudden boom of an engine.

Ramon.

He ran toward where he thought the Suzuki might be, but it didn't appear. The engine noise grew louder, then dropped, gears changing. Conroy ran back to the Rover. Keely was huddled in its lee.

"Get in, he's getting away," he shouted at her. She scrambled in by the rear door while Conroy threw himself behind the Rover's steering wheel and started the engine. Ramon would be returning along the trail, he wouldn't go deeper into the desert — or would he? Choose. Along the trail, then. Conroy swung the wheel. The track was almost impossible to see. You weren't ever supposed to drive in a dust storm or a sandstorm.

"Goddamnit," Conroy swore. "I let him get away." The air conditioner was clattering badly; the engine had taken a hit.

"There was only one of you," Keely gasped, hanging onto the seat back as the Rover thrashed its way over the sand spits drifting across the track. "What could you do? What *are* you doing?"

"Following him. The beacon —"

He looked down. The beacon's readout was dark. "Look under the dash," Conroy told her.

She climbed into the front seat and peered beneath it. "There's bits of metal and plastic all over the place," she said. "And I think the back of the radio transmitter's smashed."

"We'll keep going. He's got to stay on the track."

They floundered through the wind for three or four kilometers. There was no sign of Ramon ahead of them. Then, without warning, Conroy began to smell hot metal. He looked at the instrument panel. The coolant temperature reading was low, but the oil temperature was high in the red.

"That's that," he said flatly. "We've lost our radiator. Cardoso must have hit it." He pulled up quickly and turned the engine off, hoping it wouldn't catch fire.

"Now what do we do?" Keely asked.

"Wait for the storm to pass. There's an emergency desert kit in the back. Or so Deakin said when we started watching Cardoso. It's supposed to be in that locker behind you."

He climbed into the rear seat, leaned over its back into the cargo space and unlatched the locker. Inside was a jerrycan of water, about ten liters of it; a medical pack containing salt tablets, aspirin, bandages and ointments; matches; reflective panels for signaling to searching aircraft; a couple of large packs of clear plastic sheeting; a mirror; a compass; smoke flares; a knife; two wool blankets; and a roll of string.

"Could be worse," he said. "We'll be okay for a day or two."

"And then?"

"Then we'll be in trouble. But we'll be found before then."

"I don't suppose we could walk out? It can't be much more than thirty kilometers to the coast road."

Conroy frowned. "Don't even think about it. This is one of the worst deserts in the world. We have to stay with the Rover, no matter what."

"What about going back to see if Deakin's transmitter works?"

Conroy considered. "We might try that, if nobody turns up by tomorrow evening. The trouble is, Abu Dhabi doesn't know where we were going. They'll start looking pretty soon, but it's a hell of a big desert."

"How long is this storm likely to last?"

"I'm not sure. In the Egyptian desert they can go on for a day, or days sometimes. I don't know if they're like that here."

"Oh, no," she said. "The tape recorder. It's in Deakin's Jeep. What if it was smashed and we lost the tape?"

"The tape's likely all right. But how much we got on it I don't know. Remember how bad the reception was."

"Yes. I'm sure they said something about who Ramon was here to see, but I couldn't for the life of me make it out."

"Neither could I. Maybe the computers can make something out of it."

"But we've got two more names. Menocal, Portela. Where are they, I wonder?"

"I wonder where Ramon is, more to the point," Conroy said.

Ramon was piloting the Suzuki through the hissing yellow murk. The trail was almost impossible to see because of the sand flowing along the ground, like the pelt of some huge sliding desert mammal. Visibility wasn't much more than a dozen meters. It was that, plus the fact that there were only two rounds left in Cardoso's revolver, that had decided him against ambushing his pursuers.

There wasn't a hint of anyone behind him. Ramon hadn't thought there would be. The bigger of the two strange vehicles had been hit in the radiator, he was pretty sure; he'd seen the spark from the grillwork as Cardoso's last shot struck it, almost at the instant he brained Cardoso with the rock. He'd had Cardoso's *dishdasha* up and was grabbing in the colonel's pocket for the Suzuki keys almost before Cardoso hit the ground; then the revolver fell at his feet, an unexpected bonus. By the time the others got themselves sorted out, Ramon was over the lip of the roadside dune, waiting to see what would happen. The poor visibility and the distraction of one of the pursuing men with his presumably dead compatriot had given Ramon the opportunity he needed.

He'd have preferred to kill that one, as well, but it hadn't been advisable. And there might have been another person in the big vehicle, he wasn't sure. With any luck at all they wouldn't be found for hours, maybe days. Maybe never. He still wasn't sure who they were; they'd been wearing Arab dress as far as he'd been able to tell. PLO maybe, working with the DGI; he knew there was a PLO office here, like the one in Havana. Perhaps they'd been Cardoso's backup, but didn't want to get involved. Until it was too late.

Something else was bothering him, though, had been bothering him for some time. He identified it at last as he slammed the Suzuki over a hump of sand drifting across the track.

How did they follow Cardoso so easily? Out here, in this muck?

Jesus Maria, there's a beacon on the car.

He stopped in a hurry and jumped into the swirling sand. Felt under the wheel wells, under the frame. Nothing.

I have to find it. They may have backup waiting out there somewhere.

He wriggled under the Suzuki, searching. Still nothing. He kept looking. Finally he found it: a small metal box right up past the exhaust pipe. The pipe burned his hand and he swore under his breath as he tugged the magnets loose. He slithered from under the Suzuki and dropped the beacon into the sand. If they were looking for him, they'd think he'd stopped to let the storm blow itself out.

As he climbed into the cab, he thought again. If they'd got one bug into the Suzuki, they might have got two.

Search again, every nook and cranny. Finally he located it under the dash: a tiny FM transmitter. Ramon cradled it in the palm of his hand, staring at it. Cardoso, you half-wit, he thought. So sure of yourself and your PLO friends.

He tossed the bug out the window and sat for a moment, trying to remember the details of the conversation he'd had with the colonel. He had said next to nothing, he was sure of it. But Cardoso had spoken four names: Portela, Menocal, al-Bakr. And his own: Ramon.

It wasn't likely the first two names would help the PLO, if that was who they were. Not at the moment, anyway. And his own ... well, Cardoso would have told them who he was anyway. What worried him was the reference to the arms dealer. Could they stop the shipment somehow?

He didn't think so. He'd seen the size of al-Bakr's warehouse, and the vast quantity of containers and stores inside it; the Arab obviously dealt in merchandise other than arms. The PLO couldn't do anything at this point. They'd have no idea what his shipment looked like, what it contained, and even less where it was going or how. It was probably already gone.

He had to get out, though. And he had only four hours to escape the desert and reach the airport. That was a risk, the airport. But he'd have to take it, and trust to the Filipino passport and the fact that everyone looking for him would think he was out here in the middle of a sandstorm.

A compass was fastened to the Suzuki's dash. Ramon studied it. He'd watched Cardoso's direction carefully on the way in, and he thought he knew approximately where he now was in relation to the coast. He'd risk going across country, not the least because there might be someone waiting for him at the junction of the track and the coast road.

He hauled at the steering wheel and gingerly drove the Suzuki off the track, heading west by northwest.

Toward nightfall the wind dropped and the air began to clear. Conroy allowed half a liter of water between them. The air was cooling off in a hurry; it was just comfortable now, which meant that in a few hours it would be icy. Conroy had spent an hour trying to fix the transmitter, but it was damaged beyond repair.

"Will they send out a plane in the morning, do you think?" Keely asked.

"Probably." Conroy was staring out the windshield into the rapidly darkening eastern sky. A lot of the dust had settled, and he could see stars.

"It's awful about Deakin. I liked him. Why did that have to happen?"

Conroy made a helpless gesture. "I don't know. Usually I think there's no good reason for anything."

"Did you ever think there was a reason?"

He nodded slowly. "I guess so. Once. In a way this is my fault."

"Because you kept Ramon's mother from being killed once upon a time?"

"Yeah."

"That was when you thought there were reasons?" she asked.

He nodded again in the gathering dark. "I suppose I still think there are reasons. But only everyday, prosaic ones. Not *real* reasons. Not big ones."

She was studying him, eyes solemn. "It must be awful to live like that."

"Maybe. I don't think about it much."

"Why not?"

"I did for a long time. Then I got tired of doing it because I couldn't figure it out. It was driving me crazy."

"It's odd," she said. "You're odd. You're this huge lump of contradictions. You're like two different people sometimes. Opaque. I think it's because you don't want what you think you want."

He gave a short laugh. "What do I really want?"

"I have no idea. It's what makes you so ... peculiar."

"You're a couple of degrees off dead center yourself."

"I know," she said. "Maybe it's because I think there *are* reasons. I don't understand them, but they're there. As though there were things outside us that help us or try to hurt us, that we can't see. Just sense them, sometimes. My father had the Sight, I think. He almost never talked about it. But he always seemed to know when something good or bad was going to happen."

"You've got it, too?" he asked.

"Sometimes, I think. I'm not sure."

"It's going to get cold soon," he said, unwilling for some reason to pursue the subject. "I'll get the blankets. You can sleep in the back, I'll take the front."

"Chivalry? You're bigger, you should have the back."

"It doesn't really matter. Actually, I was wondering whether we should head to the other spot and see if the transmitter in Deakin's Jeep still works. It's not that far, but we'd have to do it at night."

"You said we should wait till tomorrow evening."

"Probably we should." He was dragging the blankets out of the rear. "Want one?" he asked.

"Okay." She wrapped it around herself. They settled down

in the seats. There was silence for a few minutes.

"I've never seen stars in the desert before," she said. "They look so close."

"Yeah," Conroy said. "They do."

Another silence. Then she said, "I suppose, in the movies, this is the suitable opportunity for the hero and heroine to make love for the first time."

Conroy started in surprise. The idea had occurred to him, but it hadn't got any further than the back of his mind, and he'd been determined to keep it there.

He laughed to cover some discomfiture. "I imagine that's the way the screenwriter'd handle it. But this is reality." He paused, wondering. She didn't move toward him or make any other sign. "I don't think it's a good idea," he said finally. "It doesn't feel like the right time, does it? And there's too much else going on. We can't get distracted."

"To tell you the truth," she said, "I feel the same way."

He felt an irrational pang of annoyance. It was she who'd brought the subject up. There it was again: their mutual tendency to strike sparks from each other. He remembered how close they'd been to open hostility the first time they met.

She was looking at him. "Are you annoyed with me because I agreed with your chivalrous gesture?"

He was glad the darkness hid the flush he could feel spreading over his cheekbones. Damn the woman anyway. She'd said he was opaque, and now she saw through him. "No. Of course not."

"Mm," she said. He couldn't tell whether she believed him.

"Look," she said suddenly.

He could see a very faint, pale blur above the horizon to the northwest. A vehicle's lights.

"He hasn't come back for us?" Keely said nervously.

Maybe not, maybe it's our people, Conroy thought, but then again maybe it isn't. "Help me get as much stuff together as we can," he ordered. "We'd better get out of sight."

They packed the essentials quickly in one blanket and struggled up the dune to the south of the disabled Rover.

Conroy used the other blanket to brush out their tracks as they went. He could hear the car's engine now, laboring in low gear as it fought its way through the fresh sand blown over the trail. He stopped at the top of the dune and threw himself down, peering over the crest, holding the Beretta carefully out of the sand. Keely was just behind him.

The vehicle's light came into view around the curve of a dune a hundred meters away. Because of the glare, Conroy couldn't tell what kind of car it was, nor who was behind the wheel. He waited tensely as the machine approached the Rover and stopped several yards from it; now he could tell that it was a Daihatsu Jeep. Two men slipped over the tailgate and crouched on the ground, using the Daihatsu to screen themselves from the Rover. Conroy could see that they were carrying machine pistols.

"Who?" Keely whispered.

Conroy shook his head. They were in European clothes, but that wasn't significant.

Then, suddenly, the two men raced forward in an assault crouch, bracketing the Rover, their guns ready. In an instant they were at the doors, one front, one back, wrenching them open, gun muzzles thrusting inside.

"Nobody," one yelled in English at the Daihatsu.

Conroy got to his knees. "Sebastian! It's Conroy! Up here!"

The two men on the track looked up, startled then discomfited as Conroy and Keely slid down the face of the dune to meet them. They could easily have been ambushed from Conroy's position.

"Where the hell have you been?" Sebastian asked. He was the leader of the second surveillance team. "We spotted Cardoso's Suzuki in Abu Dhabi an hour and a half ago. Abandoned. Nothing in it. No bug, no beacon, nothing."

"How did you find us?" Keely asked in a rush.

"Luck, partly. And that wrecked Toyota by the junction of the track and the coast road. It was a long shot, we were going to use a chopper in the morning."

"Any sign of the Suzuki driver?"

"No. God knows where Cardoso is now."

"He's up the track about six kilometers, dead." Conroy

said. He took a deep breath. "So is Deakin. Cardoso shot him. The guy we were really after got away. It was my fault."

There was a brief silence. "Ah, shit," Sebastian said. "What a goddamned mess."

Dallas
April 13

■

Southeast of Dallas there lay, within a few meters of the surface of the earth, a deep bank of sand and gravel laid down by the waters of an ancient inland sea. The deposit was large enough to be a profitable source of aggregate for road subsurfaces and concrete, and it was on its western edge that Faustino (more commonly known as Miguel Darias) had established his gravel pit and construction yard. The yard was fenced, and the machinery Faustino stored there was additionally protected by a pair of Rottweiler attack dogs that ran free behind the wire when no one was in the yard.

Some fifty meters from the fence gate and not far from the edge of the gravel pit was the yard office, a long, narrow building that had been set on concrete block foundations. It was painted white, and the windows had heavy shades. The red light of the westering sun threw the shadow of the yard office far across the sandy gravel of the yard, almost as far as the equipment shed, and turned the worn yellow paint of a small bulldozer to a pastel orange.

Faustino was not inside the office, but underneath it. The trapdoor to the underground room was carefully concealed, and only a search by someone who suspected it was there would have revealed it. In the room beneath the office floor were a couple of chairs, a heavy wooden workbench and a file cabinet. The file cabinet held nothing but old work orders and contracts; Faustino never kept anything dangerous on paper, but was perennially short of storage space for his legitimate documents.

On the workbench was a large radio transmitter and receiver. The transmitter was wired into a high-quality tape deck, which Faustino used for burst transmission, and the tape deck was wired into a digital encryption processor, which was an electronic version of the spy's old one-time pad. Faustino's contacts with Havana were as secure as modern technology could make them. Burst transmission compressed several minutes of information into an electronic bleep less than a second long, and even if the burst was intercepted by the listening ears of the National Security Council, — an unlikely event, given the amount of radio traffic humming through the atmosphere — the information would be indecipherable without the unique key provided by the encryption processor. For added security the transmitter also used frequency hopping, which sliced the burst transmission into tiny segments and sent these out on randomly selected, varying radio frequencies.

Faustino was not using the transmitter; he sometimes came down here when he needed to think. At the moment, he was thinking very hard. He had destroyed the hard copy of the message he'd received from the DGI in Havana yesterday evening, burned it and ground the ashes to powder in the ashtray next to the transmitter, but he could see the words as well as if he were still staring at them.

Cardoso had vanished. The people in the UAE — likely PLO, although this was a guess on Faustino's part — had mislaid him somehow. According to the transmission, Ramon Linares had also vanished. It was doubly important now, Faustino's instructions ran, for him to locate the two men Cardoso had let slip through his fingers in March. With all possible urgency, the message had said. Faustino knew what that meant: take risks. If he was dilatory in the search, he'd be in serious trouble. He was already in fairly hot water for letting Ramon Linares make fools of the DGI and the cartel, although Faustino couldn't see even now how he could have known what the man was going to do. It was Cardoso's fault for having recruited him in the first place.

Nevertheless, it was Faustino's head on the block right now. It was unjust and irrational, but there it was.

He considered his options. He'd been looking for Joel

Portela and Luis Menocal — Cardoso had given him their real names and a pair of photographs — since the colonel left Dallas, but he'd been doing it in the usual methodical, careful way that afforded him maximum security. That was how he'd survived on enemy soil, inconspicuous and unsuspected, for all these years. But now he was going to have to edge a little more into the open.

He was going to have to pick up Portela's woman and question her. He'd exhausted all the immediate leads he had; no doubt, given time, he'd pick up the men's trail, but he wasn't being given the time. As soon as he had realized this, last night, he'd made certain telephone calls from pay phones; the two men he'd asked for would be at the rendezvous point in Dallas within an hour.

He secured the transmitter room and the office, let the dogs into the yard and set out for the city. The meeting place was off the Route 175, in a small plaza on the southeast outskirts of Dallas, just outside a fast-food emporium specializing in fried chicken. Faustino pulled up beside a gray Ford. He recognized both men in it; he'd worked with them once before. One was an Anglo, the other was a Venezuelan; they went by the names Otto and Carlos and nothing else. Both were bland of face and ordinary in physique, characteristics useful for their profession. Faustino got into the Ford's backseat. Otto was munching on a chicken leg, and the smell of cooking grease eddied through the car.

"I need a woman picked up and brought out to my yard," he said without preamble. "Immediately."

"Okay," Otto said. "Where are you going to be?"

"Not very far away," said Faustino. He produced a photograph, one Portela had obtained from the girl on the usual romantic pretext. "Her name's Teresa Bosque," he said, handing it over. Carlos and Otto took a look at it.

"Not too bad," said Otto. The woman in the photograph was wearing a bathing suit and was smiling at the camera; she was full-figured, with a round face, full lips and black hair. She had the beginnings of a double chin, but was pretty in a slightly overripe way.

"What's the trouble about her?" Carlos asked.

"I want to ask her some questions. A boyfriend of hers has

gone missing, and we want to find out if she knows anything about it."

"Does she?"

Faustino shrugged. Cardoso had said that Portela wouldn't have dropped the slightest hint about where he was going, but three weeks had gone by and he might have taken the risk of contacting her in that period. Even well-trained men did stupid things from time to time, especially when there was a woman involved. And there was always the off chance that she was more directly involved in this than Cardoso had imagined.

"That's what I want to *ask* her," Faustino said irritably. "Memorize the picture and give it back."

They did so. "Where?" Otto asked.

He gave them the address, a high-rise about two kilometers away, and described its interior layout. "I'll lead you to it and park in front, in the visitors' lot," he finished. "Tell her you have a letter from Jorge, he's still in Panama and can't get back. She'll open the door. Then bring her down the side way, by the fire stairs. Then pull around to the front. When I see you've got her in the car, I'll move out. Follow me after that."

"Okay. She live with anybody?"

"No."

"That's good. Money."

"Ten thousand each," Faustino said, handing an envelope over the back of the seat. "Half now, half on completion."

Carlos eyed him. "That's more than a snatch."

Faustino stared hard at him. "She's got to be killed afterward."

"Oh," Carlos said. "In that case." He shoved the money into his jacket.

The very last light was gone from the sky. "Let's go," Faustino said, opening the car door. "Follow me."

He pulled out of the plaza parking lot, making sure the Ford was tucked safely behind him. Driving carefully and scrupulously obeying the speed limit, he turned onto Belt Line and after a kilometer left it to make his way into the palisade of new high-rise apartment buildings southwest of Route 175. Bosque's building was set back from the boulevard,

with a visitors' parking lot in front and the residents' lot
to one side. Faustino found a place in the visitors' lot and
backed into it. The Ford had disappeared around the side of
the building. A couple of minutes later Otto entered the
vestibule; Faustino was able to watch him through the glass
doors. Otto studied the call board then pressed a couple of
buttons at random. There was a brief pause. Then he tugged
on the interior door, which obediently opened. Faustino
smiled sardonically. There was always someone in these
places who'd let an unknown caller in.

Otto vanished around a corner, heading nonchalantly for
the elevator bank.

"This is the first break yet," Johnny Reyes said softly from
behind the steering wheel. "You don't suppose those two
guys are Portela and Menocal?"

"They were on pretty good terms with Darias, if it was
them," Conroy said. "I think it's somebody else."

Reyes inclined his head. "So do I. I wish to hell we had
more people. We can cover them if they split up, but there's
no reserve."

"Yeah," Conroy said. Reyes had driven their Chevrolet
into the front parking lot of the high-rise across from the lot
Darias had entered, and Conroy could just glimpse the right
rear fender of the target's car, a black Malibu. The other car,
a gray Ford, had moved into the far parking area and was
lost to sight.

Darias had been under surveillance since that anonymous
telephone call alerting the FBI to Cardoso's presence in
Dallas, but the watch had so far been fruitless. Darias was
certainly trying to coordinate some kind of search, but he
was being extremely careful. His home telephone and the
telephone in his office at the construction yard were tapped,
but he had used neither for anything but legitimate business.
According to the FBI surveillance reports Conroy had read
after he arrived in Dallas, Darias had used pay telephones
several times, and had managed what might have been two
brush contacts. There was also the possibility that he had
made use of dead drops, although Reyes was frustratingly
unsure of this. The Dallas FBI office was short of manpower,

as always, and maintaining tight surveillance on a single individual for weeks on end was very costly, not the least because it drew resources away from other investigations that promised more immediate results. Had it not been for Rupert Lipton's interventions in Washington, Darias would have been dropped way down the list of priorities some time ago; he wasn't providing the FBI with anything useful.

To complicate matters, the FBI hadn't liked having a CIA spook hanging around on the outskirts of the investigation, even if it was the CIA that had precipitated the investigation. Three days had passed before Conroy and Reyes got onto a first-name basis; up until that time they had either been formal or avoided referring to each other by name at all. Fortunately, the FBI agent was beginning to accept Conroy's presence with better grace now that they'd been working together for a week, especially since Conroy provided another pair of trained eyes. Reyes was a third-generation Mexican-American, fifteen years younger than Conroy, a skinny, thoughtful man with a thin, curved nose and a mane of black curly hair, which spilled over the collars of the checked shirts he favored. They were all long-sleeved shirts, which Reyes wore with the cuffs rolled halfway up his forearms.

Conroy's presence in the investigation did have a certain legal foundation. An old executive order of President Reagan's, never rescinded, permitted the CIA to carry out domestic operations to collect significant foreign intelligence, as long as the operations weren't directed against United States citizens on American soil. Fortunately for Conroy, there was some doubt as to the validity of Miguel Darias's citizenship. Although he held a U.S. passport giving his birthplace as Mexico, there seemed to be no clear record of his naturalization. This would provide good enough reason to pick him up, if it became necessary, but letting him run promised far more.

Or at least it had. Reyes, Conroy knew, was on the point of reducing the surveillance to occasional checks. Tonight there were two surveillance cars besides the Chevrolet Reyes and Conroy occupied, and this represented a significant portion of the field office's perennially stretched resources.

Maybe, Conroy thought, this really is a wild-goose chase. Maybe Miguel Darias has nothing to do with Menocal and Portela. Ramon Linares is God knows where, and those other two may be with him, or nowhere near here at all. I've been thinking all along it was Portela or Menocal who called the FBI in March and put us onto Cardoso and Darias, but maybe I'm wrong. Maybe it isn't connected at all.

But I'm sure it is, somehow. Darias saw Cardoso; Cardoso suddenly upped and went after Ramon and found him. Who told Cardoso Ramon was going to the UAE? Not Darias. Darias would have reported it to Havana, and Cardoso would have gone directly to the Emirates. He wouldn't have risked coming to Dallas at all. So who told Cardoso, or did he figure it out for himself?

And then there was the disaster in Abu Dhabi. What do we know from eavesdropping on Ramon and Cardoso in the desert? Only that there *were* two others, Portela and Menocal, and that they were working with Ramon. Cardoso said he'd caught them. But Ramon didn't believe him. And neither do I. I might have, but that phone call to the FBI won't let me be convinced. Menocal or Portela — it was one of them who called. So they're still on the loose, and Darias is trying to find them. We follow Darias to one of them, that one leads us to Ramon. That's the theory.

He shook his head. He was stale from gnawing at the possibilities; he'd been doing it for a week and a half, since returning from the UAE.

Conroy winced. That had not been a pleasant home-coming: Deakin shot dead, Cardoso with his head bashed in, presumably by Ramon, and Ramon vanished, who knew where? The State Department had been furious; relations with the Emirates were always delicate, and if the UAE authorities found out about the killings in the desert there would be a serious diplomatic reaction. Cardoso's body had been quietly disposed of, as were the damaged vehicles, but making Deakin's death look accidental was more difficult and much more distasteful. The cover-up seemed to have succeeded, but that it had been necessary at all was an embarrassment. Lipton, Vickery and Garland all wanted Ramon's head on a plate, and they wanted Conroy to give it to them. Until he did, Caracas and the promotion to station chief could wait. Keely had been drawn into it, too; she was in Washington right now, helping try to forecast what Ramon was most likely to do.

Conroy, in spite of everything else that was happening, was beginning to miss her.

"Hurry up and wait," Reyes mumbled. "What the hell are they doing over there?"

Teresa Bosque had just gotten out of the shower and was only half dressed when she heard the knock at the apartment door. "Ah, damn," she muttered and pulled a sweatshirt over her head, yanking it down over the waistband of her jeans. She left the bedroom and hurried along the hallway, reaching the door as the person outside knocked again, more insistently this time.

She put her eye to the peephole. The fish-eye lens distorted the features of the man outside, but he looked harmless, even bland.

"Who is it?" she called.

"Carlos Ramirez," he called back. The words were Spanish-accented. He waved something white. "I've got a letter from Jorge. He asked me to bring it to you. He's still in Panama, he can't get back yet."

Without any hesitation she undid the safety chain and the dead bolt. Jorge had been gone for nearly three weeks, and he'd said he'd call from Panama, but he hadn't; she'd been starting to get a little worried about him.

The man named Carlos stepped into the apartment and handed her the envelope. As she took it and instinctively backed away, a second man appeared from behind Carlos and also stepped through the door. He closed it behind him with a solid thud. Teresa opened her mouth to shriek but Carlos's hand was already stopping her. He spun her around, his arm around her neck in a fierce grip. The other man had a gun and was jabbing it at her face.

"Keep quiet, or I'll kill you right here."

Teresa went limp with terror and shock. Her mind refused to accept that this was really happening. Surely in a moment they'd vanish, a dream.

"I'm going to let you go in a second," Carlos said from behind her. "Don't shout or try to run."

He released her slowly. The other man's gun was poking her under her jaw. She didn't dare move.

"Got to get something on her feet," Carlos said. "Look for some shoes, Otto."

The man named Otto opened the hall closet and kicked around on the floor. He found a pair of canvas slip-ons. "These yours?" he asked.

She nodded, wild-eyed and white.

"Get them on."

She managed to do so although she was shaking violently. "What are you doing?" she whispered. Even in her terror she realized that this was not a simple robbery.

"We're taking you downstairs," Otto said slowly and clearly. "We'll each have a gun ready. Don't try to run away, because we'll be on each side of you. Don't try to get help from anybody else, or we'll kill them. That's what we do for a living. We kill people. Understand? We kill people."

She made a small, horrified sound of submission in the back of her throat.

"Come on," Carlos said. He retrieved the envelope from the floor where she'd dropped it.

They had a car outside the fire door. Carlos slid behind the wheel; Otto shoved Teresa into the backseat and got in beside her. The Ford began to move.

"That Ford's coming out," Reyes muttered. He was slumped behind the wheel watching the apartment entrance through a small pair of binoculars. At this distance and at night, it wasn't much of a risk. Conroy, carefully watching Darias's Malibu, saw its taillights come on.

"Darias has switched on his engine," Conroy said. "They're moving out together."

Reyes grabbed a hand-held transceiver from the seat beside him and spoke briefly into it. Then he started the Chevrolet and waited while the Malibu drove onto the street. It was followed half a minute later by the Ford. Darias and the two men were traveling together, all right, although keeping some separation.

Conroy frowned. "I think there's a third person in the back of the Ford."

Reyes trained the binoculars. "It's a woman. Wait a minute. There's a guy in back with her. Only one in the front."

"Damn it," Conroy said. "Did she come willingly?"

"Doesn't look like it," Reyes said, and slipped the Chevrolet into gear.

They drove for hours, or so it seemed to Teresa. Neither of the men spoke. She wanted the driving to go on and on; as long as they were moving, she knew she was safe. But after an indeterminate time that suddenly seemed horrifyingly short, the car was slowing down and turning from the main highway onto a side road. Teresa could see taillights ahead and realized that they were following another vehicle.

The car ahead of them stopped, and Carlos stopped behind it. She could see a wire fence and a gate in it, and heard dogs barking angrily. The driver ahead of them opened the gate and called to the dogs; they came bounding up, huge and shadowy in the headlights, and the man put them into the back of his car. Then they all drove onward. Teresa saw a low white building ahead. The cars stopped.

"Okay," Otto told her. "You can get out now. But if you run he'll set the dogs on you. They'll tear you apart." He said it with considerable relish, and she shuddered. The other driver, the man with the dogs, must be in charge. Maybe she could persuade him to let her go. She felt terrified enough to do almost anything.

The men had turned off the car lights; the only illumination remaining was from a dim bulb mounted high on one corner of the building. The third man, the one Teresa thought was the leader, was standing on the low steps in front of the door. He had something in his hands; as the others pushed her toward him she saw it was a roll of wide adhesive tape.

"Bring her here," he said roughly. They did so, and he bound her wrists in front of her with the tape. He wasn't much taller than she was, but much stockier, about fifty years old. He was well-shaven and smelled of cologne, not sweat, and his hair was neatly clipped.

Oh, God, she thought, it's drug dealers. Jorge is in trouble with them, oh God oh God.

"You want us to come in?" Otto said.

"No. Wait out here in the car. Don't come into the office, not for any reason at all. I'll leave the dogs in my car so you can get out to take a leak if you need to. Keep an eye on things."

"Is she going to be noisy?" Otto asked. He sounded hopeful.

"You won't hear much," the short man said. He opened the door and pushed Teresa ahead of him into darkness. She stumbled as he switched the lights on, and she saw that she was in some kind of office. There were calendars on the wall advertising heavy construction equipment.

He didn't have a weapon visible, but Teresa didn't try to resist when he pushed her onto a chair and began moving a desk against the wall. He was far stronger than she was, for one thing, and her instinct for self-preservation was telling her to cooperate. His manner didn't have the tinge of sadism that Otto's had.

He was lifting a trapdoor. "Down," he told her, gesturing.

She obeyed. The steps were steep but she negotiated them in spite of the trembling of her legs, and she found herself in a square underground room. The lights were on, and she saw a bench full of machines that looked like an elaborate sound system.

"Sit down in the chair," he ordered, and when she did so he taped her ankles to its legs and ran a band of tape around her chest and the chair. Then he stepped back, satisfied.

"What do you want?" she asked, her voice tremulous. "Please let me go."

He leaned against the bench. "Where is the man Jorge?"

"I don't know, really I don't."

"Are you trying to protect him?" he asked quietly.

"No, I don't know where he is." She realized that she was starting to cry. "He called me a while ago. He said he had to go home to Panama for a while. His father was sick."

"I see. When did he call you?"

She gulped back a sob. "I don't remember exactly. Three weeks."

"No letters, no cards, no telephone calls since then?"

"No. Nothing at all. Please let me go."

"I think you're protecting him."

"Oh, God, no, I'm not. Please believe me. Let me go, I won't say anything."

"Hm," he said. "I don't think I can believe you quite so easily."

"David," she said desperately. "David might know where he is."

"David Wright?"

She looked at him in shock. "Yes. Ask him, he might know, oh, *please*, I don't know where Jorge is."

"David Wright's dead," the man said briefly. "He didn't know where Jorge was, either. Look, Teresa, I don't want to torture you. But I'm going to have to know for sure if you're telling the truth."

"What are you going to do?" she whispered.

"This room is almost soundproof," he said. "Are you sure Jorge never contacted you?"

"He didn't, he didn't."

The man shook his head disbelievingly and picked up a plastic bag from the bench beside him.

"At least the damned dogs are locked up," Reyes whispered. "That makes things a bit simpler."

He and Conroy were lying outside the fence of the construction yard, peering through its heavy mesh. To their right the fence bent southeast where it ran along the edge of the gravel pit. In front of them was the road leading into the pit, and beyond that the rear of the yard office. Darias's Malibu with the dogs in it was parked just to the right of the office building, and on the far side of the Malibu was the Ford. To Conroy's and Reyes's left, some twenty meters away, was an implement shed whose rear wall was about a dozen paces inside the fence.

"The two wiseguys are still in the Ford," Conroy whispered. He had the binoculars. "Keeping an eye on things. The third man and the girl must be inside."

"We're going to have to move in," Reyes muttered.

"Yeah," Conroy answered. They'd agreed on the way out

here, as they carefully followed the Ford and the Malibu, that the woman was likely a prisoner, and that she'd definitely seen the faces of her captors. That meant they were going to kill her when they'd finished doing whatever it was they were doing to get information out of her.

He heard Reyes issuing orders over the transceiver to the other two surveillance teams. Reyes and Conroy had come in on foot to reconnoiter; unfortunately they hadn't been able to reach their observation point in time to see Darias and the girl leave the Malibu. From the positioning of the two guards outside, however, the girl was almost certainly within the yard office.

What they were doing was risky. An FBI tactical team was on the way, but it wouldn't be here for a good twenty minutes. Reyes had decided it would be better if the guards were disposed of before the tactical team arrived; the team's approach would be hard to conceal, and he didn't want the two men in the Ford to reinforce Darias inside the yard office.

Reyes finished his orders. "Over to the left," he whispered to Conroy. "We'll put the shed between us and them before we go through the fence."

Conroy crabbed along the fence until he was in position, took his Beretta out of his shoulder holster, and snapped off the safety. Reyes laid his semiautomatic shotgun carefully on the sand and went to work with the bolt cutters, opening a meter-high slit in the chain-link fencing. Conroy slipped through it, Reyes following.

They worked their way along the left side of the implement shed toward the rear of the yard office, keeping the office between them and the car in which the pair of guards was sitting. The only light in the yard came from a fixture on the far side of the building, making it into a featureless silhouette, its back wall in deep shadow. As far as Conroy could tell there were no windows on this side, or if there were they were completely shaded.

"Okay," Reyes whispered as they reached the southeast corner of the yard office. The Malibu was visible from their position, but the dogs were out of sight inside it and quiet. The Ford and the two guards were beyond the Malibu and just out of sight around the corner of the building.

Reyes hefted the transceiver and barely breathed into it. "Ready here."

A faint, affirmative double click as one of the FBI men pressed his transmit button.

"Go," Reyes whispered into the transceiver.

Conroy peeped around the corner of the yard office. Well away down the access road a set of headlights came into view. Behind those would be the second FBI surveillance car, traveling with lights extinguished.

Conroy gingerly put his head out barely far enough to make out the two guards in the Ford; they had seen the lights and were squirming around in the front seat to watch them approach. At any moment they might dash for the yard office.

Conroy made a rush for the Malibu while their backs were turned. He kept low, below the level of the car windows, and ducked behind the driver's door. From inside he heard a low growl; the dogs had sensed sounds outside.

A second later and Reyes was beside him. Conroy popped his head up, using the outside mirror for cover, and looked through the Malibu's windows, praying he wouldn't find himself face to face with a barking Rottweiler. He didn't. The guards were still looking toward the access road at the slowly approaching headlights. One of them was starting to open his door, the passenger door.

"Go," Conroy whispered, and he and Reyes pelted around the Malibu toward the Ford ten meters away. The guard opening the passenger door was half out of the car; neither he nor his companion had looked around yet.

Christ, they're sloppy, Conroy thought.

He and Reyes were only three meters from the men when the one behind the wheel turned and realized what was happening.

"Fuck!" he yelled. Conroy stopped dead two meters from the open driver's window, the Beretta in both hands and the muzzle pointed into the man's face.

"FBI," he snarled. "Get your hands on your head."

The passenger was staring into the black barrel of Reyes's shotgun. "Stand right there," Reyes ordered. The man held still as if paralysed.

Darias must have heard that shout, Conroy thought. Damn it, damn it.

It was at that precise instant that one of the Rottweilers reacted to the yell. The dog began throwing itself violently at the Malibu windows, barking savagely. The other one started up as well. For a few moments Reyes and Conroy were exposed, vulnerable targets for someone firing from the office. Conroy yanked the driver's door open, jammed the muzzle of the Beretta under the man's jaw and dragged him out of the car, throwing him into the dirt and using the open door for cover. Reyes was doing the same on the far side of the Ford. Neither of the guards was showing any sign of resistance; they'd been hit too quickly and were confused and vulnerable. On the seat inside the Ford there was a full arsenal: a couple of machine pistols, grenades, a shotgun.

"Keep your face in the dirt," Conroy whispered to his prisoner. He was feeling the man for weapons, trying not to think about Darias inside the office. He found an automatic in a shoulder holster and ripped it out as two FBI surveillance cars swept into the yard. They skidded to a halt, one behind the other, a little way from the Ford, making a protective wall. The drivers tumbled out, armed to the teeth.

Still no reaction from the office. Conroy couldn't understand it. Surely to God Darias had heard something. Maybe he was lying low, hoping to achieve a better moment of surprise.

One of the FBI men, Robertson, arrived beside Conroy. Conroy kept the Beretta pushed under the guard's ear while Robertson snapped handcuffs over his wrists. "Thanks," Conroy said. The guard was cursing in a steady undertone.

"Shut up," Conroy growled as he and Robertson dragged the man to the protection of the other cars. The dogs were still racketing inside the Malibu. Reyes was already in shelter, his prisoner shackled and lying facedown on the ground with his legs spread wide apart. The other guard joined his companion, under Robertson's careful scrutiny. The third FBI man, Visuña, was just getting off the radio.

"Backup will be here in ten," he said, keeping his voice down, although Conroy thought the dogs were making noise enough to be heard in Dallas.

"Okay," Reyes said. "Why in hell hasn't Darias reacted? He has to have heard *something*."

"Maybe he's not in there," Robertson offered. He poked the Anglo-looking prisoner with a boot toe. "You. Is Darias in there?"

"Fuck off."

"That's useful," Conroy said dryly.

"Shit," Reyes said, "maybe there's a back way out. Raul, get around there and make sure he doesn't skip."

Visuña scurried away, keeping low and using the Ford and the Malibu to cover himself. After a couple of moments he called Reyes on the transceiver to report that there was no sign of an exit in the back of the yard office.

"Stay there anyway," Reyes ordered. "Goddamnit," he added. "I'm going to shoot those dogs if they don't shut up."

At that instant the animals stopped barking for perhaps two seconds together. Then they started again, but not before both Conroy and Reyes heard from the office, very faint but unmistakable, a woman screaming.

Half an hour of air-deprivation torture, the bag seventy seconds on, ninety seconds off, hadn't produced any concrete results. Faustino was beginning to believe that Portela really hadn't contacted her after all. But he was, he discovered, beginning to warm to the work.

He looked at the gasping woman. "Tell me, Teresa," he said quietly. "Or I'll have to go on with something different. This is minor compared to what I can do."

He listened. The dogs were still barking, he thought, although the sound filtering into the underground room was very faint. Faustino considered going up to check the yard, but then realized that Otto or Carlos was likely wandering around outside; that would have set the animals off.

He swung the chair around to face the bench of radio equipment, crossed over to the bench and picked up a heavy-duty soldering iron. "This becomes hot enough to melt metal," he observed, and plugged it in.

She screamed, and kept on screaming until he went over and slapped her. "All right," he said. "Enough. I won't use it." Her reaction had made him decide that she knew nothing, and he felt some distaste at himself for wanting to go on tormenting her. It wasn't professional.

But she'd reached the end of her life, whether she knew it or not. It was time to take her upstairs and turn her over to the other two for disposal. He'd make sure they killed her quickly, where he could observe it; he didn't want them fooling around with her and delaying the business. She could go into the footings at the new apartment building; a few shovels of sand to cover her up and when the concrete was poured tomorrow she'd be gone for good.

Faustino put a gag into her mouth and started cutting her loose from the chair.

Conroy and Reyes were on the steps of the office, Conroy on the handle side of the door. The dogs were barking again, and he couldn't hear anything from the interior, but there was a window just to the right of the door, and a very faint glimmer seeped past its heavy curtaining. So there was a light on inside; that would help.

He felt the surface of the door. It was a heavy exterior one, clad in metal. No kicking that down, he reflected. Break your foot.

He glanced at Reyes, who nodded ruefully. The FBI man was holding the shotgun high across his body, ready to go in. Here's where we earn our pay, Conroy told himself.

Very gingerly, he tried the doorknob. It turned. But there might be a dead bolt; Conroy pushed a fraction of an inch. The door gave. It was unlocked, then. He made sure it was barely off the latch, took a deep breath and kicked it open. Reyes threw himself through the opening, crouching low, the shotgun sweeping an arc across the room to his left. Conroy was on his heels, down on one knee in the firing position, covering the right half of the building's interior. In the space of an instant he noted, first, that there were no interior partitions for a man to hide behind, and second, that there was no one in the big room but himself and Reyes.

"Goddamnit," Reyes muttered. "What the hell?"

Conroy blinked in the harsh fluorescent light. There really was no one there: just filing cabinets, a workbench with some tools and a roll of electrical cable on it, three battered metal desks with the usual office paraphernalia, a few wooden chairs, calendars and work sheets hung on the walls. The windows were curtained with thick cloth.

Something didn't feel right. Conroy walked softly a couple of meters toward the desks. Two were out in the room, but the third had been pushed against the wall, leaving an open space of bare linoleum tiles. Conroy studied the tiles intently. Then he went down on one knee and began running his fingertips over them, pressing down.

One of the tiles flexed. Conroy picked at its edges, and with considerable difficulty pried up a corner and peeled the tile back. Underneath was a steel ring folded into a metal socket: a lifting handle.

Conroy looked at Reyes. Reyes grinned and pointed significantly at the floor. *He's down there.*

With the girl, Conroy reminded himself. And does he know we're here?

Faustino knew someone was there, but he wasn't sure who. It was faintly possible that Otto or Carlos was wandering around in the office, in spite of his orders to stay out. He had remembered, too late, that he'd been in such a hurry to get Teresa Bosque into the underground room that he hadn't locked the office door.

He was standing at the foot of the steep stairway — more of a ladder, in fact — with Teresa in front of him. He'd been about to prod her up the steps when he heard the faint thumps from above.

That was unlikely to be Otto or Carlos, he decided. They were smarter than to disobey orders; they knew it could get them shot.

I'm a rat in a trap, he thought. But maybe whoever it is won't find the door.

He was too realistic to think he could negotiate his way out using the girl as a hostage. If it was the Americans, they'd have sharpshooters all over the place, and if it was the cartel — Faustino couldn't imagine why this would be, but you never knew — they'd kill the girl as a matter of course. He didn't think he could stand one of the Americans' prisons. Perhaps it was time to fight. That way his honor would at least be intact.

There was a creak, and a seam of illumination opened in the dimness above him. Faustino drew his revolver, reached out to his left and shut off the lights.

Reyes hauled slowly on the electrical cable they'd taken from the workbench. The other end was looped around the metal ring of the trapdoor, and the cable led from that over the top of a filing cabinet, which provided a hoisting point. The method allowed them to raise the trap without standing in the line of fire of someone underneath it. Conroy was leaning over the top of another filing cabinet and was sighting his Beretta on the steadily opening gap between the floor and the trapdoor.

No sound issued from the entrance to the underground chamber. As far as Conroy could tell, there were no lights on down there, either. Maybe we should wait for the backup, he thought. But that scream. What was he doing to her? If we wait, she might die.

The trapdoor was at a forty-five-degree angle.

Darias fired upward through it, twice. Conroy's ears rang; tile shattered and rattled against the desks and filing cabinets. The door, thick with sound insulation, swung past its equilibrium point and banged against Reyes's filing cabinet.

Well, at least we know he's down there, Conroy thought.

"You missed, Darias," he called out. "Send the girl up and come out yourself. You can't stay down there forever."

"Go to hell, Yankee."

"Come on, Miguel. I know you're DGI. A spy we might make a trade for. Not a murderer."

"Try to fool somebody else. Havana hasn't got any Americans worth trading."

"Are you going to try to make some kind of deal for the girl?" Conroy called into the dark hole in the floor.

"Okay. A car and a plane at the airport. Flight plan for Cuba."

"Don't be ridiculous, Miguel. You're a trained intelligence officer, not a terrorist. If you behave like a terrorist, the DGI'll say it never heard of you. Remember who you are."

Silence from below.

"You and I don't do things like that, Miguel," Conroy

called. "If you hurt the girl, there'll be no possibility of a trade. Texas has the death penalty, remember. And intelligence people aren't terrorists. You're a DGI man, Miguel Darias. Aren't you?"

Conroy could hear the sounds of engines outside. The tactical team was arriving. If they'd brought stun grenades one could be dropped down the hole to incapacitate Darias for a vital few seconds, but the devices weren't all that safe to use in a narrowly confined space, and Conroy was worried about the girl.

"It'll count in your favor if you give yourself up," Conroy called. "Come on, Miguel. I know you're a professional or you wouldn't have had this long a run. Don't screw it up now."

Another silence. Conroy felt that he was running out of persuasions. He was opening his mouth to try again when Darias called from the room below:

"All right. I'm sending the girl out. Don't shoot at her."

"Okay. We're waiting."

Slowly, a dark head and a tear-streaked face with wide and terrified eyes emerged through the doorway. Conroy saw a gag in the woman's mouth; her wrists were bound in front of her. She reached the top step and stumbled away from the hole, almost falling. Reyes scurried from the cover of his filing cabinet and dragged her behind it. Conroy heard muffled sobs of mingled terror and relief.

"That's fine, Miguel. Now you. I want to see your hands first."

No answer. Conroy frowned.

The gunshot made him jerk back, but no bullet punched upward through the floor.

"Oh, shit," Reyes said.

"Yeah," Conroy answered. He peered carefully into the hole. At the bottom of the steps, about three meters below him, lay the huddled body of Miguel Darias. His head was bloody.

"Damn it, he did shoot himself," Conroy growled. "Aw, hell. Maybe he's still alive. See if there's somebody out there with paramedic training."

*

There was. Darias was not quite dead, but the heavy bullet had caused a lot of brain damage. An ambulance hauled him away and the FBI men began searching the office. Reyes had got the girl calmed down and settled in the back of the Chevrolet, which he had fetched from its hiding place outside the yard.

"She's willing to answer some questions," Reyes told Conroy. Conroy was leaning against the Malibu and glumly surveying the outside of the office. He was wishing Darias hadn't shot himself. He was wishing Keely wasn't far away in Washington. "Okay," Conroy said. "She's the best we've got, now."

"Darias might live."

"Even if he does he won't be answering any questions for a while."

"Probably not." They were walking toward the Chevrolet. "Do you think she actually knows anything about this Portela and Menocal you're so itchy to catch? Or this Ramon Linares?"

"I hope so," Conroy told him. Reyes had been briefed only sketchily with regard to Ramon; the FBI agent knew Ramon was a Cuban renegade suspected of planning some terrorist strike, but that was as far as it had gone. "But I wish to hell we knew what Portela or Menocal looked like," Conroy added.

"Maybe we'll find something in Darias's stuff."

"Yeah, maybe."

They were at the car. Reyes got in beside the woman — her name, she had said, was Teresa Bosque — and Conroy slid into the front. "You feeling better, Miss Bosque?" Conroy asked. The dogs were still barking. "I'm Michael Conroy," he added. "I work for the government."

She nodded hesitantly, still badly shaken.

"You're all right now," Reyes assured her. "We've got them all."

She closed her eyes and opened them again. "They were going to kill me," she whispered. "Just like that. I didn't matter. Just like an animal."

"You're safe now," Conroy said. "Nobody will bother you again. But we need to know why they abducted you. Is it okay if I ask you some questions?"

She nodded tremulously. Reyes got out a notebook and a pen and switched on the dome light.

"Fine. The name of the man who had you inside was Miguel Darias. Had you ever met him before?"

A shake of the head. "No. Never."

"What did he want to know from you?"

"He — he kept asking where Jorge was. I think he wanted to have Jorge killed."

"Can you tell us who Jorge is?"

"Jorge Oliva. He's from Panama. I met him about two months ago, he ... he works in a bar downtown. The Blue Ox. That's where I met him. Is he an illegal immigrant? He said it was all right for him to be here."

"Perhaps. Did you see a lot of him?"

"He was, well, he was sort of a boyfriend."

Something she doesn't like to discuss, Conroy thought. Why?

"Where do you work, Miss Bòsque?"

"I'm a secretary for Hughes Aerospace in the research division."

Reyes and Conroy exchanged glances. "Did you ever discuss your work with him?" Conroy asked.

"No. Some of it's, well, company classified. But he never asked me about any of it."

"Never asked for a document of any kind, even a nonclassified one?"

"No."

He hadn't really started to work on her, then. She was lucky.

"Is he a spy?" she asked suddenly. "Are you saying Jorge is a *spy*?"

"We don't know for sure," Conroy told her. "It's partly what we're trying to find out. Did he seem to be mixed up with drugs at all?"

"No, never. He never even used grass."

"Did he have any friends?"

Again the hooded look. "A few. People he met at the bar. He was one of the bartenders."

"Nobody else from Panama?"

"Not that I ever met."

Was it Portela or Menocal? Conroy wondered. Or neither? This was like stumbling through a dark maze, trying to navigate only by one's sense of direction.

"When did you last see him?"

"About three weeks ago. Then he called and said he had to go back to Panama for a while. His father was sick. He never called or wrote or anything."

"Do you know where Jorge lives?"

"Yes. It's over near Chalk Hill Road. I can't remember the name of the street, I just know where it is. An apartment building."

"Does he own a car?"

"Yes. An old one, a Chrysler, I think. It's brown. It never worked right. He was always mad at it."

"Have you tried to telephone him?"

"Yes, a couple of times this week. But there wasn't an answer."

"Do you have a key to his place?"

"I'm afraid not."

"We ought to go over there," Reyes said to Conroy.

"I think so," Conroy said. "Would you be willing to show us where it is, Miss Bosque?"

"Okay."

"Is there anything else you'd like to tell us?" Reyes asked.

"I can't think of anything," she said. There was that tremor of withholding in her voice again. Never mind, Conroy thought. We'll pursue it later.

"Johnny, you'd better drive," Conroy told Reyes. "Bring anybody else, just in case he's still there?"

"I'll get Visuña and Robertson to tag along," Reyes said. He produced a brief grin. "I wonder how the guys are going to get the dogs out of that car. Too bad we have to miss it."

The dashboard clock was showing close to eleven when Reyes turned the Chevrolet into the parking lot of the building Teresa Bosque had pointed out. The other car with Visuña and Robertson stopped on the street.

"Do you know which window is his?" Conroy asked Teresa.

She craned her neck and peered up at the building. "It's

on the third floor on this side. I think it's the second one from the left end. It's apartment 303, anyway."

"No lights on," Reyes observed. "Okay, Miss Bosque, you'd better wait in the other car."

They deposited her for safekeeping with Visuña and took Robertson along for reinforcements, although Conroy's instincts told him that the man calling himself Jorge Oliva was long gone. The apartment superintendent was watching television and was annoyed at being disturbed, but grudgingly took them upstairs with his passkey.

"You open it," he said, at the head of the fire stairs, and handed over the key. "I'm not going to get my head blown off."

"Do you know if he's in there?" Reyes asked.

"How in hell should I know? I don't keep track of the tenants. He's paid up on his rent to the end of the month and he doesn't make anybody complain and that's all I care about. His rust bucket of a car's out there, that's all I know."

So there won't be any use putting out a search for the car, Conroy thought. If he's gone, he's gone with somebody else. Menocal. Or Portela. Or the other way around. This is going to drive me crazy.

The three men stood away from the door and Reyes banged on it. No answer, no sound from within. He knocked again. Conroy noticed a rank, evil smell on the air, faint but distinct. The skin over his backbone crawled.

"Zip," Reyes said. Still keeping clear of the door opening, he unlocked it and pushed it open. The stench came out. Conroy gagged and heard Robertson doing the same behind him.

"Holy fuck," Reyes swore in a strangled voice. "Somebody's dead in there."

Hell and damnation, Conroy thought, there goes one of the two remaining leads. But who killed *this* one?

Holding his jacket sleeve over his nose and mouth, Reyes entered the apartment, fumbled for the hall light and snapped it on. Conroy followed, trying not to breathe. The smell was thick as a wall, but there was no body on the living-room floor.

A short hallway led off to the right; a closed door stood at the end of it. "Maybe there," Conroy gasped.

It was the door of the bedroom. Conroy stopped and found the light switch. On the bed was a body lying face up, tongue protruding. Where there was exposed flesh the skin was swollen black and blue and yellow. The stink was vile. The body was wearing a T-shirt that had once been white; on the distended front of the shirt were the words PRACTICE SAFE SEX, I'M SAFE.

Reluctantly, Conroy approached the bed. There didn't seem to be any blood. Strangulation, then.

"Which one is it?" Reyes asked from behind him.

"I don't think it's either," Conroy said. "Not unless one of them had long blond hair. But male."

"Who then?"

"Maybe Bosque can help. Unless you want to search it for ID."

"Jesus, not if forensics will do it. Maybe she knows somebody blond."

They left Robertson to wait outside the apartment and headed for the fire stairs. The superintendent was waiting in the stairwell. "Is he there?" the man asked.

"Somebody is," Reyes said. "But you're going to have to get the apartment fumigated. He's been dead for a couple of weeks. Didn't anybody complain?"

"Dead?" The man stopped short.

"Yeah, murdered, it looks like. Didn't anybody smell anything at all?"

The superintendent was looking ill. "A week ago there was a complaint. I thought it was the garbage dumpster in the parking lot."

"It wasn't," Reyes told him, leaving him behind on the stair. "Stay out until the police get here," he added unnecessarily.

Teresa Bosque was in the backseat of Visuña's car. She rolled down the window as Conroy and Reyes approached. "Was he there?" she called.

"I don't think so," Reyes said, leaning on the car roof and speaking through the open window. "Does Jorge have a male acquaintance with long blond hair? Wore a T-shirt saying 'Practice safe sex, I'm safe'?"

Her eyes widened. "David? David Wright? Is he up there?"

"Yes. Is he a friend of yours?"

She hesitated, vulnerable. Conroy said, "You'd better tell us the rest. This is getting serious. It won't go any farther if it's not important."

She looked down. "We — well, we sometimes made a threesome. In bed."

Conroy sighed. He'd hoped she was hiding something significant; instead it turned out to be this, a minor sexual aberration.

"Is David in trouble?" she asked, looking up. Even in the poor light Conroy could see that her cheeks were flaming with humiliation.

"No," Reyes said kindly. "I'm afraid he's dead, Miss Bosque. But Jorge isn't there. And I'm afraid the police are going to have to ask you a lot more questions."

Mexico–Texas
April 22

■

Ramon took his foot off the accelerator, allowing the van to slow down. Ahead of him lay the squalid belt of shantytown and tumbledown slum that formed an aureole for the border town of Piedras Negras. Only a few years ago, the town had had a population of about thirty thousand; now there were four or five times that many people, human jetsam driven up against the fortress wall of the American border by the collapse of Mexico's economy.

The Americans were of course doing their best to keep them out, Ramon reflected as he took the road signposted for the border; it avoided the worst of the shantytown. Having induced the Mexican capitalist government to pillage its country's oil wealth for the sake of the United States, the American bankers were now eager to have the so-called development loans repaid. The fact that every coin of repayment was being extracted from the skins of the Mexican poor was of no consequence; they were squeezed until they had nothing left, and then were allowed to stand in places like Piedras Negras with their faces pressed to the windows of the rich man's house, looking in with their hollow eyes. A house, Ramon reminded himself, that the lookers had helped pay for. Were still helping to pay for.

His face remained calm, but within himself he seethed. He wanted to leap from the van, rush into the barrio, shout to these people what had been done to them, make them understand who had authored their misery, help them storm the hateful barriers of America, inflict on the Americans what they had inflicted on the rest of the world.

He knew even as he wrestled with the emotion that he could shout for hours to the morning sky and they would not hear him. They had been oppressed and hungry for so long that they had lost their dignity; now they were harmless. That was one of the Americans' great protections against those they had raped: after they had ruined the people's bodies, they stole their pride.

These people will do nothing until the cause is given back to them, Ramon thought as he turned the van toward the Mexican customs post on the near side of the bridge crossing the Rio Grande. I am the one to give it back to them.

The Mexicans at the customs post were lax; they looked at his tourist card, his passport and vehicle registration and checked the bills of sale he had so carefully prepared before leaving the United States for Tampico to collect the weapons shipment. They did have him pry the top off the box containing the surveying equipment, but took only a cursory glance inside. Ramon decided that they were more interested in locating smuggled antiquities than smuggled drugs. After a couple of minutes of document stamping they waved him through, and he was on his way across the toll bridge into the United States. The town at the far end of the bridge drew nearer. Eagle Pass: a small town, no larger than Piedras Negras once had been. There was no barrio there; Mexicans who managed to penetrate the border, legally or otherwise, did not stay.

One more step on the way, Ramon thought. If I pass the customs checkpoint, that will be the biggest hurdle until the final one.

He wasn't tired. He wanted to make the journey from Eagle Pass to the new base in southern Texas without stopping, so he had slept in the van last night in Nueva Rosita, eighty kilometers south of the border. Once he was across the border he had almost seven hundred kilometers to go, most of it over secondary highways. But he should be there around dark.

He was almost to the customs building. There wasn't much traffic at this time on a weekday morning. Ramon drove carefully into one of the truck lanes and stopped behind a big eighteen-wheeler. It was here that he was in most danger: from customs search, and because of the identity he was using.

He was carrying the original Panamanian documents Faustino had given him when he arrived in Dallas. Ramon didn't like the identity; he'd been using it too long. But his identity papers had to agree with the van's registration, and he'd had to have a driver's license to buy the van in El Paso and register it, and the only driver's license he had was the Panamanian one. The American passport al-Bakr had furnished was good for crossing borders, but it alone would not get him a new license; for that he needed a new social security card, and on top of that he'd have to take a driving test. The process was cumbersome and time-consuming, and it might attract attention.

Menocal had bought the second van they needed with his Faustino-supplied license, and for the same reasons. They'd agreed that the cartel and the DGI were unlikely to blow the identities to the Americans because Ramon and Portela and Menocal knew too much about their operations in the United States. Also, the risk of the DGI catching up with them was fairly small, given where they were hiding, so on balance Ramon thought the papers were still usable. He had no choice but to use them, in any case.

A customs officer appeared at the driver's window. He gave Ramon a quick look up and down and said, "You have something to declare?"

"Yes. Light drilling and surveying equipment. It's second hand."

"Okay. Pull over there and let me have a look."

Ramon did so, got out and opened the rear doors of the van. "Citizenship?" the customs officer asked.

"Panamanian." Ramon handed over the necessary documents: work permit, visa, passport. The officer inspected them carefully. "How long you been in the States?"

Ramon had memorized the passport information long ago. "Eight years."

"Okay. Just a minute." He went into the customs office. There'd be a watch list, passport numbers the Americans were looking for. But if the Panamanian passport was clean, he'd be all right. Ramon stared straight ahead.

A couple of minutes passed. The customs officer came out alone, carrying the documents. He handed them to Ramon and said, "Okay. You got bills of sale?"

Ramon produced them. "Surveying and drilling equipment, huh," the customs man said. "How come you're bringing it in from Mexico?"

Ramon smiled ruefully. "I am trying to start a company. It was cheaper to go to Ciudad Victoria to get the equipment than buy it here."

"Yeah, well, there's duty even if it's secondhand."

"I understand that."

"Two crates? Open them up."

Ramon went at the crates with a pry bar hammer, removed the tops and stood aside. The officer peered into the crate containing the missiles and lifted the ends of a couple of the drill bits to look underneath them. Ramon was in position for a blow from behind the officer; if he had to, he would kill the man and make a run for it.

"Fine," the customs officer said. "You can seal that one up." He looked into the other. "This is electronic stuff?"

"Yes. It's for surveying. I was lucky to find it secondhand."

"Uses lasers, doesn't it," the officer said knowledgeably, making Ramon start before he could prevent himself. Fortunately he was still behind the man.

"Yes." Was it some kind of a trap? "It is very accurate."

"All right," the customs man said, straightening up. "You can put the lid on. Come into the office and we'll work out the duty. Has to be cash or certified check."

"Cash," Ramon said. It had been so easy, so unbelievably easy. He wanted to shout for joy.

He picked up Route 90 at Del Rio, a green spot in the desert, and kept heading northwest. A few kilometers farther on the highway crossed the waist of the vast Amistad Reservoir. The brilliant indigo water was dotted with the tiny white triangles of sailboats, flitting to and fro over the drowned land like midges. And a few kilometers to the south, Ramon thought, there are people who drink water so filthy that

Americans would not set it in front of their pet dogs.

On the far side of the reservoir the semiarid lands reasserted themselves. Ramon drove on under the slowly ascending sun. The van wasn't air-conditioned, but in April it wasn't necessary; Ramon kept the van windows open so the warm spring air could blast in. He was very happy, driving alone like this. He drank bottled water he had bought in Mexico, but didn't bother looking for somewhere to buy food. Once, in a town called Dryden, he stopped for gasoline and bought a couple of chocolate bars. Then he drove until midafternoon; he was very careful not to exceed the speed limit by more than five or six kilometers an hour.

At the junction with Route 285 he turned right, to the north. Mesas and low peaks layered themselves on the horizon, blurred duns and greens and grays. Occasionally he saw cattle browsing the short grass, and once in a while a sheep ranch, but the vegetation looked desiccated and the animals thin. He vaguely remembered reading in a Dallas newspaper that there had been higher than normal temperatures here for three years, and that the constant heat and drought were driving the ranchers off the drying soil. Even in their new harshness, though, the landscapes had a weird, parched beauty; as the sun declined the colors of the mesas and hills became muted, the grays turning to blue and the greens to emerald, the duns to deep brown.

About thirty kilometers south of Fort Stockton he turned off the highway and began to follow a secondary asphalted road east. The sun was only a few degrees above the horizon, and a small mesa to Ramon's left threw a long shadow across the grassland and low, sweeping rises; the flats between the rises, so featureless under a high sun, were now ridged and textured by the slanting orange light.

Ten kilometers along the road stood the house and sheds and outbuildings of a sheep farm. The farm was one of those going under because of the drought, all its stock sold off for slaughter and only the land and buildings left. Ramon had rented the place from its desperate owner, who was now working in Fort Stockton to make enough money to hang on to at least his land. The owner had accepted Ramon's reason for wanting the farm without any questions; it was a plausible

enough reason to Ramon, although the owner had snorted
with disbelief when Ramon told him he and his cousins were
going to try to run sheep in spite of the drought.

The yard of the house was deserted, but there was a light
in the kitchen window. The house was two stories tall,
sheathed in wooden siding that had once been painted white
but was now badly peeling under the effects of sun and wind.
A veranda ran all the way across the front. Ramon pulled up
by the veranda and eased himself stiffly out of the driver's
seat. The front door of the house banged open and Menocal
came out, waving cheerfully, a grin softening the solemnity of
his dark and narrow face.

"Ramon!"

Ramon waved wearily back. Now that he was here he felt
his shoulders aching from the hours behind the wheel. "I
made it. Is everything all right?"

"Yes, everything. Joel is making something to eat. Did you
get what you wanted?"

"Yes. It's all in here."

Menocal left the veranda and peered past the driver's seat
into the back of the van. "That's it?"

"Yes. Don't worry, it doesn't need to be big. You picked
up the machines?"

"Two days ago. There was no problem. We assembled
them yesterday. Can you tell me what the weapons are
now?"

"After supper. I'm hungrier than in Yemen."

"It should be ready. But you know how particular Joel is
about food."

"Where's the other van?"

"In the smaller shed, with the Bronco."

Ramon followed Menocal into the house. The interior was
not quite bare; some of the furniture had been left behind by
the owner, enough to sit and sleep on. Portela was in the
kitchen, cooking on a propane stove, a wooden spatula
dwarfed in his huge hand. The long room smelled wonder-
fully of chili peppers and frying beef. Portela waved the
spatula happily at Ramon, spattering sauce. A couple of
bottles of red wine and a big bottle of rum stood on the table.
"Have a drink," Portela said. "This is nearly ready." He

sloshed a can of kidney beans into the mixture in the pan.

"No trouble at Tampico?" Menocal asked, pouring Ramon a water glass full of wine.

"No. The documents worked fine. Same at the American border. Did you have any trouble getting more guns?"

"Full automatic weapons are a problem. We have rifles and semiautomatic shotguns, but aside from the pistols we brought from Dallas, that's all."

"That'll be enough," Ramon said. "The idea isn't to get into a firefight. We're losing if we have to do that. The idea is stealth, not a battering ram."

"What is it we're going to do?" Portela asked. He was shoveling the chili into some chipped enamel bowls.

"After supper," Ramon said. "I've got a lot to tell you. Some things you've never imagined." He grinned at them, teasing.

"You always make us wait," Portela grumbled.

"You won't wait much longer," Ramon told him. "None of us will." He shoved a spoonful of chili into his mouth. The spice burned against his palate. "Mm," he said, the sound muffled.

"Too hot?" Portela asked anxiously.

"No, precisely right. Something to be said for American food."

"We never see beef like that at home," Portela said wistfully.

"Remember where it comes from," Ramon reminded him. "Americans eat like this because they pillage the rest of the world. In Piedras Negras there are children starving. The Americans want to eat up the whole planet, they don't care about anyone else."

"Should *we* even be eating like this?" Portela worried.

Menocal put his political cadre's expression on his face. "Yes. Lenin said the last capitalist would be hung with a rope he sold to the Communists. We won't help the masses by starving ourselves until we're too weak to fight. This food is like the capitalist's rope; we use it against him."

"Exactly," Ramon said.

They ate in relative silence, sharing out the wine. When they were completely full, Portela moved the dishes to the sink — they were using water from big plastic jugs because the well was dry — and sat down expectantly. The wine was gone. Ramon filled their glasses with rum. "There was no trouble with assembly?" he asked.

"No," said Menocal. "All the parts were there and everything fit."

Ramon had a mental checklist of everything that needed to be done or made. "The false license plates?" he asked. These were to be constructed from plastic sheet, using numbers cut from a real plate to make molds in which the heated plastic would be shaped. Paint would complete the illusion.

"I worked at it till I got it right," Menocal said. "From a meter you can't tell they're not real."

"Good. Camouflage nets?" These were patches and strips of cloth secured to gardeners' plastic mesh.

"Done."

"Paint for the vans?"

"We've got it, and brushes. The finish will be a little rough, using brushes."

"That's all right. It won't matter." He downed the rum. "Let me have a look at them. We can move the weapons into the shed at the same time."

They went out to the van and hauled the crates to the sliding doors of one of the farm outbuildings, a large implement shed. Portela unlocked the doors and shoved them easily aside. "There they are," he said.

Ramon looked at the spidery machines with satisfaction. There were two of them, ADR Commander lightweight gyroplanes, a single-seater and a two-seater. They looked like a cross between a helicopter and an ultralight aircraft, with a two-blade top rotor instead of wings and a five-blade pusher propeller to drive the vehicle forward. Fully loaded, the gyroplanes could get off the ground in less than thirty meters, if the rotor was prespun from the engine, and they could fly as slowly as ten kilometers an hour in still air, or cruise at a hundred and twenty. They had a useful payload, over and above the pilot and fuel, of two hundred kilos. They could be disassembled to fit into the back of one of the vans, and reassembled in ten minutes with only six hand tools, and they could be fitted with floats, wheels or skis. They were so small that they were next to invisible on radar, and so spidery that they were extremely difficult to spot visually from any distance. They were a superb delivery platform for certain kinds of terrorist weapons.

Ramon walked around them, taking a closer look. Portela had already installed the altitude telltales. He had bolted two heavy-duty flashlights to each machine, one flashlight on each side of a strut. Their beams were angled downward, so that when their spots of light were superimposed on a surface, the gyroplane was exactly seven meters above that surface. It was a much more accurate measurement than the altimeter could give.

"Do these work well?" he asked Portela, indicating the lights.

"Very well. It was a good idea."

"You can teach me to fly one, then?" Ramon asked.

Menocal nodded. Both he and Portela, as part of the purchase package from ADM in El Paso, had trained for several hours on ADM machines exactly like those in the shed. The gyroplanes, being nimble and cheap to operate, were now used widely for crop dusting, and Menocal had bought them ostensibly for this purpose.

"It's really very easy," Menocal was saying. "We had some dual instruction, but we could have learned without it. They're very stable and safe." He waved a hand at the floats stacked against the shed wall. "I wish you could be trained on water."

"I don't intend to be flying," Ramon said. "Although I want to know how. Are they stable enough for an aiming platform?"

Menocal frowned. "They bob if there's any wind. It would be better to set down for a few seconds, if that's possible."

"It should be."

"How far away will the target be?" Portela asked.

"Three thousand meters."

They both stared at him in surprise. After a moment Portela said, "What have you *got* in those boxes?"

"Bring them inside and I'll show you. Do the lights work in here?"

"Yes."

"Then shut the doors."

They did so. Ramon got a wrecking bar and pried the tops off the crates. He pointed to the one with the laser targeting system. "Try that one first."

They carefully unpacked it, frowning at first as they took out the ordinary surveying equipment, then muttering in growing excitement as they saw what was underneath. "Where did you find this?" Portela said reverently as he placed the laser projector on a sheet of plastic packing to protect it from the dust of the shed floor.

"From a man who supplied weapons to us in Yemen," Ramon said. "Now look in the other one."

They unpacked the drill bits and lifted out the HVMs and launching rails. "These will reach three kilometers?" Menocal asked doubtfully.

"Yes. We'll use two on the target, slung under the single-seater gyroplane. The guidance system we'll carry on the two-seater. The third missile is for practice."

"How long do we have for practice?"

"Ten days. That should be enough time. Then we have to move to the target area. There's C4 and detonators in that crate, too. That's for something else."

They removed the explosive and the detonators and put the packages, well separated, on a bench at the rear of the shed. "Are you going to tell us the target now?" Portela asked.

"Lock up and come back to the house."

He went ahead of them and got the maps from the personal gear he'd left in the house before going to Tampico. They were U.S. geological survey maps; he'd obtained them in Dallas. When he came downstairs, Menocal and Portela were sitting at the kitchen table, glasses of run in front of them.

"Now," Ramon said, pouring a shot of the liquor for himself, "I have to tell you everything that's happened up to now. To begin with, Colonel Cardoso is dead. That's why I wasn't worried when I got back from overseas and you told me he was looking for me."

"You killed him?" Portela asked.

"Yes." He went over all that had happened since he left

them on the shore of the Gulf of Mexico that night. They hung on every word. When he had finished, neither of them spoke for a good half minute. Then Portela said wonderingly:

"You are Che Guevara's son?"

"Yes. On my honor, and my mother's honor." He thought: Is my mother still alive? What will they do to her with Cardoso dead? They'll know I killed him.

"I can see it in you," Menocal said. "Now that I know, I can see it."

He sensed how their attitude had changed. He was much more than their old commander now; he was the heroic past come alive in front of their eyes. Ramon felt the most curious sensation, as though he had shed some kind of skin and turned into a different sort of being, or as though the foundation of the world had shifted in some essential manner.

The feeling slowly ebbed. He cleared his throat and said, "It's important that we're carrying on Che's work, but we still have to prepare properly. We have a lot to do. I think we'd better get some sleep. Tomorrow Luis will teach me how to fly, and Joel, you should get started mounting the launch rails on one of the gyroplanes."

"But the target," Menocal said protestingly. "You still haven't told us what the target is."

Ramon blinked. For some peculiar reason he'd forgotten all about telling them, or that he hadn't told them. Perhaps it was the rum. He passed a hand over his eyes and said, "I'm planning a diversion, but we'll talk about that later."

He unfolded the maps and laid one on the table. "That's where it will be," he said, pressing a fingertip to the place.

Menocal and Portela looked down at the map, the greens and blues and browns.

"Pad 39-B," Ramon said. "About three weeks from now. The space shuttle."

Texas–Washington, D.C.
May 2

■

T hey were almost finished training.
  The Texas horizon was sharp as a painted line, gray-green against azure. Not a cloud in the noon sky, all moisture distilled from it by the sun, clearer than water. Ramon flew through the bright light, feeling the gyroplane bob as it rushed through small thermals thrust up by patches of bare, sandy soil. He loved this, the flight low over the earth, the dun and sage green fleeing beneath the machine he rode.

He was flying the two-seater, making sure he had the feel of it. They had all trained on the single-seater, which was armed with the missiles, and on the two-seater, which carried the guidance system. The guidance system was much lighter than the HVMs. It consisted only of the laser beam projector — a device rather like a chunky rifle, with a magnifying electronic sight mounted on it — and the battery power supply and transformer unit. The whole package was called, in weapons technology jargon, a "laser designator."

Tactically the operation was quite simple: Menocal would fly the two-seater, Ramon would illuminate the target with the laser beam, and Portela would fly the single-seater and fire the missiles as soon as Ramon had the target properly designated. The difficult part was to keep the narrow beam of laser light precisely on the target from a distance of over three kilometers. To try to aim the laser while the gyroplane was bobbing around in air currents would be to invite a miss, even with the magnifying sight, so Menocal was to touch down and stop momentarily while Ramon held the designator's sight on the shuttle. But he would need to keep the beam steady for no more than three seconds after launch. The two missiles — their hypervelocity tag was no exaggeration — would strike within that time or even a second less, depending on how long they needed to accelerate to their maximum speed, a detail that wasn't in the documentation.

Ramon could see Menocal and Portela up ahead, Menocal standing by the single-seater and Portela already in the pilot's seat. Ramon slowed the gyroplane almost to its stalling speed, which with the slight head wind was no more than a fast walk. Satisfied with his control, he accelerated again. The engine behind him buzzed happily. The mufflers had been developed from those used on Japanese motorcycles, and even at cruising speed the engine noise was muted.

He landed a few meters from the other machine and waved to Menocal. "We can test," he called. He set the brakes and slid into the passenger seat.

Menocal nodded and hauled on the rewind starter of Portela's machine. The engine caught with a clatter then settled into an even buzz. Menocal trotted over to the two-seater and strapped himself into the pilot's seat. He engaged the rotor spin, and when the blades were whistling at the right speed over their heads he thrust the throttle forward and released the brakes. The little machine trundled forward, gathering speed for perhaps thirty meters, then bounced into the air.

Portela was already off the ground and just ahead. Ramon could see the long dark sliver of the single test HVM on its launching rail bolted above the starboard undercarriage. They'd also had to install a light metal heat shield to protect the pilot from the missile's back blast when it fired.

The two gyroplanes bobbed along side by side, flying the length of a long swale between two ridges. The swale was a good ten kilometers from the nearest main road and six or seven from the house, and it was closed at its far end by a rise of ground higher than the ridges, with a sheer rock face on its near side forming a low bluff. Closed into this long corridor they were as secure as they could be from curious eyes.

Ramon had selected a paler blotch on the side of the bluff as his target. He set the laser projector against his shoulder and switched it on. The rock wall leaped toward him in the sight, and he shifted the cross hairs to a knob of shadow that would serve as a target. Where the cross hairs rested would be a small spot of laser light, although from this distance Ramon could not see it easily. But the missile guidance system would.

It was very hard to hold the cross hairs in one place, no matter how steadily Menocal tried to fly the machine. They'd each tried it, and the aiming problem had made them decide that the only way of insuring accuracy was to land.

Menocal, who had the best eye for ranges, was responsible for setting down at the appropriate point. Ramon felt the gyroplane slow suddenly, and dip, then he felt the vibration of the wheels as they ran along the ground. The machine stopped. Suddenly he could hold the target with no difficulty whatsoever.

"Fire," he called over the burr of the engine.

Beside him, Menocal raised his arm to Portela, who was floating some six meters off the ground to their left. Portela pressed the firing switch.

The HVM snapped away from its launching rail, trailing a meter-long plume of flame. There was no smoke trail, only the flame, which in this bright sunlight seemed as innocuous as the flare of a match. Ramon heard a low hissing roar, not nearly as loud as he had expected.

One.

Two.

A bright spark appeared in the viewfinder and a burst of flame spurted around the cross hairs. A small plume of dust rose from the rock wall and slowly began to dissipate. The rumble of the missile engine died away. Ramon switched off the sight and lowered it. It was a distinct anticlimax. For the first time, doubt struck him. Perhaps the weapon wasn't the one for the task, after all.

"That wasn't much, was it?" Menocal said. He sounded disappointed.

"Fly over there and we'll look," Ramon ordered him stolidly.

They landed at the foot of the bluff. The impact point was several meters up the slanting rock wall, but there was enough footing for Ramon to climb up to it.

The rock was badly scorched where missile propellant had splashed on impact and burned. More or less in the center of the scorch was an irregular hole about twenty centimeters across and too deep for Ramon to see the bottom. Heat glowed from it. Radiating from the hole were deep cracks running away across the granite in a spiderweb of jagged lines.

If this thing will shatter a granite cliff, Ramon thought wonderingly, it will tear the insides out of any machine. I don't think I need to worry.

He turned and looked at Portela and Menocal, who were staring hopefully at him. "It will work," he called. "It will work very well." He scrambled down the rock face to join them. "Back to the house," he said. "We're leaving tonight."

Conroy was supposed to pick Gemma up from the airport — her flight from Italy was due in at seven — and he asked Keely if she wanted to come along. He felt somewhat as though he was a much younger man, bringing an equally young woman home to meet the family for the first time.

But that's ridiculous, he told himself as he waited for Keely's reply. Gemma's opinion's important to me, but not *that* important. It's just that I'm out of practice with this sort of thing.

He realized, though, that it was very important to him that Gemma and Keely took to each other. Gemma was the only family he had.

"I'd like to meet your sister," Keely said. "As long as you're sure I won't be intruding."

Conroy laughed. "Of course not. Gemma's very sociable. She likes people."

"Sociable, unlike you?" Keely teased him. They were getting into Conroy's Toyota — he'd bought it a week previously, after returning from Dallas — and were about to leave Langley for Washington. Keely was staying at the Watergate Hotel; she'd been dividing her time between

Boston and Washington for the past month, since she and Conroy had returned from the Emirates. Lipton and Garland felt that with Cardoso's death the threat to her had diminished, and Conroy thought this was probably true, although the idea of her being alone in Boston still made him slightly nervous. In Washington she'd been working with a CIA task team to identify Ramon's most likely targets and his probable approach to them, given his background and psychology.

The targets made a long list, and they were spread all over the United States, which was maddening when it came to finding a way to intercept him. Conroy was part of the task team, handling liaison with the FBI. The FBI was taking Ramon more seriously now, since a search of Darias's house and construction yard had turned up clear evidence of espionage activities, although they were still unconvinced that Ramon offered a serious terrorist threat. As far as the Bureau was concerned his organization didn't appear to be big enough to have good resources. Darias was no help. The DGI man was still in a coma, and if he ever did come out of it would have severe brain damage.

"I'm not really that unsociable, am I?" Conroy asked, twisting the key in the ignition.

"I've never heard you mention much of a social life."

"Well, no."

"I suppose I'm much the same way, to be quite honest," she said as he drove toward the exit. "I have a few very close friends, but most of my time's taken up with work."

Conroy tried to think of close friends. Gemma, and there the list ended. Keely was a friend, and then again she wasn't, exactly. They struck sparks from each other, there was no doubt about that, but right from the first they'd had a perverse tendency to fight with each other. If they'd been stranded in the desert a little while longer, Conroy thought, they might have resolved their prickliness, but it hadn't happened. And since returning to the United States they'd either been separated, or too involved in the problem of Ramon Guevara to address what was hanging in the air between them.

"You know," he began, and stopped.

"What?" she asked.

"Nothing."

She looked at him oddly. "Well, —" she said, and then lapsed into silence. "This is incredibly frustrating," she said.

"It is? What?" Maybe she's going to broach the subject finally, he thought. I suppose this is as good a time as any.

"Ramon. What he's going to do. We have this list of targets, and we don't ... What are you looking so peculiar about?"

Conroy rearranged his features. "Just Ramon. You're right. It's driving me crazy, too." He took a deep breath. "We know what he looks like, but we don't know the identity he's traveling under. We know from Teresa what one of the others looks like, although not whether it's Menocal or Portela, and we know the DGI identity of that one, although he may not be using it any more. Apart from that, we don't know a damned thing. The two leads we had — Cardoso and Darias — are either dead or as close to it as makes no difference. Although there's one bit of progress. I was going to tell you. Johnny Reyes has managed to cull the Mexican border customs declarations."

"Is that a long shot?"

"It's not as long as some of the others. As far as we can tell, Ramon doesn't have a big organization. If he bought weapons in the UAE, the seller likely arranged the shipping for him. You recollect we put a watch out for anything coming in from the Middle East into American seaports or airports, and nothing turned up. So that means he's using an alternate route, overland from a third country. That's either Mexico or Canada. He'd be less conspicuous coming in from Mexico, so that's where Johnny has been concentrating."

"But surely he couldn't smuggle something as large as the weapons he'd need for a big attack. It would be too much of a risk. Although," she added thoughtfully, "he's the sort of personality who would take that kind of chance. He'd risk everything on one throw of the dice, if there was no other way."

"Johnny thinks Ramon might have been cool enough to run his cargo through customs disguised as something else, fill out the forms, pay the duty. That's why he's having the declarations checked. The profile would be a single Spanish-American — maybe two — in a medium-size truck or van, a few crates in back, very plausible story about what's in the crates, and if they're opened they look exactly like what he says they are. He dutifully pays up the customs dues and vanishes."

"How far along with the declarations is he?" she asked. The hills of northern Virginia were rising ahead of them.

"Not very. There were a lot of them that fitted the profile. They're all being checked out, every driver and shipment. Theoretically we should end up with one declaration that *doesn't* check out. For example, the address is fake, or it's real but the person's vanished. With a name, we can get the vehicle registration and description, and that'll narrow the search."

"It all seems very reasonable."

Conroy gave a sardonic snort. "It's just a sample of the possibilities we have to cover. There are lots of others. Maybe he did come in through Canada. Maybe he's working with another cartel renegade, and the weapons were flown in. Maybe he came in by small boat in New England. Maybe he didn't come at all. All of it has to be checked."

"In other words, if he is here, we might not catch him before it's too late."

"That's a possibility. The only consolation is that there aren't any really new ways of getting something through the border. All these have been used one time or another. It's not that the DEA and the FBI don't know how these people do things. They do know. But the haystack's a big one, and there's only one needle. The Mexican border crossing is the most likely one for Ramon to use, so that's the point of concentration right now."

"Mm," she said.

"Anything new on the targets?" Conroy asked. They weren't far from the airport turnoff.

"We just keep adding more," she said tiredly. "Nuclear power plants are the big worry, although they're hard to damage because of the containment buildings. The fact that he was in the UAE to buy weapons seems to rule out poisoning a major water supply, and bacteriological agents and gas are hard to direct with the precision a soldier like Ramon would want. He's likely going to try to blow up something or somebody. The White House or the Capitol are two obvious targets. Airports are an old standby. We thought about refineries, but they're likely not political enough for him, he'd want a clearly defined symbol. There's a GATT economic summit in Miami in ten days, with a lot of foreign politicians running around."

"He'd have a hard time getting through the security for that."

"I know. But it's the kind of strike he'd favor. It would embarrass the United States horribly."

"Yeah."

"And there's the Soviet Embassy here, and the Soviet UN Embassy in New York. It just goes on and on. There's a shuttle launch scheduled for May seventh. That would be to his taste, as well."

"He'd have a hard time getting close enough to the launch pad to do any damage," Conroy observed. "He'd have to hijack a tour bus or fight his way in, and there's enough security to stop anything like that."

"Unless he's worked out something nobody's ever thought of," she suggested.

"I suppose it's possible," Conroy said. He turned the Toyota onto the ramp leading to the airport access road.

"I keep remembering how wrong we all were about Ramon and Cardoso working together," she said. "Your people, Rupert, you and I. We were all so sure it was to stop any movement toward reform in Cuba. But that wasn't it at all. Are we wrong about Ramon again? Underestimating him? He's got next to no money compared to other terrorists, and he's got the CIA and the DEA and the FBI and the cartel and the DGI after him, but nobody can seem to catch him. He's always one step ahead of everyone."

"I know," Conroy muttered. "He's very good at it."

"Do you know what I did while you were in Dallas?"

"What?"

"Rupert insisted, because of what happened in Miami. He arranged for me to take a weapons course with the FBI. I thought I'd be nervous about handling the things, but I wasn't. I turned out to be quite a good shot. Rifles and hand-guns."

Conroy was startled. The image of Keely blazing away with a pistol was one that had never entered his mind. "Are you carrying one?" he asked.

"Oh, no. I haven't gone that far. I hope I never have to."

"So do I," Conroy said with feeling.

They found a space in the short-term parking lot and trudged into the terminal. Gemma's flight, according to the monitors, was on time. They went to the arrivals area. "We could all three have supper after we get out of here," Conroy said. "How about it?"

"Won't your sister be exhausted?"

"Possibly, but I've never known Gemma to get off a plane and not be hungry."

"Let's see what she says."

Gemma was among the first out of customs. She saw Keely beside her brother and an expression of surprise flitted across her face. It was replaced immediately by the instant's appraising scrutiny that women reserve for each other.

Each of them must have passed the other's preliminary inspection because Gemma broke into an easy, unreserved smile and Conroy felt Keely's arm relax in the crook of his elbow. "Hi, Michael," Gemma said. "My God, that's a long haul from Rome. I'm starving. Hello," she said to Keely. "Michael, perform introductions, for heaven's sake."

Conroy did so. He sensed quickly that the two women liked each other, and he breathed a sigh of relief. "Feed me, Michael," Gemma said, turning from Keely. "I slept most of the way across the Atlantic so I missed dinner, and I'm famished."

Conroy exchanged a glance with Keely and winked.

They ate on the way into Washington, in a restaurant not far from Gemma's house in Georgetown. The women, both of them from the academic world, had established a quick rapport with each other, finding among other things that they had some acquaintances in common.

Over coffee, Keely excused herself. When she was gone Gemma leaned across the table. "Where did you find her,

Michael?" she asked. "She's perfectly wonderful."

"It was sort of an accident," he said carefully. "There's a think tank out at Langley's she's involved with. We spent some time overseas on business. It just growed, I guess."

"Does she do the same work you do?" Gemma asked. "Even though she's Irish? I noticed she was reticent about why she was here in Washington, and I didn't want to pry."

"No, she's, uh, civilian. She's a specialist in revolutionary history and the psychology of revolutionaries. There's something she's working on."

"With you?" Gemma asked.

"Yes."

"Is there anything else going on?"

"Yes. But not ... well, we haven't really discussed it."

"I thought so. But it shows all over both of you. You never took your eyes off each other during dinner."

"Gemma," he protested, laughing self-consciously.

"All right, I'll shut up. Subject closed. Make sure you treat her well and keep her safe, Michael, or you'll be living in hotels when you come to Washington."

"I will. Uh, speaking of which, I haven't got a place of my own yet. I've been away a lot. Again."

"You're welcome to stay as long as you want."

"Thanks."

Keely came back to the table, and they left the restaurant. When they reached Gemma's house Conroy unloaded her single suitcase — even for a three-month absence, Gemma traveled light — and hauled it into the house. The three of them congregated in the kitchen while Gemma unwrapped a treasure she'd brought from Italy. It was a little pottery oil lamp, no more than a hand-span from its stubby handle to the wick opening.

"It's real," she said, "not a reproduction. It's Roman, first century AD. Marco got me the export permit. They're not really that uncommon. They were so cheap in Roman times they used to throw them away if they broke."

Keely touched the incised curves decorating the lamp. "I wonder who lit the way to bed with this?" she murmured. "So long ago."

"Speaking of collapsing civilizations," Gemma said, "how

were the cherry blossoms this year? I gather I missed them."

"Not good," Conroy told her. "Maybe a little worse than last year. I don't know about the birds, I haven't been watching."

Gemma was about to say something when the telephone rang. She picked up the kitchen extension, exchanged a couple of words and handed the receiver to Conroy. "For you."

"It's Johnny," Reyes said in Conroy's ear.

"Hi, Johnny." This wasn't a secure line; he presumed Reyes was aware of it. "Where are you and what's up?"

"I'm still in Dallas. We got a very probable hit on the declarations. Real lucky. Seventeenth we checked."

"By God. How probable?"

"I'd say about ninety percent, unless we're paddling up the wrong creek completely. There's an address in Dallas, and I've got somebody on the way to check it out now. We're also looking for vehicle registrations under that name. Nothing yet, but you know how fast things can move. You want to come down?"

"Just a minute." Conroy thought hurriedly. They were running into walls here, and there wasn't much more he could do in Washington. He was restless from inaction and sitting in committee rooms. But Keely?

"You want to go to Dallas?" he asked her.

She looked startled. "I was supposed to go to Boston tomorrow. I really have to, Michael. I'm committed to hear three Ph.D. thesis oral exams. I can't be away or the exams will have to be postponed."

"Oh. Okay." Disappointed, Conroy turned to the telephone. "I'll be down tomorrow."

"Let me know when and I'll pick you up at the airport," Reyes said.

"Right." Conroy hung up.

"You're going to Dallas?" Keely asked.

"Uh-huh."

"Oh."

Gemma looked from one to the other. "I'm getting jet lag," she said. "I'm going to bed. See you in the morning, Michael. Good night, Keely."

"Good night."

They stood awkwardly in the kitchen together. Keely said, "What did Johnny Reyes find out?"

He told her Reyes's news. When he finished, she said, "His guess was right, then. That's how Ramon came into the country with his guns or bombs or whatever. This man is Ramon."

"Johnny thinks so. The rest of the people will have to be checked, but Johnny thinks this guy looks good."

"But where is he?"

"That's the problem. But it might be solved in a hurry. That's why I want to be there."

"Tell the truth, Michael," she said. "You don't want to sit in an office any longer. You want to be part of the hunt."

He nodded slowly. "I suppose so."

"When will we see each other again?" she asked.

"Soon. It's hard to be sure . . ."

She looked so woebegone all of a sudden that he reached out and put his arms around her. "Oh, hell," he said. "I'm sorry."

"I want all this to stop," she mumbled into his shoulder. "I just want us to be together. Without all these — these complications."

"So do I. Keely, I love you."

She disengaged her face from his shirt and looked at him. "I know. I love you, too."

"Now what?" he asked, and kissed her.

After a moment or two she drew away, put her arms around him and held him tight. "I feel awkward here. Let's go to the hotel."

As they pulled out of the driveway, Conroy was seized by a wild exhilaration. He drove fast and one-handed, his other hand clasped in Keely's, but every light was against them. At the third red, she started to laugh. "Isn't it always the way?" she said. "If we were on our way to a meeting, they'd be nothing but green. Never mind. It's nice to anticipate."

They reached the Watergate and parked. A short, plump woman with eyeglasses and a fur coat rode up in the elevator with them. Keely leaned against Conroy and Conroy slid his arms around her waist, clasping her to him. The woman looked studiously at the floor indicators, a faint purse of disapproval at her mouth. Conroy tried to keep a straight face but couldn't. By the time the elevator reached Keely's floor the woman was looking quite alarmed.

"What *were* you doing to her?" Keely asked as the elevator doors closed behind them. "Leering at me behind my back? Or at her?"

"Neither," Conroy said. "I just kept grinning, that was all."

"No wonder you frightened her. You can look quite demonic when you grin."

The suite was dimly lit by light reflected from the sky outside. Keely snapped on a lamp and closed the curtains. "There," she said.

"I don't suppose," Conroy said, grinning, "that I could persuade you to kiss me again."

"You might try," she said, and when he had stopped doing so for a moment she reached to the bedside table and turned off the lamp.

Texas
May 4–5

■

Joe Hendry stopped the pickup in front of the house and switched off the engine. In the sudden hush — the pickup's muffler was going — he looked doubtfully at the front door, which was standing wide open. There weren't any vehicles in the yard, and the place had an empty feel to it.

"Assholes," Hendry muttered as he got out of the truck. "Can't even shut the goddamn door when they go out in the morning."

He walked around to the side of the house and stared at the outbuildings and the big shed, remembering when the corral beside it had been full of sheep, all bleating their heads off. Couldn't even run sheep nowadays, the drought was so bad. He didn't think even goats would make it. The spic he'd rented the place to must have been crazy, thinking he and his cousins could make this place go again. If that was what they were really doing. Hendry had his doubts, but Francisco Ramirez had been willing to sign the lease, and he'd paid two months' rent up front in cash.

Hendry turned glumly away from the corral, went onto the veranda and banged on the open door. No answer, but he smelled old food, so he went inside and headed for the kitchen. Dirty plates sat on the table, and there were more in the sink. A cooking pot encrusted with what might have been stew was shoved to the back of the stove. There were several empty wine bottles on the table, and a rum bottle with a little rum still in it. Hendry opened the bottle, wiped its neck with his palm and drank the rum.

Upstairs there were no personal belongings. Hendry came down again and stood at the foot of the stairs.

"What the fuck," he said plaintively.

He went outside into the morning sunlight to check the outbuildings, leaving the big shed till last. Behind the old chicken coop was the fifty-gallon oil drum he'd used for hauling water before he and the sheep finally went under. Inside the drum was a lot of burned junk smelling of carbonized paint and plastic. In the dirt behind the big shed there were a lot of narrow tire tracks, as though the spics had been using a heavily loaded wheelbarrow. The tracks headed past the corral and disappeared on a patch of sun-dried earth.

Hendry went around to the front door of the shed he used for a garage. He'd come out to the ranch to get his extension ladder; God help the spics if they'd been using it or any of the other tools he'd left here.

He hauled the sliding door aside, stepped around it and stopped, blinking with surprise. "What in hell's name?" he said.

Inside the shed was a Ford Bronco, green and white. Hendry walked around inspecting the vehicle. There weren't any plates on it. He looked in the glove compartment, the map pockets in the doors and under the seats. No registration, no papers at all. The thing was clean as a whistle.

"The bastards have blown," he mumbled. "What about my goddamned lease?"

They'd been up to something funny, all right. Illegal, Hendry mused. And he'd been counting on that lease money to keep him going.

Maybe I could keep the Bronc and keep my mouth shut, he thought. Naw, I'd have to put plates on it and it might be stolen. Sell it under the table, maybe. Wouldn't get much. The fact is, those bastards done me out of twelve thousand dollars. Sonofabitch. I'll have the law on them goddamnit.

He tried the telephone in the house, but it was dead; they hadn't bothered to have it connected. Hendry slammed himself furiously into the pickup truck and shot out of the yard dragging a rooster tail of dust and gravel. He forgot the ladder completely.

*

Reyes and Conroy didn't get to the sheep ranch until some twenty-four hours after Hendry reported the abandoned Bronco and the vanished Hispanic named Francisco Ramirez. It was the same name that had been on the customs declaration from Eagle Pass, and the name of the man who had rented the apartment in Dallas. The FBI had had the name flagged for the state police computers, and when Hendry's report went in an alarm came out. Reyes and Conroy had flown as far as Pecos then rented a car for the journey southeast to the sheep ranch. It wasn't easy to find, in spite of the telephoned directions given by the state police in Fort Stockton.

"You figure this is the road?" Reyes asked as Conroy navigated the bumpy surface.

"There's something up ahead," Conroy said. "Looks like a house. Barn, maybe."

"Yeah, okay, I see it. If that's not it maybe we can ask directions."

A minute later Conroy said, "That's it. I can see a police car by the house."

Conroy stopped the car near the veranda. A state trooper had seen them from his car. He got out and sauntered over to Reyes's window. He was young and he looked cheerful enough, but Conroy noticed that his hand was never very far from his gun. "You the folks from Dallas, sir?" he asked.

Reyes showed his identification. The trooper relaxed and looked questioningly across the car at Conroy behind the wheel.

"That's okay," Reyes said. "He's my driver."

Conroy snorted. "Is Hendry here?" he asked.

"Yes, sir," said the trooper. "He's round by the back of that little building over there. I don't know if you'll get much out of him. He can't touch anything because of evidence, and he's madder'n a nestful of wet hornets."

"We'll handle it," Reyes said confidently.

Together he and Conroy went around to the rear of the shed. Joe Hendry was sitting on an inverted wooden box and leaning against the shed wall. He appeared to be in his late fifties, a long-limbed, gaunt man with a tanned face. He was wearing regulation Texas gear: Stetson, denim jeans and

work shirt, cowboy boots. A broad leather belt with a heavy
brass buckle encircled his narrow waist.

"Well," Hendry said, looking up. "If it ain't the FBI."

He didn't show the signs of unease and eagerness to coop-
erate that a lot of people did when confronted with the
Bureau. Conroy wondered whether it was because he was a
Texan.

Reyes displayed his badge. "I'm Special Agent Reyes," he
told Hendry. "This is Special Agent Conroy." Conroy
nodded.

"Okay. You want to get this over with so I can use my
own goddamned property?"

"As soon as possible," Reyes said. He started asking questions. Conroy listened intently, relieved that Hendry was
going to cooperate despite what the trooper had said.

A man named Ramirez had rented the sheep ranch, paid
two months immediately, in cash. He was going to try to run
sheep on it, with his two cousins, no, Hendry had never seen
the cousins. Ramirez had been driving a gray Ford van, not
new, a long box type. Texas plates. Hendry had only seen
him twice. The man had come to Hendry's rooming house in
Fort Stockton, and Hendry had brought him out to look at
the ranch. He'd signed the lease the next day. That was it,
until Hendry came out here and found the place deserted.

Reyes showed him an artist's renderings of two faces. One
was Ramon, taken from the original DEA photograph of the
Cuban standing beside the Cessna; the other was a composite derived from Teresa Bosque's description of Jorge Oliva.

"That's Ramirez," Hendry said, pointing at Ramon. "I
dunno 'bout the other one."

"Fine," Reyes said, putting the photographs away. "We're
just going to look around for a while."

"You going to be long with all this?"

"It depends on what we find," Reyes informed him. "We
might want to send out a lab team from Dallas."

"Jesus H. Christ," Hendry snapped. "What exactly has this
person done?"

Conroy saw the mask slip, revealing for an instant an intelligent man beneath the camouflage of Texas redneck. "Hang
on a minute, Johnny," he said. "Mr. Hendry, can you tell me

how you *felt* about Ramirez? Was there more to him than a Hispanic who wanted to start a sheep farm?"

Hendry, eyes narrowed, studied Conroy for a moment. "Okay," he said slowly. "Since you've had the wit to ask. There was something different about him, all right, now that I think about it. It was like he was under pressure inside. Like a boiler that's about to go, it looks quiet but it ain't. He moved real quick all the time. Not that he was jittery, you understand — he wasn't. And he watched everything, like he expected something to jump out of the bushes at him but it didn't worry him because he was ready for it. I never saw that anywhere but Nam. Some of those Special Forces guys looked like that. But under it all, something was pushing him. Like there was something he had to get done before it was too late. Is that why you're after him?"

"Yes. That's why."

Hendry snorted. "You'd better get looking, then. Because if I read him right, he's going to keep you busy as a man with one hoe and two rattlesnakes."

Conroy grinned at him and they began their search, starting with the house.

There was nothing revealing there except a stack of El Paso newspapers, consecutive dates, covering the past three weeks, and a couple of Dallas editions. Reyes checked through the front pages. Articles had been clipped from two El Paso papers and one from Dallas. Reyes made a note of the editions and pages.

"Might give us an idea of targets," he said as they left the house. "Be lucky if they did."

They checked through the garage, being careful to touch the Bronco as little as possible because of fingerprints. The serial number plate had been removed. Reyes got himself filthy looking for the stamped engine block serial number and finally located it.

"At least they didn't drill it out," he said, emerging greasy and irritable from the engine compartment.

"Can they do a registration search on the engine serial?" Conroy asked.

"Yeah, but it takes time. The computers aren't set up that way, damn it ... and the thing might not be registered in

Texas. We'll start here, though. Let's look around outside."

Hendry and his pickup had vanished, although the trooper was still in the yard, sitting in his cruiser and looking bored. By the side of the large shed Conroy went down on one knee.

"What?" Reyes asked.

"What kind of tire tracks do you suppose these are?"

Reyes looked at the narrow imprints. "Wheelbarrow?"

"Did you see a wheelbarrow?"

"No. We'd better cover them up with a box or something. The forensic people can trace the make, maybe."

They used the box Hendry had been sitting on. Then Conroy found an old oil drum behind what had once been a chicken coop.

"Johnny," he called. "Somebody's been burning stuff in here."

Reyes joined him and they peered into the malodorous drum.

Conroy sniffed. "Plastic. Smells like burned paint, too."

Reyes fumbled around in the bottom of the drum and came up with a blackened glass bottle. "Looks like the ones they put plastic model paints in," he said.

"Can we empty the drum?"

"Okay. Forensics will be pissed off, but what the hell. They won't get out here for a day, at least, and we've got to keep moving."

They tipped the drum over and raked out the debris. Some of it was melted plastic or bubbly plastic ash. There were a couple of scraps of carbonized cloth, several metal tubes and a triangular shard of metal sheet.

"Paint-brush ferrules," Reyes said as he fingered one of the metal tubes. "Have we got artistic terrorists, or what?"

"Damned if I know," Conroy muttered. He was fingering the blackened scrap of metal. It had one straight edge but the other two appeared to have been cut with tin snips; there was embossing on one of the cut edges and an embossed rim on the uncut side. Conroy tilted the scrap to catch the light.

"Looks like a D, then an A," he said. "I think this is part of a license plate. What state ends with D, A?"

Reyes thought. "Nevada. Florida. Are there any others?"

"None I can think of. What's he doing? Getting rid of a Florida plate? One he stole?"

Reyes's eyebrows were knitted together. "Maybe. But ... plastic, paints. Could he be making fake plates out of plastic? Painting them the right colors? He could have cut up a real plate to make a — well, some kind of mold to form the plastic over. That way he'd have plates that only he'd know about. That really screws us. The Ramirez name gave us the license tags for the van he bought, but if he's replaced them with good fake ones. . . ."

Conroy shook his head despairingly. "Jesus, he's cunning." He thought about Keely's lists of targets. There were a couple in Nevada: an air base that included a nuclear weapons dump, the Hoover Dam on the Arizona-Nevada border.

The Hoover Dam would be a nice one, Conroy thought, but I don't know how he'd crack that short of using a nuclear weapon. And he hasn't got one of *those*, at least I don't think so.

"What're you thinking about?" Reyes asked.

"Those newspaper clippings. I don't think we can wait for your forensic people to find out what they were. Let's see if the trooper will let us use his fax machine."

He would. Reyes put in the request, then they searched the house and yard for more scraps of the cut-up license plate, but without result. Conroy eventually found himself standing behind the large shed, gazing across the great sweep of the land. With the buildings out of sight behind him he might have been looking at the Texas plains as they had been five hundred years ago, before the Spaniards came. No sheep, no cattle, no fences.

No complications, Conroy thought. I think I like it better out here. What was it Keely said? That I don't want what I think I want? I'm not even sure what I think I want any more. Caracas. . . .

"The info's coming in!" Reyes was calling from behind him.

Conroy tramped toward the cruiser. Reyes was listening intently to the beep of the cruiser's fax machine, which ended as Conroy reached the car. Reyes tore off the transmission and gestured Conroy away from the car, away from the trooper's hearing.

"It's the GATT conference," he said. "All three articles were about the GATT economic conference. That's what he's going to hit."

"That makes sense from what we were talking about in Washington," Conroy said. "He'd see the northern economies as exploiting the Third World. This is the sort of target to make the point."

"Yeah, well, I'm glad he isn't going after the shuttle. They've got one of these plutonium-powered satellites going up day after tomorrow. You know, the type that's supposed to wipe out Florida if it goes splat?"

"I heard," Conroy said. "Some scientific group was trying to get an injunction against the launch."

"Doubt if they will," Reyes said. "They never have yet."

"Are you going to get the forensic team out here?"

"Yeah. I'm curious about those narrow tyre tracks. Need to lift some prints, too, unless they wiped everything down."

"I'll head for Miami as soon as we get to Dallas," Conroy said. "And I've got to call Washington about this."

"Okay. Let's get the hell out of here," Reyes said. "This was easier than I thought it would be. Some days you just get lucky."

Don't we just, Conroy thought. "I don't like it," he said.

They were getting into the rented car. "Why not?" Reyes asked.

"Ramon left a clear trail. That's not like him."

"Everybody makes mistakes," Reyes said, and started the engine.

Florida
May 6

∎

Rain was falling, a streaming downpour. Inside the van the air was so wet that Ramon felt he could squeeze his hand closed on it and see water drip from between his fingers. The windshield and side windows were badly fogged in spite of Portela's intermittent attempts to swab them clear, and outside the windows the streetscape of Miami was no more than an indistinct, rain-streaked blur. The asphalt was layered with water, and most of the cars spraying through it had their lights on although it was only shortly after noon.

The van was parked at a meter on a side street just off North Miami Avenue, not far from the Omni Mall. This was the van Menocal had rented, the one they had painted dull green at the sheep ranch in Texas. The other van, which had been gray when Ramon crossed the border from Mexico, was now biscuit-colored. If Menocal hadn't run into any trouble it should now be parked two blocks from the rear entrance of the huge Miami Convention Center down by the bay. It hadn't been possible to get any closer than that.

Ramon had checked the GATT conference's security perimeter on foot last night after they arrived in Miami. The security zone extended for a block around the convention center, and they weren't allowing any traffic inside the zone except vehicles with some kind of pass stuck to their windshields. Ramon had thought about stealing such a pass but had decided against it. He wanted a diversion that looked like a demonstration of revolutionary anger; whether it did any damage was quite immaterial.

Although, he reflected, watching drops of condensation chase each other down the windshield, that five kilos of C4 over the van's fuel tank will certainly make them sit up and take notice. Assuming the timer's accurate there'll be a big bang at three this afternoon.

He'd instructed Menocal to insert all four of the little timer detonators al-Bakr had supplied, just to be sure the thing would go off.

"He should be turning up any time now," Portela said, looking at his watch.

"Yes," Ramon answered, and looked at his young captain. Portela looked quite calm and relaxed, his big hands resting quietly on his knees. Ramon felt a rush of affection for the man and his courage. On the long drive from Texas to Florida he had talked to them plainly about their chances of escape, which were not really very good. Their reaction was matter-of-fact, which he'd expected; they were soldiers.

"Anyway," Portela had said, "at least the Americans don't let their women cut the balls off prisoners, like the Yemeni hill men did. Remember?"

Ramon had nodded. He remembered.

He handed Portela this morning's newspaper, which had been lying on the seat between them. "Look in there and see if anything's changed," he said.

Portela began flipping through the limp pages. "No change in their schedule, according to this," he said.

"Good."

A central cab pulled up just ahead of them, stopping in the traffic lane. There was a short pause while the passenger paid the driver, then Menocal was trotting toward them through the rain, his poncho pulled over his head. Portela shoved the door open and moved over to let Menocal climb into the cab beside him.

"Everything's fine," Menocal said in a rush, slamming the door and exuding a smell of wet cloth and rubber. "I parked it in that lot we picked out. Right at the side. There's a clear line of sight to the back of the convention center. Maybe it'll jiggle them a little."

"Let's hope so," Ramon said. He started the engine and moved into the traffic. From behind he heard a crack and click of metal as the partially disassembled gyroplanes shifted with the motion. The two machines were a tight squeeze in the cargo space of the van, but there was just enough vertical clearance for them once the rotor heads were removed. The rotors, broken down into their component blades, were strapped to the van's roof rack under a plastic tarpaulin, which also hid the camouflage nets. The three men had been sleeping in the back of the other van and using service stations to shave and wash in. It was important that they did not look like vagabonds; Americans put so much store by appearance.

He settled down to drive. Portela fiddled with the radio and tuned into a Miami station playing Gloria Estefan. Ramon found himself tapping the steering wheel in time to the beat. As they curved up the access ramp to the north-south expressway the rain slackened off, and a few minutes later the sun came out. The city glistened and steamed under a sheet of humidity. Menocal opened a window and let the warm damp air rush in; it smelled fresh and oceanic.

Better to travel than to arrive, Ramon thought. Is it? Of all the times in my life that I've been truly happy, this would be one of the happiest. Nothing to do but drive for a few hours, without immediate responsibility, all preparations made and made as well as I could manage, and the anticipation of what we are going to do tonight, or to be precise early tomorrow morning. And there is no reason to believe anyone knows we are here or suspects what we are going to do.

Mother, do you sense that I've almost succeeded? Have Cardoso's people struck out at you because they couldn't find me? Or have they let the cancer take you? Did it move faster than you thought it would? Will I ever know?

If there was a cloud on his horizon, that was the cloud. He had steadfastly refused to imagine what might have happened to his mother because of what he had done and what he was doing. Not knowing whether she was alive or dead was the most difficult. He had thrust that question out of awareness and kept it out, preferring instead to imagine her alive, as he had last seen her, waving to him from the doorway of the house in Puerto Real as he tramped up the lane toward the bus and his future.

But she knew what might happen, he reminded himself. We talked for hours about it after she told me how we might strike back against the counterrevolution. I was willing to die then, she said, in Bolivia. I am still ready to die, and I *am* dying, Ramon. Why wait to act when my end is inevitable? What would it achieve? *Think*, Ramon. I always taught you to think. Think now.

Once he had accepted the fact that she was going to die no matter what he did, everything was much easier.

"Hungry?" Menocal asked, fumbling behind the seat and surfacing with a box of doughnuts. "There're a few left from last night. Capitalist luxury," he added with a grin.

They ate the sweet confections and drove on through the afternoon sun. Humidity draped haze over the horizon. They were now well out of Miami and following Route 1, although the Florida turnpike would have been a faster route north. Ramon's self-protective instincts had warned him against using the toll road; if by some freak the authorities were searching for him the men in the toll booths would have been told to watch. In any case, he didn't want to arrive too soon. They were safer, he felt, when they were on the move.

He kept an eye on the dashboard clock. The Miami radio station was fading out. Portela found a stronger one, from Fort Pierce, a little to their north. At a couple of minutes to three Portela said, "I wonder how long it will take them to put it on the news outside Miami?"

"A few minutes, half an hour. I don't know."

The clock ticked over to three. "There," Menocal said. The music played on, uninterrupted except for commercials.

The announcer broke in at sixteen minutes past, just as they were rolling into the outskirts of Fort Pierce. A large car bomb had exploded in downtown Miami, not far from the convention center. None of the GATT delegates had been harmed, but an uncertain number of people had been killed and more injured.

"Good," Ramon said. "Look for a public telephone."

"There's one," Portela said after a minute, pointing toward a convenience store just ahead on their right.

Ramon drove into the parking lot and stopped. The telephone would do; it was several meters from the store entrance and he was not likely to be overheard. He got out, leaving the others in the van, and fished in his pocket for the handful of quarters and the slip of paper with the telephone number of radio station WLMB.

The operator told Ramon to deposit a sum of money, which he did. When he got through he asked for the newsroom.

Clicks and hums. "News."

"You must write this down," Ramon said. "It is about the explosion in Miami. Are you ready?"

The man was fast off the mark. "Okay. Can I tape it instead?"

"Be quick."

A few seconds' silence. "Go ahead."

"This is the Guevara Brigade," Ramon said clearly. He looked around; there was no one near. "We are responsible for the bomb aimed at the exploiters of the masses of the world. This is the first shot of the new revolution. There are five more such bombs in Miami. You will not find them in time. Goodbye."

He hung up and went to the van, where Portela was eating the last of the doughnuts.

The parking lot attendant had been filleted by the glass in his booth when the bomb detonated, and the walls of the small enclosure were marked by trails of blood drying slowly in the humid air. Conroy could smell the sweetish rusty odor of it as he and Reyes showed identification at the police line and were waved through. Keely, white-faced, stayed behind the barriers among the curiosity seekers and the television news teams, waiting.

The firefighters had had to use a lot of foam to put the gasoline fire out — the blackened and truncated van must have had a full fuel tank — and the dirty white substance dribbled over the wreckage in the parking lot like soot-streaked soapsuds. Eight other vehicles had been burned out by the explosion and the fire, but it was clearly the van that had been the focus of the explosion; its entire rear half had been ripped off and fragmented.

Reyes stopped to survey the mess, and Conroy did likewise.

He looked down and found himself standing next to a small puddle of bloody water. Next to it lay a scrap of twisted metal with paint on one side. Conroy picked it up and inspected it.

"Was it him, do you think?" Reyes asked. "The bastard."

There had been half a dozen people in the lot, leaving or approaching their cars, when the bomb went off. One had been inside a station wagon and been burned small and black.

"I think so," Conroy said. He handed Reyes the swatch of sheet metal. "Look at this."

The scrap was only slightly scorched. Probably it had been blown out of the van body by the explosion. A layer of buff paint had been partly stripped off, revealing dove gray underneath.

"The van Ramon bought in El Paso was gray," Conroy said. "He must have painted it. What's left over there looks like it might be the same model."

"He's a smart bastard," Reyes said. "So he's got another vehicle."

"Not likely stolen, either," Conroy reminded him. "There're three of them as far as we know, Ramon, Portela and Menocal. This was Ramon's van probably. The one calling himself Jorge Oliva hasn't turned up in any of the vehicle registration searches. So if they've got a legally registered vehicle, it's under the third guy's name."

"Which we don't know."

"Right," Conroy said gloomily. "And he could have bought a house trailer, for all we know."

"Piss on it for the moment," Reyes said. "I see Merrick over there. Come on."

Conroy followed, glancing back for a moment to see if Keely was still there. She was. The three of them had been in the convention center security headquarters at the time of the detonation, which had sounded like no more than a faint, dull thud, but Conroy had known immediately what it was. He and Reyes and Keely had raced outside in time to see the greasy column of smoke rising into the blurry sunlight two blocks away. There had been several ambulances in and around the convention center, just in case somebody's deputy trade minister had a heart attack, and the crews were ordered to the scene even before the fire trucks arrived. The last ambulance had left about five minutes ago, carrying the burned person from the station wagon.

As well as Merrick, several other security people — the conference had been under the protection of the Secret Service, the FBI and the Miami police — were already clustering around the van's wreckage, staring gloomily at it. Although the fire was out the metal was still too hot to touch.

Gary Merrick looked over his shoulder as Reyes and Conroy approached and nodded, stern-faced. Merrick was FBI, head of the antiterrorist unit for Florida; he would have been near the GATT conference site even if Reyes and Conroy hadn't sounded the alarm about Ramon Guevara's expected strike.

"Hello," he said. "You think this was your boy?"

Conroy had not been sure how seriously the alarm had been taken by the FBI in spite of the warnings furnished by the CIA analysis team, of which Keely was a member, and the pointers furnished by the findings at Hendry's ranch. He and Reyes had flown to Miami yesterday evening; Garland had already arrived with key members of the analysis team including, not to Conroy's total surprise, Keely. Lipton had wanted her there for her experience with revolutionary psychology. Keely told Conroy that Washington was terrified that there might somehow be a bloodbath at the convention center, in addition to the economic experts there were present three foreign ministers, a clutch of trade ministers and undersecretaries too numerous to mention. Keely and Reyes and Conroy had been up most of the night with the Secret Service people and Merrick's teams, working out possible scenarios for Ramon's attack and methods of countering it.

Our mistake, Conroy reflected as he looked past Merrick at the smoldering wreckage of the van, was that we expected him to be more determined and selective. Instead he seems to have opted for simple terror.

"Yes," he said to Merrick. "I think it's him. We just found something that points that way."

Reyes handed over the shard of painted steel. "Buff?"

Merrick said. "We were looking for a gray vehicle with plastic Florida plates. Everybody was."

"It's been painted," Reyes pointed out.

"Yeah. I see." Merrick handed the scrap to one of his men. "Make sure the lab gets that. Well, at least he missed this time. I wonder where the hell he is?"

A gray-suited agent appeared at Merrick's elbow. "WLMB, got a message from somebody claiming to be the perpetrator, sir," he said briskly.

"What is it?"

"A male person telephoned the station and stated that he was a member —" the agent consulted a slip of paper "— of the Guevara Brigade, and that the Guevara Brigade claimed responsibility for the bombing. The person also stated that there were five more such bombs in the Miami area. He then hung up. The WLMB staffer was able to tape the call."

"A real campaign," Merrick observed dryly. "Maybe he studied with the IRA. Unless it was a crank."

"No," Conroy said. "Not if he said he was the Guevara Brigade. That was Ramon, all right."

"Jesus," Merrick said. He was sweating in the humidity; they all were. Conroy was wearing a lightweight suit so that the jacket would conceal his Beretta, and his shirt was clinging to his back. "You think he really might have five more bombs?" Merrick continued.

"He might," Conroy said uncertainly. None of these men, except perhaps Reyes, knew Ramon as he did. This did not fit with Conroy's image of the Cuban.

"Don't you think so?" Reyes asked curiously.

"I don't know for sure. This smells like a diversion. I think he's going to do something else."

"I'd say five more bombs was something else," Merrick observed dryly. "He's not making idle threats. Where there's one bomb there may be more. We're going to have to go on that basis."

"Yeah," Conroy said. "I know. But suppose," he said in a rush, "it's a diversion. The other main target in Florida is the shuttle launch just after one o'clock tomorrow morning. Suppose that's really what he's after."

"They've got good security at the cape," Merrick said.

"Nobody's allowed within five or six kilometers of those pads when there's a launch. How could he get at it?"

"I don't know. I'm trying to think like he does."

"I hope to hell that isn't it," Merrick said. "They've got one of those plutonium-powered satellites on board. You know, the ones the ecologists keep making such a stink about."

"The power units in those things are supposed to be secure even in a launch pad explosion," Conroy said. "Aren't they?"

"So NASA says. Would your boy be interested in finding out if they weren't?"

"Don't know," Reyes said. "It's possible he's not even aware of it. The story didn't get into the papers until after he left the Fort Stockton area."

"Well, maybe he isn't, then," said Merrick. "Nobody's paying much attention to it this time around except a couple of the Florida papers. NASA's launched six of the things so far without any trouble."

"Mm," Conroy said. "Look, I want to go up to the cape anyway. Gary, can you lend me a car with a telephone and radio so I can keep in touch?"

Merrick winced. "I'm short of transportation as it is."

"CIA will be eternally grateful."

"Oh, hell, all right. I'll get you one. Give me a few minutes."

"Okay. Thanks a lot."

"Can you get into the launch area?"

Keely could likely pull strings with Lipton. "I think so. Johnny, can you come?"

Reyes looked doubtfully at Merrick, who said, "I need all the help I can get, if there's another five packages like this one. I can spare you a car, that's all."

"Okay," Conroy said as gracefully as he could. "I'll be back in a few minutes." He'd wanted Reyes along, if only to serve as a sounding board for his suspicions. What was troubling him was that he might still be misjudging Ramon. There was no clear indication that he was planning any kind of a strike at Cape Canaveral; if he was, it might not be the shuttle. It might be one of the Air Force launches, the unmanned Atlas Centaurs or Deltas; one of the former was scheduled to lift off from the Cape Canaveral Air Force Station tomorrow afternoon. There'd be less security for those than there was for the shuttle, Conroy figured.

The problem is, he thought, as he hurried toward the police barricade and Keely, I'm not really sure enough of anything. I don't *think* Ramon's interested in a bombing campaign, not from what Keely's told me about the way he thinks. But who can predict how another person will think, especially one as skewed and cunning as Ramon? She's smart and intuitive, but still....

He reached her and ducked under the barricade. "This is horrible," she said. She was clearly very upset. "This wasn't what I thought he'd do at all. How could I have been so wrong? This is the work of a thug. If we'd realized that, these poor people...."

Might be alive, he finished for her silently. "We can't blame ourselves," he told her brusquely, taking her arm and starting toward the convention center. "It's not possible to predict everything. And I'm not sure this isn't a diversion."

She looked at him. "Oh?"

"Does it feel right to you?"

"No. It doesn't. He's more than a thug."

Perverse, Conroy thought, that we don't want him to be only that. We'd prefer him to be demonic, which I think he is. "I want to go up to the Cape," he said. "Can you get hold of Lipton and persuade him to arrange it so I can get into the launch area? I'll ask Garland if I can find him, but Lipton would likely carry more weight with NASA."

"Do you think the shuttle's in danger?"

"I don't know. I want to go up there, that's all."

"I think I can reach him from the security office in the convention center," she said. "He's probably been on the line already, after this."

"Yeah," Conroy said. He squeezed her arm. "It's going to be okay. Try to find out if NASA's doing anything special about security."

"NASA was warned when you said Ramon was coming to Florida," she told him. They were a block from the convention center, and a Miami police officer, bulky in a flak jacket and carrying an assault rifle, was hurrying toward them. Conroy and Keely were wearing identification badges with photographs, but he stopped them anyway and compared their faces to the photographs before letting them pass. "But," she went on as they entered the convention center, "I don't know how seriously they took it." NASA, Conroy recollected, had its own security forces, well equipped and by all accounts well trained.

Their badges were checked three more times by Secret Service agents before Conroy and Keely reached the security center. Television screens glowed everywhere, displaying sensitive parts of the huge complex, watched constantly by security staff and Secret Service personnel. There was a good deal of tension in the air, a result of the bombing. Apparently, though, the conferences were continuing without interruption.

Garland was nowhere to be found; somebody said he was closeted somewhere with the chief of the Secret Service team. At loose ends for the moment, Conroy waited in one corner of the big monitoring room while Keely tried to contact Lipton; he could see her frowning behind the glass partition of one of the cubicles along the side of the room. After two or three minutes her face cleared and she began to talk, presumably to the chairman of the National Security Council.

A newspaper was lying on a filing cabinet. Conroy leafed through it. On the back page of the front section he found what he was looking for: another attempt by a coalition of scientists, ecologists and antinuclear activists had — again — failed to obtain an injunction to stop the launch of the plutonium-powered satellite. The coalition said NASA was inviting disaster by continuing with the launches; a NASA spokesman said that the fuel cells would remain intact "even in the event of a major launch pad incident," by which he presumably meant the shuttle blowing up. The judge had agreed with the spokesman. There was a small diagram and a technical description of the satellite power pack, which Conroy read with some attention. He tore the article out and stuffed it in his pocket.

Keely came back. "Rupert will clear it," she said. "He'll

make sure they're expecting us."

"Us?" Conroy said, startled.

"Of course. I'm going, too."

"But ... aren't you needed here?"

"Not really. The FBI and the Miami police can judge at least as well as I can what's vulnerable. I suggested to Rupert that so long as you were going up there, I should go along. One never knows when one is going to need an intelligence analyst." She tried to say it lightly, but there were lines of strain around her mouth. She looked, for once, as old as her thirty-nine years. Conroy wanted to throw his arms around her and hold her tight, but didn't.

"Okay," he said, although he had mixed feelings about her coming.

"He sounded odd," she added.

"Who? Lipton?"

"Yes. He seemed to have expected Ramon to be caught trying to get into the complex. He was very upset that it hadn't happened that way."

"It might have. We thought it was likely. Not much wonder Lipton's upset. We missed Ramon, after all."

"Yes," she said. "We did. Do you need to tell Garland we're leaving?"

Conroy pondered. It had never been clearly spelled out whom he was to report to; by default, he'd stuck with Vickery. "No," he said. Garland might want him to stay put for some obscure bureaucratic reason, and Conroy was of the opinion that obtaining forgiveness was often easier than obtaining permission. "I'll leave word at the message center."

The sun was edging toward the western horizon as the van passed through Mims, traveling north on Route 1. To the east of the highway, Ramon knew from his careful perusal of the geological survey maps — the wonderful maps that were a soldier's dream compared to those he'd had to cope with in Yemen — was a strip of land some two kilometers wide, and beyond that lay the upper reaches of what was called Indian River, although to Ramon's eye it was not really a river at all, but a broad, shallow bay. Beyond the bay was the huge, irregularly shaped landmass known as Merritt Island.

The island stretched over sixty kilometers from its broad northern end to its slender southern tip. At the top of the island, as seen on a map, lay a region of sloughs and ponds and salt marshes sprinkled with low trees and bushes; this was the Merritt Island National Wildlife Refuge. East of this low-lying terrain was another body of water, named Mosquito Lagoon, which was separated from the Atlantic Ocean by a slender strip of land composed of sand dunes, marsh and a ribbon of beach on the ocean side. The lagoon was peppered with patches of land, some no more than marshy hummocks, some large enough to be called islands, which divided it into a maze of creeks and channels and shallow inlets.

South of the wildlife refuge, and across the bottom end of Mosquito Lagoon, lay the John F. Kennedy Space Center. There was no distinct southern shore to the lagoon; it dissolved vaguely into a stretch of sloughs and ponds, which reached to within a thousand meters of the service towers of Pad 39-B, where the orbiter *Atlantis*, mated to its huge external fuel tank and rocket boosters, gleamed white in the early evening sun. Five kilometers southwest of the pad rose the vast cliff of the Vehicle Assembly Building, dwarfing the angular facades of the Launch Control Center next to it. Florida State Highway 3 ran right past the assembly building and the control center, although here it was called the Kennedy Parkway. Above the complex the highway entered the wildlife refuge and, leaving that, passed northward along the isthmus that divided Indian River from Mosquito Lagoon and connected Merritt Island to the mainland. Eventually Route 3 intersected with Route 1 a few kilometers past the Brevard-Volusia county boundary line and well to the north of Merritt Island. Ramon was making his approach from the north.

He slowed down slightly to glance at the road map. Route 1 should swing right just ahead, and not far past the bend should be the intersection with Route 3. He laid the map on the dash and sped up, but was careful not to travel more than five kilometers over the speed limit.

"We're timing the light well," Portela said. None of the men in the van had spoken for a good half hour. Ramon knew they were all starting to feel the preattack tension, the heightened awareness that comes when all the plans have been made and all the equipment and the men are in position and there is nothing left to do but wait.

"Yes," he said briefly. "It's good." The curve was ahead, then the straight leg for a few kilometers. The highway was passing through a stretch of marshy land. There was the junction with Route 3; Ramon turned right. Ahead of them now, although hidden, were Merritt Island and the space center.

After a few more minutes he slowed down again. Menocal had the survey map out and was studying it carefully.

"The road should be just ahead. A hundred meters," Menocal observed.

"I see it," Portela said after a moment.

Ramon turned onto the side road. It led into a region of palmetto and straggling undergrowth and quickly lost whatever surface it once had, becoming a potholed track twisting among the skinny tree trunks and skirting dark pools of standing water. Eventually it petered out almost entirely and was no more than a set of parallel ruts threading the undergrowth. Through the scrub to his left Ramon saw water: Indian River. He coaxed the van off the track and under the low tree canopy until it was more or less hidden among the bushes, then turned off the engine. "We're here," he said.

The three men sat silent for a moment, then Menocal said practically, "Do you think the light is the way we want it?"

"It's hard to tell under the trees," Ramon said. "We should go down to the water and look."

He was feeling extraordinarily relieved. He had reconnoitered this place very hurriedly in early March, flying from Dallas and back in less than thirty-six hours, before Faustino was likely to miss him, and he had been worried that it would not serve his purposes as well as he remembered, or that somebody would have built a house on it in the meantime, the way Americans did. But it still worked.

The land ended not in swampy mud but in a lip of earthen bank about half a meter above the water. Trees overhung the surface, and a hundred meters away from the bank was a line of low islets. The islets were among the reasons he had chosen this place from the maps then reconnoitered it in person: the Intracoastal Waterway with its traffic of pleasure boats ran a few hundred meters offshore, and the islets would screen Ramon's preparations.

"The light's good," he said, squinting at the evening sky. "But I think we'd better not waste any time. Let's put them together."

They hurried to the van and started to unload. First the four pontoons, which had been strapped to the inside walls of the van to give space for the gyroplanes' fuselages, then the fuselages. They carried the parts to the shore and bolted the floats to their supports. Menocal and Portela returned for the rotor blades while Ramon made sure all the control cables and fastenings were tight and properly adjusted. He also put fresh batteries into the big flashlights of the altitude indicators, installed the red filters over the lenses and made sure the flashlights were securely fastened to the airframes. He had practiced this so many times at the sheep ranch that the procedure was almost automatic.

As soon as the blades were fastened to the rotor heads they slid the little machines into the water, using wooden beams for skids. The gyroplanes, unloaded, rode high and buoyant on their pontoons. The light was diminishing rapidly.

"Arm them," Ramon said. He glanced appraisingly at the sky and the water. There had to be just enough light to allow them to pick a good landing zone — this he had not been able to reconnoiter — but darkness also had to be far enough advanced to make the gyroplanes indistinct against the eastern sky.

Menocal and Portela brought the crate containing the missiles down to the water. Ramon helped slide them onto their launching rails, then tested the batteries and firing circuits and connected the wiring. Menocal checked the laser designator and found it satisfactory. Then they checked each others' work, and Portela went over the gyroplane airframes and control cabling.

The tests were complete. The weapons were ready. Menocal took the tools and beams to the van and locked it, and they ran through one last equipment check.

Camouflage nets, for the remainder of the daylight and in

case the shuttle launch was delayed until past dawn tomorrow. Two small FM radios, for monitoring the count-down the local radio stations carried. A flashlight, for signaling the moment at which the target was properly designated, and a spare. Weapons: a .357 Magnum revolver each. For each man: two canteens of water, a pound of chocolate and a pound of dark rye bread in a waterproof bag.

"Time to go," Ramon said. "One last look at the map."

They peered at it in the failing light. "Here is where we are," Ramon said, pointing. "Three kilometers right across from here is Vanns Island. It looks as though there's an expanse of water a hundred meters wide just beyond it. That's where I want us to land. Use maximum cruising speed; that way we'll be there about two minutes after takeoff. Joel, you'll go in first, as we planned, since your machine is lighter. If you can't get in, then we can't, so the alternate landing zone is to the south, here, where there's more water. But it's more exposed, so I'd rather not use it. All right? And before we take off, we must watch for masts on the other side of the islands, there. I don't want to fly over a boatload of American bourgeoisie."

The others nodded. Ramon folded the map and slipped it into the plastic sealer bag.

The gyroplane bobbed as he stepped onto the float and got carefully into the seat. Menocal and Portela had been tutored in water takeoff and landing by the manufacturer, but they hadn't had a chance to refresh their skill.

Joel said it was easy, though, Ramon reminded himself.

Menocal was starting Portela's machine while Portela strapped himself in. The engine fired quickly and settled down into its hornet buzz; from the other side of the string of islets it would sound, Ramon judged, like the motor of a small boat. He held the plane to the bank while Menocal started their engine then dropped into the pilot's seat. Menocal grinned at Ramon and waved to Portela, who began to maneuver away from the riverbank to clear his rotor. Ramon saw him scan for masts then engage the prespin. The rotor began to turn and the gyroplane started to accelerate over the surface of the water, leaving twin white Vs of wake.

Now their rotor was turning, and Menocal pushed carefully on the throttle. The little machine slowly gained speed. Ramon watched Portela ahead of them. From land the planes would lift in thirty meters, but with the drag of the floats to overcome the takeoff run was almost doubled. There was a good ripple on the surface to help them unstick, though; Luis had told him that getting off from perfectly calm water was more difficult than from slightly rough.

There. Portela was airborne, moving very slowly and turning gently to head across the river.

Their own plane, more powerful than Portela's but heavier, seemed to be taking a long time to reach flying speed. The floats were trying to climb their own bow wave, and when Ramon looked down he could see the dark water rushing past beneath him, flecked with streaks of foam. He willed the gyroplane into the air.

They crossed the remnants of Portela's wake with a jounce, then suddenly the motion smoothed out and the plane picked up speed. They were off. The horizon ahead of Ramon tilted, and suddenly they were flying over one of the islets toward Vanns Island. Portela was about a hundred meters ahead, no more than three meters above the surface of the water. Even at this distance his machine was hard to see against the dark eastern sky.

Ramon looked up and down the channel of the Intracoastal Waterway. He could see the white hull of a boat a long way away to the south, but nothing in the other direction. It was a good bet that they were making the crossing unobserved. Another minute or so and they'd be landing.

The island shore slid by underneath, and Menocal gained a meter or two of altitude to clear the low vegetation. Portela was already halfway across and slowing down. Menocal drew the throttle back. On the far side of the island, true to the map, was a sheet of water. Its surface reflected the last light of the sky, silvery rose and much brighter than the dark land and marsh surrounding it. Portela had slowed to his minimum possible airspeed, and there was an onshore wind from the Atlantic that enabled him almost to hover above the water surface. After a moment of scanning the ripples from a meter up, he let the machine slowly descend. It mushed into the water, perfectly upright and stable. Ramon saw him wave in invitation.

Taking advantage of the same wind, Menocal slipped down out of the darkening air to land forty meters from Portela's machine. Ramon clapped him on the shoulder. "Beautiful," he called over the engine's hum. "Now, over against the bank. Once we have the camouflage nets up, we're safe."

They reached the grassy verge, and Menocal switched off the engine. "We're almost there," he murmured softly in the quiet. "Almost to the shuttle."

Ramon nodded. "Just a little farther," he said. "Not really very far at all."

Merritt Island, Florida
May 6–7

■

"What do you think of that?" Conroy asked. He fished the newspaper clipping about the satellite out of his jacket and handed it across the car to Keely. Outside, the humid Florida night fled by, velvet and damp behind the sodium glare of the lights of the Bennet Causeway. They were nearing the east end of the causeway, where the Canaveral Barge Canal entered Indian River; on their right lay the speckled lights of the town named, like the land on which it stood, Merritt Island.

She opened the glove compartment so that its light would illuminate the clipping. "Oh," she said. "Yes. We considered that possibility when we were making up the target list."

"Would it be tempting?"

"Certainly. If he breached the fuel capsules it could be very bad. But I don't know whether he'd realize that."

"But NASA says the capsules can't be breached," Conroy said. "Not in a pad explosion." The interchange with Route 3 was coming up. He slid the FBI car into the lane for the northbound exit.

"I do know the NASA engineers rammed one of the capsules into a stationary target at high speed," she told him. "Almost three hundred miles an hour. The capsule wasn't even dented."

"What about heat? Could the capsule casings be melted?"

"I'm trying to remember," she said. A pause. "They say not," she resumed. "The capsules are iridium metal. It melts at some ridiculously high temperature like two and a half thousand degrees centigrade. The solid boosters burn at less than that."

"The newspaper article says the iridium capsules are inside graphite blocks," Conroy observed. "Graphite's just carbon. It'd burn, but it wouldn't be hot enough to touch iridium. But what about the liquid fuels in the external tank? Those are liquid hydrogen and liquid oxygen. That's about as hot as you can get, isn't it?" They were on the exit ramp now, almost on the highway leading north toward the space center.

"It's above the melting point of iridium," she told him. "But an explosion in the external tank wouldn't expose the capsules to that heat long enough to melt them, because an oxyhydrogen fire burns upward, not downward. So if there were an explosion, the capsules would fall down, to the pad, and the oxyhydrogen would go up. Not enough contact to be dangerous."

"Or so they say."

"Yes. So they say."

"We must be crazy," Conroy said. "Taking those chances. Suppose they're wrong. What *would* happen if the capsules were breached in a pad fire?"

"That was what worried me when we were discussing it," Keely said. "No one knows for sure. It's not the sort of thing you can easily test. But plutonium-238, the isotope of the metal that's on the satellite, is the most carcinogenic substance known, and it's most dangerous when you breathe it in. Assuming the capsules were cracked open, a pad fire could send a lot of plutonium compounds into the air. Depending on the size of the plume and the direction of the wind. . . ." He sensed her helpless shrug.

"What was the worst case they looked at?"

"This is classified," she said, half joking. "It was in one of the Nuclear Regulatory Commission reports the task team was looking at."

"I'm CIA." He grinned at her.

"If you say so. I don't remember the details, but it said that if half the plutonium in that kind of power supply were released in the form of oxides, rose to more than three thousand meters, then spread downwind in a plume across central

Florida, the central part of the state would be uninhabitable for several centuries."

Conroy digested this. It seemed unreal, a plot concocted by a mad scientist in a 1950s horror film that had swamp monsters in rubber suits. "Christ," he said. "And I let you come up here with me."

"You didn't *let* me come with you," she reminded him sharply. "I don't need your permission to do what I feel I need to. I'm an academic and a theoretician, but I've been right about Ramon when others have been wrong. And I called Rupert for us."

"Sorry," he said humbly.

"I know you're just trying to take care of me," she told him. "But I managed nicely for quite a few years on my own. I'm perfectly capable of taking care of myself, Michael." She paused. "Except when I called you from Miami that first time. That was different. I admit to that."

"Everybody should know when to call in the experts," he teased her, then became serious. "I thought plutonium was bad for a lot longer than a few centuries."

"That's the 239 isotope," she informed him. "It has a half-life of about twenty-five thousand years. This 238 is worse in the short term, because the half-life is much less, about eighty years, and that makes it a lot more radioactive."

"Oh, boy. Deaths?"

"That would depend on the wind, the height of the plume, the time of day, whether people were inside or out, whether they were evacuated before the fallout came, all sorts of things. If it blew over Orlando, for example, and people walked around in it and breathed it, they'd almost all die of cancer sooner or later. It doesn't kill quickly, you see. It waits in the bone marrow and the liver and the lungs."

"Jesus," said Conroy. "A city of walking dead people."

"Yes. Like those towns around Chernobyl. There could also be immediate deaths from radiation poisoning around the launch pad, where the isotope concentration was thickest."

"The stupid bastards," Conroy said. "No wonder they classified it. How crazy do you have to be to take these kind of chances with a whole goddamn state? Florida'd be shipping Day-Glo oranges for the next two hundred years," he added with black humor.

"We're part of it," she said. "We know, and we don't say anything. That's because we want to believe it will never happen, and we don't want to end up in jail for saying that the sky is falling, especially when we're not really sure it's going to."

"Ramon couldn't breach the capsules, anyway."

"I don't see how."

"We may be up here for nothing," Conroy said. "He may just be trying to blow up Miami."

"I've never seen a launch, anyway," Keely told him. "I'm rather looking forward to it."

"We'll be there in a few minutes."

The first security gate was around a dogleg in the highway. Conroy identified himself and Keely. Evidently Lipton had done whatever it was he was going to do, because the guards were expecting them and gave them a vehicle pass to put on the dashboard. The men were armed with Colt assault rifles and wore flak jackets and web gear.

"Are those people Special Forces?" Keely asked.

"No. NASA has its own bunch. Kennedy Space Center Security. There's also a specialized antiterrorist team here called the Reaction Force. They're supposed to be good."

"Do you see anything like extra security?" she inquired.

"I don't know what extra would be. There's a helicopter up north, though. I can see its searchlight."

They stopped at a second security gate. In the distance they could see the brightly illuminated monolith of the Vehicle Assembly Building — called the VAB — with its vast American flag and the NASA insignia painted on the side, and in the night beyond that a small, bright blur that was the floodlit service structure of Pad 39-B. At this remove the shuttle was not visible.

They were passed through a third security gate, and the VAB loomed closer. The third gate was just outside the complex of low buildings and parking lots that surrounded the launch center and the assembly building. Even from several hundred yards away the huge structure hung over them like the face of a sheer cliff, gleaming white where the lights illuminated its base and reaching up forever into the night, its summit shadowed and indeterminate as though it might not really end at all but be the base for some fantastic tower that rose to the stars.

"I had no idea it was so big," Conroy said as the guard perused Conroy's CIA card and the one issued to Keely by the National Security Council.

"Everybody says that the first time, sir," the guard told him. "You get used to it. When you pass the gate, turn right off the highway and go right to the back of the VAB complex. The road curves around to your left. The Launch Control Center — the LCC — is back there — it's got a lot of glass windows on the bottom two stories. You can park near the entrance on this side. I'll call to let them know you're coming. Just wait in the car and someone will be out to get you."

They followed the guard's directions. As Conroy parked the car a heavyset man came out of the LCC's brightly lit entrance and waved to them. Conroy and Keely got out of the car and walked over to him. He wore civilian clothes but had a distinct military bearing; his gray hair was clipped short above a wide, tanned forehead. Conroy recognized in the guarded blue eyes the look of the security professional. "Hello, Mr. Conroy, Dr. Fitzgerald," said the man. His voice, light and tenor, was at odds with his looks and size. "I'm Clay Whiddon. Chief of Kennedy Space Center Security. You want to come in where we can talk?" He didn't smile or offer to shake hands.

"Thanks," Conroy said.

They followed Whiddon inside and through a series of anonymous white corridors to a very ordinary small office. "Security center's on the other side of that wall," he said, sitting on the edge of his desk as though he didn't expect them to be with him long. "Sorry, but I can't let you in there at the moment. I don't want my people distracted. What seems to be the trouble?" He still wasn't smiling.

"Did you get a call from Rupert Lipton?" Keely asked.

"No, I didn't. Somebody above me said I was to talk to you two. Some kind of information. That was all."

Hell, Conroy thought, bureaucracy. Whiddon thinks we've

been foisted on him, political pressure. No wonder he isn't falling over himself to make friends.

"We've come up from Miami," Conroy said. "There was a bomb explosion there this afternoon."

"I heard about that. That was the group we were warned about yesterday, was it?"

"I think so," Conroy said. "But I'm worried it might have been a diversion."

"You're worried they might be after *Atlantis*?"

"Yes," Keely said. "It's the sort of thing he'd do."

"Who's 'he'?"

Doesn't anybody tell anybody anything? Conroy wondered. "Ramon Guevara," he said. "Che Guevara's son, an illegitimate one. He's been putting something together for several months. It might be a strike against the shuttle."

Whiddon blinked at Conroy disbelievingly. "He'd never get near it," he said positively. "There's only one grade of security here when there's a launch, and that's the highest grade. Nobody's within five and a half kilometers of the pad at lift-off, which is going to be at a quarter to one this morning. They're getting the crew aboard right now. Am I supposed to tell them to scrub the launch because of some possibility that Che Guevara's son is out there with a weapon? Do you know how dumb that would sound? This place is flat as a plate, there's nowhere to hide."

"What about the marshes up north?" Conroy asked.

"Come in by boat, you mean? Too slow. My choppers would spot him. I've got a pair out watching the perimeter right now, and one outside here in reserve, just in case. And he couldn't get a boat closer than about three kilometers, anyway. He couldn't hit anything from that distance, not with the weapons terrorists use."

The man's confidence was maddening. Ramon could very well be in Miami, waiting for his next explosion, or he could be out in the darkness beyond the lights, waiting. "I know Ramon was in the Middle East," Conroy said. "He didn't go there to buy C4."

"What's he got, then?"

"I don't know."

"Look," Whiddon said, "we're doing everything we

normally do. There's nothing else I can assign to the patrols, not this late in the game." He switched his gaze to Keely. "You mentioned Rupert Lipton," he said. "The National Security Council chairman?"

"None other," said Keely.

Conroy could see Whiddon thinking. The post he held would have political dimension; there would be people his superior would not want him to offend. And as far as Whiddon could know, Keely and Conroy might be close to Lipton, close enough to be worth catering to.

"Well," he said in a much more friendly tone, "I don't think there's any danger from Ramon Guevara, even if he is old Che's kid. Tell you what I'll do. I'll give you a pair of VIP passes and take you out to the reserve chopper. The pilot'll fly you around for a while. Not many people get a chance to see the space center from the air the night of a launch. If you want, you can watch the lift-off from the press stands. There's a couple of camera crews out there setting up right now. How would that be?"

Conroy and Keely exchanged glances. Hers said: We might see something. We might sense something they don't.

"Sure," Conroy said. "It'd be great."

"Okay. Come with me."

The reserve helicopter was stationed a few meters northeast of the parking lot. Pad 39-B was about five and a half kilometers away. Conroy could make out the chubby white cigar of the orbiter and the much larger orange sausage of the external liquid fuel tank on which it rode.

Inside the olive-green UH-1 helicopter, which had a searchlight mounted under its nose and an M60 machine gun on a flexible mount inside the left-hand cargo door, were two troopers from the Reaction Force. The pilot was a woman with long blond hair and a perfect oval face, strikingly incongruous above the battle dress and combat gear she wore. The other trooper, a man, looked like a younger edition of Clay Whiddon, right down to the cropped hair and chilly blue eyes. Whiddon introduced them quickly. The pilot was Joanna Ridley, the man Orville Platt. Whiddon made sure they knew Conroy was CIA and that Keely was (although she wasn't) a member of the National Security Council. Conroy could sense Platt's evaluation of them, if not Ridley's: a CIA spook and a Washington think-tank theoretician, not much better than civilians. Nevertheless, they seemed willing enough to fly the perimeter.

"This okay with you?" Conroy asked Ridley. She was in the left-hand seat, Keely in the right. There was a fold-down jump seat behind Keely's, into which Conroy had somehow shoehorned himself. Platt was in a harness between the open doors in the cargo compartment, one arm draped over the machine-gun mount.

"Yeah, it beats sitting on the ground. I don't like being in reserve. Nothing to do. Lemme show you where the headsets plug in. There, put this one on, Dr. Fitzgerald. Okay, the turbines are warm so here we go."

The rotors clattered overhead, and the Huey rose into the dark. Ridley flew in a wide arc toward Pad 39-B, but didn't approach too closely. "There it is," she said, voice scratchy over the headset. "Isn't that a pretty sight for sure?"

"For sure," Conroy said. The orbiter gleamed under the lights. Conroy thought about what was in its belly and grimaced.

Ridley took them up to the boundary of the nature refuge and flew along it some forty meters up, sweeping the ground once or twice with the searchlight. Clumps of vegetation, irregular patches of water. A man in camouflage could be hiding down there, Conroy thought, and we wouldn't see him unless he moved.

He looked northward. Another helicopter searchlight drifted up there, but the other machine was much higher than the one he was in.

"Why isn't that helicopter flying lower over there?" he heard Keely ask. She'd noticed it, too.

"Nesting season," the pilot drawled. "We're not allowed to fly low except in an emergency, 'cause the rotor down wash and the noise freak out the birds and they leave home. New regulation."

"Oh," Keely said. "Can you see anything from that height?"

"Not a damn thing, Dr. Fitzgerald. As the count goes down we bring the choppers in closer anyway. At five minutes before lift-off we all come in and check the ground approaches to the pad."

"What do you do then? At lift-off, I mean?" Conroy asked.

"We all set down for a minute. Don't want anything in the air around here at launch."

"Speaking of things in the air," Keely said, "I suppose you've got ways to keep a light plane from flying in just before a launch and hitting the shuttle with an air-to-air missile."

"Yeah. You can't see them, but there's Navy jets out there with lookdown radar. Any plane comes in too close — I can't tell you how close — they jump on him."

It's all so carefully done, Conroy thought. Why can't I shake this premonition?

Ridley flew them down the line of the Kennedy Parkway, out across a long gulf of water — the Banana River, she said — and back to her reserve position at the LCC. "You staying to watch the launch?" she asked as the turbine whined slowly down and her two passengers wriggled out of their seats.

"Uh-huh," Conroy said.

"The press stands are over there."

"Any objection," Conroy said, "if I brought my car over here and we watched from it? It's got a phone and radio in it I want to be close to."

"Sure. Go ahead."

They sat in the car, looking at the faraway bright towers and the indistinct dart of the orbiter. Conroy tuned the car's civilian radio to a local station that was carrying the count-down. There hadn't been any unexpected holds; lift-off was still scheduled for a quarter to one.

"Forty minutes to go," Conroy said. He called the Miami convention center security office, hoping to talk to Reyes, but they didn't know where he was. They promised to have him call back as soon as he turned up.

"Is Ramon doing this by himself?" Conroy asked as he replaced the receiver. "Or is he following somebody's orders? I can't believe Castro would go off the rails this way."

"I think he's alone," Keely said. "There's often a streak of romanticism in these people. Romanticism gone wrong. Ramon sees himself, I think, as a romantic hero like his father, doomed but fighting to the end for what he believes in. Most people lose those notions in a hurry when they find themselves on a real battlefield. But there are a few who don't, and they can be very determined and dangerous. They feel they have some special destiny, you see, and they turn themselves into a symbol in their own imaginations. It's a kind of madness, because it doesn't take account of reality."

"God protect us from true believers," Conroy muttered.

"Yes," she said. "Exactly."

Time passed.

The sound of the radio was no more than a cricket's chirr in the darkness under the camouflage nets. The helicopters with their lights had never approached closer, Ramon estimated, than ten kilometers, and they seemed now to have gone farther south. Nevertheless their presence was making him reconsider his intention to attack in daylight if the launch was delayed. The American security was tighter than he had thought it would be.

But according to the radio the countdown was proceeding without delay. He'd make the decision later, if he had to.

All three of them were under the net covering the two-seater. Ramon shaded the penlight with his hand and checked the survey map again. Here in the slough behind Vann's Island they were twenty-four kilometers from Pad 39-B; it was almost time to move into the jumping-off position. One of Ramon's worries — that one of them would fly into the water in the dark in spite of the flashlights they'd rigged as makeshift altimeters — had been relieved by the Americans; there was enough of a sky glow from the space center lights to the south to provide a horizon. Between that and the flashlights he thought they could keep their altitude and orientation accurately enough.

"Time to go," he said quietly. "We fly straight toward the Americans' lights."

After they removed the camouflage nets and secured them behind the gyroplane seats he tested the wind. It was out of the east, blowing inland across their intended flight path, but he judged it to be moving without gusts at no more than ten kilometers an hour. This time he and Menocal took off first, with Portela following. Ramon navigated.

The altitude lights, he was pleased to see, worked perfectly even on the water. Once Menocal adjusted their height to superimpose the two dim red spots of illumination, they were flying at precisely seven meters above the surface. At their present speed they'd be in the air for no more than seven or eight minutes.

Menocal gained two meters of altitude as scraps of land whipped by underneath. Then came a longer stretch of land. Ramon read the memorized map in his head. This was Pardon Island.

More water; the machine dipped again. The islands were easier to see because the glow in the sky above the space center was reflected in the lagoon's surface. Ahead were narrow strips of land: Cucumber Island, Turtlepen Point.

Four kilometers and set down, Ramon thought. He counted the seconds off in his head. One minute, two kilometers. Two minutes. A streak of black on the dim water ahead, Gallinipper Point. He pressed Menocal's shoulder. The plane slowed, almost hovering as it passed over the slip of land. On the other side was a basin about five hundred meters across and open to the south. The dull red spots of the flashlight beams separated, drew apart. The gyroplane plopped down onto the water, and Menocal turned it toward shore to get out of Portela's way. Within two minutes they were snuggled up to the bank, the camouflage nets loosely draped over the rotors again. If Ramon stood up under the net, he could just see the illuminated top of the pad service tower. The helicopters were nowhere near.

He put the radio to his ear and listened. The Americans were starting a predetermined five-minute hold, after which the count would resume at nine minutes to zero.

"Looks like everything's fine," Conroy said. The LCC had resumed the count. The radio station was feeding the LCC orbiter communications directly to the audience, punctuated by the announcer's explanation of what was going on. Conroy thought the man sounded a trifle bored; NASA had been sending up a shuttle about once a month for two years now.

"Event timer started, over."

"Roger, *Atlantis*, out."

The announcer talked for a minute about the satellite on board and the safety factors built in to the power supply. Then he said, "Now they'll retract the crew-access arm. Seven minutes to launch."

The man shut up for a few seconds. Then the crackle of the orbiter communications loop:

"*Atlantis*, this is control. Initiate APU prestart procedure, over."

"Roger, out."

The announcer did his best to fill the ensuing minute of silence by explaining the functions of the auxiliary power unit. He broke off as the loop came alive again.

"Control, this is *Atlantis*. Prestart complete, powering up APUs."

"Roger, over."

"APUs look good, out."

"Six minutes," the announcer said.

"Six minutes," Ramon said. "Let's go."

The camouflage nets were already off, lying on the bank by the water. Menocal started the engines, and the two gyroplanes began taxiing across the basin, the two-seater in the lead. Ramon switched on the laser sight, peered through it for an instant to make sure it was on, then held it across his chest like a rifle. The plane accelerated.

"Four and a half minutes," said the announcer. "They are now on internal power."

The car telephone bonged. "Yeah," Conroy said into it. "Conroy." He didn't take his eyes from the orbiter.

"It's Johnny." Reyes sounded agitated. "Listen, we finally got a make on those tire tracks. The manufacturer supplies them for about a dozen other outfits. One of the outfits makes ultralight aircraft. Gyroplanes. They come with wheels. Or floats."

"Oh, my God," Conroy blurted. "Do they know that up here?"

"We're telling them now. Or trying to. Some trouble getting through to the security center. You'd better try. This might be it."

Conroy slammed the telephone down and looked out the window past Keely at the reserve helicopter. Keely had a worried expression on her face. "What?" she asked.

"Ramon's coming in by air," he said. "From the north, the swamps." He could see Platt sitting in the cargo door of the Huey. The trooper was watching the shuttle, unconcerned.

"The message isn't getting through," he said in horror. He flung the door open and raced toward the helicopter. He heard Keely's running footsteps behind him and wanted to tell her to go back, get inside the control center, but couldn't spare the breath. "Platt!" he shouted from a dozen meters away. "Start the engine! There's an attack coming in from the north."

Platt looked startled and disbelieving as Conroy came up. "What the hell are you talking about? We haven't heard anything from control."

"Damn it," Conroy yelled at him, "there's a guy out there in an ultralight, I don't know what weapons he's using, but he's coming. For God's sake call Whiddon and tell him to pick up his call from Miami. Or let me tell him. For Christ's sake, I know what I'm talking about!"

Platt's face lost the disbelieving look and he scrambled to his feet. "Okay. Come up front."

Conroy clambered into the helicopter cargo bay. Faintly from the press stand he heard a loudspeaker say, "Oxygen vents are now closed. Two minutes fifty seconds."

Keely was right behind him. "Go back to the LCC," he said. "Please. It'll be safer there. Even if the plutonium goes up."

"No," she said stubbornly. "I'm not leaving."

There wasn't time to argue. He put his head into the cockpit. Platt shoved a headset at him; he saw Joanna look over her shoulder at him for an instant, then her hands were moving across her instrument panel to the engine switches.

"Whiddon here. What the hell's going on out there, Conroy?"

"Haven't you been talking to Miami?"

"No. We're busy here. Would you please get off this circuit?"

"Send your people north, for God's sake," Conroy said, keeping his voice even, although he didn't know how he was managing it. "Ramon Guevara's in an ultralight out there somewhere."

"Jesus," Whiddon said. "Are you sure?"

"As sure as I can be."

"What's he carrying?"

"I don't know. Tell them to abort the launch."

"I can't do that on your say-so, for Christ's sake. We're only a minute from main engine ignition. You don't know for sure he's there."

"At least tell them."

"Okay. Now tell Ridley from me to go out and look. I'll vector the other choppers. But they're down south. Get going."

Conroy tore the headset off. The rotor blades were clattering overhead. "Whiddon says go north and look," he shouted at Ridley. "Up to the sloughs."

Ridley gave him the thumbs-up, and the Huey lifted.

The two gyroplanes were slowing down. Portela and his missiles were hanging well back, as they had practiced. Ramon had the radio around his neck and the volume well up so he could hear the count over the hum of the engine. Ahead was the palely reflecting band of Max Hoeck Back Creek. Pad 39-B was no more than three kilometers away. Ramon could see the white dart of the orbiter quite clearly.

"Land," he called to Menocal. The gyroplane dropped slowly to the water, settled. Menocal ran the float tips against the near bank and held them there with the engine, stabilizing the little machine. Ramon stood up so he could see over the bank, braced himself against the seat and put the laser sight to his eye. The shuttle leaped toward him, seeming no more than six hundred meters away. He took a deep breath, exhaled half of it and fixed the cross hairs in the center of the orbiter's cargo bay. The gyroplane engine was just ticking over.

"Main engine ignition," said the radio.

Fire bloomed in the night.

"Now," Ramon said clearly.

Menocal blinked the flashlight at the single-seater, which was drifting slowly across the marsh to their left.

Portela fired the missiles with half a second of delay between them. They shot out of the launching rails trailing plumes of flame, which were overwhelmed and obliterated by the glaring light from the orbiter engines three kilometers off. Ramon kept the cross hairs steady on the cargo bay.

"Solid booster ignite," said the radio. "Lift-off."

The first missile hit the orbiter, then the second.

Conroy had shoved Keely into the right-hand seat as the Huey rose. He hunched behind her seat back, peering into the night. Platt was in the cargo compartment, snapped into the gunner's harness behind the M60 machine gun. Conroy noticed a pump-action shotgun clipped to the inside of the door next to Keely's seat; on the opposite door, by Ridley, was a Colt assault rifle. At least we're well armed, Conroy thought.

"I don't see anything," Ridley said. The helicopter was clattering over the ground some thirty meters up, flying due north. Pad 39-B was directly to their right. "Are you sure —"

A small, bright spark appeared ahead of them. It didn't appear to accelerate at all; it was just suddenly there, moving at tremendous speed across their line of flight. A second spark followed it. There wasn't even time for Conroy to blurt more than "Look!" before the sparks disappeared into the glare of the shuttle's engines. For a moment nothing seemed to happen. Then, abruptly, the light from the engines doubled and redoubled into an incandescence that threw every leaf and branch below them into staring relief.

"I see something!" Keely cried.

The shuttle was already rising when the first missile struck. Because Ramon was keeping the laser sight quite still, and because the second weapon was a split second behind the first, there were two distinct impact points.

The first missile, traveling at almost fifteen hundred meters per second, pierced the upper skin of the cargo bay about halfway along its length. The weapon's nose cone broke up with the impact, as it was designed to do, and the depleted-uranium penetrator slug inside the missile body continued on into the bay, where it struck the power module of the satellite. The iridium capsules containing the plutonium power cores were strong enough to protect the cores against most kinds of impact, but they were useless against a weapon designed to breach any known tank armor.

The penetrator slug crashed into the row of capsules, splitting open the iridium casings and shattering the power cores inside. If the cores had been pure plutonium metal the slug would likely have bounced out of the module immediately on striking the first one, but they were not; they were a hard, brittle mixture of ceramic and plutonium intended to reduce the chemical reactivity of the metal, which in its pure state was quite high. As a result, the slug smashed half the capsules open and scattered their contents before it finally diverged from its original course and exited from the underside of the power module as a misshapen incandescent lump of uranium. On its way through the power module it also ignited the graphite casings of the capsules, starting a hot carbon fire around the pulverized ceramic-plutonium debris. The slug then struck the floor of the bay, but went no farther.

The second missile hit the gimbals of Number Three Main Engine and smashed the engine off its mounts. Metal fragments from the impact penetrated one of the high-speed turbopumps of Number Two Main Engine — the pump's turbine was running at thirty thousand revolutions per minute — and the pump tore itself apart. Fuel from broken feed lines poured into the inferno at the stern of the orbiter, and ignited.

The total loss of two engines unbalanced the shuttle assembly beyond the ability of the computers to control. Instead of rising slowly along the length of the service tower, the vehicle began to topple sideways, rotating along its axis as it went. The nose of the external tank ripped open against the top of the service tower and the tank exploded.

In the orbiter cabin, Payload Specialist Alan Kawada saw a very sudden, very bright light outside the left window. Through his headphones he heard Commander Lacey say,

"What —" and then the cabin slammed against the service tower and disintegrated.

Conroy knew that something terrible had happened to the shuttle, but like Keely he had seen the flicker of movement in the darkness ahead, and the Huey was racing toward it at the best speed Ridley could coax out of her machine. The other helicopters would be on their way, but Ridley's was closest.

They shot over a broad finger of water. The searchlight was on, Ridley controlling its direction with a small joystick. The beam swept over a slough, climbed the scrub and palmetto of an islet, snapped down again.

"There's the son of a bitch," he heard Ridley scream. Conroy could see more distinctly as the helicopter closed: a dark moth of a machine, its propeller disk a faint blur in the searchlight. It dodged down and to their left.

"Dragon One to base," Ridley was saying urgently. "We have him. Coordinates approximately ... damn it, it's too dark. Northwest of Pelican Island, flying northwest, target speed one-twenty klicks, in pursuit."

"Dragon Two and Three are on the way," Conroy's headset said. He recognized Whiddon's voice.

Ridley, somehow, was flying the Huey and managing the searchlight, but it obviously wasn't easy. Keely reached out for the joystick. "You fly," Conroy heard her say clearly. "I know how it works now."

Ridley gave up the joystick. She'd lost the gyro when it dodged away, and Keely swept the light beam to their left, in the general direction of its disappearance. There it was again, much closer. It was a single-seater, flying very low.

Platt had seen it. Even through the headset Conroy heard the hammer of the M60, and flashes of tracer swept over the gyroplane. "Don't kill him, damn it!" Conroy shouted. "Knock him down, we need to know where the others are."

"Advise, base," Ridley said. "Did you hear that?" She'd turned the Huey onto the gyroplane's track, masking the M60.

"Knock him down if you can, Dragon One," said Whiddon. Even over the circuit, Conroy could hear the shake of horror in his voice. "Affirmative do not shoot down."

"I copy," Ridley said. "Platt, hold your fire."

"There's another one!" Keely exclaimed. "I saw it ahead of the other one, I'm sure."

"This one first," Ridley said. The Huey was almost on top of the gyroplane, about fifteen meters above it. "I'm going to knock the bastard into the water with my rotor wash."

The gyro dodged left again, seeming to turn almost at a right angle. Ridley swore and banked after it, overshooting. "Base, the sucker turns faster'n the Huey does. Other Dragons copy."

"Copy," Whiddon said. "Copy," said two more voices over the circuit.

Keely had the gyro in the light again. It had turned to the northwest after its dodge. There's something up there he wants to reach, Conroy thought. An escape route, a car, something.

"Not this time," he heard Ridley mutter. "This time he'll turn right, keep the light on him."

She had anticipated the gyro's next evasion perfectly. The little machine twitched to the right, and the Huey was suddenly above it. The Huey's rotor wash blasted downward over the gyroplane's spinning blades. Conroy saw the pilot slow down suddenly, as though trying to make the helicopter overshoot, but the attempt was futile. Deprived of lift by the violent down draft, the gyro staggered and fell twenty meters into the dark, roiled water below. Ridley moved away a little to allow Keely to train the searchlight on the spot where the machine had gone down. There was nothing to be seen but the concentric rings of water beaten by the Huey's rotor wash, and in their center a pair of upturned floats.

"The other one," Conroy said urgently. "He's out there ahead of us."

"Throw a flare float," Ridley told Platt over the intercom. A moment later a glaring white light was burning on the water below them, and Ridley turned the Huey northwest. "How far ahead of the other one was he?" she asked.

"I couldn't tell exactly," Conroy said. "But not very far."

They clattered steadily away from the holocaust of Pad 39-B.

*

The later analysis of the catastrophe stated that almost everything that could conspire to worsen it did in fact happen. When the shuttle rotated and toppled, it sandwiched the orbiter between the external fuel tank and the latticework of the fixed service tower. The oxyhydrogen explosion, instead of scattering the various parts of the vehicle for thousands of meters around the pad, rammed the orbiter cargo bay and the satellite's plutonium debris downward and into the tower lattice, where it lodged. The left solid booster shattered when it struck the tower and separated into its component fuel segments, which joined the orbiter wreckage heaped around the bottom of the tower. The right booster, detached by the explosion from the external tank, pivoted outward and lodged against the movable portion of the service tower, which had been swung back for the shuttle's launch. It hung there for a few seconds like a colossal inverted Roman candle, then its thrust and the weakening of the tower from the external tank explosion brought the whole mass of the towers and the entrapped wreckage thundering down across the launch pad and the crawlerway in an avalanche of flame and molten metal.

The exposed plutonium was undergoing certain chemical transformations. The missile's impact and the shattering of the cargo bay had intimately mixed it with carbon from the graphite blocks that had once surrounded it, and as it was exposed to the inferno of the burning solid fuel it began to form finely divided plutonium monocarbide, a compound with extremely high resistance to heat. Quantities of plutonium dioxide also formed, but at such temperatures it broke down quickly, allowing the plutonium to recombine with the carbon of the graphite and form more of the monocarbide.

While this was happening, tons of water from the sound-suppression system were still pouring into the baffles underneath the launch pad. Much of the water turned to superheated steam, which forced its way up through the ruined towers and the masses of burning plutonium. The monocarbides, with several other plutonium compounds formed by the heat and the various materials of the shuttle, were drawn upward by this steam and the combustion gases from the solid booster fuels. The smoke and steam and plutonium rose toward the night sky in a vast gray-white plume that soon reached through three thousand meters and kept rising, although it was slowly beginning to be blown inland by the wind from the sea. The cloud was violently radioactive.

Menocal was still flying doggedly northwest. As far as Ramon could tell, they hadn't been seen. But the Americans had caught Portela, shot him down, or so the machine-gun tracer would indicate. There was a flare burning back there on the water, almost invisible in the glare from the burning launch pad beyond it. Even at a distance of fifteen kilometers Ramon could see his fingers quite plainly when he tilted his hand to catch that hellish light. It illuminated the gyroplane as well, but in his elation Ramon didn't care.

"What does it look like, Ramon?" Menocal called plaintively from the seat beside him. They were flying low, with the flashlights off, and Menocal couldn't take his attention from controlling the machine.

Ramon twisted in his seat to look back. "Magnificent," he called over the engine's hum. "There is a great pillar of smoke and a pillar of fire under it. The rocket crashed and burned. They never thought it could happen to them. We've struck our blow, Luis. We've done it."

I've started the revolution again, Ramon thought. In the name of my father, and the masses of the earth. All I need to do now is stay free and alive long enough to tell them who did it. Then I no longer matter.

"Is Joel all right?" Menocal asked.

There was no point in upsetting Luis. "Behind us somewhere."

Ramon looked behind again. There was a light there, not the flare on the water, and it was growing brighter.

Conroy saw it before Keely or the pilot did, in the sickening light from the pad behind them. "Over there!" he cried into the intercom. "Eleven o'clock. To the left and ahead, Keely!"

She trained the light and caught the gyroplane in its beam. Five hundred meters away, Conroy thought. Beyond it, dimly catching the light of the flames behind them, was a line of trees or bushes, Conroy wasn't sure which. The distance closed rapidly, but the gyro made no attempt to evade. A hundred meters. Fifty. Still no evasion.

Two bright sparks from the gyro, one right after the other.

He's trying to shoot out the light, Conroy realized as Ridley made the Huey jink. The gyro disappeared suddenly as the searchlight lost its target with their evasive action. Then he saw it again, a spindly moth in the far-off firelight. A two-seater.

"He's heading for shore," Ridley called out. "I don't know if we'll catch him."

The shoreline was much closer than Conroy had thought. Perhaps three seconds later the gyro splashed down into the water and overturned. The Huey shot overhead, climbing and banking as Ridley fought it around to pass the impact point.

Menocal had misjudged his height and flown the gyro right into three meters of water, digging the float tips in and flipping the machine end for end. Fortunately he'd slowed down for the landing, and the impact wasn't severe enough to do more than stun Ramon for a few seconds. He found himself hanging upside down in his seat belt, surrounded by warm brackish water, and with his mouth and nose full of it.

After a quick struggle with the belt release he twisted out of his seat and away from the gyro, letting natural buoyancy direct him toward the surface. Gasping and choking, he broke into air. Menocal was already out, striking the water to keep himself afloat.

"Ramon?" Desperately.

"I'm here. The shore. We can get away. Go north, the van's up there."

The Americans' helicopter blatted overhead, the finger of the searchlight probing downward. Ramon ducked beneath the surface and swam for the bank a little way off. He reached it and dragged himself onto the scrubby grass and weeds. The undergrowth and low trees started a meter beyond the bank; he rolled into their cover. The helicopter swung over the water and hovered, searchlight trained on the overturned gyroplane. Then it moved overhead, the light raking through the leaves, flying slowly inland. Through the screen of vegetation Ramon could make out a clearing, brightly lit by the searchlight beam.

Menocal had disappeared. Ramon jumped to his feet and began thrashing his way through the undergrowth, heading north. He had no idea how far he had to go.

"They got out," Keely said. "I saw them get to the bank as we came over."

"There's a clearing the other side of those trees," Conroy said urgently. "Put Platt and me down there and track them from the air as much as you can. If they get away in the undergrowth, we may not catch them for days."

He heard Keely's sharply indrawn breath over the headphones, but she said nothing.

"Platt? Okay?" Ridley asked.

"Yeah." The voice was flat and hard. "Do it."

"Jump from the skids," Ridley said, turning the Huey. "I'll stay a meter up. We'll blink the light when we see somebody. And take the Colt," she added, gesturing to the weapon clipped to the door beside her seat.

Conroy grabbed the assault rifle and scrambled into the cargo compartment. Platt was already out of his harness and standing by the right-hand cargo door. The helicopter settled.

"Let's go!" Platt shouted at him, and Conroy was on the skid, dropping away from it with the Colt in his right hand, feeling the ground come up and hit the soles of his feet. He staggered once and ran for the tree line to the north. Behind him the helicopter rose and passed overhead, the light sweeping the trees. Platt, almost invisible in his camouflage suit, was crashing through the low bushes to Conroy's right.

The helicopter's light blinked. Conroy and Platt slowed and moved apart, weapons ready. The undergrowth made them half-blind; it was the worst kind of fighting. Like Bolivia, Conroy thought, trying to get the old skills into his eyes and ears and feet.

He couldn't see Platt all of a sudden; a thick wedge of

brush had become interposed between them. The Huey was moving on. Conroy stumbled over a tree root and recovered in time to see the light beam blink, swing to point fifty meters to his right and blink again.

They've separated by accident or on purpose, he thought. The Huey was dead ahead of him, almost in a hover. She's lost one of them, Conroy thought. Where the hell are the other choppers?

As if in answer another light sprang into being on his right; he hadn't heard the machine approach because of the noise Ridley's machine was making. The light blinked.

They won't get away now, he thought. One helicopter each.

Ridley moved suddenly, and the light blinked again. Conroy squinted through the leaves overhead. Keely seemed to be pointing the beam to the ground a hundred meters farther on. Conroy ran through the weeds, keeping low.

He burst into a narrow gap among the trees, no more than ten meters across, and pelted across it as fast as he could. Beyond was a narrow band of palmetto, and beyond that a small clearing. There was a man in the middle of the clearing, not more than twenty meters from Conroy. He had stopped and was aiming a pistol at the helicopter that was thundering above him.

Ramon.

He saw Conroy as Conroy saw him, and he was quick as an adder. He threw himself prone as Conroy fired and missed. Conroy brought the Colt's muzzle down.

Ramon's revolver banged twice, the noise almost inaudible in the roar of the helicopter's blades, and Conroy felt something hit him very hard in the side, just below the rib cage. He staggered backward and his fingers lost all their strength. He dropped the Colt. He knew vaguely that he was on his knees and that Ramon was still aiming at him. This is how I end, he thought.

He looked despairingly at the helicopter and saw the open copilot's window and a series of muzzle flashes, one, two, three. Ramon's arm dropped and his suddenly ruined head fell onto the grass.

Keely got him, Conroy thought as he toppled forward. Good for Keely. Good for her.

Charleston–Puerto Real
May 8–15

■

He seemed to be spending a great deal of time somewhere where it was dark. Sometimes there were voices, sometimes images of fires and black water and thunder. A lot of the time there was pain, and sometimes something that made the pain go away.

Little by little, though, he sensed himself rising nearer to the light, and then there was a time when he opened his eyes, becoming aware as he did so of what eyes were, and that he possessed them, and looking up at a white plain. He recognized it after a while as the ceiling of a room. Then someone said, "He's awake," and he knew it was Keely. He saw her face above his, and then he dropped away into the dark again, although not so far as before.

Later (he didn't know how much later) he found himself properly awake. Keely was still there, or had gone away and come back.

"Hello," he said, through a painfully sore throat. "Where am I?"

"Charleston," she said. He noticed that there were tears running down her cheeks. "Gemma's here, too. You're going to make it, Michael."

"Was I not going to?" he asked.

"Nobody was sure. But now you are."

"Ramon?"

"He's dead."

He remembered what she'd done. "Thank you," he whispered.

"Rest now," she told him.

*

A couple of days later his throat didn't hurt nearly so much and he felt a good deal stronger. He was awake and partly sitting up when she came in. She kissed him. "Good morning," she said. "This is good to see."

"I feel better," he told her. "Keely ... what happened afterward? The pad fire?"

She looked down. "Perhaps we should wait till you're stronger."

"Tell me."

She closed her eyes and opened them again. "It could have been worse, I suppose. Most people were inside when the cloud came, because it was at night. They evacuated Orlando, but a lot of things went wrong. The cloud went all the way across Florida and some of it's still traveling. As far as Texas. The radiation plume ... well, there's a band across Florida a hundred miles wide that no one can live in for the next two centuries. At least."

"How many deaths?"

"Twenty-six right away at the space center. A lot of people were killed in the evacuations, in the panic. The long-term exposure to the plutonium, nobody knows for sure. The figure the experts seem to believe is a hundred thousand over the next twenty years."

It had all been so futile. "We were so close to catching him," he said. "So close."

"You did everything you could."

"I suppose so." Everyone had failed except Ramon. "The other two?"

"Both dead. The first one drowned. Platt shot the other one. I can't say I'm sorry. They deserved to die. When I saw him shoot you ..." She trailed off. Then she said, "I would have killed him with my hands, if I could have."

He found her hand. "It's okay."

"I wish it were."

He let go of her fingers. "What?"

Instead of answering she looked at her watch. "Wait," she said, and went to turn on the television set bracketed to the wall facing the bed. After a moment of fiddling she found the channel she wanted: Headline News.

The top-of-the-hour reports were beginning. The announcer was looking grave; behind him were shots of crowds in streets, streets Conroy recognized after a moment as being in Havana.

"Events in Cuba have taken a stunning turn," the announcer was saying. "It appears that a concerted attempt to overthrow Fidel Castro has begun in the past few hours, an attempt apparently led by forces in the government frightened of the United States' reaction to the terrorist attack of May 7 that resulted in the destruction of the space shuttle *Atlantis* and the devastation of central Florida. The Cuban government has denied any involvement in the attack, but American State Department sources say that the three dead terrorists have been positively identified as Cuban Army officers. More from our correspondent in the State Department —"

Keely switched it off. "The rest will be cover-up," she said, sitting down wearily in the chair beside the bed.

"Why?" Conroy asked softly.

"It was Torras," she said. "And Lipton. And Garland. They were working together. Torras sent Ramon on his way with the knowledge of the other two. Like that crew in the White House basement, the Iran-Contra business. The same sort of thing."

"Jesus, Keely."

"I know. The idea was that Ramon would be caught as he went for the GATT conference, and the finger would be pointing at Fidel. Torras and his friends would then do exactly what they're doing now." She gestured at the television. "But no one allowed for the possibility that Ramon would do something else entirely. He outmaneuvered them all. The political result for Cuba is the same, of course. At the cost of.... I already told you the cost. Remember the meeting in Gemma's house, when we were all there? Lipton was so overbearing about a Cuban terrorist attack being intended to strengthen the grip of the Cuban Communist Party. And you suggested it was the other way around, that the attack was intended to weaken it. He jumped on you, remember? He didn't want you getting too close to what he was really up to."

"How did you find this out?" he asked. She couldn't have been in on it, he thought. She couldn't have been.

"Garland collapsed after the shuttle disaster. He couldn't handle it. He went to the attorney general. The attorney general and some others questioned me; they thought I might have been Lipton's courier. Maybe I was. Sometimes I carried documents. Maybe they had secret writing on them, those little boys' games some men like to play. But they believed me when I said I didn't know anything about it. Garland had already told them that, I guess. Anyway, I pieced it together from what they asked me and from what they told me. They'll want to talk to you, too. Soon."

This had already occurred to him. "And Lipton?"

"I don't know. Probably he'll resign. What can they charge him with? He knew Ramon was coming, and he did try to stop him. Using us. He didn't try quite hard enough, but that would be hard to prove. I think it will all be swept under the rug. They got what they wanted, didn't they? No more Castro."

"He would have been dead of natural causes in a few years," Conroy snarled. "Why in hell couldn't they wait?"

"Because for all their cunning, they're really very stupid."

"Torras? What's happened to Torras?"

"I don't know. Probably he'll surface with a nice post in the new government."

"The bastard."

"They didn't know what they'd turned loose, did they?" she said sadly.

"To hell with them all," Conroy said. "I'm finished with them. People do these things, like I've done and Ramon's done, over and over again, and no one ever seems to learn. I'm sick of it."

"You'll resign? After it's all swept up?"

"Yes. As soon as I can. What are we going to do after that?"

"Stay together, of course." She managed a weak smile. "You don't think I'd turn you loose after all this, do you?"

"I was hoping you wouldn't."

A pause. "Michael," she said, "I'd like to resign from Harvard and go to Ireland and stay there for a while. There

are some things I feel I need to recover from. Will you come
with me?"

"Yes. What about the diplomatic work?"

"Never again," she said. "Not ever."

"Yes," he said, "I'll come with you."

A light breeze out of the east blows a scrap of paper down
the empty main street, past the town hall and the fire station.
Three sparrows bob and weave on the pavement, pecking for
food, their shadows foreshortened in the early afternoon sun.
On their feathers, as on the ground and the buildings around
them, lies a fine, almost invisible dust. The sparrows are
already dying.

Farther along the street the ice-cream parlor is deserted,
spanking clean and neat for the day's customers, who will
never arrive. The town square with the quiet elegance of its
colonial buildings lies silent; wind-borne dust is already
beginning to silt in the angles of the windowsills and the
crevices between the bricks.

At the end of the main street, its white facades and dark
green tower roofs and gilded spires brilliant in the sun, the
castle stands empty. No one now living will ever come to
Disney's bright illusion again.

On an island nine hundred kilometers to the southeast,
Marita Linares sits by the window, waiting for the nurse to
come to put her to bed. She cannot walk any more, and the
nurse helps her from her bed to the chair by the window
every afternoon so she can look out at the sea. In spite of
what Ramon has done, Marita still lives in the yellow stone
house by the white beach, and the nurse lives with her. This,
she knows even through the blur of the painkillers, is not
because they wish her well. It is because they know she is
going to die soon, so they do not need to kill her, and
because they do not want her in a hospital to talk to anyone
about what her son has done.

They say Fidel is gone, she thinks. Or going. This was
what Torras wanted all along. Perhaps I should have known.
But it doesn't really matter. Fidel is of no importance, none
at all, beside what my son had done.

He succeeded against all the odds, she thinks as she watches the sea and the seabirds. Soon there will be others to carry on after him. He showed them what can be done. There will always be others. We will always be there, haunting the oppressors' dreams, waiting in the depths of the clearest sky.

She hears the nurse's footsteps on the stair and takes a last look from her window. Out on the horizon, alone against the sky's darkening blue, there is a cloud no larger than a man's hand.